WAYWARD WINDS

MICHAEL PHILLIPS

BETHANY HOUSE PUBLISHERS
MINNEAPOLIS, MINNESOTA 55438

Published by Bethany House Publishers
A Ministry of Bethany Fellowship International
11400 Hampshire Avenue South
Minneapolis, Minnesota 55438
www.bethanyhouse.com

Printed in the United States of America by
Bethany Press International, Minneapolis, Minnesota 55438

ISBN 0–7642–2082–9
ISBN 0–7642–2044–6 (pbk.)

MICHAEL PHILLIPS is one of the premier fiction authors publishing in the Christian marketplace. He has authored more than fifty books, with total sales exceeding five million copies. He is also well known as the editor of the popular George MacDonald Classics series.

Phillips owns and operates a Christian bookstore on the West Coast. He and his wife, Judy, have three grown sons and make their home in Eureka, California.

Contents

——— ◆◆◆ ———

There was a man who had two sons. The younger one said to his father, "Father, give me my share of the estate...." Not long after that, the younger son got together all he had, and set off for a distant country....

Introduction
Progress, Rivalries, and Alliances
◆ ◆ ◆

*A*s you open this book, those of you who are continuing on in THE SECRETS OF HEATHERSLEIGH HALL series may want to skip ahead and get started with the story rather than spend time with a long introduction. Hopefully later you'll find yourselves coming back for some historical background.

For those of you coming to this book without having read *Wild Grows the Heather in Devon*, I offer these introductory thoughts and observations in the hope that it will help you enjoy the book, and series, more thoroughly. This is a "historical" novel, and the early years of this century were historically very complex.

The story opens in Edwardian England during the opening decade of the twentieth century. These were happy times for the British people, an era of prosperity and British world domination.

It was a new era. Queen Victoria was dead. Her son Edward was on the throne. Prosperity and progress were in the air.

The past half century had been an enormously expansive and creative fifty years of ideas and change. Science had explored the perplexing puzzles of the universe, and seemed on the verge of resolving most of them. Man's place in the order of things, according to the evolutionists, was accurately understood for the first time. The development of machines, the harnessing of electricity, and the explosive growth of invention had created an industrial power that seemed capable of accomplishing nearly anything man could envision. The automobile was barely fifteen years old, and now men were flying aeroplanes in the sky. The last reaches of the globe's unknown corners had been explored. Advances in medicine and health care made life better and easier. Once dreaded diseases were slowly being conquered. A rising humanitarianism reduced human suffering on any number of levels. Women were stepping forward to occupy newly "emancipated" roles in the world. Work for most was easier and shorter. More people had more money and were working less to get it. In art and literature, music and philosophy, medicine and science, philosophy and politics . . . in *all* ways culturally the nineteenth had been a century of genius. As the twentieth century opened, therefore, expectations were high that the result of all this progress would be more of the same, with yet more lofty achievements.

Have I made it sound like a utopia? It wasn't. There were problems too. All this progress came with a price.

Industry and modernization, and the raised standard of living of workingmen, brought new lines of division into society. No longer was the world defined merely by the fortunes of the very rich and the very poor. A third socioeconomic class had been born. It was called the middle class. This change benefited millions and contributed to the overall good. It carried with it, however, a consequence—the rising expectation of the masses.

Today you and I tend to take what is called the middle class for granted. That's where most of us spend our lives and we think nothing of it. But back then this change, in a sense, turned all of society on its ear. A huge middle class was something altogether new—what today's politicians would call a new "constituency," with needs and demands that had to be addressed.

With the explosive growth of cities, mounting numbers entered this new middle class daily. With this growth came social and political power, creating a whole range of new cultural conditions. Steadily new voices made themselves heard, demanding larger and larger slices of society's affluence. Not far behind was their cry for political representation. In such a climate were communism, socialism, and many diverse forms of liberalism born.

Unfortunately, the reality lagged behind the ideal. Every new constituency wanted change more rapidly than the institutions of their governments were prepared to give them. We recognize that very same problem in our own day, and it was equally true back then. Some of the more radical elements sought a wholesale overturn of society; others sought to gain their ends through the vote. In Great Britain the rising expectation of the masses led to the birth of the Labour Party and the suffragette movement. In Russia it would lead to revolution.

One thing was certain—the voices spawned by industry and modernism *would* be heard. Sound familiar? Everyone wants his or her voice heeded more than anyone else's. These new demands would not go unmet. The eighteenth and nineteenth had been centuries of kings and queens, autocrats and tsars. The question was: To what extent could the old order survive in the new?

And there were other problems too. The most serious was the most obvious: The world was on a collision course toward war . . . but no one knew it.

You and I have the benefit of hindsight. As you read this book, you know World War I is looming on the horizon, just like you know the *Titanic* is going to sink. But the characters in the story, just like the men and women living in the years prior to those events, *don't* know. And nothing could have been further from their minds. Understanding that, I think, makes their lives and responses all the more intriguing.

Calm appearances of society often mask turbulent undercurrents destined one day either to cause the collapse of that society from within or its destruction from without. Such social fissures had already begun to ripple through the underpinnings of a European exterior of equilibrium and tranquility long before the nineteenth century gave way to the twentieth. For yet a while longer they remained unseen. But slowly these cracks were widening.

But as I said, few knew it. One of those who did was Winston Churchill, whom you will meet in this story. We think of him as a hero of World War II. But as you'll discover, he was an integral member of England's leadership core during World War I as well.

Historians speak of the end of one era and the beginning of another. Yet rarely does a particular moment of history so thoroughly divide all that has come before with all that came after with such definitive finality as those years in Europe between 1910 and 1914. The chasm yawning between the new order which was approaching and the Europe of the old guard of recent memory, though but a few years separated them, was a gulf not of a decade or two, but of centuries.

As the twentieth century opened, Europe had reached stability and equanimity, which, built on a foundation of what was considered enlightened thinking, many assumed to be permanent. Wars had always been fought, of course. There had been terrible wars throughout the 1800s. But since Napoleon's time these had all been small and localized. In Britain especially it was now felt that such an uncivilized way of dealing with disputes lay in the past. From these present times forward, reason and moderation, dialogue and diplomacy, would henceforth solve men's difficulties. Yet the enforcement of this reason must still be backed up with military muscle. All the nations of Europe therefore built up their armies and navies, with greater and greater numbers of troops and ever more lethal and sophisticated weaponry.

Another factor was at work as well in the midst of these social, political, and military changes at the turn of the century. It was a force which, though it seemed perhaps healthy and invigorating to the human spirit, at a deeper level appealed to the basest emotions of egotism, pride, arrogance, and aggression.

That force was nationalism.

In many ways, national pride had been the inherent ideology of the nineteenth century. Every country and race in Europe was ruled with its own private ethnic passion. Though not so visible as that between Arab and Jew, European antagonisms and hatreds made the blood run no less hot in the veins of Teutons, Gauls, Poles, Anglo-Saxons, Serbs, Croats, Slovenes, Bulgars, Bohemians, Slavs, Bosnians, Ukrainians, Russians, and Turks. Now these many diverse and passionate bloodlines rose to new heights in this age of patriotic fervor. Each desired its independence. Each lusted after its perceived right of territorial possession.

As you read, I think you will find yourself amazed at how contemporary some of these disputes are. Today's newspapers are full of the very same ethnic rivalries and territorial disputes that led to World War I. You'll read about the first Bosnian crisis and the second Bosnian crisis . . . and we're *still* in the midst of a Bosnian crisis! The same regions are being fought over today. Almost a hundred years later we find ourselves wondering if two world wars and a protracted cold war succeeded in solving anything.

In spite of the optimism of reason, therefore, the nations of Europe continued to be ruled by complex military treaties and agreements. In the midst of a heating conglomeration of rivalries, all intent was to strengthen one's own position and preserve the delicate and ever precarious borders with one's neighbors.

The map of Europe had been redrawn in 1871 after a short series of wars climaxed by German unification. The next forty years saw rapidly shifting alliances between the nations of Europe. There was the Dual Alliance, then the Mediterranean Entente, then the Austro-German Alliance, then the Three Emperors Alliance, then the Austro-Serbian Alliance, finally the Franco-Russian Alliance.

Treaties, treaties, treaties.

Documents tried to predict every conceivable conflict that Europe's hundreds of diplomats and advisors and negotiators could imagine. Every nation bartered and hedged against the others, trusting none, not even trusting its allies, only using them to gain its own ends while at the same time hopefully clipping the wings of its adversaries.

Again, to really understand these times, we have to go back a hundred years and realize how different things were. Militarism still dominated much of the world, not the peaceful harmony which exists between the powers of Western Europe today. And alliances we take for granted today were much less stable back then.

At the heart of Europe, the German temperament was neither a placid nor compliant one. Germany's rise under Bismarck in the 1870s and 1880s was of particular concern to France and England. She had grown into a formidable power which, if left unchecked, could become a force in Europe that none could contain. Since the great Bismarck's time, Germany's industrial might had become considerable, and its military had grown into the strongest on the Continent. Bismarck's successor, Kaiser Wilhelm II, nephew of Great Britain's King Edward VII, was well known to be expansively minded.

Gradually it became clear to many in Britain that Germany's aim was nothing short of domination of the Continent. Britain and France, therefore, as the two chief western powers, sought to curb further German territorial ambitions. Germany observed their attempt and interpreted it not as defensive but aggressive, and spoke against the threat of its own encirclement. And with France and Russia now allies, she perceived this threat as a serious one.

With every shift in outlook, every incident, every change in leadership, every nation in Europe scurried to adjust its position. Times remained peaceful, but those who understood the shaky state of European diplomacy could not help being jittery.

At the end of the first decade of the new century, out of these constantly modifying rivalries and alliances had emerged the Triple Alliance—formed in 1882 between Germany, Austria-Hungary, and Italy—and the Triple Entente—formed in 1907 between Great Britain, France, and Russia.

The point of conflict where these shaky alliances all converged was in the east, in the Balkans, that dubious, debated, and long-contested region adjacent to three empires—the Russian, the Turkish, and the Austrian—and sitting at the critical juncture between the Black and the Mediterranean Seas. The three largest of the Balkan states, therefore—Serbia, Bulgaria, and Romania—though not major powers themselves, became the focus of all Europe's diplomatic maneuvering.

To Germany the scenario was simple: If the Balkans fell into Russia's hands, the German-Austrian empire would be virtually encircled.

To France and Great Britain, the opposite scenario was equally clear: The Balkans must be preserved in order to prevent Germany or its ally Austria-Hungary from controlling Europe's eastern seas.

But no forces of world climax bring about change merely in the abstract. It is across the pages of human life that history is written. *Individuals* make up the stories of the times in which they live.

History is people.

Its events are only what those people *do*. Its themes are no lofty vagaries, but the inner forces that drive men and women to make the choices that cause events to flow one into another. These impact other men and women, who make yet more choices . . . and thus are families and nations set upon courses from which there is no turning back.

Since the release of *Wild Grows the Heather in Devon*, I have received a great deal of mail representing a huge variety of responses. One reader was so outraged by a certain fictional conversation that I was sent the book itself back in the mail (without accompanying word of explanation) with the offending pages all glued tightly together! On the other hand, I have received probably a dozen letters from readers *praising* that very same glued-together section, telling me what a help it has been to their spiritual understanding.

It is sad that some Christians are so afraid of ideas that they are angered just to hear another viewpoint voiced than their own. Disagreement I can understand . . . *anger* at different points of view bewilders me.

In any event, I remind you again that we are trying to explore a historical period to discover what we might learn from it. This is not a treatise for or against women's rights, socialism, spy networks that disguise their motives or any of the other topics or societal forces involved.

And finally, as I did prior to the previous book, I remind you that this is a series. The whole story is yet to be told. I hope you will enjoy the history, the leisurely pace, the people we get to know, and this interesting period we are exploring together.

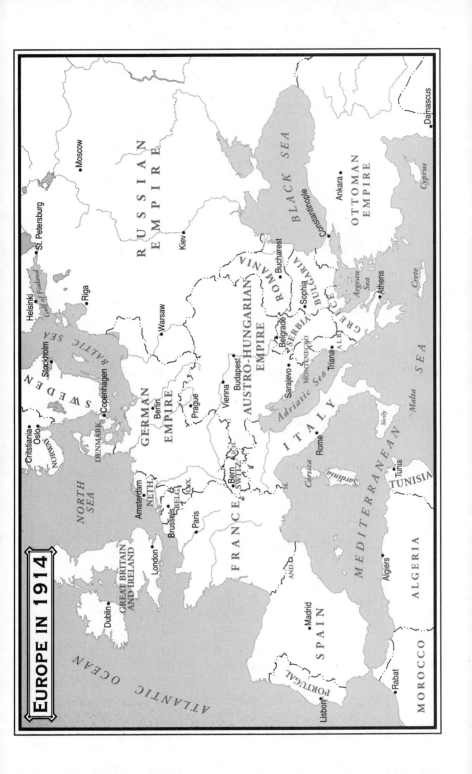

EUROPE IN 1914

ATLANTIC OCEAN

NORTH SEA

GREAT BRITAIN AND IRELAND
Dublin
London

NORWAY
Cristiania
Oslo
SWEDEN
Stockholm

Helsinki
Gulf of Finland
St. Petersburg

BALTIC SEA
Copenhagen
DENMARK
Riga

Moscow

RUSSIAN EMPIRE

Kiev

Warsaw

GERMAN EMPIRE
Berlin
Prague
NETH.
Amsterdam
Brussels
BELG.
LUX.
Paris

FRANCE

Vienna
Budapest
AUSTRO-HUNGARIAN EMPIRE
Bern
SWITZ.
LIECH.

Prague

ROMANIA
Bucharest

SERBIA
Belgrade
Sarajevo
MONTENEGRO
BULGARIA
Sophia

BLACK SEA

Constantinople
Ankara

OTTOMAN EMPIRE

Damascus

Cyprus

ALBANIA
Tirana
GREECE
Athens

Aegean Sea
Crete

ITALY
Rome
Corsica
Sardinia

Adriatic Sea

Sicily
Malta

MEDITERRANEAN SEA

SPAIN
Madrid

PORTUGAL
Lisbon

AND.

TUNISIA
Tunis

ALGERIA
Algiers

MOROCCO
Rabat

Prologue

A Mystery and a Prayer

1908

A woman with hair of pure white sat regarding the top limbs of pines as they swayed against a grey sky. The day was a melancholy one, and her mood grew reflective.

The plain wooden rocker slowly creaking beneath her motion carried even more years in its joints than she. Her days were many, and they had carried out their work well. Out of her eyes shone the peace one's season upon the earth is meant to produce. An ancient Bible rested open in her lap.

Her gaze, however, had drifted up from its pages a few moments ago, through the window, and out upon the wooded Devonshire countryside in which sat the so-called cottage she had always called home.

It was in truth far more than what is typically meant by the word, but was rather at one time the gamekeeper's two-story lodge of a sizable estate in southwestern England, constructed sometime in the early eighteenth century. Though it bordered the estate and had once been numbered among the manor's holdings, the cottage was no longer listed among the assets of the present lord of the manor of Heathersleigh Hall, Sir Charles Rutherford, descendent of the long Devonshire line of ancient name.

The old couple who occupied the cottage had for years been considered by many of the locals an odd lot. Children in Milverscombe a generation earlier had feared the very name *McFee*, and were careful not to venture too far west of the village. The years since, however, largely because of their close friendship with those at the Hall, had made the two aging McFees among everyone's favorites, in no small measure due to the spiritual esteem in which they were held.

The onetime eccentric reputation of the pair was no doubt enhanced by the fact that through the years the history of the strange property in the woods had been clouded in obscurity. It was a cottage, like the great Hall to which it had once been connected, that possessed secrets no one alive was aware of, not even its present owners. There were those who harbored suspicions. But as yet they had been unable to obtain the proof they sought. And as they lived in the city and did not have free access to the region, they had to bide their time until suitable opportunity presented itself. Notwithstanding such stories, rumors, and unanswered questions, many of the less fortunate in the nearby environs were indebted to the McFees more than was generally known.

The woman in the chair was not contemplating such things, for she knew nothing of them. Her grandmother's Bible lay open on her apron to the second Gospel. She had just read the words, "Unto you it is given to know the mystery of the kingdom of God: but unto them that are without, all these things are done in parables: That seeing they may see, and not perceive; and hearing they may heed, and not understand . . ."

A warm, gentle rain fell, preventing work this afternoon in her expansive flower beds which spread out from the white plastered walls of the cottage in all directions, by now half surrounding the barn where her husband spent a good deal of his time. Her mind, however, was not occupied with the growing things of her garden. Her thoughts and meditations were full instead with the greatest growing thing in the universe: the *human* plant, created in the image of the One who made flowers and people, cottages and galaxies all together.

A persistent breeze had kicked up a few minutes earlier. It drew her attention to the treetops, and now carried the drops of rain sideways in occasional splatters against the panes of her window. A more vigorous storm seemed likely. Her husband had commented over tea an hour ago that a windy night was in store for the downs. He was now busy outside preparing for it.

The sound of the droplets and the movement of the pines brought to her mind inexplicable reminders of Sir Charles and Lady Jocelyn's daughter.

How well she recalled the day nine years ago when the young mistress of Heathersleigh had been with them for lunch at the cottage. They had tried to explain the things of God to her. But she had been one of the unseeing . . . the unhearing. For now all remained in parables.

But it would not always be so. The Lord's voice had broken through into the soul of Master Charles. So too would his daughter one day hear divine whisperings into her own soul.

With such thoughts, prayer was not far behind.

"Lord," whispered Maggie McFee, "I pray that you would keep the hand of your care on dear Charles and Lady Jocelyn. You've done such a great work in their lives and in their family in recent years, and Bobby and I are privileged to have been part of it."

She paused briefly.

"But now, Lord," she went on in a moment, "it's her daughter you've brought to my mind this day. What gusts will be needed to turn the sails of the girl's ship back to the home of your Father's heart?"

As those of the faith's humble folk often are, her entreaties were unintentionally poetic. Because her heart spoke, she did not pause to consider the prophetic bent of her words.

"Send the breath of your Spirit upon her," she continued, "even as you are now breathing upon the countryside with your stormy rains. Remind dear Amanda where she came from, and where we are all going in the end. Send your flurries, Lord—blow the fog from her brain . . . and carry her home."

The elderly woman fell silent.

The simple prayer had roused her faith. She knew the wayward winds in the girl's life would give way to the Spirit's homeward currents in due time.

"Open her eyes," she added, "to understand the mystery."

PART I

Hidden Currents

1909

1

House of Light

A lone figure made his way up a rocky, treacherous path to a flat plateau, on whose meager soil grew a thin layer of green grass overlooking an angry sea.

The site was solitary and had been chosen for precisely that reason.

Late afternoon winds whipped clouds and water into a fury together. The latter remained blue yet a while longer. Its incoming waves pounded noisily on the rocks of the shoreline, sending the white spray of final impact crashing halfway up the jagged bluff. Sky and sea would both doubtless be black within hours as the impending storm drew steadily nearer the coast.

Behind a red-roofed house and two or three outbuildings rose the whitewashed column of a slender lighthouse, built to keep ships off the shoals of North Hawsker Head on the eastern reefs of the Yorkshire moors. Recently, however, it had been turned toward a more sinister and clandestine purpose.

Slanting flurries threatened to blow the walker into the North Sea below. But he won his brief battle against the elements, reached the top, and made for the house, where dry clothes, warm fire, and stout Irish ale awaited him.

He opened the door and entered ahead of a hearty gust from the squall.

"Is the dinghy secure?" asked a voice when the door was shut.

"Ay," answered the newcomer, "but the nor'easter'll be down upon us er' midnight, I'll warrant. 'Tis soaked I am from the water an' spray, but the wee craft'll ride it out safely."

As the Irishman went in search of fresh attire, the conversation in progress in the lounge continued. The subject was not of particular interest to him anyway. Doyle McCrogher had been hired because of his knowledge of boats and lighthouses. He also knew the peculiarities of this stretch of coastline, its tides and weather patterns, its caves and currents and hidden shoals, better than any local, it was said, for a hundred miles. Why this was so, his employers had not paused to inquire, for he was a native of Wexford on St. George's Channel in southern Ireland. But McCrogher's reputation as a practical, mechanical man familiar with the ways of earth, sea, and sky was enough for them.

The strange and obscure politics of the new century mattered nothing to the Irishman. If he was well fed and well paid, and his pantry kept supplied with Guinness, his loyalties could be bought and he could keep his mouth shut. Thus far he had remained silent.

"You were wise to postpone the meeting," commented a woman's voice as McCrogher disappeared. "The sea would have been far too dangerous." She was the only female among three or four men, appearing mid-fiftyish, tall, robust of build, and with a commanding countenance. "When do you now expect the count?" she asked, the merest hint of forgetfulness in her speech betraying her national roots, though England had been her home for years.

"When the weather clears and the seas calm," answered her counterpart, a man of approximately the same age, whose tongue could not have given more perfect representation to the Yorkshire dialect of his upbringing. From the thin grey moustache to the mode of expression to the manner in which he prepared his tea, the acknowledged leader of this small enclave was to all appearances and in all ways external an Englishman. What was not immediately apparent from his mere appearance was his subtly powerful, almost hypnotic personality, which was able to sway the minds of others to his purpose. His allegiances, like the woman's, lay elsewhere. "Probably next week," he added.

"I do not know whether I shall be able to get north again so soon," she said.

"Do not trouble yourself. This storm has set our plans back a few days, but there will not be a great deal of substance to discuss. It is chiefly an opportunity to see how effective McCrogher is in bringing our colleagues ashore, and whether the activity is noticed. This delay concerns me, however. We cannot afford to be at the mercy of the weather and turbulent seas. In any event, the real work will come later."

A sudden blast of driving rain against the windowpanes brought a temporary lull to the conversation.

"It would appear McCrogher's northeaster has arrived well before midnight," commented now a third member of the company, a London painter in his late thirties who was not on his way to fame and fortune by virtue of the brush. A philosophical man, his associations in certain shadowy art and literary circles had stimulated more interest in recent years in the winds of revolution than in flowers and fruit on canvas. He had traveled extensively in Russia and Germany—by what financial means none of his associates quite knew—had become fluent not only in their languages but also in the currents of change blowing everywhere in the east, and had returned to his native England with strong views he deemed best to keep to himself except in these select circles.

The pounding of rain upon the tile roof put the English among them in the mind for tea.

Gradually they rose and wandered to the kitchen. Fresh water was boiled, and each prepared his or her preferred drink.

2

Plans and Schemes

*T*hirty minutes later the conversation in the lounge of the house with the red roof had resumed. Three members of the group held cups of tea, the lady a glass of light red wine, and a certain greying Welsh aristocrat, of ancient family with dubious links to the Continent, had decided to join McCrogher—who sat behind the others with pipe and brew paying little attention—with a glass of dark brown Guinness.

"Your comment, Barclay," the final member of the coterie was saying, "about whether our activities are noticed, brings up one of our pressing needs."

The eyes of the others remained focused on the Oxford professor of economics.

"It pinpoints the necessity," he went on, "that we have eyes and ears everywhere. If the government perceives something as threatening, they will not advertise that fact in the *Times*. There are critical times ahead requiring redoubled efforts to expand the network. We must have sympathizers everywhere. Wherever word might leak out, possibly exposing us, we must have people who will learn of it, that we might respond swiftly and silently."

"You are right, of course," rejoined the other. "Many have been brought within the sway of our control in recent years without recognizing our influence. But as events move toward their climax, we in the Fountain of Light must widen our enlightening work over the perspectives of yet many more, whether or not at first they apprehend our ultimate purpose."

"I have hopes in that regard for my—" began the lady, then stopped herself. Barclay knew, of course, but it might not be best to divulge her personal plans to everyone just yet. "Let me just say," she went on after a moment, "that I concur. We must infiltrate as many aspects of society as possible, as our counterparts in the east have successfully done."

The conversation, as was not uncommon among them—especially when they retreated northward on the coast to gather in this comfortable setting—went on for some time, considering many possibilities and diverging in many directions. Abstract analysis was meat and drink to their collective spirits. Yet when it came to the dissemination of their unconventional philosophies, they could be devilishly cunning.

"We are a select few who have seen the truth in advance of the masses." Again it was Barclay speaking. "Yet we have not been chosen to keep the mysteries of the cause to ourselves. We must spread them vigorously, though silently at present, as people are brought to us with hearts receptive to the new destined order which is to come."

"What do you propose as our next step in this regard?" asked the ever practical Welshman.

"Science and the military are vital, as well as the political arena," replied their leader. "Not only do we need eyes and ears, on a practical level we need expertise. Writers, economists, historians, of course, are all useful. My official position allows me great latitude to move abroad freely. I am constantly on the lookout for such individuals. I would especially like one familiar with modern invention. Such could greatly aid our efforts."

Gazing outside as night slowly descended, the others pondered his statement. A silence fell among them.

3

A Name From the Past

———— ♦ ♦ ♦ ————

*Y*ou know," said the professor at length, "an old acquaintance comes to my mind just now as we are talking, a fellow I knew years ago in the navy. He would bring a perfect combination of assets."

"Why do you think so?" asked the lady.

"He is well known and highly thought of in political circles."

"That would dovetail very nicely with my position. Anyone we would know?" asked Barclay.

"You won't believe it when I tell you," smiled the professor. "Yes, I think you will all be familiar with the name. He became quite an important man after my acquaintance with him, although his recognition has fallen off in recent years."

"Then get on with it," said the Welshman.

"I'm talking about Sir Charles Rutherford."

"You mean the Devonshire M.P. a few years back?"

"None other."

Glances and nods went about the room.

"What were his politics?" asked the Welshman.

"A liberal when I knew him, with socialist leanings."

Expressions of approval were voiced, punctuated by a few more affirmative nods.

"You may indeed have hit upon something, my friend," said the leader. "As I recall, he once spoke up on behalf of positions decidedly in a direction, shall we say, that would suit our purposes nicely. That, along with his being such a respected voice . . . yes, I like the possibility. Do you know if he had any connection with the intelligence community when he was in Parliament?"

"I have no idea."

"His perspective on international affairs?"

"I never spoke to him about philosophical things, or the world situation. And, of course, it was all quite different back then."

"Do you think he might be amenable to meeting with some of our Austrian friends, discreetly of course?"

"We certainly might make some overtures and see which way the wind is blowing in his thinking these days."

"Now that I think of it, I read something about him not long ago," said the Welshman, "something about being appointed chairman of a government commission to investigate the practicalities of taking electricity into rural areas. Bit of a whiz with technological things, isn't he—electricity, telephones, and all that?"

"Sounds like he could be an ideal addition, just as you said earlier," added Barclay. "What about family?"

"Actually, I've lost track of him since our navy days," replied the professor. "I really don't know. Married, that's all I know, to the daughter of old Colonel Wildecott, who spent most of his career in India."

"Any other family?"

"There was a sister, I believe."

"Whose sister?"

"The Wildecott girl's."

"You mean Rutherford's sister-in-law?"

"Right—the colonel's younger daughter."

"Are the two women in touch?"

"I really don't know."

"What about Sir Charles and Lady Rutherford themselves?"

"Now that I think of it, there is a Rutherford chap at university, bright young boy."

"Relation?"

"I'd never considered it. I suppose it's possible."

"There are Rutherfords everywhere—I know one high up in the Bank of London."

A few more glances went around.

"There is also a daughter," said the woman at length, offering her first remark in some time.

"You speak as one who knows. Do you have more information on the Rutherford family than you are telling us?"

"I know only that there is a daughter, eighteen or twenty, who is presently in London, and *not* on close terms with her family."

"An interesting fact. It might prove useful."

"Should we make preliminary contact?"

"Leave that to me," said the professor.

4

Hidden Dangers

♦♦♦

*H*igh above the English coastline, storms swirled far more turbulent than the one presently coming from Scandinavia across the north sea. Indeed, the silent clouds moving steadily but inexorably westward from the regions of Serbia, Romania, and Bulgaria were thick and black and worldwide in their scope.

Few, however, apprehended the threat.

For millennia it was in the nature of things for the nations of Europe to mistrust, even hate one another. The English, the French, the Germans, and the Russians had been natural enemies longer than anyone could remember, despite the numerous family alliances of the ruling classes. They were four distinct cultures, with distinct histories, languages, and ethnic backgrounds, all attempting to dwell beside one another on a continent which any of the four would have been happy to dominate.

They would thus, as they had for centuries, be constantly antagonistic, constantly suspicious, constantly trying to protect and defend themselves. If in this present age the Kaiser was the greater menace to England, it was not so long ago that Napoleon had sought to bring all of Europe under his dominion.

However, it was not only nationalism, liberalism, the rising expectation of the middle class, and the political instability of the European power structure that made this a dangerous time. There were unseen currents of deceit and deception lurking silent but lethal beneath the surface of European affairs, such as the recent naval invention called in England the submarine, in Germany the U-boat.

Masquerading under a cloak of truth and enlightenment, one of the most secretive of those forces dedicated to the undermining of existing powers was the underground network which called itself the Fountain of Light. The obscure philosophy of its adherents concerned itself not with governments but with a new order they believed would arise in time out of all nations and would transcend national loyalties. They were not revolutionists as such, as were their counterparts in Russia, yet they found the overthrow of autocratic and monarchal systems necessary to pave the way for this new order. Those who were not prepared to sell their souls for the cause were considered the enemy. Their origins had roots eastward, and thus their sympathies lay also in that direction. Their number had now spread and infiltrated into all the nations of Europe.

Their sleepers had been in place throughout the Continent and Great Britain for years, in some cases even for decades, silently wooing loyalties and affections toward their cause. Some had been implanted from outside. Others were recruits from native populations, whose mannerisms, habits, and occupations gave no hint of subversive loyalties. These "moles" occupied ordinary roles and came from every element of society, blending in with their surroundings so as to be politically invisible. Politicians, students, men and women of the working class—anyone might be recruited. Especially prevalent in England were Austrian sympathizers from the intelligentsia and the aristocracy.

Certain select individuals of its number had for years moved back and forth on the Continent and to England, planting seeds, making contacts, and subtly courting new loyalists, while at the same time establishing a smooth-functioning communications network between its various branches. Luring by friendship, they won over many who had no inkling what would ultimately be demanded of them.

Always new recruits were sought. In numbers was power. They would use whoever suited their purposes, but were especially on the lookout for persons of stature, reputation, and influence. Such could advance their cause most readily.

The opening decade of the twentieth century, therefore—notwithstanding its prosperity, modernity, and the free flow of new ideas which filled it with challenge and optimism—was in many unseen ways a dangerous age.

And as England and the rest of the world approached a climax when the world would be changed forever, the Rutherfords of Devonshire stood, too, in a peril they could have no way to foresee.

5

A Mother's Prayer

*T*he sun beat gloriously down on the earth, calling its children, the flowers, to straighten their slender stalks and raise their colorful faces upward into the light. So too does the Creator of suns and flowers, and men and women, call his children to lift their faces and hearts to the radiance and warmth of his Life.

Lady Jocelyn Rutherford walked slowly across the meadow from the Devonshire estate which was her home. She was one of those human blossoms who had learned, not without pain, to behold the light of her heavenly Father's smile. And now in her heart she carried the reflection of his love with her always.

The daisies and buttercups were out today in wondrous white and yellow profusion on their canvas of green. The happy sight had lured her from the house.

As she began she had not been thinking of the similar day fifteen years earlier. But now as she strolled through the profusion of summery growth, Jocelyn remembered the occasion so long ago when she had walked near here with George and Amanda as children. She had been heavy with Catharine inside her at the time and recalled how weary the walk made her. The first daisy of the season had revealed itself to both youngsters, and they had raced up the knoll toward it.

The reminder of the innocence of that day momentarily stung Jocelyn's heart.

"Lord," she prayed quietly as she went, *"my mother's heart is so sore when I recall the happy times of my once carefree daughter. I miss those times, Lord. And I miss dear Amanda."*

Merely thinking her name in silent prayer brought a lump to Lady Rutherford's throat. She paused, glanced away across the downs, as if the motion and air and sunshine might keep the tears from rising too far.

The daughter for whom she prayed, her second child, had been in

London three years. Jocelyn had not seen her since the day of her somber and strained departure.

"She was so full of life, Father," she whispered after a minute or two. *"Fill her with your life again. Remind her of the happy times we had together. Bring to her remembrance the love and vitality of our family, the walks and rides and laughter, and especially how her father and I loved her. Plant within her a longing for the peacefulness of Devonshire, that when the time is right she will remember Heathersleigh . . . and know it is always her home."*

Jocelyn arrived at length at the top of the same little knoll up which the two children had run, and where Amanda had plucked the daisy that had so captivated her for a brief moment. She knelt down, amid many blossoms now. Yet when her hand reached out, it picked a new bud not quite open. She gazed tenderly at it for a moment.

"Here is my daughter, Lord," prayed the mother, *"not yet fully in bloom. Restore her childlikeness, even in the midst of the great city's tumult. Protect her, watch over her. Shine your light upon her—yes, and send your rains as well, that when the time comes for her to truly bloom, she will open the face of her heart toward you, and know you to be her Father."*

PART II

♦♦♦

London Society

1910-1911

6

Sister Suffragettes

◆◆◆

*C*hants of "Votes for women . . . votes for women!" filled the air.

Marchers filled a busy London street from one side to the other. It was Friday, November 18—soon to be known as Black Friday. Most of those present were dressed nicely, as was the custom of women who had time on their hands.

Half the protesters carried placards. All noisily proclaimed the case for women's rights.

Their bannerettes read "Asquith Has Vetoed the Bill" and "Where There's a Bill, There's a Way." The marchers had been summoned because it had at last become painfully clear that British Prime Minister Herbert Henry Asquith intended to do nothing to move what was known as the Conciliation Bill on to its vital third reading in the House of Commons.

The bill, which would have given about a million women in Great Britain the vote, it was now clear, was merely designed to mollify the suffragettes. After passing its first reading, Mr. Asquith allowed it to languish, and Mrs. Emmeline Pankhurst had finally had enough. Her husband, the late Liberal barrister from Manchester, had been the author of the first women's suffrage bill in Great Britain in the late 1860s, and had remained at the forefront of the fight for women's rights throughout his life. His wife had then taken up the cause where he left off. By this time, the name Emmeline Pankhurst had become synonymous in Great Britain, not merely with women's suffrage itself, but with growing militancy. She had become a political force to be reckoned with, and everyone in Parliament knew it.

The fact that little more than half the women, and none of the men who chanced to pass, paid these protesters heed only roused the passions of the orators yet higher.

As they went, more women joined them, and gradually the crowds on the sidewalks also increased. Toward the rear, a handful of rabble-rousers and students with nothing better to do, young men mostly, seemed intent on disruption.

Perceiving the opportunity for a good time at the expense of the demonstrators, these hecklers followed along, tossing out comments of rebuke. The taunts and shouts began good-naturedly. But now, with the activists returning in kind, throwing challenge back to challenge, some of the jeers grew lewd, others angry. But still the women kept on.

Meanwhile, the police, who had been alerted of the march in advance, were already on the way. In the distance a few sirens and whistles sounded their approach.

The year was 1910, and the suffragette movement in England was picking up steam. Whether the island kingdom would witness the advent of universal suffrage anytime soon may have been doubtful. But proponents of the cause were certainly making themselves heard around the world—not only in Britain, but in Finland, New Zealand, and across the Atlantic in America.

Beside Emmeline Pankhurst and her two daughters Christabel and Sylvia marched their twenty-year-old protégée, Amanda Rutherford.

That the daughter of Sir Charles and Lady Jocelyn Rutherford of Devonshire had so actively joined their cause gave special delight to the leaders of the movement. Their enthusiasm was heightened in that Rutherford himself—former leader in the House of Commons and, prior to his sudden and unexpected retirement six years ago, considered by many a leading candidate for the premiership in the 1905 elections—had given no public statements to discourage speculation that perhaps he was in support of his daughter's position.

Sir Charles and Lady Jocelyn had been thorough modernists prior to their conversion to the Christian faith during their daughter's seventh year. And though the change in their lives at the time was total—leading to Charles' retirement from Parliament and Amanda's alienation from the rest of the family—they yet recognized their daughter as a free moral agent accountable for her own decisions. They had not prevented her leaving once they saw that her mind was set. If their daughter was thankful for anything about her parents, she was grateful for that.

Amanda Rutherford was now making the most of that freedom.

During the years between her twelfth and seventeenth birthdays, the increasing constraint of the family's new spiritual values created more and more estrangement from father and mother, as well as from brother and sister. Other than the judgment her parents had shown in allowing Amanda the freedom to leave home, she viewed her family as hopelessly prudish and backward in their thinking.

Her older brother George showed every sign of entering adulthood the perfect image, as Amanda thought, of his father—obedient, dull, and unimaginative. He was good-looking enough, she supposed, and quite a skilled horseman. But the fact that he had full parental favor resting upon his shoulders was enough in itself to make Amanda resent him. Father and brother were typical of the weak sort of masculinity to which women were forced to spend their lives in meek compliance. That George had almost immediately given himself submissively to their parents' new religious perspectives annoyed her all the more.

Where her younger sister Catharine stood on matters of so-called faith, Amanda didn't know, and cared even less. The two girls had never talked about it. But Catharine probably went along with all the Christian nonsense too. That was the trouble with them all—they were stuck in the dreary Victorian past.

Amanda tried to convince herself that she loved justice, that she cared for the downtrodden and unprivileged, that she was a pioneer for modernism in the new century. But her activism was mostly just a means to an end—a way out of the drab and constricting confines of Heathersleigh Hall. If she was a wild sprout on the Rutherford family line, she certainly did not recognize herself as such, but rather saw herself as a bold and progressive thinker who would have an impact in society and the world. Notwithstanding her childish words to her father about becoming prime minister one day, Amanda Rutherford had matured enough to realize that Great Britain's government would probably not be headed by a woman in her lifetime. But still she remembered Queen Victoria's words on the day her father had been knighted. Amanda had never forgotten her vow to "turn the world on its ear" in one way or another.

Her opportunity had arrived in 1907. Shopping in Bristol, mother and daughters chanced upon a suffragette rally at which the two Pankhurst girls were speaking to a small crowd of ladies. Hearing their words and ignoring the protestations of her mother, sixteen-year-old Amanda had crossed the street and was immediately entranced with what met her ears. Not only did the message find sympathy with her fiery spirit, the two young ladies, whom she later discovered to be Christabel and Sylvia, seemed not that many years older than herself.

By the end of the afternoon a friendship among the three young women had sprouted which nothing would be able to dim.

How different can be two persons' perception of the same event. To Amanda the encounter signaled the beginning of her emancipation. To her mother it signaled the end, she prayed temporarily, of her relationship with her daughter.

Even now, three years later, it caused Jocelyn Rutherford renewed pain and a few tears to recall the conversation which had followed two or three months after the Bristol incident, when Amanda had presented herself to both her parents in the drawing room of Heathersleigh Hall.

◆◆◆

I received a letter from Sylvia Pankhurst today," she said. "They are moving to London and have invited me to live with them there and join the movement. I have decided to accept their offer."

A heavy silence followed. The announcement was the last thing either Jocelyn or her husband had expected so soon after Amanda's seventeenth birthday.

"This comes as quite a shock," she managed to say after a moment. "Surely . . . you must realize that we need time to think it over."

"I told you when Father resigned from Parliament," Amanda went on, "that I was determined to make *my* life count for something. Your beliefs are not mine. I want to make a difference in the world, and this offers me an opportunity. The world is changing. The Pankhursts are in the middle of it. I want to be part of it too."

A brief conversation ensued.

"You are making a serious mistake, Amanda," said Charles Rutherford in a soft voice after the cool exchange.

"Not in my eyes," she replied.

"That will not prevent you from the consequences of it."

As father and daughter spoke, the mother did her best not to cry, but the struggle was proving unsuccessful.

Ignoring the fatherly injunction, the daughter went on.

"I am asking for nothing," Amanda said. "I know George is

the eldest and is your favorite—"

"Oh, Amanda—don't say such things," Jocelyn pleaded. "You must know that we love you."

Amanda drew in a deep breath but managed to conceal her annoyance at the words that sounded hollow in her ears.

"I am requesting nothing, Father," she repeated. "I know Heathersleigh and all that goes with it will be George's someday. But if it is your plan to give me any portion of your inheritance, I would like to ask you to give it to me now so that I may use it to begin my new life in the city."

Again a lengthy silence followed.

"Whatever you wish, my child," the lord of the manor said at length, even more softly than before.

Jocelyn was unable any longer to keep the tears from flowing. Thankfully the strained interview did not last much longer.

———————— ♦ ♦ ♦ ————————

A month after that talk with her parents, Amanda Rutherford, with all her worldly possessions and a cheque from her father for three thousand pounds, had departed from Devonshire to begin a new and exciting life in London.

Amanda had now been in the city almost three years. Father and mother had not seen her since.

7

Unwelcome Face

———————— ♦ ♦ ♦ ————————

From a high office window, two eyes gazed down on the street to the scene playing itself out between suffragettes, hecklers, and police.

The watcher was but nineteen yet already held a position of growing importance in the offices of the bank located on the ground floor, in which establishment his father had risen to prominence as a vice-president. This latter fact in no small measure explained the professional prestige of the youth. No one particularly liked him, yet few begrudged the increasing stature of his position. Most recognized clearly enough his genius for any and all things financial. He would be a vice-president himself before long, they said, probably before he was thirty. It might well be that one day his father would work for *him*.

The votes-for-women movement amused the youth. Even if they succeeded in convincing Parliament to grant them suffrage, which he doubted, men would still control the financial institutions of the land. Alongside that, what would the vote matter? These silly and arrogant women were engaged in a futile exercise which wouldn't change the course of events one whit. When they had had enough they would return to their needlework and teas.

He was about to turn away and resume work at his desk. Suddenly his eyes riveted themselves on one of the loudest and most outspoken of the suffrage advocates. He sprang bolt upright in his chair. The next instant he was on his feet and leaning closer toward the window.

It couldn't be! he thought. *What could she possibly be doing here?*

The resemblance, however, was too striking. He must have a closer look.

He spun around, left the office, and hastily made for the stairway.

On his way to the street level, the young banker fell into quick reflections. It was not that he was particularly anxious to see the goose. He had despised her since he could remember.

He had to admit, however, that she had grown into a decently pretty young lady. She was dressed fashionably and appeared at ease in the city. It might prove beneficial to obtain her favor. One never knew where profit was to be gained. Opportunities ought not be squandered. He had never considered it before, yet who could tell what advantages there might be in a closer approach than their childhood had afforded?

By the time he emerged from the bank onto the street, the tumult which had aroused the attention of the ambitious youth was disappearing along Whitehall. He fell into step behind them, hurrying to keep up, trying to get closer to the front.

By the time they reached Parliament Square, hundreds of women and a great number of police had been assembled for what everyone knew would be a contest that would last the rest of the day. A thick line of policemen kept the marchers well away from the Houses of Parliament, which was exactly where Mrs. Pankhurst and her troops wanted to go.

One or two of the signs had already been wrested from thin feminine hands and thrown to the ground and trampled underfoot.

The scene showed danger of becoming ugly.

Several of the rowdiest hecklers were pulled to one side by the police. Another officer attempted to calm the gathering peacefully before it got further out of hand. The suffragettes, however, made matters no easier, shoving and pushing and trying to break through the line.

"We know our rights," insisted Emmeline Pankhurst. "You are exceeding your authority if you try to force us to leave."

"I am exceeding nothing, lady," rejoined the man. "I'm telling you to break this up peacefully before I run in the whole lot of you along with those roughs there."

He pointed to the two his colleague already had in tow.

"Go ahead—arrest us," rejoined Pankhurst defiantly.

"I've a mind to do just that if you push me further!"

"The publicity will do us more good than these speeches to this crowd. It will make front-page news. Then the whole country will hear of it!"

The shrill sound of the man's whistle summoned several officers to his side. "In the meantime, I want all your names," he said. "—Men," he added, now addressing his fellow policemen, "I want a list of every woman involved in this thing. Any who refuse, throw them in the wagon and we'll haul 'em back to headquarters."

The officer's words were more bluff than substance. The clever Mr. Churchill, though at one time a vocal supporter of the suffragette movement, had given the police their orders—don't arrest them except for extreme provocation. But at all costs, *keep* them on the other side of the Square.

The women, however, were not about to be easily deterred. In wave upon wave they pushed and shoved against the police line. The large crowd which had gathered yelled and cheered and taunted, inciting both police and women to higher pitches of energy and anger. Before long the whole of Parliament Square became a battleground. Women were kicked and knocked down, the placards and bannerettes trampled. But they would not give up their attempt to push the police line back and gain access to the gates surrounding the Houses of Parliament.

An inexperienced policeman had hold of one especially defiant young lady by the wrist. Half dragging, half pulling, he was attempting to lead her toward the wagon where, despite the home secretary's orders, some arrests were starting to take place.

"It's all right, Knox—I'll take her from you."

The officer turned to see a well-dressed businessman at his side. The man was a trifle stout in several of the wrong places, indicating a life of ease—notably stomach, neck, and jowls—though he was not fat as he had been as a child. He looked hardly more than a boy himself, yet spoke with an air of confidence and breeding such as comes with wealth.

"Oh, it's you, Mr. Rutherford, sir," he said. "You really know this'n?" he added in disbelief.

"I'm afraid she's my cousin. I'll see she causes you no more trouble today."

"All right then, Mr. Rutherford. But get her out of 'ere, or the cap'n'll 'ave me 'ead."

The man relinquished the woman's wrist to her rescuer. He led her, still struggling, away from the scene.

"I don't need any of *your* help, Geoffrey!" said Amanda irritably, without benefit of greeting, though the two had not seen each other in years. She tried to twist herself loose, but found Geoffrey's grip stronger than she gave him credit for.

"I would think a word of thanks might be in order," smiled Geoffrey condescendingly. "After all, I just saved you from going to jail with the rest of your troublemakers."

"Better jail than going *anywhere* with you!"

"Come, come, Amanda—is that any way to talk to me after all this time?" Gradually he loosened his hold. "I didn't know you were in London. How long have you been in the city?"

"Almost three years. Let me go, I tell you!"

Finally Geoffrey released her arm. In the few seconds which had transpired, Amanda calmed sufficiently to realize she did not especially want to spend the afternoon either behind bars or at the police station. She'd already spent two afternoons there last month, and she wasn't sure it had done the cause any good. She therefore continued to walk slowly along at her cousin's side, glancing back every few seconds at her comrades and the police.

She and Geoffrey had never got along. Whether this had to do with the annoyance of Geoffrey's father toward his cousin, Charles Ruth-erford, whom he supposed unworthy of both the Rutherford estate and the title that went with it, or was the mere product of a rivalry between two selfish children, neither had ever bothered to consider.

Whatever the cause of their lifelong antipathy, Amanda was not the least bit anxious for Geoffrey's company. But right now it seemed the best option. She would make good her escape as soon as the police were gone.

"Three years! I can't believe I haven't seen you. I must say," re-marked Geoffrey as they went, "that you have both changed a great deal and yet not changed at all."

"Just what is *that* supposed to mean?" rejoined Amanda testily.

Geoffrey let a superior smile play around the edges of his lips.

"You are just as feisty as ever," he replied, "though you have become a very nice-looking young lady."

He took in her grey boots, wool suit, and small grey hat with dash-ing feather slanted back at an angle.

"And I commend your dress and hat," he added, "—they become you well."

"Coming from you, I'm not sure whether to take that as a compli-ment or not," replied Amanda, neither softened nor flattered by his words. The Geoffrey Rutherford she used to know always had an angle. She hadn't liked him any more than he had her.

"Would you like to come back to the bank and see Father?" asked Geoffrey.

"Not in the least."

"I know he would love to see you again."

Amanda could not prevent herself from bursting into brief laugh-ter.

"*Him*—love to see *me*! You have finally gone too far, Geoffrey," she said. "Now I *know* you're lying, as you always used to. He was always too jealous of my father to like me."

She turned and, without another word, walked briskly off down an adjoining sidewalk away from him, yet also away from the ongoing ruckus back at the Square.

"But you haven't told me where you are staying," Geoffrey called out after her. "How will I get in contact with you?"

Amanda did not stop or reply. Nor did she give the slightest indi-cation she had heard him.

Geoffrey stood watching as she disappeared.

It doesn't matter, he thought. He would find her. There were ways. *The minx! She always was high and mighty.* He would show her!

Slowly the young financier walked back toward the bank, turning many things over in his mind. This had been a fortuitous meeting indeed.

He would talk to his father, thought Geoffrey as he climbed back up the stairs to return to his office. He would know the best strategy to pursue.

Behind him in Parliament Square, the battle of Black Friday did not end until darkness. Many serious injuries resulted, mostly on the side of the women. The demonstration had not been peaceful. Blood had even been shed. A certain Miss Ada Wright had been knocked down so many times that, as the site was cleared, a number of her anxious friends gathered about her where she lay unconscious.

The confrontation resulted in Mr. Asquith's promise to make a statement the following Tuesday.

The ladies waited patiently. But when the statement came, it proved utterly unsatisfactory in furthering the cause.

On the following morning, therefore, on Wednesday the twenty-third, a second army of women led by Mrs. Pankhurst marched into Downing Street. This time the police were not prepared. Sylvia Pankhurst, standing on the roof of her taxi, shouted and urged the women forward.

Belatedly, a mounted detachment of police reinforcements rode into the scene. Both the prime minister and Home Secretary Churchill appeared.

The "Battle of Downing Street" lasted late into the afternoon. By day's end the total of arrests since the previous Friday had climbed to 280.

The suffrage movement had clearly entered upon a new and militant era.

8

Machinations

The atmosphere in the home of Gifford Rutherford was thick with long-awaited opportunity. The wealthy London financier and his son sat alone together in the drawing room after dinner. The father poured his son a liberal portion of expensive brandy and took a seat opposite him.

Gifford raised his glass. Geoffrey returned the gesture.

"To our cousin, the fair daughter of he who calls himself *Sir* Charles Rutherford," said Gifford. The sarcasm of his tone was unmistakable.

"And to Heathersleigh," returned Geoffrey.

The father nodded in approval of this addition to the toast. Both drank deeply from their crystal glasses.

Gifford Rutherford was proud of his son, all the more so in how much the boy reflected himself. Gifford had raised him to be a chip off the old block, and this recent development demonstrated just how completely he had succeeded. He had all but given up on the thing, and now here Geoffrey had shown himself just as shrewd as ever the father could have hoped. Gifford may never himself be acknowledged as either the lord of the manor of the family estate or a knight like his cousin Charles. But it would yet give him enormous satisfaction to see his son one day secure the title for their branch of the family. How to get around Amanda's brother was still an obstacle, but this would certainly bring them immeasurably closer.

"Would you seriously be willing to marry the girl?" said Gifford after a long and thoughtful silence.

"She would not make an altogether bad match," replied his son.

In truth, Geoffrey's best chance of marrying at all was for some social-climbing debutante to marry him for his money—not the best means for finding husband or wife or love of any kind. He had not shown himself of a character that attracted members of the fairer sex. He had been chubby for so long that most of those who knew him well, including Amanda, still tended to see him in that light. Though he was not tall, two or three inches under six feet, he had in fact begun slowly to trim down in the last couple of years. If this trend continued, he might begin to attract more feminine notice, though it was too early to tell. He had a plentiful head of black hair which he kept liberally oiled to his scalp, a custom which did not help toward that end.

The thought that perhaps a liaison with Amanda might be arranged for their mutual benefit—he providing her money and prestige in the business world, she placing him a step nearer control of Heathersleigh—was not an option Geoffrey found completely distasteful. He did not love her, of course. He did not even like her. But he had long ago learned from his father the valuable lesson of expedience, that most vital foundation stone in the world where Mammon rules. And the idea of having a large and prestigious estate from which to administer his financial empire, without a great outlay of funds, was powerful inducement to look at the matter practically rather than sentimentally.

"You may be right," conceded the father with thoughtful expression.

"What ought to be my next move?"

"That will require careful consideration," replied Gifford. "It will no doubt behoove us to look into the finances of her father, in the event that we might uncover something my previous investigations have missed. I shall also set some inquiries in motion to see what she is doing in London. If there is a rift in the family, that might also work to our advantage."

"What about George?"

"Yes ... hmm—we will have to examine his affairs too. Let's see, how old would the fellow be? Around twenty-one or twenty-two, I should think—old enough that we might be able to make some skillfully thrown dirt stick to him."

"I heard he is to graduate from Oxford next year."

"Ah, yes—the university life always contains secrets that can be exploited. Good boy, see what else you can learn, what alliances he has formed with his college fellows."

They spoke awhile longer in general terms. Suddenly the father's face lit up.

"Would you consider taking her to the Kensington Lawn Tea at the Gardens in the spring?" he said.

"She would never agree to it," replied Geoffrey with something resembling a laugh of incredulity at the mere suggestion. "She cannot stand me."

"Then we shall just have to be persuasive," rejoined his father. "We will make inquiries, find out where she is staying. Then I shall send her an invitation to come round for a visit—one she will not be able to refuse. I shall have a little chat with her."

9

Kensington Gardens

The scene at the Kensington Lawn Tea in late April 1911 was everything its organizers could have hoped for. The day shone warm and fragrant, profuse blooms spread color everywhere, and the soft sounds from the small string ensemble added the perfect classical touch to the gathering. Members of London's highest circles and most of its aristocratic families milled about.

Sufficient time had now passed that the event was unmarred by occasional reminders of the death a year earlier of King Edward VII. Edward's forty-six-year-old son, the new George V, was said to be in Kensington Palace with Queen Mary even now. He was reportedly planning to emerge later in the day. Their coronation was scheduled for June 22, two months from now. Even without the new king, the gala spring celebration would be talked about for weeks.

Amanda Rutherford, however, was not particularly enjoying herself. Here she was at the heart of London society—all she had ever dreamed of—but on the arm of her cousin Geoffrey! She had dressed carefully. She knew her cream-colored crinoline was perfect for both the event and for her.

It should have been her father—*he* was the one who belonged here! He could have been the prime minister. She should be on the arm of *Prime Minister Rutherford*—not this slimy creature! She would never forgive her father for turning his back on what had been the brightest political career in the empire. He had promised to make her a lady of London. But he had reneged on that as well.

The idea of her hand touching Geoffrey, even through the sleeve of his jacket and her glove, and her carrying on with pleasant demeanor as if his presence was anything but detestable . . . it was enough to make her skin crawl. She was beginning to regret ever agreeing to this. At the time, however, it had seemed a small price to pay for the chance to attend a gathering so close to the Crown. All her life she had dreamed of this very thing. The fact that a sizable anonymous donation was to be made into the bank account of Emmeline Pankhurst to advance the cause of women's rights had also added to her motivation to accept the offer.

The invitation from her father's cousin Gifford three weeks earlier had been entirely unexpected. Curiosity, more than any desire to see him, had prompted Amanda to accept it.

◆◆◆

I understand you are involved with the Pankhursts," said Gifford after the exchange of initial trivial pleasantries.

"That is correct," replied Amanda.

The banker took the information in with a knowing nod. He appeared deep in thought.

"I am curious as to how you found my whereabouts," Amanda added.

"I am reasonably influential in London," replied her father's cousin. "Many things besides money are at my disposal. Speaking of finances—how is your, uh—your cause . . . how are you faring?"

"Money is always needed."

"What would you say if I made it possible for you to obtain a donation?"

"I would want to know what you wanted of me in return. I would not expect you to contribute for the sake of family ties, nor out of concern for the advancement of society," Amanda replied with a hint of sarcasm in her voice.

Gifford smiled. He had not underestimated his cousin's daughter in the least. It seemed he and Amanda understood one another perfectly. He rather liked this young firebrand. She might make a very suitable daughter-in-law at that.

"It is a small thing, really," he said at length. "You know of the Lawn Tea coming up next month at Kensington Gardens?"

Amanda nodded.

The two continued to talk for another few minutes.

"Of course, you understand Geoffrey must not know that there are finances involved in our little arrangement."

"He will suspect something."

"You leave that to me. If you want the donation, you must say nothing."

———— ◆ ◆ ◆ ————

Amanda had agreed. Now here she was paying a price she wasn't sure was worth what Mrs. Pankhurst was to be given in exchange. But the day would soon be over, and Geoffrey would once again be out of her sight. And she had had her opportunity to mingle with high society.

"Good afternoon, Rutherford," said a voice nearby.

Geoffrey turned toward it.

"Oh, it's you, Halifax. I didn't know they let the press in."

"No less than bankers," rejoined the newcomer with a smile. "I'm here because my dear mum secured me an invitation," he added.

"She doesn't approve of your profession, I take it?" asked Geoffrey politely. It was with difficulty that he tried to act interested.

"A bit too plebeian for her—all the riffraff associated with newspapers, you know. Ah, wouldn't dear old Mum be proud of me if I were a banker like you!"

"Sarcastic flattery will get you nowhere, Halifax."

"I don't need to flatter *you*, Rutherford. I'll never need money from your bank.—But aren't you going to introduce me to this lovely young lady on your arm?" he added, turning toward Amanda.

As he spoke, he tipped his hat and gave just the slightest bow, while locking his eyes onto Amanda's. She answered his penetrating gaze with a smile of her own, her first of the day.

The young reporter had learned from a tender age that things were not always what they appeared. This applied to relationships as well as events. He thus lost no opportunity to gain new acquaintances, no matter what prohibitions toward intimacy appearances might indicate.

The fact that a lady was on the arm of another nowise deterred him from approach. One never knew what might come of it. Such assertiveness had made of him not yet a *good* journalist, but nevertheless one whose name was gradually coming to be known throughout London. He possessed a certain knack for discovery that lent itself well to his chosen profession, of which his wealthy dowager mother approved more than she was willing to let on.

She had financed his Cambridge education, biding her time and keeping her own plans quiet for the present. These had, in fact, been well under way for years, which he suspected not in the least. So much the better if he could make the cause his own without knowing of her hand in some of the very associations he kept from her. His university affiliations could not have gone in directions more perfectly suited to her ends. He had fallen into circles full of liberal thinkers, several Marxists among them—the sort of company Amanda's father had kept two decades earlier—and involved himself with two or three failed student publications. He left Cambridge after two years and was now working for the *Daily Mail*. Thus far he had been able to keep his leftist leanings from his editors. Both mother and son had secrets from one another, yet the same forces drove each toward common goals.

The young lady who had caught the eye of young Halifax from across the lawn a few minutes earlier was certainly one he could not ignore for the rest of the afternoon. She was slightly above average in height, five feet six or thereabouts, with lovely brown hair, curled nicely and bouncing at the shoulder. She seemed altogether mismatched with the young banker whose acquaintance he had made two or three times. She was good-looking, though not so beautiful that her features would in themselves have drawn him. She was carefully dressed and knew how to comport herself. But she carried herself with a purpose and determination that he could detect even from a distance. It was her energetic and confident bearing that kept his eyes returning in her direction as the day progressed. He could tell she was a strong young woman—in what ways he would have to discover later. For that fact alone he must know her.

On her part, in the few seconds she had to gather a first impression, Amanda judged Geoffrey's acquaintance to be something over six feet, and probably twenty-two or twenty-three years of age. His lean frame fit his height, though he filled out the expensive tailored grey suit well enough to keep from looking ill fed. He possessed an ample supply of very black hair, parted down the middle, thick and dry rather than pasted down onto his scalp, as was the custom with so many young men—Geoffrey for one. He was handsome enough, though not what she would call dashing. He appeared comfortable with what she gathered had been an aristocratic upbringing. In his expression she detected a hint of what she could only call the unknown, which added to the intrigue about him, especially alongside her cousin. In this setting she would never have guessed him for a newspaperman. His eyes did rove about, it was true, which *might* have been a sign of a mentality awake to people and events around him—necessary for any seeker of news, especially one who sought to commit ideas to print. But he was not searching for news as much as for pretty faces, a character weakness which his previous words to Geoffrey indicated well enough.

"This is my cousin," replied Geoffrey to the question just posed. "—Amanda Rutherford. Amanda—may I present Ramsay Halifax."

"Charmed, Miss Rutherford," said Halifax, still holding her eyes. "Are you of the Rutherfords of Devon?"

"The same," replied Amanda.

"Heathersleigh, I believe the old family estate is called, is it not?"

"You are remarkably well informed, Mr. Halifax."

"And the present lord of the manor would be. . . ?" he began in questioning tone.

"Would be my father," said Amanda, completing the sentence.

"Ah, now it begins to become clear. The two scions of the Rutherford family coming together in harmony for the Kensington Tea!"

Neither Amanda nor Geoffrey offered comment.

"But if my memory serves me . . ." Halifax continued, then paused, glancing over Amanda's face again with index finger pressed to his lips, "—I have the feeling I have seen you someplace before."

"Surely, Halifax," chided Geoffrey, beginning to tire of the newsman's presence, "you can be more original than that!"

"No—I mean it. I'm sure I know your face. Did I see you in the *Times* about something or other?"

"You may have," answered Amanda. "There were reporters and photographers at one of our rallies two weeks ago."

"Rallies?"

"She's a suffragette, Halifax," put in Geoffrey. "Come on, Amanda," he added, attempting to move away.

"That's it!" exclaimed Halifax, ignoring him. "You were next to the

Pankhurst girls. There was a picture on page three. So—you're part of the radical new women's movement!"

"You disapprove?"

"I didn't say that."

"Your tone implied it."

"Don't assume too much, Miss Rutherford. Journalists have to walk both sides of many fences, and I'm better at it than most of my colleagues. Besides, you suffragettes have been relatively quiet since last November's Black Friday and the Downing Street ruckus."

"It is said that the government plans to pass the Conciliation Bill later this spring or early in the summer. We can be patient."

"Is it true that Mr. Churchill actually had one of his wife's close friends run off like a common tramp during the Downing Street affair?"

"That's the report," answered Amanda.

"What about your father?" said Halifax in a slightly more journalistic tone. "It was a shock to the whole country when he resigned from the Commons."

Amanda did her best not to display her own emotions at the memory. She did not comment.

"Although I must say he is managing to keep himself in the news, what with an occasional speech at university about modern inventions. And he's become one of the country's leading experts on the practical uses of electricity, from what I hear. What do you think about your father's new approach to social involvement, or should I say *non-involvement*?"

"I prefer not to think about it at all," replied Amanda.

"A noncommittal answer," laughed Halifax. "Just what I should have expected from the daughter of a former M.P."

"Please do not read diplomacy into my words, Mr. Halifax. I really am completely uninterested in my father's affairs."

Geoffrey, who had been growing more and more uneasy relegated to the role of listener, finally broke up the conversation.

"Nice to see you again, Halifax," he said. "Come with me, Amanda."

10
A Surprise at Hastings

◆ ◆ ◆

$\mathscr{A}$manda sat down on the side of her bed, removed her shoes, and lay back with a deep sigh. The day had certainly ended more hopefully than it had begun.

During the drive home in Geoffrey's expensive new motorcar, she had wished she was riding with Ramsay Halifax instead.

Anyone but Cousin Geoffrey!

Yet she supposed she owed him at least a minor debt of gratitude for taking her to the Gardens in the first place. She had wondered after two or three years if she was *ever* going to meet anyone in London besides the Pankhursts! And now, thanks in part to Geoffrey and Cousin Gifford, she had made the acquaintance of the mysterious journalist from the *Daily Mail*.

"Amanda dear," said Mrs. Pankhurst the following afternoon at dinner, "you remember the meeting this Wednesday down in Hastings. You will be with us, I hope?"

"Yes, of course," answered Amanda.

"We shall take the train down in the morning. The event is scheduled for two o'clock."

"Is it indoors or outdoors? What shall I wear?"

"Your finest!" chimed in Sylvia. "I am. For once no one will be throwing things at us!"

"Or yelling obscenities," added Christabel.

"Indoors, to answer your question," said Emmeline. "The southern England committees have all joined to rent a large facility in Hastings. We will be speaking to every woman in the cause for miles. They will come from everywhere between Cornwall and Dover. And not a man among them!"

"That's a relief," said Sylvia.

"But how will it help?" asked Amanda.

"To rally the troops, Amanda. Imagine five or six hundred women, on fire for women's rights, taking the message to every city and town across southern England!"

When it occurred four days later, the Hastings Women's Suffrage Rally turned out to be everything Emmeline Pankhurst had hoped for. The hall was packed with enthusiastic supporters, and, except for a few hecklers outside, once the round of speeches and music and hoopla and organizational meetings began, the day went off without a hitch.

Only one of the prophecies concerning the day proved inaccurate, that voiced by Emmeline herself. Just moments before she was scheduled to begin the opening address to the crowd of ladies, her daughter Sylvia came hurrying backstage to speak with her. The noisy hubbub of the hall filling with women finding their seats could be heard through the heavy curtain.

"Mother, there is a man out there!"

"I don't think one man will cause us too many difficulties," smiled Emmeline. "Dear Mr. Pethick-Lawrence could use some company. If only more men shared his vision for our cause. We need more male supporters. Who is he?"

"I don't know," answered Sylvia. "But he is sitting in the middle of the front row!"

"Well, if he interrupts," laughed Mrs. Pankhurst, "I shall call upon every woman in the place to throw him out!"

The unknown intruder, however, uttered not a peep throughout the proceedings. When the daughter of former M.P. Charles Rutherford was introduced, Amanda walked to the podium. Instantly, she saw the man whose presence had so unnerved Sylvia.

His eyes bore straight into hers. A slight smile spread over his face. With difficulty she flustered her way through her speech in support for the cause of women's rights.

As soon as the gathering broke up, which was to be followed shortly by a meeting of all the committee chairwomen, the uninvited guest sought her out. Amanda sensed his approach but did her best to pretend she did not see him.

Such a presence, however, was impossible to ignore. The small group of women nearby quieted. Slowly Amanda turned. His eyes again stared straight into hers.

"Mr., er ... Mr. Halifax," she said, attempting without success to act surprised, "whatever are *you* doing in a hall full of ladies?"

Some of the women tittered. The newsman took it in stride.

"My paper ran a piece yesterday announcing your little shindig," he answered with a good-natured grin. "I thought I ought to come down and report on the affair firsthand."

"And what will you report?" asked Amanda. She drew in a steadying breath which she hoped would be invisible. Among so many women, she must *not* let it show that she was nervous around a *man*.

"I must say I am impressed at the turnout," replied Halifax, gesturing about the hall.

"What about the content of what you heard?"

"I must decline committing myself," he smiled.

"And we all know what *that* means," rejoined Amanda with significant yet playful tone. "It is a rare man who has the courage to approve of what we are doing," she added. Her voice contained more fun than jab. It was impossible not to be charmed by the man's smile.

"I told you when we first met, Miss Rutherford, that I was adept at walking many sides of many fences."

"Did you say that?" she laughed.

"I think I said *something* like it," Halifax rejoined. "So don't be too quick to judge my opinions. I think you will find me more open-minded than most men, even most progressives."

Seeing that she was apparently acquainted with the stranger, the three Pankhursts now joined Amanda. Mrs. Pankhurst did little to hide her curiosity.

"Emmeline," said Amanda as her mentor approached, "I would like you to meet Mr. Ramsay Halifax—our lone male listener today. Mr. Halifax—Emmeline Pankhurst."

"I am honored to meet you, Mrs. Pankhurst," said the journalist, extending his hand. "I have followed your career for some time with interest."

"Mr. Halifax is a reporter for the *Daily Mail*," added Amanda.

"Now your presence makes sense," said Pankhurst, shaking his hand and allowing a smile of heightened interest onto her face. Publicity was the stock-in-trade of the movement she was spearheading. "These are my two daughters—Christabel and Sylvia."

"Charmed," said Halifax, shaking each of their hands in turn.

"You are doing a story on our cause?" said Pankhurst.

"Actually, no," replied Halifax. "I am here chiefly because of my acquaintance with Miss Rutherford."

A moment's hesitation followed.

"Ah, I see . . . well, we are happy to have you here in any case," said Mrs. Pankhurst. "There are many men, you know, who support our cause. So you are welcome anytime. I hope your paper will see fit to give the event the attention it deserves."

"I will speak to my editor about running a feature piece."

"This is the largest such gathering yet.—But now you must excuse me. I see they are waiting for me across the hall. I am pleased to have met you, Mr. Halifax."

"Likewise, Mrs. Pankhurst," he replied, with a respectful nod of the head.

Both Pankhurst daughters smiled, then turned and followed their mother. Amanda and the journalist were left alone for the first time.

"How did you come down from the city?" he asked.

"By train," Amanda answered.

"Do you have more duties here?"

"If you mean more speeches," laughed Amanda, "no—I am through for the day."

"What would you say, then, to accepting an invitation to ride back to London with me?"

"I don't know—do you mean on the train?"

"Of course not," he laughed. "Anyone can ride the train. I mean by motorcar. It's a lovely day—we'll have a drive up the coast to Dover, then back up into town.—What do you say?"

Amanda did not have to think for long.

"I say that I will accept your invitation, Mr. Halifax!"

11

Larger World

❖❖❖

A warm sun shone down on the two people walking as they made their way across the grassy coastal plateau of Capel-le-Ferne a mile east of Folkestone.

The drive in Ramsay Halifax's bright new Rolls-Royce convertible touring car across Romney Marsh, and then along the shoreline of the Strait of Dover, made the suffragette rally in Hastings seem another world away.

The wind blew Amanda's hair in a thousand directions as she and Ramsay Halifax laughed and talked and sped along in the greatest invention, according to Ramsay, of the modern age. He had driven up the steep hillside from Folkestone, pulled off the road and parked, jumped out and run around to open the door for Amanda.

"Come with me," he said. "—I want to show you one of my favorite places!"

After the windy ride, as they walked slowly away from the car, suddenly all became quiet and still. The grass underfoot was springy, soft, and thick. From this vantage point the sea was not yet visible, though the unmistakable aroma of salt spray in the air gave evidence that it was nearby, accented by the faint cries of gulls in the distance.

Halifax paused, reaching out his hand to Amanda's arm.

"Stop right here," he said. "Now look around you—"

Amanda obeyed.

"—and imagine yourself out in the middle of a wide, flat moor."

He waited a moment.

"Can you picture it?"

"I think so," she replied.

"All right . . . now come with me."

He reached out his hand. She took it, and they continued forward.

After another ten or fifteen paces, only yards in front of their feet the grass ended abruptly at a sheer cliff dropping some five or six hundred feet straight down to the water's edge. The earth seemed to give way utterly. As if appearing from out of nowhere at the end of the bluff, the vast blue of the sea stretched out as an infinity far before them.

Amanda gasped. Her hand tightened on Ramsay's.

"Don't worry," he laughed as they stopped. "It's not *quite* a straight drop. There are several precipices and juts to catch you if you fall."

"Don't say such a thing!" said Amanda, still struggling to catch her breath and steady her quivering knees.

They waited a few moments, then once more Halifax urged Amanda gently forward.

"Believe me, there is nothing to fear," he said.

They reached the edge. She now saw that indeed the edge was not exactly a perpendicular drop-off, but that the surface gave way to the white cliff below them by degrees.

They sat down, legs over the grassy incline, and remained several long minutes in silence.

Far below and to the right, the city of Folkestone stretched away from the water's edge toward the inland hills. Ships and boats of all sizes came and went from its harbor. Smoke drifted lazily upward from its red and grey rooftops. Forward, their gaze met only blue, broken by a few clouds in the distance. Closer by, seagulls played on the gentle breezes. Their shrill cries and the occasional distant drone of a ship's horn were the only sounds to meet their ears.

"Oh, Ramsay—it's breathtaking!" exclaimed Amanda. "I've seen the Channel many times, but never like this."

"Imagine it on a stormy day. The coastline can be wild too."

"Do you come here on such days? I would think you would be afraid."

"I come here in all weather. I love the sea during a fierce storm, with the wind howling and waves shooting up off the rocks."

"I can see why you say it is one of your favorite places. How did you discover it?"

"Just the way you and I did today," he replied. "I was driving along here one day and decided I wanted to have a look at the Channel. I walked away from the road. Suddenly I found myself at the edge of the world, with this stupendous view stretching out in front of me."

"It is wonderful—now that my heart is out of my throat and back where it belongs!"

Halifax laughed. "Part of the magic of the place is that there is a *little* danger associated with it," he said. "But do you know why else I enjoy it here?"

"Why?"

"Because I consider it a *significant* spot—perhaps one of the most significant places in all England."

"*Significant?*" repeated Amanda. "I'm not sure I understand you."

"Look there," said Ramsay, pointing with his arm out across the Channel in a southeasterly direction.

"I see nothing but water."

"Squint—way off there in the distance . . . can you see it?"

"All I can . . . oh yes—I *do* see land. I thought those were clouds on the horizon."

"It takes a clear day, one like this. But that is the coastline of France you're looking at, from Cap Gris Nez to Calais."

"How far is it across?"

"Twenty-two miles from Dover, probably twenty-three or twenty-four from here."

"It's not that far really, is it?"

"Far enough to have kept England and the European continent separated since 1066. Twenty-two miles of water is better than a thousand miles of open terrain. No European general or dictator in nine centuries has been able to conquer that twenty-two miles."

"So why do you call this a significant place?" asked Amanda.

"Because at this exact spot, like no other I know of, you can see just how narrow the Channel really is. Now that the modern age has come, that distance will shrink all the more."

"Shrink—what do you mean?"

"Like the motorcar," Ramsay replied, nodding his head back toward where his Rolls was parked. "Look at us—today we've gone from London to Hastings, here to Folkestone, and we'll both be sleeping in our own beds back in London again tonight. We've toured nearly all southeastern England in a day! We could never have done such a thing thirty years ago. Industry and transportation, progress and invention—they're changing everything, Amanda. The motorcar is just the beginning—aeroplanes will fill the sky before we know it. You shall no doubt ride in one someday."

"Now you're sounding too much like my father," said Amanda, with disinterested feminine scorn. "He always used to talk about such things."

"My stepfather spoke well of your father once or twice in my hearing."

"Your . . . stepfather?" said Amanda.

"Lord Halifax—he died two years ago."

"I'm sorry."

"He was old—a genial enough man. But he and I were not especially close."

"But you—"

"My mother married him when I was a boy. She wanted me to take his name. But all that's in the past. I'm more excited about the future," Ramsay went on enthusiastically. "I tell you, Amanda, aeroplanes *will* fly over this Channel within a very short time, back and forth from

England to the Continent, as if this narrow stretch of sea doesn't even exist. Mark my words, the time is coming when England will no longer remain separate from the Continent as it has for centuries. More and more will our fortunes and our future be bound up with those of France and Germany and Austria-Hungary, and even Russia."

The sound of the word "Russia" sent a chill up Amanda's spine. Even though its royal families were intricately related, and their two nations had generally been friendly enough, the huge colossus at the eastern edge of Europe remained full of dark mystery in her ears. It was difficult to imagine modern and progressive England having to do with an ancient eastern power ruled by tsars.

"*France* and England might draw closer," she said, almost with a shudder, "but Russia seems too remote and different and far away."

"Russia is England's ally now," said Halifax. "It's a changing world. Change is happening on the Continent more rapidly than most English realize. Especially in Russia. Forces are at work there that very few understand, even though socialism began right here in England. Conflict is coming, and England will not be able to avoid being drawn into it."

The talk of changing times unsettled Amanda. She could not have said why. Though she prided herself on being part of the *avant garde,* she was uncomfortable when events moved beyond her capacity to influence or understand them. Women's rights were one thing. Alliances with Russia were another. She didn't like the sound of it.

"Why are the cliffs white?" she asked at length.

"The rock here is mostly chalk."

Again it was quiet. Halifax glanced down at his watch. "Almost four-thirty. It's probably time we thought about getting you back to the city. We don't want Mrs. Pankhurst upset with me."

He rose, took Amanda's hand, and pulled her to her feet and safely away from the cliff. She sighed deeply, taking one last gaze up and down the coast. They turned and walked back to the car.

"Emmeline won't worry about me," said Amanda. "She's not my mother, after all. She lets me do as I please."

12
Two Fathers

———— ✦ ✦ ✦ ————

*C*harles Rutherford and his twenty-two-year-old son George, home for a weekend visit during his final term at Oxford, were busily stringing wire in the second floor of the north wing of Heathersleigh Hall, the last portion of the great stone mansion yet to be outfitted with electricity. As happy as he was for his son's education, it was always a boon to the father's spirits to have him home, even if briefly.

Both were eagerly anticipating the summer months. Already plans were being laid between them for the completion of the electrical project, as well as the installation of a telephone at the Hall. Charles' work on the prime minister's commission allowed him not only to keep pace with developments elsewhere in the country, but to have a hand in directing them as well. As more and more electrical and telephone lines were strung outward from London, Charles' dreams were being fulfilled almost more rapidly than he had dared imagine.

George came bounding down the stairs from the attic.

"What would you think, Father," he said, "of running a line up into the garret?"

"A little soon for that, isn't it, George?" replied Charles, looking up from where he sat on the floor pulling a length of wire through the hole he had recently bored from the other side of the wall. "We haven't even finished the main house yet."

"I know. But I want to have light operational up there later this summer. I found a spot where I can drill down easily through the floor and connect with the junction we made this morning between the library and the armory. The wire will hardly be seen. Then the current will be in the garret when we're ready to install lights."

Charles laughed. "You seem to have thought it through. Sure, go ahead, George."

"Thanks, Father!"

"If I need you, I'll pound on the ceiling with Morse code!"

George turned and hurried back to his project. Charles watched him go with a pleased smile. As the last words of his son continued to sound in his brain, gradually the smile faded and his thoughts turned reflectively toward his second child.

Neither did the last words *she* had spoken to him ever leave his thoughts. He would not forget them should he live to be five hundred years old.

"I have no respect left for either of you," she had said. *"I can't say there is much feeling left in my heart for anyone around here. I hate it here. I have hated it for years."* Then had followed the letter which, at least for the present, had ended hope of relationship in the near future. *"I am not interested in your God,"* she had written, *"in your prayers, or in either of you."*

The letter had come two and a half years ago. Yet to a sensitive nature like Charles Rutherford's, the words plunged anew every day like a knife blade into his father's heart.

What a contrast between the two—George who loved him and embraced his role in his life, and Amanda who found all thought of parental supervision hateful and confining. He had been the same father to them both, thought Charles. What could account for the difference?

Will Amanda ever want to call me father again? he sighed. *Will the very word always be hateful to her, or will she one day soften to the idea of someone above her to whom she can be a daughter?*

With the thought, prayer was not far behind.

Amanda had asked him not to pray for her. But that was one request with which he could not, and would not, comply.

"O God, Father of us all," Charles groaned inwardly where he sat, *"though her mind is set against all reminder of it, stir Amanda's heart toward daughterhood. Probe and prick her in the deep places of her being where we are all children, because we were made to be children—your children. Help her to warm to the idea of your Fatherhood, though her brain may resist for yet a season. Take away the hate, the bitterness, the resentment that somehow has come to reside in her as a result of my influence in her life."*

As he prayed, the imagery of growing things came into his mind, as it often did when he and Jocelyn prayed for their children, as had been their custom for years, in the heather garden next to the wood east of the Hall.

"Till the soil of Amanda's heart, Lord," he now prayed. *"Send your warming sun upon it. Break up the frozen ground of her independence. Though the*

thought of me remains odious to her, though perhaps she does not want to call me father, turn her heart toward your Fatherhood. And I am not, after all, her true father, Lord. You only gave her to me for a little while, to help her become your daughter. Forgive my inadequacy to the task. It would seem I have failed both her and you, Lord God. Yet I know you did not expect me to be a perfect father, only one who sought to obey you. I began late to do so, which is my life's deepest regret, and even now I do so but feebly."

Charles paused and sighed at the reminder of his shortcomings as a father.

"You are the only perfect Father," he prayed again, *"and you will yet be that perfect Father to our dear Amanda. You will take up my imperfect fatherhood into your plan for her, and use it in your miraculous way to perfect Amanda's daughterhood in you. Carry out that work, heavenly Father—not only in Amanda, but also in George, in Catharine, in Jocelyn . . . and in me. Turn my heart, too, more and more toward your Fatherhood. Create ever more deeply in me the longing to be a child. Make me more fully your obedient and thankful son."*

13

An Invitation

◆ ◆ ◆

*L*ife with the Pankhursts rarely lacked for excitement.

Visitors came almost daily for information, interviews, and business. Passersby came to heckle. Still others just stared into the windows of the home where dwelt the radical women firebrands.

But mostly the excitement came from Emmeline Pankhurst's activities themselves. Her most favored method in the women's campaign was to push the limits of the law so as to make *news* for the cause. Every day the possibility existed that Emmeline might not return home for tea, or even for bed that night.

Enough stories circulated about Mrs. Pankhurst, exaggerated by the London press, to keep public curiosity at a high pitch. The demonized drawings in the papers made people want to see her for themselves.

The perceptions created in the papers were not actually so far from the truth. Emmeline Pankhurst was passionately obsessed with the suffragette movement. It was the sole topic of conversation at every meal. The guests who appeared for tea were either new recruits or prospective donors to the cause. In the household in which Amanda Rutherford had cast her fate, women's rights dominated every moment, every breath, every waking thought.

Mornings she and the others folded and prepared leaflets and placards. Afternoons they distributed their wares, marching, speaking, protesting, and otherwise appearing around the city to make the cause known to wider numbers. Once or twice a month they gathered in front of the Houses of Parliament while the M.P.s arrived for the day's session, bullying and badgering to cajole the lawmakers to listen to their pleas.

At first the involvement in something that seemed so important thrilled Amanda. It was a new and exciting life. She had always dreamed of living in London. Now here she was in the very middle of it. Yet though outwardly she despised her upbringing and everything her parents stood for, she could not erase the good breeding she had received. In spite of what she tried to tell herself, there were times she found herself balking at the unladylike things the cause required. She did her best to convince herself that she would eventually get accustomed to the boisterous, rude, and radical behavior.

The invitation arrived at the Pankhurst home a week after Amanda's outing with Ramsay Halifax between Hastings and Dover. Its words were simple enough, but they would change her life.

"Amanda," called out Sylvia from below, "—Amanda, come downstairs! A messenger is here for you."

In surroundings where Emmeline Pankhurst was a woman of national reputation, Amanda could not imagine what a messenger could possibly want with *her*. She hurried downstairs thinking to herself that there must be some tragic news. Sylvia and Christabel stood waiting at the front door in anticipation. Outside a young man in top hat and tails held an envelope and the thornless stem of a peach-hued rose.

"You are Miss Rutherford?" he said.

Amanda nodded.

He handed her both envelope and flower, then turned without another word, and strode across the brick walk to a waiting single-horse carriage. Within moments he had disappeared down the street.

Amanda stared bewildered after him.

"Well . . . open it!" said Christabel impatiently.

The words brought Amanda to her senses. With trembling finger she tore at one edge of the envelope, then pulled out a single sheet from inside. She took a deep breath and read:

To: Miss Amanda Rutherford

Amanda,

I would be pleased if you would do me the honor of accepting an invitation to accompany me to the Derby and the Reception that follows. The race is scheduled for Saturday next, the eighth, at two o'clock in the afternoon. Unless I hear otherwise, I shall call for you at eleven.

Yours cordially,
Ramsay Halifax, Esq.

Amanda handed her the card. Christabel scanned it quickly.

"Who is he?" Christabel asked excitedly.

"Someone I met at the Kensington Lawn Tea—the man who was at Hastings, remember. I came home with him."

"A good-looking man too! Will you accept, Amanda?"

"Of course," replied Amanda, heart pounding. "How could I turn down an invitation like this!"

"The Derby is one of the premier events of the social season," said Sylvia. "Not that I care about such things, but some people do. If Mother received an invitation like that, she would probably smuggle in a piece of dynamite and throw it onto the track before the race!"

"I plan to enjoy myself," laughed Amanda.

Already her girlish enthusiasm was mounting. Nothing like *this* ever happened at the Pankhursts'. Nothing like this ever happened to *her*. All of a sudden women's suffrage seemed unimportant and far away.

"In fact," she added with a giggle, "I think I will go to Harrods this very afternoon. I simply must find a new dress!"

"Oh, but Harrods is too expensive."

"Money is no object!" rejoined Amanda. "I can't be seen in rags for such an occasion!"

"Rags—what are you talking about? You have beautiful dresses."

"But I *must* have something new and stylish for the Prince of Wales Horse Race."

The conversation at lunch an hour later left Amanda wondering if her hostess approved of her attending the Derby as a spectator, as one of the social elite.

"Amanda dear," Emmeline said, "I understand you have been invited to the Derby."

Amanda nodded, thinking to herself that if given such an opportunity, Emmeline would probably try to disrupt the race with a demonstration, or, as Sylvia had said, with dynamite.

"You know Emily . . . Emily Davison?" asked Mrs. Pankhurst.

"Yes, I believe so. Was she at Hastings with us?"

"That's right," replied Emmeline. "She has always dreamed of attending the Derby. Do you suppose your friend might secure her an invitation?"

"I . . . I don't know."

"Do ask, will you, Amanda?"

"I don't really know him that well. I doubt I will see him before Saturday."

"But you will try, won't you?"

Awkwardly Amanda agreed.

Immediately after lunch she set off for Harrods. Already she was having second thoughts. Sylvia was right—Harrods *was* expensive. Though she did her best to conceal it, her money was dwindling more rapidly than she liked. She had already dipped into the account far too deeply for gowns and other costly apparel, half of which she had never even worn. She had so relished in the freedom of being on her own and having money in the bank, she now realized she had squandered far too much of it on foolish expenditures.

But she would start exercising more caution later—*after* next week's reception at Epsom. For this occasion she would look her best!

Amanda tried on dress after dress. The Pankhursts were fashionable enough, but they had other things on their minds than men and society. And the luncheon conversation left her with an oddly uncomfortable feeling. Sylvia obviously wouldn't approve—she didn't believe in marriage at all, much less social outings with men. Amanda needed to get away from the house for a while. She was glad to be alone for the rest of the afternoon.

The dress Amanda chose *was* far too expensive, but it was so beautiful she could not resist—absolutely perfect for the occasion! The long skirt of rich navy blue contained tiny pink stripes running lengthwise through the fabric, highlighted with a bodice of light pink silk, with loose ruffles about the neck. A navy blue jacket fit snugly over the blouse. After a tailoring session the following day with Harrods' dressmaker, the overall effect showed off her slender figure beautifully. She chose a fashionable straw hat and matched it with pink and white flowers, along with pink and navy ribbons.

As it turned out, Amanda neither saw nor heard from Ramsay Halifax again before the eighth. Neither did she see Emily Davison, nor did Mrs. Pankhurst bring up the subject of the Derby again.

Halifax called at the door of the Pankhurst home precisely at 11:00 A.M. He was shown into the parlor.

Before Amanda reached the top of the stairs, Emmeline greeted him. She and Halifax were chatting freely by the time Amanda made her descent. For once Amanda hoped she would hear nothing about the cause. She wanted to step into another world on this day—the world of high London society. She did *not* want to have to think about rights and votes and feminism.

"—the *Daily Mail*, that *is* interesting," Emmeline was saying. "It was your paper that first coined the word 'suffragette,' was it not?"

"My editor himself," laughed the personable young man.

As Amanda reached the bottom of the stairs and entered the drawing room, Mrs. Pankhurst had just begun introducing her escort to another young lady of somewhat wild green eyes and bright red hair. Her orange dress clashed with both and hung from wide but slender shoulders without accenting any of her feminine curves. The overall effect was not unlike a human scarecrow with red straw stuck on top.

"Amanda . . ." she said, glancing up as she walked in, "—you remember that Emily is going with you.—Mr. Halifax," she added, turning again toward the journalist, "I would like you to meet Emily Davison. Amanda *did* speak with you about Emily's accompanying the two of you?"

Not wanting to embarrass Amanda but clearly caught off his guard, Halifax fumbled for words.

"I . . . didn't exactly," he said, shaking Miss Davison's hand, "—well, but—"

"I promise I will be no trouble, Mr. Halifax," interrupted Emily in a thin, high-pitched voice that fit the image created by her appearance. Then, without awaiting an answer, the newcomer immediately walked outside and toward the car. Halifax and Amanda followed, the former perplexed, the latter irritated, by the sudden change of plans.

"Do enjoy yourselves," Mrs. Pankhurst called out in an uncharacteristically genial tone.

By the time Halifax was comfortably behind the wheel, with Amanda next to him on the front seat, Emily Davison had stationed herself securely behind them with an expression on her face that even Ramsay Halifax apparently decided it would be best not to argue with.

Almost inaudibly he sighed, then drove off.

14

The Derby

♦♦♦

*T*he drive south to Epsom remained quiet and strained. Halifax did his best to keep up a conversation with Amanda, though with limited success. Not a word was spoken from the backseat.

They arrived shortly after noon. Crowds and vendors were already gathering throughout the auto and buggy park. Though Ascot, which would be run two weeks later, remained a far more exclusive horse race, the overwhelming popularity of the Derby had long before necessitated that it be shared with the masses, and it was widely attended by a great cross section of society. Halifax parked the automobile, and the trio walked toward the main entrance across the wide expanse of lawn. Only moments after they were inside the grounds, Amanda suddenly realized she and Ramsay were alone.

"I am sorry for the inconvenience of that intrusion," she said. "I had no idea such a thing was going to happen. I cannot believe Mrs. Pankhurst did that!"

"No harm done," laughed Halifax. "Bit of a strange one though, I must say. Are all your suffragette friends so wild-eyed?"

"I've only met her once," replied Amanda. "I really know nothing about her."

"I assume she is *the* Emily Davison?"

"What do you mean *the* Emily Davison?" repeated Amanda.

"You don't know?" said Halifax.

"I guess I don't. Know what?"

"It didn't strike me until we were on our way, then I began to re-member an incident from last year. Seems your friend was discovered beside the Parliament Street Post Office with a pile of paraffin-soaked rags and matches—all ready to set the place ablaze. That's when all the militancy began. Prior to that, even your Mrs. Pankhurst had been rea-sonable enough."

"I've never seen Emily around the house."

"What's done is done—we will enjoy ourselves nonetheless for it.—Ah, Witherspoon!" he exclaimed, observing an acquaintance walking toward him.

"Halifax," said the other with a nod. The two men shook hands.

"May I present Miss Amanda Rutherford, daughter of Sir Charles Rutherford—"

At the words, Amanda cringed inwardly. She wanted to be known for *herself*, as a suffragette, not as her father's daughter.

"—Amanda, meet Lord Leslie Witherspoon."

"Charmed, Miss Rutherford," said Witherspoon. "Tell me, what does your father think of the situation in Morocco—will France go to war with Germany?"

"I really could not say, Mr. Witherspoon," replied Amanda, bristling again. "My father and I do not discuss political matters. Actually, I have not seen him for some time."

"What about you, Halifax," persisted Witherspoon. "What do you think? I'll wager some of *your* friends are closely watching events in the east," he added with a grin that seemed to imply more than the words divulged.

"What I think, Lord Witherspoon," said Ramsay, laughing off the question, "is that Miss Rutherford and I came today to watch the horses, not talk continental politics.—By the by, have you seen my mother?"

"I do believe I saw her, old man," replied Witherspoon, glancing around. "About here someplace with old Harry Thorndike's widow, I believe."

"Right . . . we'll find her. Cheers, Witherspoon."

As Halifax led Amanda away, he leaned toward her ear with a low voice. "He'll talk your ear off if you let him!"

"I'm glad you rescued me from such a fate," she laughed. "What did he mean about your friends?"

"Oh, nothing—just my news colleagues . . . always watching events.

Looking for a story, you know.—Ah, there's Mum now. We'll be sitting in her box for the race."

They walked across the lawn in the direction of two women.

"Ramsay dear," said the younger and taller of the two, glancing toward them as they approached. "This must be Amanda."

"Yes, Mum—Amanda Rutherford, my mother, Lady Hildegard Halifax."

"I am pleased to meet you, Lady Halifax."

"I have heard so much about you, Miss Rutherford dear," said Ramsay's mother, shaking her hand with uncommon strength and vigor. The voice which met Amanda's ears was low, and contained an accent which could not have originated anywhere in Britain. The very sound of it reminded Amanda of mystery. "I would like you to meet my dear friend, Mrs. Thorndike," added Ramsay's mother.

"How do you do?" said Amanda, now shaking the hand of the older woman. She took Amanda's palm in her soft fleshy fingers and gave it the slight up-and-down motion that passed for a handshake between women of the British nobility.

"I was sorry to hear about your husband's death," said Amanda, turning again to Mrs. Halifax.

"Thank you, my dear," she replied. "It was not altogether unexpected. It was two years ago, and he was my second husband. I am twice a widow. However, I have managed to adjust to life without dear Burton. And dear Lady Thorndike, widowed near the same time as myself, has been staying with me since shortly after our husbands' deaths."

The brief silence which followed gave Amanda the chance to take in the woman's features. She judged Ramsay's mother to be somewhere in her mid-fifties, several inches taller than her companion, stout yet with a solid, robust, Germanic stoutness rather than a soft plumpness. Her face seemed to wear several expressions at once, as in layers, as of one whose awareness of people and events about her was deeper than she allowed herself to divulge.

"Excuse me, will you a minute, Mother, Amanda?" came the sound of Ramsay's voice intruding into her thoughts. "I see someone over there I need to speak with."

He walked off across the lawn. His mother's eyes followed him, squinting slightly when they fell upon the man Ramsay met. Whatever she was thinking, she said nothing. Soon she and Amanda and Lady Thorndike were engaged in more of the meaningless chatter of which such gatherings are comprised, though Mrs. Halifax seemed at the same time to keep an eye subtly roving about the crowd.

"There is Sarah Marlowe," said Lady Thorndike in a low voice of disdain. "However in the world did *she* get an invitation? Do you know her, Hildegard?"

"I believe I met her one afternoon at your house for tea, several years ago," replied Ramsay's mother.

"Oh yes, I remember now.—And there's the prime minister's wife," the English socialite went on. "We really should speak to her. Won't you excuse us, Miss Rutherford?"

Lady Thorndike waddled off toward Mrs. Asquith. Lady Halifax followed. Amanda hesitated, glancing around momentarily for Ramsay. In the second or two that followed, she found herself standing alone. She was about to set out to overtake the two women, when she heard her name. She glanced in the direction of the voice.

It was Geoffrey's mother Martha bustling her way!

"Why, Amanda dear," said Gifford's wife, "what an unexpected delight."

Amanda was not surprised to see Cousin Martha with billows of flowing fabric trailing behind her. Indeed, the indistinct form presented to her eyes matched the indistinct image of the lady in her fading memory.

"Hello, Cousin Martha," said Amanda.

"Won't Geoffrey be upset at himself for not coming with me," said the woman. "If he'd only known *you* were going to be here."

Silently Amanda breathed a sigh of relief at the answer to the question she had been afraid to ask—whether Geoffrey was here too.

"Who are you with, dear?" asked Mrs. Rutherford.

"I came with Ramsay Halifax. Perhaps you know his mother?"

"Oh, so you are with Lady Halifax's party," said Mrs. Rutherford.

"I came with her son Ramsay," repeated Amanda. "I only just met Lady Halifax for the first time a few minutes ago."

"Oh . . . I see," said her cousin, drawing out the words with obvious inflection of significance. An awkward silence followed.

"How, uh—how are your mother and father, Amanda dear? You were not at Heathersleigh the last time we called."

"I've been in London nearly three years."

If Martha was astonished at the news she did not show it, though how much she knew of Gifford's approach to the girl was doubtful.

"We try to make the trip to Devon every few years," she went on as if nothing were so strange in what Amanda had said. "My dear husband considers it his duty to visit the old family estate upon occasion."

"I've been busy myself here in the city," rejoined Amanda, unconsciously glancing around for sign of Ramsay. This was already becoming tedious.

"I hear—though I cannot believe such a thing myself, but there are those who say you have had some association with that Pankhurst woman," said Martha. "What a dreadful business. I'm sure I don't understand a bit of it."

Amanda pulled herself up slightly. "What you hear is true," she said.

What would the dull woman say if she told her about the afternoon she had spent in jail!

"There you are, Miss Rutherford!" came the voice of Ramsay Halifax to her rescue. "I've been looking all about for you. Mum said she lost track of you. It's time we were in our seats. The announcements are about to begin."

Amanda turned to go. "Good-bye, Cousin Martha," she said.

"We must get together for tea now that you are in London," the billowy lady called after her.

The rest of the day passed pleasantly enough. The horses ran without major upset. Amanda saw neither Martha Rutherford nor Emily Davison again. The odd-looking young woman did not return home with them, and both Ramsay and Amanda were left wondering why she had accompanied them to the Derby at all.

15

Setting the Bait

❦he conversation in the home of the London Rutherfords that same night, as Martha reported to her financier husband what she had seen and heard at the Derby, had nothing to do with the winning thoroughbred or his odds.

As Gifford listened, he realized he had underestimated the little shrew. He had taken too much for granted, assuming that their previous talk and the girl's acceptance of Geoffrey's invitation to the Lawn Tea insured a deeper loyalty between their two houses than she apparently did.

He could not confront her too boldly, however. If he accused her of playing false, she would bolt. He knew her kind well enough. He would lure her into his web by giving her something she wanted—something more than a donation to a cause she might not be that interested in anyway.

Geoffrey would also have to play his hand more aggressively, thought Gifford. It would not do for the girl to get involved with other men, or the cause of his son might be lost. Wealth notwithstanding, the father knew as well as anyone Geoffrey's limitations as a potential suitor. To make this match would require more cunning than he had initially thought.

"I'm worried about Amanda, Gifford," said Martha as she prattled on about the day. "She knows absolutely nothing about society etiquette."

"Yes . . . hmm, I see what you mean," mumbled her husband as he turned the thing over in his mind.

"And to have dealings with those suffragettes!"

"It *is* unfortunate to see such an attractive young thing falling in with such influences. I must admit," Gifford went on, assuming the dignified tone of wisdom, "that I find it impossible to understand how some parents can neglect their most basic responsibilities. I would never have thought such about my cousin Charles."

"I had not exactly thought of it in such terms," replied Martha, "but now that you say it . . . yes, it *is* rather shocking. And *why* would they have been so neglectful? That is what I cannot understand."

"Who can say? But then . . . the results would seem to speak for themselves. It is scarcely any wonder the poor girl is estranged from them. She is languishing for lack of proper training and upbringing. Whatever pretense they tried to put over on others publicly, I don't know what other conclusion to draw other than there was simply a lack of love in the home."

"It is *such* a sad thing to see."

"Perhaps we ought to help," suggested Gifford.

"What could *we* do?" asked Martha.

"I don't know, my dear," he replied with feigned innocence. "But it is clear my cousin has not done his duty by the poor girl. Perhaps we ought—"

He stopped for effect.

"—yet it is hardly *our* place," he added.

"Our place to what?"

"I was just thinking," replied Gifford, the engines of his brain beginning to spin more rapidly, "—I was thinking that, since we live in London, and since the girl *is* here, and the season is now in full swing . . . perhaps *we* should take it upon ourselves to present her to society. She is our cousin after all, one generation more distantly removed, of course, but blood is blood, and I have always thought of her as the daughter we never had."

"Oh, that is a wonderful idea, Gifford," exclaimed Martha. "How delightful it would be to take her to the season's round of balls and parties."

"I'm sure Geoffrey would not mind *occasionally* being seen with her," suggested Gifford, casually lifting an eyebrow. "Once I explain the thing to him, I'm certain he would be glad to help—for the sake of the family, of course."

"And I could take her shopping for suitable attire," said Martha excitedly. "Perhaps we might even make a dress together."

"I think you are absolutely right, my dear," said Gifford. "That is a very good idea. It is kind and selfless of you to suggest it."

"Oh, what fun we shall have!"

"Perhaps we ought to have a talk with the dear girl. Why don't you invite her for tea next week?"

16

Garden of God's Blossoms

A warm sun beat down upon the luxuriant flower garden which surrounded and spread out in every direction from Margaret McFee's cottage.

Maggie was perspiring freely. From her lips could faintly be heard the hum of various hymns spilling one into the other. Rarely did she enjoy herself so much as when on her knees amongst her children, God's blossoms, as the sun lured from them multitude fragrances to perfume the air, her hands black with the Creator's rich earth, the food for all growing things.

As was often the case when she worked here, Maggie's thoughts were on the Lord's words from Matthew: *"The kingdom of heaven is like unto treasure hid in a field; the which when a man hath found, he hideth, and for joy thereof goeth and selleth all that he hath, and buyeth that field."* She could not dig or cultivate the ground without being reminded of the mystery of growth which God had implanted into the very earth itself. The parable spoken by the Lord indeed pointed to the greatest treasure of all—the power of life itself—which lay buried invisibly in the soil and, in combination with the sun and rain, could perform such wonders as were displayed in her garden.

What were her flowers but that same treasure of the heart hidden in *this* field? And God had given it to her! To Margaret McFee, growing these radiant treasures was more priceless than had her digging uncovered a stash of gold.

She heard her husband approach behind her. She turned and greeted him with a smile.

"On such days as this, Bobby," she said, "I'm so thankful for the cottage. I know we don't deserve it, but I can't be any less glad that it's ours."

"'Tis nothing wrong with the ownership of a fine thing," rejoined Bobby. "God gives us material possessions to enjoy. 'Tis meant to make us happy, so long as we ne'er worship the possession rather than the Creator who gives it."

"Well, this garden does make me happy," said Maggie. "I feel closer to him when I'm here."

"'Tis no doubt one o' the reasons he's given it to ye."

"It's the Lord's provision, but it came from the old bishop."

"Ay—to yer grandmother through the church. So in a manner o' speaking, 'tis kind o' like from the hand o' the Lord himself."

"It was God's provision," repeated Maggie, "of that I am certain, whoever's hand delivered it. But my mother said that her mother would never talk about it when she asked her about the affair. She only said, 'It's in the Book. The mystery's in the Book.'"

"What did she mean?"

"The mystery of the kingdom, the mystery of godliness, is all I could ever think. Once or twice my mother said she thought it had something to do with the Hall."

"'Course it had to do with the Hall. This grand cottage that's now ours used t' belong t' the Hall."

"True enough, Bobby. But it's more than that she was meaning, I'm sure of it, though it's puzzled me all my life long. 'Everything's not as it should be at the Hall,' she said."

"And ye have no idea what she was meanin'?"

"None. I don't think my mother knew herself. She was just repeating what my grandmother said to her."

"Then we best not only be prayin' for Master Charles and Lady Jocelyn and young Amanda and the others, like we have been," said Bobby, "but for the Hall itself."

Maggie raised herself from her knees, moved to a clear spot between planted beds, then sat down on the warm earth and folded her hands and closed her eyes.

"Lord," she said aloud, "we pray for this whole Heathersleigh estate, the parts that are in it now and that once were in times past. Whatever's not right, whether it's known or unknown, work your healing and whole-making purpose."

"We ask ye, Lord," now prayed Bobby, "that ye'll make all come right in the end, with the Hall and this cottage, and the whole estate and all the people connected with it. Do yer will in yer time."

"We ask you again to take care of the dear child Amanda," prayed Maggie. "Her heart's not right with her mother and father, Lord. How can she ever be happy with such wrongness sitting like a lump of blackness inside her?"

"Give Master Charles and dear Lady Jocelyn yer grace to bear this burden without lettin' their trust wither. Give them courage to stand and be strong in the midst o' their pain."

"Amen," added Maggie.

17

An Offer

◆ ◆ ◆

*W*hy Amanda accepted the invitation of the wife of her father's cousin, she wasn't exactly certain.

Yet on the Wednesday following the Derby she found herself approaching the forbidding stone house on Curzon Street from the cab which had just left her in front of the gate. She hoped Geoffrey wasn't home. She found it difficult to breathe in his presence.

A servant showed her into an old-looking drawing room. It seemed to billow like her aunt's clothing. The drapes covering the front windows were entirely too full and let in none of the outside light. The room was so dim that Amanda's eyes found it difficult to adjust. Cushions and lap blankets and antimacassars lay over all the couches. Her aunt was seated, engaged at something or other at a table with mounds of fabric spread over it.

"Hello, Amanda dear," she said. "Come in."

Amanda approached tentatively.

"I am so glad to have you here," said Martha. "I have looked forward to your coming. I never have much to do for myself, you know. So occasionally I busy myself with making bandages for the hospital—that's one of my little causes."

The words fell strangely on Amanda's ears. Cousin Gifford's wife involved in a humanitarian cause—she would never have dreamed it. The image of hospital bandages was altogether inconsistent with the picture of Martha Rutherford as a plump and intellectually vacant socialite.

"I go every week and take flowers and visit those less fortunate. We must all do something for others, you know."

In spite of herself, a smile of genuine goodwill escaped Amanda's lips. "Thank you for inviting me to tea, Cousin Martha," she said.

Amanda found herself for the first time drawn in a strange way to the flustery lady. If anything, she deserved pity for having to live with Gifford and Cousin Geoffrey!

"Oh yes, the tea," said Martha. "Pull that cord over there to let Louisa know we are ready."

Amanda did so while Mrs. Rutherford rose from the table and walked to one of the couches in the center of the room.

"Come over here, dear," she said. "You can sit across from me and we will have a little talk. I do like to see people when I speak to them. It saves so much trouble if you can see their faces." As she spoke, she motioned Amanda to one of the chairs across the small tea table from her. "People often speak in riddles," she went on, "and I'm not keen on riddles. But I am keen on faces."

Amanda sat down, removed her hat, and set it down beside her. The brocade chairs appeared ancient but were well taken care of. Her cousin seemed to read her mind.

"Yes, things in here are indeed quite old," said Martha. "But I don't let the sun in and that keeps them from deteriorating. It's the sun, you know, that makes things old before their time. As true with the complexion as with the furnishings."

A minute or two later the door opened. The woman named Louisa entered carrying a tray of tea things. A young servant girl followed with another tray of breads and cakes and various spreads. They set both trays down on the table between them. Steam rose from the teapot, and the aroma of fresh tea gradually filled the room.

"When I saw you at the Derby last week," Martha began as they waited for the tea to complete its brewing, "I must admit to some surprise."

Amanda cocked her head quizzically but said nothing.

Martha continued. "I do keep track of such things, you see," she said. "I had seen your name on none of the lists, and of course you are a little older than most young women . . . but I assumed you planned to continue waiting, perhaps until next year. But then suddenly . . . there you were, and as I say, I was quite surprised. Not shocked, I would not say *that*, but certainly surprised.—I think the tea is ready. Would you like to pour?"

Amanda took the pot and poured the contents into the two cups which stood waiting with milk in them.

"Cousin Martha," she said as she did, "whatever are you talking about?"

"Why, about being presented, of course. You have not been properly introduced to society, my dear."

Now Amanda understood clearly enough. She knew the fact to which Martha referred only too well. It was one of her chief ongoing grievances against her parents—their refusal, as she saw it, to let her grow up and enter society like other young women her age. They had wanted to control her life all the way into adulthood! If she'd have let them, they would have kept her an old maid living at Heathersleigh until she was forty!

"I must admit I have been curious why your parents have done nothing to bring you out. I know Devon is some distance from the city," Martha went on. "But then for a family of our standing—well, it would just seem that . . . and with a young woman of breeding and noble name as attractive as you, my dear—well, it all should have been undertaken when you were seventeen or eighteen. Your presentation to English society—had you been *my* daughter—would have occurred the first season after your seventeenth birthday. I know some would say it doesn't matter so much these days. But it *is* very proper."

Amanda stared down into her cup of tea. Martha's words pricked at wounds she would rather not talk about.

"And then when I realized you were actually living in town—Gifford told me he had seen you one day when I was out. Well . . . imagine. I did not think about it again until I saw you on Saturday."

"I appreciate your concern, Martha," said Amanda, the reminder of her own irritation making her unusually sympathetic to what appeared a genuine feeling of compassion on her cousin's part. "You need not worry about me."

"But perhaps it is not too late. Tell me, my dear—do your parents have plans to bring you out?"

"I strongly doubt it," replied Amanda stiffly. "Even if they did, *their* plans could hardly interest me now."

"It is unfortunate. But your father and mother *have* behaved oddly these last few years. They do not seem to care for society at all."

Amanda nodded but said nothing.

"I'm certain if I had title and property as your father does, I would make the very best use of it," Mrs. Rutherford went on. "But the social season has only just begun, dear. The Lawn Tea and the Derby are behind us, but most of the spring's events are yet to come. And you *were* seen with my Geoffrey at Kensington Gardens, which is a good beginning."

"The beginning of what?" asked Amanda cautiously. She wasn't sure she liked the idea hinted at—future appearances with Martha Rutherford's son!

"You are a lovely young lady," replied Martha. "I would love so much to see you make a showing. Perhaps I might help."

"Help . . . in what way?"

"I could arrange—I have no doubt my Gifford would use his influence to secure the invitations we would need, and Geoffrey would no doubt be willing, occasionally perhaps, to accompany you . . . as I was saying, I am certain we could arrange for you to be presented at the court."

Suddenly Amanda's attention was arrested. "The *court*?" she repeated.

"I can see you now," said Martha exuberantly, "at all the parties and balls in London. I felt so sorry for you when I saw you at the Derby with a young man without yet having been presented. Your parents have apparently overlooked this necessity. But that is no reason why we of your family, who are more familiar with the etiquette of London, should not help you now. What do you think, my dear?"

"Cousin Martha," smiled Amanda, "are you concerned for my reputation?"

"Of course, dear."

Part of Amanda was already tingling with the very thought of Cousin Martha's suggestion. Had she not dreamed of such since before she could remember? Yet another part of her attempted to remain sophisticated and aloof, pretending she didn't care. She had spent the last three years accepting the fact that such opportunities were never going to come to her. This was so sudden, so unexpected.

"This *is* 1911," she said, as two sides battled for supremacy within her. "Things are different now, Cousin Martha. At Mrs. Pankhurst's house we do not worry about what society may think. Many former traditions must be cast aside for women to be looked upon and treated as equals."

"Oh, but . . . the Pankhursts! Surely, dear, you must see—they are a different breed. They are not like us. Of course *they* wouldn't care for such things. Their heads are too full of politics and social change to know how to be women. Don't you care what men think? Don't you want to be attractive and to be invited to balls? Don't you want to be married one day? No man will want to marry a militant, Amanda. Not all traditions are so bad."

The words pricked deep. Of course she cared. Those were the very things she had so yearned for as a girl. Though trying to convince herself she didn't care, Amanda silently felt the pain every year when the season began. She saw young gentlemen and ladies going to the theaters and great houses, while she stood on the street with placards in her hands.

And yet just when she had all but given up on such a thing for herself, suddenly here was an opportunity to enter into the very society whose customs and behavior her parents and even Emmeline Pankhurst disdained.

"There are other ways for women to exert a force in the world," Martha was saying. "Some of the greatest influences come in quiet ways that are more pleasing and make women appear so much nicer than those pictures in the newspapers of women shouting with their hair all undone, and being handled by policemen. We are all women together, Amanda. We may not be able to vote, but we have influence in other ways. The Pankhursts will not further you in society, my dear."

Amanda slowly nodded, though her gaze remained in her lap.

"There is so much for you to learn, and I would like to teach you," said Martha. "This year's season is well on its way, but I can arrange to have you presented soon, and in the right way. You can accompany me to the theater and to receptions. At the end of it, you could attend the coronation in June. By then everyone who is anyone in London will know the name *Amanda Rutherford*."

Amanda now sat up a little straighter in her chair. Her cousin was offering her a chance for everything she had always dreamed of. Even to see the new king and queen, and this time not as a small child as she had been when her father was knighted, but as a woman in her own right!

What would the Pankhursts say? she thought to herself. If *they* got within blocks of the coronation it would not be to enjoy the pomp and ceremony, but to disrupt it.

A brief silence followed.

"Yes, Martha," said Amanda slowly at length. "It is very kind of you to offer to help, and to do this for me. I . . . I think I would like that very much."

"There will be, of course," said her cousin, "expenses involved. You have a nice shape and an eye for fashion—that was a lovely blue suit you had on at the Derby. *Do* you have money, my dear?"

"I, uh . . . yes—yes, of course," replied Amanda.

Martha Rutherford, however, was skilled enough at reading faces, as she said, to see Amanda's eyes dart away uncomfortably as she replied.

"Never mind, dear," she said with a motherly smile. "I will speak with Gifford about the matter. I assure you there will be no difficulty."

When Martha Rutherford later reported on the conversation to her husband, it was with some difficulty that the banker hid his delight. Whether or not he possessed a legitimate *legal* claim to Heathersleigh— and who could tell whether he would *ever* be able to get to the bottom of it—the pathway leading through his simpleminded cousin's daughter was clearly the most direct means to attain his objective.

Yes, he thought, his wife had done well. Better than she would ever know!

18

Society

◆◆◆

*E*ven in the modern times of 1911, the majority of the country's aristocracy measured the passing of every new year by the events and functions of the English social calendar. Though the newly powerful business class of which her husband was a part paid such things little heed, Martha Rutherford was no businesswoman.

Like most of her breed, the wife of Amanda's father's cousin loved the *old* ways of society.

Martha Rutherford's mother had been a social climber of sorts, not too successful it is true, but sufficiently to have passed on to her daughter the hunger for that level of society fated to remain forever just beyond their family's reach. She had long ago made peace with her station in life. It did tend to get dreary, however, when everyone vacated the city each fall for the north and west. When overhearing dames and ladies in conversation, poor Martha found herself longing for an estate like Heathersleigh. How fashionable it would be to leave London for one's country villa when Parliament adjourned in August, and then return to the city for the winter and spring social seasons.

Though not titled like his cousin, Gifford Rutherford was of sufficiently ancient name and certainly of sufficient net worth to give himself and his wife the necessary prestige to move about with ease in the lower echelons of society. These days wealth had *nearly* as much to do with one's rung on the ladder of status as did title. On that score Gifford's standing was secure enough. He could have bought any five country estates he had wanted. But without title, people talked. The snubs were not particularly subtle toward those who tried to appear more *landed* than they had a right to be. Invitations dried up, conversations cooled. Better to be rich *without* an estate than to pretend. Money was useful as far as it went. But there were some circles into which not even a fortune could buy.

Gifford had already pushed propriety ever so slightly with his purchase of Lord Berkeley's former home on highly fashionable Curzon Street only a quarter mile from Park Lane. Eyebrows had gone up around Mayfair at the time, but most accepted the fact on the basis of what everyone recognized as the changing mores of the modern age.

In years gone by, self-respecting English "gentlemen" had little in the way of occupation to bother with, other than making sure the income from their estates came in on time. The diversion of sporting events was what really got the blood going. The year's social events in London originally came to be associated loosely with the schedule of the House of Lords, whose members anticipated their adjournments no less than schoolchildren awaiting holiday. Their recesses were scheduled for the precise purpose of enjoying those sporting events.

The *real* business throughout the fall months was the hunt. It wouldn't do to have to attend to politics when the foxes were running and the hounds must be after them, and when grouse and pheasant and deer were plentiful.

Grouse season opened in mid-August, when Parliament adjourned. Everyone who was anyone headed north, either to their own "grouse moor" in Scotland, or to that of an acquaintance. Those who weren't fortunate enough to have a lodge in Scotland retreated to their lodges elsewhere in the country. Partridge season began in September, the pheasant season in October, and on the first Monday of November at last came the traditional opening of the fox season.

After the weather turned too cold for such outdoor pursuits, only then did the lords and their ladies think of locking up their hunting lodges and vacating their country estates and returning to London to prepare for the opening of Parliament. A modest round of winter social functions followed.

The height of the London social season opened, however, a few months later, after the return of Parliament from its Easter break and another brief visit to the country. Throughout spring and early summer the city witnessed a constant round of parties and horse-racing events, when the intent of the ladies was to be seen in their newest dresses and finest jewelry.

This was the time of the year when the new crop of maturing young ladies was officially presented to society. Fathers and young men throughout London used the occasion to survey the landscape for the most suitable matches. When the reign of Queen Victoria was at its height, young girls throughout the empire dreamed of nothing more than being presented at the royal court as the most exciting possible debut of all into this magical world of balls and beaux.

The annual exhibition at the Royal Academy of Art came in May, and was usually the first major gala event of the season. A whirlwind of dinners and balls, parties and breakfasts, followed. The Derby and Ascot came in either May or June, followed in July by the Henley Regatta and numerous cricket matches. As the summer progressed and the weather warmed, talk between men gradually turned toward the grouse, and between the women to what new engagements the season had witnessed and who they were planning to visit in the fall. For when August arrived, it would be time for the whole year's cycle to begin all over again.

19
Amanda's Coming Out

*T*he wife of Gifford Rutherford did not care for the twentieth century's modernism. The new informality and equality between the classes, not to mention between the sexes, was not for her. If the fabric that held society together broke down, where would England be then?

And voting—heavens!

In Martha's eyes, the idea of women wanting to vote was much ado about nothing. Who could possibly care about voting! Let the men handle the world's affairs and good riddance.

For Martha Rutherford, Amanda represented a link to the social circles she had once longed to be part of, yet who had only been familiar with its lower portions. Nor had she had a daughter of her own, a fact which hadn't helped propel her higher. To be able to take the girl under her charge would give Martha grounds to insert herself into the very middle of it, and now to a greater extent than her *own* position had previously justified.

Amanda was, after all, the daughter of a Knight Grand Commander. Her father's standing as lord of the manor of Heathersleigh did not quite make him a peer. But it was certainly far more title than Gifford could lay claim to. Along with Charles' high parliamentary reputation, and the fact that Amanda would be two or three years older than most of the year's new debutantes . . . Martha had no doubt that within weeks Amanda would be the talk of London.

It might even turn out in her favor that she had waited so long to come out. It would add to the interest shown her. And *she* would be there at Amanda's side!

Amanda's reasons for wanting to be part of the glamorous society scene were not so very different from her cousin's. All her life she had dreamed of attending a ball on the arm of her father. They had talked about taking London by storm. He had then shut himself off from all that in favor of his religion. And she had been shut out of it in the process. She had hoped coming to live with the Pankhursts would involve her in the life of her girlish fancies. In reality she spent more time in streets than in ballrooms. Now all at once Cousin Martha had made it possible to rekindle those former dreams.

Martha and Amanda Rutherford, an unlikely pair, each had a large store of personal hopes as together they entered into the round of social events during the remainder of the spring of 1911. Both were caught up in shopping and fittings and plans. Amanda's spirits rose higher than they had been in a year. As her name began to circulate, new invitations began to pour in.

Martha's husband Gifford watched it all with amused satisfaction. He shrewdly appeared now and then, carrying himself with detached fatherly demeanor. He would imperceptibly deepen Amanda's dependence upon him for her newfound and rapidly climbing social standing. He was willing for the perception to spread among their associations, though nothing was *said*—the girl must not hear it prematurely—that Amanda and his son Geoffrey had an "understanding" as to how things were between them.

Mrs. Pankhurst saw a change in Amanda immediately. Most days now, instead of participating in rallies and protests, Amanda was off to Curzon Street to spend the day with Martha. If she felt torn between her two worlds, she did not show it. Mrs. Pankhurst was wise enough in the ways of the world, however, to recognize the advantage one such as Amanda represented. Her value was based on the fact that she was the daughter of Sir Charles Rutherford, not because Amanda brought one more foot soldier into the ranks. A thousand young women in England would have given anything to live in the Pankhurst home. All the while, however, it never dawned on Amanda that had she been the daughter of a commoner, the invitation to take up residence with them would never have been extended in the first place.

Therefore, Mrs. Pankhurst said nothing about Amanda's fling with society. She could bide her time for the present in order to keep so great a prize safely within the ranks of their cause.

Amanda knew far less of the world than she thought. Thinking herself sophisticated in the ways of adulthood, she yet remained oblivious to the many motives swirling like an invisible dust cloud about her. Imagining that she held the reins of her fate in her own hands and had stepped with maturity into her stature as a woman, in many respects she was merely a pawn in a larger chess game with a growing range of players. Unknown to her, another was already watching for the opportunity to stealthily make use of this particular pawn in a far higher contest already under way.

She despised the fact that her father had prevented her from attaining her most cherished ambitions. Sir Charles Rutherford, however, occupied the vital and pivotal center from which many of these wheels in Amanda's life turned. It was because of *him* that people were interested in *her*. Though Amanda perceived it not, it was the power her father represented which was opening the doors now before her.

They were doors that would lead for a little while to her pleasure and satisfaction . . . but ultimately to her danger.

20

Coronation

♦ ♦ ♦

The Derby and her chance meeting with Cousin Martha began the most wonderful year in Amanda's life. Suddenly she found herself at the very center of London life. As distasteful as she found Geoffrey's presence, she was grateful for his mother's efforts to introduce her to society.

No more fitting culmination to any year's social season could be envisioned than that which took place in the year 1911, when, on June 22, George V, grandson of Victoria, and his wife Mary were crowned King and Queen of the United Kingdom of Great Britain and Ireland.

From commoners to the highest noblepersons in the land, except for a minority who would do away with it altogether, all Britain loved its monarchy. The pomp, dignity, and many-centuried history of its royalty gave the empire's men and women hope for the future strength of their nation. Whenever it was thought that the royal ceremonial coach might be seen, for wedding or christening or any occasion involving the royal family, and of course for the annual passage through London for the opening of Parliament, spectators crowded along the route, many with tears in their eyes, hoping for any glimpse of the monarch.

On the twenty-third, a bank holiday, the day following the coronation in Westminster Abbey, there would be a parade through the city such as came along only once in a lifetime. The Royal Progress would leave Buckingham Palace at eleven in the morning and wind through the streets so as to give as many as possible of the new king and queen's subjects the chance to see them.

The momentous celebration of the coronation, awaited and planned for thirteen months, at last arrived. Before six in the morning of the following day, London's streets were already lining with tens of thousands seeking good position from which to view the splendid processional from the palace in a great circle and back to Green Park.

After the procession, the ranks of society would gradually again divide along the ancient lines of nobility and rank. Those few of highest station had been invited inside the great abbey to witness the coronation itself the day before. Others of more modest standing would be included for the large outdoor reception at Green Park at the end of today's parade route. This latter event would include the family of London financier Gifford Rutherford, who had secured an invitation for four. Their cousin Amanda would be escorted by the banker's rising prominent son Geoffrey.

None of the London Rutherford party paused to inquire whether Amanda's parents, Sir Charles and Lady Jocelyn Rutherford, would also be in attendance. That the lord of the manor of Heathersleigh and his wife had been selected to receive a prestigious invitation to the coronation ceremony inside the abbey remained equally outside the scope of their reflections. Had Gifford known, it would have struck him as preposterously unfitting and backward from what should be the true order of things.

Amanda had seen nothing of Ramsay Halifax for two weeks. When she awoke on processional morning, she wondered where *he* would be today. She wouldn't be surprised to see him, though his interest in the monarchy had never seemed as great as she would expect for the stepson of a well-known peer. But Ramsay somehow seemed to turn up everywhere.

He went to the Continent with some regularity, though always remained curiously secretive to Amanda about such trips. Whenever she asked what he'd been working on, he laughed it off.

"My paper would fire me," he told her more than once, "if I leaked stories for the Pankhursts to get hold of."

"You can trust *me*, Ramsay," said Amanda with a coy smile.

"Of course. But can I trust them? You *are* one of the inner circle."

"But I wouldn't tell," she insisted.

"It's the code of journalism," he replied, "never to divulge too much. Someone in my position cannot leak information about a story prematurely."

And now he was gone again. Amanda wondered if it was another of his secretive excursions to the Continent.

Shortly after breakfast on the twenty-third, Geoffrey Rutherford came to the door of the Pankhurst home, presented his card, and asked for Amanda. Without greeting, Amanda accompanied him down the steps.

Amanda wore the blue suit-dress she had bought at Harrods for the Derby. However, today she replaced the large straw hat with a small navy hat with pink veil. She and Geoffrey walked from the house in silence. Geoffrey offered his hand, which Amanda took reluctantly. He helped her into the carriage.

"Oh, Amanda," exclaimed Martha as she climbed into the backseat beside her, "how absolutely lovely you look. That color is so becoming on you, dear.—Gifford," she added, tapping her husband on the shoulder in front of her, "doesn't Amanda look beautiful?"

Gifford nodded politely, half turning back toward the two women as Geoffrey sat down beside him. He then returned his gaze forward, glancing momentarily toward his son with the faintest upward turn of the lips. Amanda saw the silent exchange. Were they secretly laughing at Martha's chatter? Or was the expression on Gifford's face meant to communicate something about *her*?

The weather was uncertain and fitful, with brief gusts and drizzling rain. Though the bank was closed, they rode to the tall stone edifice, where during the week the fate of fortunes was determined. From Gifford's office window on the fifth floor, they awaited the processional.

Leaving Buckingham Palace, the plumed and jeweled Indian and Colonial processionals were followed by hundreds of soldiers and horsemen and dignitaries from every nation in the vast British Empire—from New Zealand and Australia and Canada and South Africa, then the ministers of the Crown Colonies and the Dominion Premiers. What seemed a thousand royal horsemen at last led the royal coach with the new king and queen. Every buckle and stirrup, every bright gleaming sword, every button on every red-and-blue uniform, every atom of polished brass and finery of gold and silver, glittered in the occasional sunlight.

The processional proceeded around Hyde Park Corner where the sun shone through briefly upon the royal carriage, by the Wellington Arch, where a Royal Pavilion had been built for foreign royalty, all of whom stood as King George and Queen Mary passed, along Piccadilly, thence through Trafalgar Square and along Whitehall past Westminster Abbey, along Victoria Street and back to the precincts of the palace, where it would arrive at length at Green Park.

The elegant coach at last came into view where Amanda and her relatives stood, with the new king and queen smiling and waving at the throng. By their very gait even the four perfectly matched white horses pulling their carriage seemed to sense the reverence of the occasion. The two most honored footmen from the royal brigade stood tall on its back, glancing neither right nor left. At such a moment nearly every Englishman, regardless of creed or station, was equally the humble servant and loyal admirer of the king.

Amanda glanced toward Martha. Tears stood in the older woman's eyes. Amanda looked down at the street again. Surprising even herself, the pride of her heritage swelled unexpectedly in her heart. She could not have said why, but a lump rose in her throat.

This was a good and proud nation, Amanda thought, whether women could vote or not. She did not want to hurt or destroy it. Not even being counted as important as men in the political arena was worth that.

Then the coach was by, and the rest of the procession slowly followed. As soon as the parade was past, the Rutherford party of four descended again to the street and returned to their carriage. They attempted to follow the route of the parade. But the throngs were too vast.

Gifford ordered the driver on to Green Park by another route. If they made haste, they would get there before the royal party and be able to see King George and Queen Mary make their arrival.

21

Reception

*E*ven the Kensington Lawn Tea, which Amanda had attended two months earlier, as much as it had impressed her, was nothing at all like this. Today's outdoor setting was as elegant as could be imagined. Endless tables crowded with food and delicacies and wines of every sort spread as far as one could see. The organizers only prayed a downpour didn't drench it all, though the sun's occasional rays poking through the clouds were hopeful.

Hundreds were already present when they arrived. About twenty minutes later, a buzz began to circulate that the newly crowned king and queen were on their way. An electric current of anticipation immediately spread through the gathering.

Across the way as they watched, Amanda saw Ramsay Halifax with a companion she did not recognize. How did he always manage to show up everywhere! If only she might get away from Geoffrey and work her way through the crowd in Ramsay's direction.

Even as she scanned the faces of those present, Amanda managed to sustain her end of various fragmentary conversations. The previous weeks of social activities since the Derby insured that wherever she went now, no end of attention came her way. To her great annoyance, Geoffrey did his best to fend off visitations from the persistent male element.

Well aware of the opportunities Geoffrey's mother and father were opening for her, during the preceding weeks Amanda had forced herself to behave with a certain decorum and geniality toward her cousin. She could not exactly be said to be friendly or warm toward him. Yet she was noticeably less cool and snappy than before, occasionally going so far even as to grit her teeth and smile at one of his banal remarks. Whether her cousin misinterpreted this subtle change might have been an important question to consider. In any event, Amanda did her best to circulate as he tagged along and generally made a nuisance of himself.

Meanwhile, Martha Rutherford beamed at how easily Amanda fit into the scene. She could not keep from priding herself on what she had done with her in such a short time.

"Oh, Martha," exclaimed one of her lady friends, "isn't it all so wonderful! And, Amanda dear, how beautiful you look.—Hello, Geoffrey," she added with a sly expression. "Your cousin is lovely, is she not?"

Geoffrey mumbled some indistinct words of reply. Amanda cringed and glanced away.

"Excuse me, Martha," she said. "I see someone I must speak to."

"Go along with her, Geoffrey, and keep her company," said Gifford.

"Please, I would rather go by myself," rejoined Amanda. That would be all she needed—to walk up to Ramsay with Geoffrey following like a puppy dog!

Amanda moved off quickly before anyone could argue further.

Before she had taken more than a half dozen steps across the lawn through the crowd, however, she was arrested by another face not twenty feet from where Halifax stood chatting and laughing.

Amanda's steps froze. Her face went pale. Slowly she retreated back to Martha's side.

"Cousin Martha," she said, "could you take me home?"

"But, dear . . . why—your face is white, Amanda. You look—"

"I'm not feeling well," said Amanda. "I really need to get out of here."

"Geoffrey will have James drive you. Go with her, Geoffrey. Tell James—"

Martha stopped.

"—Oh, but, Amanda," she exclaimed after a moment. "Is that . . . it is! There are your parents across the way."

"I don't want to see them, Martha. Please . . . I must get away from here."

Martha glanced bewilderedly back and forth between husband and son. Gifford could not have been more delighted at the turn of events. He was one of those small natures who enjoyed seeing division in a family, especially one he envied. He would be only too happy to take Amanda's side against his cousin. Apparently the rift in the family went deeper than he had imagined. Amanda's reaction only showed how much more likely they were to solidify her loyalties to his side of the family.

He nodded to his son with the same hint of a smile, and Geoffrey led Amanda away.

PART III

◆ ◆ ◆

Cross Purposes
1911

22
On the Other Side of the Lawn

* * *

$\mathscr{A}$cross the grounds, having no idea they were at the center of such a fuss, Charles and Jocelyn Rutherford moved leisurely through the crowd, arm in arm, without the slightest inkling their daughter was present at the historic occasion. Charles greeted many of his old friends from London whom he hadn't seen in years, while Jocelyn clung close to his side.

The bright red birthmark which scarred half of one side of Jocelyn's face—from the neck, across her cheek, and up to the left side of her forehead—was not the burden it had once been. She had learned to accept her husband's love and God's love, and had through them learned to accept herself and give God thanks for his unique handiwork with her. She had learned, not without tears, to see her scar as the fingerprint of God's care. Such occasions as these, however, among crowds of people, would always be difficult. She had grown up thinking that everyone was always staring at her, laughing to themselves, silently mocking the bright red side of her face. Such inward habits were difficult to break.

Charles sensed his wife's uneasiness and gave her hand a reassuring squeeze.

"I know I am loved," she said quietly, "but this is still hard."

Charles nodded. "It won't be much longer," he said. "We'll get out of here and be on our way back to Devon—"

"I say, old chap," interrupted a boisterous voice.

Charles glanced up to see its owner moving toward them with a wide grin spread over his face and hand outstretched.

"It *is* you . . . I thought so. Charles Rutherford! It is good to see you, old man."

The two shook hands warmly.

"Jocelyn," said Charles, "you remember my speaking of Byram Forbes, of the *Times*.—Byram, may I present my wife Jocelyn."

"Lady Rutherford," said Forbes, tipping his hat. "—But I forget myself," he added, speaking again to Charles. "You are *Sir* Charles now. I beg your most humble pardon."

Charles laughed. "Believe me, Byram, the title is far less significant *after* one has it than one anticipates beforehand."

"You are keeping yourself busy, I hear."

"Busy enough."

"I hear your name mentioned all the time in connection with electricity and all sorts of newfangled gadgetry. Better not let the Germans or Austrians get hold of that brain of yours. They're after liberals, you know."

Charles laughed again. "And what about you?" he said. "You must just about be editor by now."

This time it was Forbes' turn to laugh. "Not if I live to be a hundred," he said. "Too many in line ahead of me. But I manage to get the occasional interview to impress my colleagues. I had a session with the new king last month."

"I read your piece," said Charles. "Nicely done."

"Would you like to meet him? I'm certain I could arrange it."

"That is very kind of you, Byram. Some other time perhaps."

"What about you, old man? Any chance I could talk *you* into an interview? You know, a world view from the retired politician looking at the situation with balance and perspective."

"I'm afraid not," laughed Charles. "I'm out of politics now, remember."

Now a third man moved in to join the conversation.

"I say, Forbes," he said, "this can't be Sir Charles Rutherford you've cornered—the political recluse?"

"Hello, Max," smiled Charles, shaking Baron Whitfield's hand. "It's been too long . . . you're looking well."

"As are you, I must say. But you're a dreadful liar, Charles. Your eyes can't have escaped the fact that I've added a stone's weight and have lost half my hair."

Charles roared with fun. "I try to look at the man, Max, not the appearance."

"Well then, I forgive you. But London's not the same without you, Charles."

"You all seem to be managing to hold the world together just fine without me!—Excuse me a moment."

Charles turned to Jocelyn at his side. "You don't mind if I visit a few minutes with my old friends?" he said.

"Of course not. I'll just go for a litle walk."

"I didn't mean that, Jocie. I wasn't trying to get rid of you," laughed Charles.

"I would like to wander about."

"You won't be uncomfortable being alone? I'm happy to have you stay."

"Don't worry about me, Charles," she replied. "I'll go get another cup of tea and leave you men to your politics. I'll wait for you over by the pond. The ducks and geese will entertain me."

"Are you certain, Jocelyn?"

"Charles, I will be fine—enjoy yourself." Jocelyn turned and walked off with a smile.

"I'll join you in a few minutes," Charles called after her.

23

Former Acquaintance
♦ ♦ ♦

$\mathcal{M}$eanwhile the small group had been joined by another of Charles' former parliamentary colleagues, an outspoken Tory by the name of Chalmondley Beauchamp*, who now walked up alongside a man whose bearing struck Charles as vaguely familiar but whom he could not immediately place. The man seemed to be eyeing him too, with the merest hint of submerged grin about his lips.

Friendly greetings and handshakes ensued between Beauchamp and Charles. A brief hesitation followed as the count glanced back and forth between his former colleague and the man who had walked up at his side. His eyes contained the sparkle of fun.

"Charles," he began slowly, as if inviting Charles to speak, "may I present—"

He paused and glanced at Charles again.

---

*pronounced *Chum*-ley *Beach*-um

"I have the distinct feeling we're already supposed to know one another," said Charles, at last giving in to a smile of bewilderment, "but I must confess—"

"Think water . . . ships . . . midshipmen . . . admirals," said the newcomer, speaking for the first time.

"The navy?" said Charles, still perplexed, although the voice was even more familiar than the man's look.

"And that training exercise off Portsmouth, when a shipload of new recruits—"

"The *navy!*" exclaimed Charles. "Of course—Redmond, isn't it . . . give me a second . . . uh, Morley Redmond!"

"Good show, Rutherford—yes, you've found me out at last!"

The two shook hands amid laughter and good-natured comments all around the group.

"Why, we haven't seen one another in, what is it . . . must be thirty years!" Charles said, glancing around to the others by way of explanation. "We were stationed at Portsmouth together."

"I make it thirty-two," said Redmond. "I had the advantage of being able to perform some hasty mental computations after I saw you. Beauchamp and I were standing across the way, when suddenly I realized my eyes had fallen on someone I hadn't seen since I was a raw green sailor. Chalmondley noticed me staring at you and then realized it was none other than *his* old friend from Parliament. He was off like a flash. I followed . . . I tagged along to see if I could stump you."

"Well, it is good to see you again, Morley!" laughed Charles. "The joke was on me, and the two of you pulled it off very adroitly."

"It would seem the two of you have risen through the years," Count Beauchamp now said. "Redmond, your friend is now *Sir* Charles . . . and Charles, you have the honor of speaking with *Dr.* Redmond."

"I do remember hearing about your knighthood some years back," Redmond said. "Congratulations."

"And you . . . a doctor—my congratulations as well . . . surgery, medical research?"

"I'm afraid nothing like that," laughed Redmond. "I am what we call a doctor of *philosophy*—I earn my bread in the dusty halls of academia."

"I see—the intellectual crowd . . . training young minds to thrive in a changing world."

"Something like that."

"At what level?"

"Here and there, wherever I can be useful. I bounce around a bit."

"My son recently graduated from Oxford."

"I do some duty up there myself from time to time—don't recall encountering any Rutherfords."

"George studied engineering and mathematics. What field is your—"

"Oh, excuse me, Rutherford ... Chalmondley," interrupted Redmond. "I just now see someone I need to speak with. You'll forgive me if I dash off?"

"Certainly, old man," Beauchamp replied. "We'll be here."

Redmond walked off and the conversation resumed among Charles, Forbes, Whitfield, and Beauchamp. A minute or two later James, earl of Westcott, joined them, shaking hands all around.

"Any of you chaps attend Edward's funeral last year?" he asked.

Whitfield nodded; Charles shook his head.

"Should have seen it," said Westcott, "—kings, queens, and princes from all over Europe. Everyone was there. The German emperor, King Albert of Belgium, Prince Yussuf of Turkey, Archduke Franz Ferdinand of Austria, and more princes and princesses and royal highnesses than you could shake a stick at. I haven't seen anything like it since Victoria's Jubilee. This day reminds me of it somehow."

"Though Wilhelm II *isn't* here today," said Whitfield, "not even to celebrate his cousin's coronation, nor Archduke Ferdinand, heir to the Austrian throne."

"You note significance in that fact, I take it, Max?" asked Beauchamp.

The baron nodded, but for the present said no more in that direction.

24

Disquieting New Book

$\mathcal{A}$ few more friends and former colleagues came by to greet the former popular member of Parliament and Liberal leader, and the discussion about the world situation grew lively. Jocelyn sat near the pond enjoying seeing Charles mix so easily with his friends. Five or ten minutes later, Dr. Morley Redmond returned. At his side was a man Charles did not recognize, though whom several of the group apparently knew. Another round of greetings and introductions followed.

"Meet my friend Hartwell Barclay, Sir Charles," said Redmond. "—Hartwell . . . Sir Charles Rutherford, lord of the manor of the Heathersleigh estate in Devonshire."

"I am pleased to make your acquaintance, Sir Charles," said Redmond's friend. "I have, of course, heard of you and have followed some of your work."

"I'm sorry," Charles replied somewhat sheepishly, "you'll have to forgive me, Mr. Barclay, but I find myself at the disadvantage of not being able to return the favor."

"Mr. Barclay is with the foreign office and works as a liaison with the secret service, mostly on the Continent."

"I would not only be surprised if you had heard of me," said Barclay, "I would be disturbed as well. Success in the field of international intelligence, especially these days with the delicate negotiations in which we are involved, is greatly aided by keeping what we like to call a low public profile."

"But I say, old chap," Beauchamp said, turning to Charles with a somewhat lighter tone, "the country needs you. Any thoughts of returning to the political arena?"

"None whatever," laughed Charles. "I am perfectly content at present with where the Lord has me."

A few uneasy coughs and adjustments of various collars went around the circle at Charles' comment.

"But what do you make of the world situation?" persisted Beauchamp. "Now that we have a new king, will the kaiser bring the German army out of mothballs?"

"I hardly think it's been in mothballs, Beauchamp," objected Forbes. "Don't you Tories pay attention to what's up on the Continent? Wilhelm has been rattling his German sabers all around the world for twenty years."

"Nothing but bluster and show, if you ask me," remarked Beauchamp in reply. "He's just not the diplomat old Bismarck was."

"I am not so sure," rejoined Forbes. "He is an imperialist, bent on antagonizing every nation of Europe, replacing Great Britain's supremacy on the seas, and taking over the Ottoman Empire when it finally collapses altogether. I say we have plenty to fear from Berlin."

"It's not the Germans I worry about," remarked the earl of Westcott, "it's the Russians."

"Ah, but haven't you heard, James old man," put in Beauchamp, "they're our allies now."

"According to a piece of paper perhaps, Chalmondley. But there's revolution brewing there, I tell you, and no good will come of it. It's only a matter of time before that keg explodes."

"James is right," added Forbes. "But it remains the Germans who are the threat to stability and peace in Europe."

"Byram is spot on," said Baron Whitfield, "—it's the Germans all right. That's why the emperor isn't here—relations between our two nations, without Edward at the helm of Britain, are cooling rapidly. They're infiltrating everywhere. There may, in fact, be German and Austrian sympathizers among us even now."

"Nonsense, Max," laughed Beauchamp. "You're an alarmist."

"I would prefer to call myself a realist. Moles, they're called, Chalmondley. And you oughtn't be so cavalier. Watch what you say—the enemy might be listening."

"We're not at war," rejoined Redmond. "We don't have enemies nowadays."

"There are enemies of the silent, devious kind too, you know, Dr. Redmond," said the baron. "Enemies don't always carry guns. Sometimes your enemy disguises his true motive with a smile and soothing words."

"Communists too, looking for support for their revolution," added Westcott, returning to the Russian theme. "One can't be too cautious these days. It's a changed world. One hardly knows whom to trust."

"I will agree with you there," added Whitfield. "With revolution in Turkey and Austria annexing Bosnia and Herzegovina and Russia now recovering from their Japanese war . . . I tell you, it is a dangerous time. It wasn't that long ago that we were friendlier toward Germany than Russia. There are many who think England's present course wrong and would side with Austrian and German interests. But behind Austria, Germany is the greater worry, though it is likely their alliance with Austria will light the fuse. The Germans are a people who thrive on war. If there is—"

"Come, come—there's not going to be any war," said Beauchamp. "This is the age of diplomacy, or haven't you heard? Am I not right, Mr. Barclay?"

"That's supposed to be our job all right," replied Barclay. "I doubt it will come to war."

"I wouldn't like to differ with someone from the foreign office, but haven't any of you read General Bernhardi's book," asked Whitfield, "—just out?"

"The old German general?" said Charles.

"Yes, and the first German to ride through the Arc de Triomphe when the Germans entered Paris in 1870. He was a twenty-one-year-old cavalry officer then. He is a sixty-two-year-old military theorist now. His ideas ought to frighten all Europe."

"What's it called, Max?" asked Charles.

"*Germany and the Next War*," replied the baron. "The title says it as clearly as can be. He argues that war is a biological necessity, that there will always be wars, that they are intrinsic to the struggle for the existence of nations. Furthermore, he says that Germany is at the head of all of Europe, the leader of progress and culture, the most important nation in existence today."

"He actually makes such a claim!" huffed Westcott.

Whitfield nodded. "And more."

"It seems that is enough," commented Beauchamp, though without the earl's emotion.

"Germany cannot," Whitfield went on, "according to Bernhardi, be compressed and cramped into unnatural borders. She is morally entitled, by her inherent greatness above the other nations around her, to expand her sphere of influence and enlarge her territory. Such is its right as political necessity. And to attain these ends, Germany must fight and conquer."

A moment or two of silence followed the sobering words.

"Nor is this all," continued Whitfield. "Bernhardi goes so far as to call it Germany's acknowledged right to secure the 'proud privilege' of *initiating* war. He says it is incumbent on Germany to strike the first blow."

"Does he say where such a blow will come?" asked Morley Redmond.

"Where else?" replied Whitfield. "France. France must be completely crushed, he says."

"At least his sights are not set on us," laughed Beauchamp uneasily.

"Not in the first attack, but certainly thereafter."

"He doesn't think the Germans would dare cross the Channel?" said Westcott, still heated.

"Not now, perhaps. But the Germans are building ships even as we speak. The Anglo-German naval race is no secret. Where better for the kaiser to prove his supremacy than by conquering the Channel. You've heard of the development of their new generation of submarines."

"The U-boat—it will never be a threat," insisted Westcott. "England's shores are safe. Germany will never be a naval power."

"Don't be too certain, James," replied Whitfield soberly. "Imagine, a fleet of Germans lying off the coast, completely invisible. It gives one pause."

25

Private Confidence

♦♦♦

*A*gain the discussion fell silent.

"It *does* make one think, indeed, Whitfield. And I for one would like to hear what Sir Charles thinks about what the rest of you have been debating," said a new voice, whom none had seen approach as the discussion grew serious.

All heads turned to see a distinguished man walking into the circle whom every one of the number knew well enough.

The home secretary of the U.K. shook hands with everyone around the small circle.

"Nice to see you again, Sir Charles," said the gravelly voice.

"And you, Winston."

"We all miss you in the capital."

"As I said to Max a few moments ago, I am certain the country is in good hands."

"Still, as the others have been telling you, these are worrisome times."

As he spoke, Churchill gently nudged his former Liberal colleague away from the others. None of the rest of the group was inclined to object. Everything Winston Churchill said or did seemed somehow imbued with an authority few thought to question.

"You've risen far since we first met, Winston," said Charles as they walked slowly away. "I read about you often in the *Times.*"

"Meaning no ounce of disrespect, Sir Charles," rejoined the home secretary, "but I wish I could say the same of you. You might have been my prime minister now instead of Henry Asquith."

"I doubt that," laughed Charles.

"Don't be too sure. You were the clear leading candidate. When Campbell-Bannerman retired in 1908, your name would have been top on the list. I have not the slightest doubt you would have risen even higher than I had you remained in Parliament."

"I suppose we shall never know. In any event, those days are behind us. I made my decision and have never regretted it."

"*Those* days may be behind us," Churchill said when they were alone, "but new ones are ahead—dangerous days."

"You share Baron Whitfield's concerns about Germany?"

Churchill nodded. "If anything I would say Max understates the gravity of the situation."

"A strong statement coming from the home secretary."

"I am genuinely concerned, Sir Charles. It is a changing world, and I am not certain England is ready for it. We rule the seas, to be sure, but Germany's army and navy are growing more rapidly than I like. And Whitfield is right about Bernhardi's book—"

"You were listening?" said Charles.

"I like to eavesdrop awhile before I enter a conversation," smiled Churchill. "I've learned enough in my brief years in politics to keep my mouth closed until there is something important to say. In any event, the book is positively chilling. I only finished it two days ago."

"And you consider it significant, I take it?"

"Germany's so-called *Weltpolitik* represents the wave of the future—world politics, they call it. They would say it indicates only a new, forward-looking, and broader world outlook. Others maintain its design is military," replied Churchill. "Bernhardi certainly does nothing to counter that view."

"And *your* thoughts?"

"Both are probably accurate. Germany is a new nation on the world stage. I cannot fault them for desiring to be a major player on that stage. But the buildup of their armaments, and Kaiser Wilhelm's obvious expansionary interests—these ought to concern us deeply. And with the Balkans so tenuous ..."

Churchill paused and sighed.

"It is a frightening situation, Sir Charles," he went on.

"What can be done?"

"Preparedness is our only hope."

"What about diplomacy?" asked Charles. "There have been many crises during the last ten or fifteen years, all successfully averted."

"Because one party has always backed down. But when the time comes when no one is willing to do that—as it surely will—what then?"

"Will not reason prevail?"

"Reason is hardly the operative position between bullies. And if the kaiser has shown anything since coming to power, it is that he relishes playing the bully. Bismarck possessed raw power, and wielded it with dexterity, even a certain caution. Wilhelm II, however, as I see it, will be only too glad to provoke hostilities as soon as he feels in a position to win."

"What about Norman Angell's book? There is one I *have* read."

"*The Great Illusion* is itself an illusion," chortled Churchill. "The premise—the *proof*, he calls it—that war is impossible by virtue of the financial and economic interdependence of nations ... it's absurd. It is based on a faulty thesis altogether, that reason dominates a nation's actions. Much as we might hope such to be true, the fact is, when situations and crises arise, usually reason does *not* dictate action."

"What does, as you see it?"

"Pride, arrogance, nationalism, fear, belligerence ... and the bully mentality—calling another's bluff, assuming *he* will back down. It is no way for nations to behave with one another, but sadly such is the case. Nations are run by men, and men are fallible, egotistical, and often *un*reasonable by nature. The situation between Serbian nationalists and Austria is an explosive one. And with the kaiser feeling more powerful by the day . . . eventually, Sir Charles, I tell you, we are going to find ourselves in a predicament from which no one will back down. In my view, it is inevitable. It is only a matter of time."

"So I take it, you are making plans for such a crisis?"

"To the extent I am able," replied Churchill. "But England is asleep. Even within our own government, within the cabinet, within the military itself, there remains such an attitude of disbelief that the peril is genuinely serious. The army and navy are devising plans without even talking to one another. The leadership of the navy in particular is ill equipped for what faces us."

"Are you . . . making your views known?"

"When the appropriate time comes, believe me, I fully intend to make my voice heard. I may be dismissed from my post altogether, but I love England too much not to speak out."

"You have always been plainspoken," smiled Charles.

"A virtue or a vice, as the case may be, of which I might also accuse you."

"I hope you are right," rejoined Charles.

"That is one of the reasons I wanted to discuss these matters with you . . . alone," said Churchill, now lowering his voice. "We are not what would be called close friends. But I have been watching you through the years, Sir Charles. Not only are you plainspoken, you are a man whom I judge to be completely trustworthy. I would not hesitate at this moment to place my very life in your hands."

"I appreciate that confidence."

"Perilous times lie ahead," Churchill went on. "I need men who will tell me what they think without fear of the consequences. And I need men I can trust. On both counts, I have no doubts concerning you."

"What are you asking, Winston?"

"I am asking if you might consider coming out of retirement and getting involved again? The country needs men like you."

"Are you talking about politics . . . my standing again for the Commons? If so, I'm afraid—"

"I don't mean Parliament specifically. I don't mean anything specifically at this point. I have no post as such to offer you. If I did," he added, casting Charles a shrewd sidelong smile, "I have the feeling you would turn it down anyway."

Quickly he became serious again. Charles returned his smile with a nod, as if in indication that the home secretary knew him very well indeed.

"I simply have the feeling," Churchill went on, "that I might find myself wanting to call on you at some time in the future."

They strolled away from the crowd a few moments in silence. Charles saw Jocelyn ahead of them by the edge of the pond where dozens of ducks and geese swam about. He had already left her alone far too long and wanted to rejoin her.

"I don't exactly know what to say, Winston," he said at length. "You have caught me, to say the least, unexpectedly."

"Say that you will think about it," replied Churchill, "and I will be satisfied."

"Then I can say that I will pray about it," rejoined Charles. "I love my country too . . . but I have higher allegiances."

26

Memories of a Happy Day
◆ ◆ ◆

*I'*m ready to go home, Mrs. Rutherford. How about you?"

Jocelyn glanced up and smiled. "Do you think the new king and queen and all their admirers can do without us?"

"I think they just might be able to at that," laughed Charles.

"I'm glad you had a nice visit with your old friends. It was good to hear you laugh."

"Yes, I enjoyed it. But I don't miss that world, though I do miss a few of the people who are in it."

"Did you want to visit Timothy Diggorsfeld again before we left the city?"

"I thought it might be nice," Charles replied. "But this took longer today than I anticipated. I'm glad we were able to have dinner and a good long visit last evening. I'll post him a letter or call him as soon as we get home."

He took her hand and they made their way back to the field where Charles' Peugeot was parked along with the other automobiles present. They would drive to Southampton this afternoon, where they would spend the night at an inn, before continuing on to Devon tomorrow.

An hour later they had passed the western reaches of the metropolis and were motoring leisurely through the countryside. The coronation and reception had reminded them distinctly of their trip to London fourteen years earlier for Queen Victoria's sixty-year Jubilee where Charles was knighted. Now as they drove, both husband and wife fell into a melancholy and reminiscent mood.

"I still laugh," said Charles, "whenever I think of Amanda looking up to Victoria and telling her she was going to be prime minister one day."

Jocelyn smiled at the memory.

"I was so timid and afraid back then," she said.

"I almost had to drag you to come with me!"

"I'm glad you did. I'll never forget the queen's lovely eyes. The look she gave me was so tender."

Jocelyn sighed and grew pensive. "So much has changed since then," she said.

"That's when it began to change," rejoined Charles, "—the ride to the Jubilee, the ruckus I got into, then the walk the next day ... and meeting Timothy Diggorsfeld, learning about the Lord for the first time. How could I ever forget that day? How could I have imagined back then that a young pastor whom I encountered passing out anti-evolution leaflets would become my best friend!" Charles added with a chuckle. "You're right, Jocie—everything's changed, and that's when it began."

"Do you ever wonder, Charles ... you know, if we *did* do something wrong with Amanda—if what she is now going through is our fault?"

"Of course, Jocie—I wonder that all the time. Sure, I think I did so *many* things wrong with her. I was not nearly sensitive enough to what she was feeling at the time."

"But you didn't know."

"Neither of us knew how negatively she was reacting to our attempts toward spirituality. But as I look back, I see many areas where perhaps I should have given her more rope, more trust, and not tried to force her."

"You never tried to force the children to see everything exactly as you did. I sometimes thought you gave them too much liberty."

Charles laughed, though without a great deal of humor in his tone. "It does get confusing," he said. "Did I really change that much when I became a Christian? I tried so hard to teach them independence of thought. Yet Amanda now thinks I forced her into my own personal framework of belief. It is *so* hard for me to understand what happened, because I never wanted to do that at all. The very thing I wanted so badly to accomplish with my children, it would seem I failed at."

"Timothy would say we weren't forcing them. We were doing our best to *train* them according to biblical principles. All three were young at the time. Wasn't it still our duty to teach and train and instruct them?"

Charles nodded. "Timothy is a staunch believer in personal responsibility for one's choices and actions. If he were listening, he would say that Amanda is accountable for her own decisions, and that we are not to blame for what she has done. He would say the same of George and Catharine. They are following our beliefs, at present Amanda is not. But I feel tremendous guilt sometimes, thinking of all the ways I perhaps did not—I don't know—be all as a father to her that I might have . . . that perhaps I should have been."

"So do I," rejoined Jocelyn. "But don't forget, we were new Christians at the time."

She paused thoughtfully for a moment. "That's the trouble with parenthood," she went on, "—you don't get second chances. You fumble through, do the best you can. Before you know it your children are grown up, and you can't go back. And, Charles, we *did* do our best, at least the best we knew at the time."

"And you know what Timothy would say to that?"

Jocelyn nodded. "That no parent can do more than their best."

"And that parental *im*perfection is something God built into the human relational equation."

Charles sighed. "I say the words," he added. "I know in my brain that God doesn't expect perfection from me. He doesn't now, and he didn't then. Yet my mind is constantly searching out the past . . . wondering, doubting, reliving incidents, trying to think what I *might* have done differently so as not to have alienated Amanda. But I always come to the same place in the end—I don't know . . . I just don't know. And not knowing makes the grief all the harder to bear. Over and over I say to myself that I have to put it behind me, that I must stop thinking about it, stop talking about it all the time. Yet I can't help it. Something inside me is compelled to try to understand."

It fell silent for a few minutes as they both gazed out over the passing countryside. Slowly Jocelyn began to cry.

"Oh, Charles," she said at length, "I miss her!"

"I know, Jocie . . . so do I."

"I haven't seen our daughter in three years. Sometimes I think my heart is just going to break for aching to see her and hold her again."

"We've got to be realistic, Jocie," said Charles. "That day may not come for a while."

"I want to write her, pour out my heart, tell her I love her, even ask if I can come visit her."

"There's nothing I want more than to wrap my arms around her and hold her to me like I did when she was a little girl. But it's nothing we can make happen ahead of its time. She is a grown woman. Now more than ever, whatever the future holds between us has to be Amanda's choice."

"That day when we all came into London together—that was our *old* life, before we knew what it meant to walk with God. And yet that was also the last time we had a good relationship with Amanda. I don't understand it, Charles. Sometimes it weighs me down so. How could giving our lives to the Lord create such pain and division in our own family?"

"I don't know, Jocie," sighed Charles, shaking his head. "It puzzles me too. All we can do is pray for the Lord to accomplish his purposes . . . in our hearts as well as Amanda's."

Jocelyn quietly wept at the words she knew were true, yet were nonetheless painful.

Charles slowed and pulled off the dusty dirt road at the next opportunity. He stopped the car, then pulled Jocelyn close and stretched his arm around her. She continued to cry softly. They sat for five or ten minutes in silence. Gradually Charles began to pray.

"*Lord,*" he said, "*wherever our dear Amanda is at this moment, whatever she is doing, whoever she is with, whatever she is thinking, we ask that you would be there beside her, inside her—speaking, wooing, luring her to your heart. Again we pray, as we have so many times, that you would send brief arrows of light into her heart, pleasant reminders and fond memories. And, Father, in your time and in your way, we ask you to please restore the friendship that once existed between Amanda and us. Remind her of the happy times, the long talks, the laughter. In the meantime as you carry out that silent, invisible work, give us patience, give us hope. Give us fortitude and courage to trust you to be Amanda's Father in our place. O God, be a tender, caring, loving Father to our daughter. Watch over her, protect her, and accomplish your perfect will and perfect desire in her life."*

"And in ours," added Jocelyn softly. *"As painful as this separation is, dear Lord, we ask you to perfect your will in us through it."*

27

Heathersleigh Hall
♦ ♦ ♦

𝒯he estate toward which Sir Charles and Lady Jocelyn Rutherford were returning, in the middle of the county of Devon in southwest England, had been called Heathersleigh longer than anyone alive could remember.

That some former lord of the manor had been fond of the wiry plant from which was derived the name of the property was clear from the extensive patch of it planted east of the mansion. Charles and Jocelyn had reclaimed the overgrown area from the encroaching woods because of their own newfound love of growing things several years earlier. They had since expanded it into a heather garden of considerable size, which included pathways, streams, hedges, and a few small conifers. It had become one of their favorite places on the estate, where they often retreated, either alone or together, for prayer.

Their twenty-three-year-old son George, home after his graduation from Oxford, found himself wandering out of the library on the afternoon prior to his parents' return from London. He had been reading in one of several titles given them by London minister and family friend Timothy Diggorsfeld. The books were by the Scotsman, dead now six years, who had long been Diggorsfeld's favorite author and whom he had met and spoken with during one of the author's visits to London late in his life.

As George left the library, his steps took him unintentionally in the direction of a wide portrait gallery off the landing of the main central staircase. For one with such a thirst to understand mechanical things, who had explored every inch of the ancient Hall, and who had even discovered more than one hidden passage his father never knew existed, George had been curiously uncurious about the people who had dwelt in this wonderful old place which was his home, and who had come before him in the Rutherford line.

How many times had he passed through this gallery, unconsciously observing the portraits hanging on each side of him, yet walking by unseeing and unquestioning? But the book he had been reading contained just such a portrait gallery, and its mystery made him all the more aware of a possible mystery here.

Who were these people? What kind of men and women were they? What had they thought, what had they felt? What secrets of Heathersleigh Hall might they have possessed? If they could speak, what would they tell him that would satisfy George's quest for mystery?

Such questions George Rutherford had never before considered.

But suddenly on this day, the young man stopped. His attention was arrested by the look coming off the canvas from one of his old silent ancestors. Why were those two eyes—which he had walked past a thousand times since his boyhood—all at once staring at him . . . following him even as he moved? They seemed suddenly alive with mute expression. George was not immediately aware of it, but he had himself inherited a good many of the old fellow's physical characteristics, from dark brown hair and tall forehead, to wide-set eyes and lanky but ruggedly built frame. Right now George was gazing into the man's eyes, hazel like his own, almost as if he were looking into a mirror.

George paused, and returned the stare. What was the old fellow trying to say?

As he gazed upward at the face, the strange sensation came over him that this was the man who had constructed the hidden passage George had discovered leading from the library to the garret, and who had walled up a portion of the upper region of the house.

It had long been a riddle that George had not been able to solve: *Why* had it been done?

The conviction grew upon him as he studied the peculiar expression of the portrait that *this* man knew the secret.

George turned and gazed around one by one at the other faces all staring down at him from the gallery's walls.

All of these people possessed secrets. If only they could speak.

Again George returned to the portrait that had first arrested his attention. The old fellow was still staring at him with eyes that seemed alive. George walked closer, then bent forward to read the brass plate on the frame beneath the man's portrait.

HENRY RUTHERFORD, 1783–1865.

The expression of the old lord of the manor revealed a life of bitterness. George had heard stories that in his old age his great-grandfather had lost his senses. Yet . . . something other than senility stared out of that face. There was almost a look . . . of pleading mingled with hardness and anger—pleading with someone to heed his silent cry from the grave, to make right what he had done but did not have the courage in this life to repent of, yet in the next life no longer had the power to change.

Slowly George moved away, unnerved by the old man's expression. He continued along the gallery and gazed again at face after face from the past.

The sound of an automobile engine approaching on the gravel entryway outside interrupted his reverie. Already he heard his younger sister running out the front door below to welcome their parents home.

George turned and made for the stairway.

28

Brother and Sister

———— ◆◆◆ ————

A week after the coronation, Catharine and George Rutherford bounded along in their saddles, enjoying a vigorous morning romp together on the backs of their two favorite young mounts, Snowmass and Black Fire, whose contrasting equine coats bore precise resemblance to their names. George sat atop the white colt, Catharine rode the black filly.

That brother and sister were skilled equestrians insured that a good deal of galloping, racing, hedge jumping, and various pranks were included in almost any outing together. Though six years separated them, the two were indeed the best of friends. Catharine had always looked up to her older brother almost as if he occupied an equal stature with their parents, a perspective that his years away at Oxford only enhanced. He represented in her eyes the ultimate in youthful manhood.

George, on the other hand, had come during the past few years to enjoy Catharine as a true friend and equal, appreciating her lively personality and wit, since he was himself generally reserved and quiet. With the passage of his last three years at Oxford, Catharine had matured in his eyes two or three years to each of his one. Her rapid physical growth no doubt contributed to this perception, but even more her keen-brained, invigorating, alert mentality. He found her every bit the intellectual equal of many of the students he had met while away. And now, though she was merely seventeen, in his opinion she might as well have been the same age as he.

Her medium blond hair occasionally caught the sunlight such as to give it a hint of auburn. Her expression, like the shade of her hair, carried an air of occasional mystery. Such may have been accounted for by the fact that her light grey eyes perpetually sparkled as if aware of some unspoken joke being revolved in her mind. Indeed, her dry sense of humor could pop out at the most unexpected times, and kept the rest of the family, if not in constant laughter, certainly in good spirits. She had grown to be taller and more stout than her older sister, though not plump, and also better looking. A robust five ten, Catharine Rutherford had the look of one not afraid of a tussle—with horse, with difficult task, or in fun with older brother. Neither figure nor build was likely to attract immediate notice from one desiring petite and demure femininity. However, her face and spunky nature were sure to turn nearly any man's eye . . . and hold it, that is if he was a good enough judge of character to inquire to himself what lay beneath those gleaming grey eyes.

As they rode, Catharine was bent on pushing the pace, always inviting adventure, while George, at six one, sat more sedately in the saddle, as the elder statesman of the pair, thoughtful, perusing the landscape within and without.

"When are you going to get married, George?" Catharine asked, as for the moment they rode leisurely along.

"What kind of question is that!" laughed her brother.

"I don't know—it just popped out," she laughed with him.

"Then I'll answer you with the same words—I don't know. I suppose I don't think about it much."

"Everybody thinks about it, George. You can't tell me you don't."

"All right, sometimes I do."

"I knew it!"

"But it seems like something that might happen in the future."

"You're old enough to be married now."

"Maybe, but I'm in no hurry."

"Why?"

"Maybe for the same reason I waited until I was older to go to university. I wanted to get the most out of it possible. I wanted to be ready, not rush it. So many of the students I met were too young to absorb the education that was given them. If I ever do get married, I want to be ready for it. Besides, who'd want to marry me?"

"Anybody. If I weren't your sister I'd marry you in a minute."

"What a thing to say!" laughed George.

"Why not? If I were looking for a husband, I'd want him to be just like you."

"I'm very flattered. *Are* you looking for a husband, Catharine?"

"*Me*—are you kidding! I *am* too young."

"Seventeen? That's all most seventeen-year-old girls are thinking of—finding a man."

"A waste of time, if you ask me. I'm not *most* seventeen-year-olds. I happen to be Catharine Rutherford, and I won't give a man a second look until *I'm* good and ready, not because most other girls my age want to behave like ninnies and go giggling and ogling at every man they see between seventeen and thirty."

"Plenty of that goes on with young men too, though disguised."

"Most young men are ninnies themselves—except for you of course, George. It might be different if I met someone worth giggling and ogling over."

"You don't want to go to balls and parties like Amanda did?"

"Ugh—balls and parties! *Me*? Heavens, George ... you know me better than that. At least I thought you did. Nothing could interest me less."

"Well, I can't say I'm disappointed. I never found much use for that sort of thing."

"But you do want to get married?" persisted Catharine.

"Surely . . . I suppose," replied George. "I'm just not in a hurry."

"What are you going to do, then, now that you're out of university? I wondered if you would ever come home to live now that you're all grown up and graduated."

George laughed again. "I may be graduated, but I'm not sure I feel all grown up."

"You're a lot older than me."

"True. But maybe we're both still young. That's one of the things about Amanda that I never understood—she wanted to grow up so fast and get away from here. I'm not especially eager to do either."

"Do you like it here, in Devon, at Heathersleigh?"

"This is home," replied George. "I can't imagine living anyplace else. I love it here. And I suppose I will someday be lord of the manor just like father and his father, and so on. I'll probably have a stern old portrait of myself to hang with the rest." He made a face like old Henry, which brought another laugh from Catharine's mouth.

"What about being with Mother and Father, now that you're—you know, George—now that you're almost grown up yourself? Don't you want to be independent and out from under their roof?"

"Who needs independence? Father's my best friend. Why would I want to be out from under his roof?"

"I'm so relieved to hear you say that!"

"Why?" laughed George.

"I wondered if you might be like Amanda and want to leave and never come back. That was my greatest worry about your being gone at university, that you would come back all sophisticated and different, and that you would then go somewhere else to live, and I would never see you again except for visits when you'd wear starched shirts and lift your little finger when you drank tea and be all stuffy and sit around talking about boring—"

George could not contain himself any longer. Finally he burst out laughing.

"I thought *you* knew *me* better than that," he said.

"I thought I did too, but I couldn't help being nervous. I like it here too. Mother is *my* best friend, just like you say of Father. But I suppose I thought I was the oddball of the three of us children for feeling that way."

"Well, have no fear, younger sister. I promise I will never change. I won't get stuffy, and unless circumstances force a change upon me, Heathersleigh will always be my home.—Come on, race you to the top of the ridge!"

With scarcely a flick of the wrist from their respective owners, both horses immediately tore off across the grassy slope, throwing back great clods of turf behind their hooves.

29

Neighbors

The race was curtailed after only about two hundred yards, however, by the appearance of another familial riding pair, who about the same time emerged from a thin stand of pine to the right of the two racers.

George reined in. Although Catharine was about half a length in the lead, it was several seconds before she realized she was no longer being hotly pursued. She glanced back, saw George slowing to a trot, then reined in Black Fire even as she spun her around to rejoin her brother. As she did, she saw the reason for her brother's withdrawal from the contest.

George was already greeting the twenty-four-year-old heir of the marquessate of Holsworthy, Hubert Powell, and his sister, Gwendolen. Though Heathersleigh Hall and Holsworthy Castle were separated by some twenty miles, the two estates were considered almost as neighbors, not only because they were the two largest and most well-known estates in the region, but also because of the similarity in ages of the rising generations within the two families. Neither set of parents had ever been close, nor desired to be. There had been considerable interest on the part of young Powell in Amanda Rutherford at one time. However, it had been smartly rebuffed by the latter's father. The incident left such an acrid sting in Hubert's mouth that he never forgot his vow to get even somehow. What better way than to get the religious fool's other daughter to fall in love with him, for which second chance he had been biding his time until she was old enough to become interesting in his eyes.

In the meantime, remarkably, in spite of having plied his affections in more than a dozen directions, he had never married. This fact was not remarkable because he desired to marry and had not been successful. Six or eight foolish maidens would happily have married him for his looks, his dash, and his wealth, and been most miserable for it later. But the young Holsworthy heir had no inclination toward that sort of existence known as "settling down." He preferred his oats numerous and wild.

That Hubert Powell remained single was remarkable simply by virtue of the fact that no outraged father who had come to the marquess Atworth Powell demanding that his son marry his daughter had actually succeeded.

More than one *had* come, it is true, with precisely such a demand. But money has a way of mollifying much outrage. And the marquess of Holsworthy possessed it in sufficient quantities to have thus far kept the reputation of his son unsoiled and his future uncommitted.

By outward appearance, the years had been good to the future marquess. Hubert Powell was even more handsome and dashing than before. He had heard—he possessed many sources for the receipt of this sort of information—that Sir Charles Rutherford's second daughter, now seventeen and thus technically "available," had become something of an Amazon, and a beautiful one at that, whose eyes were like a wildcat's, who could ride like the wind, and who was stronger than any three normal women together.

When first he heard the report, he lost interest immediately. Who wanted a girl whose behavior resembled that of a man? He immediately set renewed inquiries afoot concerning the elder of the two girls. Now suddenly he realized how hasty had been his judgment. As the younger of the three Rutherford progeny rode up behind her imbecile of a brother, Hubert's eyes widened in fascination.

She *was* beautiful, and every inch a desirable young woman.

Knowing well enough Hubert Powell's reputation, George immediately assumed the role of knight protector, moving forward the moment the two riders came into view in hopes of placing himself between Catharine and harm's way. But the future marquess was not so easily deterred. The two eldest sons had just completed their stiff but properly cordial greetings when Catharine energetically cantered up alongside her brother. Her hair was flowing and her face flushed from the exhilaration of the ride.

"And this must be your sister Catharine!" said Powell effusively, smiling his most charming smile, bowing slightly and lifting his cap. "I don't know that we have seen one another since we were children."

"Catharine," said George with obvious reluctance, "this is Hubert Powell, and I believe you know his sister Gwendolen."

Catharine glanced momentarily toward her counterpart, then returned Hubert's smile, though cautiously. She too had heard the reports about him, and in truth George had nothing to fear. Her affections were perfectly safe. Because she was a young woman of substance, cajolery would not succeed in sweeping her off her feet. If she ever fell in love, it would be with someone of character, not superficial charm.

Already, however, Hubert was slyly angling his mount between George and Catharine, hoping to effect a pairing off, which could not better have suited Gwendolen Powell. She had had her sights on George Rutherford for years. Already, as her brother made his move, she flashed her eyes in George's direction.

"Perhaps you would like to join me for a ride, Catharine," Hubert said in his smoothest tone. "I'm sure Gwen and George would—"

"I think George and I would prefer to remain together," Catharine interrupted.

"What say you, George, old man?" rejoined Powell, turning with a quick wink toward George. "You and I are both men of the world, university fellows and all that. No doubt you and Gwen—"

"I'm sorry, Hubert," said George. "Catharine is right. We really do intend to continue on together."

Inwardly fuming at the double rebuff, Hubert did his best to maintain his composure.

"Well then, what would you say to some company? Gwen and I were heading down in your direction anyway."

"The countryside is wide open," replied Catharine. "We certainly have no objection, do we, George?"

The next instant she wheeled Black Fire about and was off down the slope at breakneck speed. George was after her before the two Powells knew what to think. Belatedly they both whipped their horses and did their best to catch up, but to little avail.

Eventually Catharine began to realize the rudeness of her swift departure. Gradually she slowed. George was soon by her side. They exchanged glances of resignation, as if to say, *I don't suppose we should just ride off and leave them.*

Neither was anxious to do so, but they now waited for the others to join them. In a minute or two the four young riders were clomping leisurely down the grassy incline side by side. The conversation among them, however, never quite successfully got smoothly under way.

"Tell me, Catharine," said Hubert, whom the quick ride had succeeded in tiring enough to moderate his anger, "what would you think of accompanying me to the Summer Ball in Exeter next month?"

"I would say that you move rather quickly from the front door to the drawing room for someone I scarcely know."

"How else will we get to know one another if we do not spend time together?"

"I would never go *anywhere* with a young man I don't know," said Catharine, "especially to a ball."

"Do you mind if I ask why?"

"I don't like balls."

"You are at the age where such things are done."

"Not by me."

"Why?"

"Because I have no interest in developing the kinds of relationships with young men that such circumstances are bound to produce."

George smiled. Powell was no match for his sister.

"Ah, it is against your religion—you think balls are evil, is that it?"

"Mr. Powell," rejoined Catharine, almost as if addressing a child, "you heard every word I said, and nothing remotely like that came out of my mouth. I simply find the atmosphere of a ball so shallow and artificial that it is the worst place I could imagine for two people to become acquainted."

"How would such a one as myself, then, approach an attractive young lady such as yourself whom he desires to get to know?"

"Talk to my father."

"What does *he* have to do with it?" asked Hubert, with difficulty keeping down his disbelief at her words.

"Everything. You surely do not think that I would become involved with a young man without my father and mother being part of it, do you?"

"I must admit . . . such a thing sounds rather old-fashioned in this modern day. Most of the young ladies I know are sophisticated and in step with the times—they have learned to speak for themselves."

"Perhaps it is old-fashioned, Mr. Powell. But I would still suggest that you talk to my father. If he approves, you could come visit us at Heathersleigh—George, myself, and my father and mother. Better yet, your whole family could come. What better way to become acquainted than for families to know one another? And in that suggestion I am speaking for myself."

Again in the company of these idiotic Rutherfords, the young heir to the Powell fortune was rendered fuming and speechless. Were they all a pack of fools together?

The ride did not last much longer. The strained silence that accompanied Catharine's remarks was followed within several minutes by a fork in the path, which, by common consent, saw two of the mounts take one direction, and the other two the opposite.

30

A Brother's Prayer

❖ ❖ ❖

*C*atharine and George came bounding into the sun-room flushed and exuberant. Charles and Jocelyn sat sipping tea and waiting lunch for them.

"You should have seen it, Mother!" exclaimed Catharine. "I don't think I've ever seen the clouds so white and the sky so blue. It was lovelier than you can imagine. I wish you could have ridden with us."

"Where did you go?"

"East, past Milverscombe and up along the high ridge that leads toward the forest."

"You were gone most of the morning," said Charles.

"George got me out immediately after breakfast and made me go with him."

"I was out an hour earlier than that," said George. "It was already warm, and the air so clean and still. I wanted a good long ride, and I knew Catharine would enjoy it."

"It sounds like she did," laughed their father.

"All except for running into Hubert Powell," said Catharine.

"How did that happen?" asked Charles.

"Sheer accident. He and his sister were out riding too."

"He didn't give you any trouble?"

"None that Catharine couldn't handle!" laughed George.

They all joined in, knowing well enough what he meant. "Good girl!" said Charles.

"She invited them all to Heathersleigh for a visit," said George.

"The whole family!" asked Jocelyn in alarm.

George nodded. "I doubt they're planning to take her up on it anytime soon."

"You should have seen Gwendolen Powell making eyes at George," added Catharine. "She is a sly one."

"How old is she now?" asked their father.

"I don't know, twenty-four, maybe even twenty-five," replied Catharine. "Old enough! And *very* pretty, wouldn't you say, George?"

"I suppose she's pretty. But she's a flirt. And there's nothing so unattractive to my eye, no matter how pretty a girl is. The instant I see that look in a girl of trying to attract notice and make me look at her, it repulses me."

"Why isn't she married?" asked Jocelyn. "At her age, I would have thought the marquess . . ." Her words fell away in indistinct question.

"There are rumors," said George.

"You mean. . . ?"

"Of more troubles in the family than Lord Holsworthy wants publicly known," said George. "It was all over Cambridge."

"Ah . . . I see," nodded his mother. "Then I think we need ask no more questions in that direction."

"We saw Mrs. Blakeley in the village," now added Catharine. "She told us to thank you, Mother, for the heather plant and rose bush. She said her little garden is beginning to bloom."

"How did she look?" asked Jocelyn.

"Better than I've ever seen her, Mother. She looked happy and well."

"Oh, I am so pleased. God bless her."

"She said to tell you to come over for a visit."

"I need to do that. In fact—Charles, when will you be working with Rune again?"

"Tomorrow."

"Then I think I will go see his wife at the same time. In the meantime, are you two horsemen ready for tea and some lunch?"

"I am," replied George. "And I'm hungry. Has Sarah—"

In answer to his question, Sarah Minsterly walked in from the kitchen.

"Yes, Master George," she said, "I *do* have lunch prepared.—Where would you like it served, Lady Jocelyn?" she said, turning toward Jocelyn.

"I think we'll just stay here, Sarah, since we already have our tea."

"Very good, mum."

She disappeared, returning a few minutes later bearing a tray of lunch things and more tea. She set down a pot of fresh water on the table, and two plates in front of Charles and Jocelyn, then returned to the kitchen for the rest. Meanwhile Charles made tea for son and daughter as they took seats around the sun-room table, which they used now and then for informal meals.

When everything was served and ready, Charles turned to his son. "Would you return thanks for us today, George?"

George nodded and they all bowed their heads.

"Lord, we thank you," George prayed, *"for this beautiful day you've given us to enjoy, and for the marvelous ride Catharine and I had. As always we give you thanks for your provision, for food, for family, for health, for the home you've given us, and the life we all have. You are good to us, Lord, and we give you thanks from our hearts. Yet as grateful as each of us four are for one another, we all know that our family is not complete right now. So we pray for Amanda too, Lord, as we do every day. Somehow let her know how much we love her. Restore her to us, that our family might be complete once again. Thank you, Lord . . . Amen."*

As always, when prayers were spoken for Amanda it could not help but make each of the four pensive for a few moments. They sipped at their tea in silence and began serving from the trays of cold sandwiches and vegetables.

"Oh, I wish Amanda could have been with us today!" exclaimed Catharine all at once. "I know she was sometimes grouchy, but I can't help it—I miss her. It's not right around here with her gone. I just can't imagine what she finds so interesting in London anyway."

Catharine shook her head and took a bite of sandwich.

"Although, now that I think about it," she added, "she would probably have made a fuss over the direction we went."

Everyone laughed.

"And no matter which horse you wanted to ride," said Jocelyn, "would have become the one *she* was determined to have."

"And she would have argued over whatever we were talking about on the way," added George. "You've got to admit that we are able to talk more freely and enjoyably than if she were picking every word apart."

"I suppose you're right," rejoined Catharine. "But I don't remember that as much as you do. All I can think of is that she's my sister . . . and I miss her."

31

Curious Invitation

◆ ◆ ◆

*L*ater that same day a letter arrived for Charles in the post. He shared its contents with the rest of the family at evening tea.

"I received the most peculiar invitation today," he said as they began eating. "I can't quite tell what to make of it."

"Who from?" asked Jocelyn.

"You remember my telling you about meeting the fellow I was in the navy with, Morley Redmond. It's from him. But it also mentions another man who was with Redmond last week. Seemed like a decent enough fellow, I suppose."

"Why do you think it's peculiar, Father?" asked Catharine.

"Listen," said Charles, "see if the tone of it doesn't strike you as just a little odd somehow."

Charles unfolded the paper.

To Sir Charles Rutherford, he read,

Dear Charles:

Our chance running into one another at the coronation reception after so many years was most fortuitous, as was the opportunity to introduce you to my friend Hartwell Barclay. I do not exaggerate when I say that he is an influential man in certain circles—though ones not generally well known to the public at large—vital to the future interests of our nation, and indeed all of Europe. He would like to meet with you, with a few select other individuals on a matter which we feel will be mutually beneficial to all concerned, as well as, I emphasize again, to our nation. The gathering will be held in Cambridge on the twenty-third of July. Will advise time and address later. I would ask, because of the nature of the times, that you keep this communication confidential. I look forward to seeing you again. I am, respectfully yours,

Dr. Morley Redmond

"I've heard of him," now said George.

"In what regard?"

"He's professor of economics at Oxford."

"Did you ever meet him?" asked Charles.

George shook his head.

"Who is the man Barclay?" asked Jocelyn.

"Redmond said he worked for the secret service," replied Charles.

"The secret service—that sounds dangerous."

"I've got it!" said George. "They want you to engineer a line of spy gadgetry—devices for listening to telephone conversations and who knows what else. Obviously they know about the electricity commission. They want to pick your brain."

Charles nodded thoughtfully. "That makes some sense," he said. "Somehow, though, I can't escape the feeling there's more to it. If that's all it is, I'll send *you*, George!"

"I may have the more recent degree, but you know fifty times more than I do! I'll be years catching up on what you've learned on your own."

Again Charles grew pensive.

"I told you too," he said, glancing toward Jocelyn, "about my conversation with Mr. Churchill."

She nodded. Charles briefly explained to Catharine and George.

"I suppose this might be connected in some way with that. For reasons we do not know, perhaps he asked about my willingness to help the country again in order to smooth the way for this request from the foreign office. Yet because he represents the other side of the cabinet, the *home* office, he cannot appear to be involved directly. It's a logical explanation."

"So will you go?" asked his wife.

"I'll have to pray about it and see. It still feels peculiar."

32

Land, Power, and Conquest

◆◆◆

*W*hat's all the fuss about over on the Continent," said Catharine. "From what you said Mr. Churchill said, do some people think there might actually be a war?"

"Some people think so, Catharine," Charles replied.

"Why?"

"Hasn't Mr. Sherborne explained it to you? I thought he kept you up on politics and world affairs."

"I suppose he has. I studied the different wars of the last century and the alliances that exist. But it's so dull coming from him. Tutors are always boring. He makes me read things I don't half understand. You always make it interesting, Father. I learn more from you in five minutes than I do from him in a week. You make learning into a story. You make history fun."

Charles laughed. "All right," he said, "let's see if we can turn the world of 1911 into a story that my little Catharine can understand."

"Father!"

"Right, so . . . Catharine, why are there disputes between nations?"

Catharine thought a moment.

"Because they each want something the other has, and both want to control the other?" she said at length.

"That's it precisely. You *do* understand the situation on the Continent."

"There has to be more to it than that."

"But you've put your finger on the foundation, Catharine, my girl. It's all about *land* and *power*. All disputes between nations start at the same point—they're because of land and power. Every nation wants *more* land and more power. And they don't want some *other* country exercising power over them."

"I see what you are saying, Father," said George. "But how does that apply, say, to America, when they were English colonies?"

"The War of Independence of the colonies was fought over *power*. The fight for independence is always a contest for control. Was England going to be in charge of the American colonies, or were they going to rule themselves?"

"I see."

"And when two countries like France and Germany, or Scotland and England share a border," Charles went on, "there is *constant* conflict. Both feel entitled to more of the land between them. They fight over it through the years, because both sides want it, especially, as is the case with Germany and France, if the land between them is rich, fertile, or of strategic importance. The Rhine River is obviously such a border. They have been battling over some of that land for a thousand years. Back and forth it goes, from one side to the other, borders constantly changing as one side gets stronger for a while, then the other."

"What about the power?" asked George. "I don't see it as clearly in that case as with the American colonies."

"When two countries fight over land for long enough," replied his father, "they generally come to dislike and resent each other. Often this animosity is increased because there are two different nationalities involved. The people of the different nationalities eventually hate each other just because they are different."

"But why?"

"There's no *reason* to it, Catharine. Of course it's illogical. The human race is sinful, and there's no other explanation than that. Different races often tend to despise each other. It's an awful thing, but true. Those feelings are increased all the more when land disputes are involved. What it usually leads to is not merely the desire to take your enemy's land, but also to conquer and control him. If it were only a matter of the land, then eventually governments and countries could peacefully negotiate borders, maybe one side would pay the other side for some bit of disputed territory, and everything would be fine. But it's not just about land. It's about power and control, fueled by nationalistic pride."

"I think I understand."

"Now that Germany is a united and growing force in Europe, the question of power and control is all the more critical. Which nation on the Continent is going to be the most powerful—France or Germany? Both want to be. And neither wants to be dominated by the other."

"Which would be best for England?"

"It's hard to say. That changes too. France has long been England's traditional enemy for much the same reasons, although the 'land' we share is the Channel. Historically, we have had much more in common with Germany, by both blood and language. Our royal houses are completely intertwined. The English monarchy is German through and through. Yet in recent years we have come to be on more friendly terms with France, and Germany now represents a greater threat to English power."

"Why have we grown closer to France?"

"For many reasons. As Napoleon and the French Revolution recede into the past, France has become a much more representative government, less authoritarian, and thus more similar to us politically and in general outlook. So gradually England's and France's interests in Europe have merged. All these things are constantly changing. Russia, too, has long been antagonistic towards England, until very recently, just in the last five or ten years. Now we have a treaty with both Russia and France called the Triple Entente."

Charles paused for a moment.

"Let's return to the example from our own history, because I think it will help you understand what is happening now on the Continent," he went on. "Scotland and England both wanted the land between them. As they fought over it, the Scots came to hate the English just because they were English, and the English came to hate the Scots just because they were Scots. So there was a nationalistic and ethnic pride involved that wanted to exercise power over its enemy.

"When bonnie Prince Charlie raised his army, he didn't merely attempt to regain *land* that England had taken from Scotland. If that had been the case, he wouldn't have needed to march any farther than Carlisle to insure that Scotland's land and border were secure. But Prince Charlie marched south almost to London. His goal was to take over and *conquer* England. He wanted both the land *and* power over his enemy. And when the duke of Cumberland chased Charlie's army back north, did he stop at the border once English *land* was secure?"

Charles paused and glanced first at Catharine, then to George.

"He pursued him throughout Scotland and massacred Charlie's whole army," replied George.

"Exactly. Both sides wanted the land *and* the power. And essentially that was the end of Scotland as an independent nation. England conquered her longtime enemy, subdued her, and made her part . . . well, not really part of England as such—we still call it 'Scotland'—but it is clear she is no longer independent. She became part of Great Britain. But it is obvious that England was the dominant force in the newly united nation, and that she had gained both the land *and* the power over Scotland.

"You see, there are always two possibilities which can emerge from these kinds of disputes—either *conquest* or *balance of power*. In the case of Germany and France, there is a balance of power. Both are independent nations of approximately equal strength. They may still be enemies, but their power exists in balance. And that's good for Europe. No superpowerful nation can dominate the others. In the case of England and Scotland, however, there was conquest. Now there is but one nation. Scotland no longer has the status of an independent and sovereign nation."

"But neither does England, Father," said George. "They're joined, with Scotland and Wales and Ireland, into the United Kingdom."

"Technically, of course, you're correct, George," replied Charles. "But practically speaking, England defeated the others and renamed the new and larger nation. England didn't really lose her sovereignty and independence in the process, she merely expanded it. But Scotland lost its sovereignty, and its parliament was disbanded."

"But what does all that have to do with the Continent now?" asked Catharine.

"This same thing is now going on over there," replied Charles, "involving several small nations that are just like Scotland used to be—fighting for their independence so as not to be swallowed up by bigger and more powerful neighbors. It is exactly the same situation. Will these states be allowed to be independent, or will they be swallowed up? Will a larger nation defeat and conquer them, or will a balance of power be preserved among many independent nations?"

"What are the small countries?" asked George.

"In the Balkans there are five states that all used to be under the domination of the Ottoman Empire—Serbia, Romania, Bulgaria, Albania, and Montenegro."

"And what is the country like England who is trying to take them over?" asked Catharine.

"There are three major powers involved," replied her father. "All three want to control the Balkans—the Turkish or Ottoman Empire, Russia, and Austria-Hungary. The Crimean War of the 1850s was fought over this same region, and the disputes were never resolved—except that Ottoman Turkey is weaker, and now Germany is considerably stronger. So you see it is far more complicated than with the England-Scotland parallel, because there are *five* states struggling for independence, and *three* major nations who want to control the region. On top of that, all these countries have allies who are also involved. It is a very dangerous situation, far more explosive than when the Crimean War broke out in 1854."

"And do the various people involved hate each other too, like you were saying earlier?" asked Catharine.

"Fiercely," replied Charles. "Far worse than has ever existed between the English and the Scots, or even between the Germans and the French. It more resembles the Jews and the Arabs. There are many ethnic races and bloodlines involved in a very small area. They all hate each other passionately—Bosnians, Serbs, Slavs, Bulgarians, Turks, Hungarians, Austrians, Romanians, some with ties more toward Russia, others more Teutonic or German in origin, and some still clinging to old allegiances toward Constantinople and the Ottoman Empire."

"Why does England care so much what happens down on the Black Sea?" asked Catharine.

"Because we have interests in the Near East, we control the Suez Canal, and because we are concerned that no other world power—such as Russia or Germany—try to take over or gain control of those interests. It is mainly that we desire to maintain a balance of power. England has no interest in *taking over* Europe, so to speak. But neither do we want to see some other nation grow so powerful that our interests would be jeopardized—especially some nation that we don't entirely trust, such as Germany or Russia."

"Are you saying that we are somewhat in the middle?" asked George.

Charles nodded. "In a manner of speaking," he said. "Great Britain often acts something like a diplomatic referee among many differing interests on the world stage, trying to keep all the nations in balance. It is a role we have occupied for centuries. England has always been different than conquering nations. England's history has no Alexander, Napoleon, Caesar, or Genghis Khan, intent on world domination and conquest."

"What about colonialism?" asked George. "Isn't the present British Empire something like the ancient Roman Empire?"

"No, no, my boy—although some modernists would like people to believe exactly that. Colonialism is much different than conquest. The British Empire is an altogether different thing than the domination of Rome or even what Napoleon sought. Britain is a colonial power but not a *conquering* power."

"And Britain has sought the good of the peoples of its colonies," added Jocelyn. "There have been mistakes, of course, but that has generally been our policy, wouldn't you say, Charles?"

"Yes and no, I suppose. We discussed just such things many times in Parliament. Mistakes . . . yes. But doing good for the native peoples of our dominions has always been a concern—a much different objective than the Napoleonic or Roman empires, where subjugation by military might was supreme. It has not been a policy that has always been carried out very well. I don't suppose the American colonists, or the natives of India more recently, have always felt that we were trying to do good for them. There are two sides to everything. But Great Britain has, to whatever degree, always tried to keep the good of its dominions in mind."

Charles paused momentarily and took a sip of his tea, now lukewarm.

"For centuries," he went on, "our role has been as the balancing hub of Europe, trying to prevent any one nation from establishing hegemony. Britain believes in balance, not conquest. That is why we are now allied with France and Russia, our former enemies—as a counterbalance to Germany and Austria-Hungary. We do not want to conquer Germany, but neither do we want to allow her to grow so strong she can conquer the rest of Europe."

"But why is the land by the Black Sea so important to everyone?" asked Catharine. "Why is everyone nervous about it?"

"Because some regions are more important than others," replied Charles. "Remember . . . conflicts originate over land. But not all land is equal. If Iceland were being disputed, for instance, it would hardly cause worldwide concern. The Shetland Islands were once Norway's possession and are now part of the United Kingdom. The dispute over the Shetlands did not lead to war."

"Those are unimportant disputed lands, is that what you're saying?" asked George.

"Surely not to the people who live there," replied his father. "But they are not strategic or possessive of great wealth. In terms of the whole world, I suppose we could call them relatively unimportant. The fate of the world's future is not going to be determined by Iceland. Would nations go to war over Greenland or Antarctica?"

Catharine and George chuckled at the idea.

"But the land around Bulgaria, Greece, and the Ottoman Empire," their father continued, "—and especially the straits between the Black Sea and Mediterranean, and the city of Constantinople—have been throughout history some of the most disputed and fought over land in all the world. These are extremely vital lands and waterways. Everybody wants to control it. Wealth is at stake. Power is at stake. It is at a place like this where land and power merge and almost become synonymous."

"Whose land is it?"

"For centuries it has been in the hands of the Ottoman Empire, which stretched across the Dardanelles into Bulgaria and Serbia, whose enemy all those years has been the Austrian Empire. However, the Ottoman Empire is now in decline. As its power has weakened, Austria has slowly advanced southward."

"How has that affected the Balkans?" asked George.

"The five states I mentioned before are all feeling more independence because of the withdrawal of Turkish power from their borders. There is even talk that they might join together and go to war against the Ottoman Empire in order to gain complete independence, much as the Americans went to war against us. But at the same time, Austria is trying to move in and bring these nations under *its* control. And, likewise, Russia feels a legitimate claim to the region because many of the peoples of these Balkan states are Slavic in origin. Russia considers it her right to protect Serbia and Romania in particular from being swallowed up by Austria."

"So it's not as simple as America fighting for its independence," remarked George. "Or even the disputes between Scotland and England."

"Not at all," rejoined Charles. "It's far more complex, and far more explosive. The whole future of Europe may be at stake. What you have is a clashing of three major powers—imperial Austria, Ottoman Turkey, and tsarist Russia—at one tiny point on the map of huge strategic importance and wealth, where live a cluster of intensely nationalistic Slavic and Germanic peoples. Not only that, it is a region of constant unrest, whose peoples are violent and frequently disputing among themselves."

It fell silent for several long minutes.

"I think I understand it a little better now," said Catharine. "But it is still confusing."

"It *is* confusing," said Charles.

"What do you think will happen?" asked Jocelyn.

"We can only hope and pray that cool heads will prevail. But the Balkan people themselves can be hotheaded. Their patriotism is extreme, even fanatic. There is Middle Eastern blood intermingled in some of these Balkan races—Turkish blood, probably some Arab. They are hostile, fighting people. When you put into the middle of that the present bellicose German outlook . . . it is frightening. What Serbia will do if Austria threatens its independence is anyone's guess. My own fear is that Austria and Russia may come to blows over the Balkans. If that happens, Kaiser Wilhelm of Germany becomes the wild card. What might he do? If he reacted impulsively and arrogantly . . ."

Charles paused and shook his head, then sighed.

"As I said," he added, "we can only hope the major powers will not allow such pride, ethnic nationalism, and arrogance to dictate their actions."

33

Family Evening in the Library
◆ ◆ ◆

With the advent of electricity in Heathersleigh Hall, Charles and Jocelyn often retired to the book-lined room in the evening after tea, to spend two or three quiet hours in the company of their favorite authors and other literary friends. What a delight it was to be able to read as if in broad daylight rather than by beeswax candlelight or kerosene lamp, especially on a cozy, rainy evening.

On this particular occasion Catharine and George had joined them. And now father and mother, son and daughter, all sat close to one another in a sitting nook which had been carved out by the rearrangement of a few of the shelves, each quietly engrossed in his own literary selection.

"This is absolutely the most remarkable book!" Charles suddenly exclaimed, shaking his head as if in disbelief and chuckling. The others glanced up. "I was skeptical at first," he went on, "and probably wouldn't be reading it at all if I hadn't promised Timothy I would. But now I can see why it's causing such a stir over in the States."

"What is it?" asked Catharine.

"It's a novel by an American pastor called *In His Steps*."

"*You* . . . reading a novel, Father," she exclaimed laughing, "—I don't believe it! *You*, who once said novels were only for romantics and women."

"Don't be too hard on him, Catharine," said George. "Between Timothy and me, we've almost got him converted."

"He's right," added Charles. "And it was dear Queen Victoria who first got me interested in the Scotsman's work with her gift at my knighting. And with Timothy raving about him all the time, how could I not keep an open mind?"

"I don't recall your reading any *other* novelists," persisted Catharine good-naturedly.

"I suppose you have me there," confessed Charles.

"But, Father, there are so many great novels with so much spiritual truth in them. I like them *better* than devotional books.—And don't you dare say it's because I'm a young woman! I'm *not* a romantic—I just learn more about living as a Christian from novels than anything else. They're more real."

Charles laughed. "After reading this Sheldon book, I understand why you say so."

"Oh, you should read Harold Wright. He's an American too. I *love* his books."

"But, Charles," now said Jocelyn, "I haven't read the book Timothy gave us yet. What's it about?"

"The most fascinating premise," replied Charles. "The pastor of a church put before his congregation the proposition that they pledge, for an entire year, to do nothing—in their businesses, in their homes, in the life of their church, in *everything* that came up—without first asking, 'What would Jesus do?' "

It was silent a moment as they considered the startling proposal.

"And what was the result?" asked Jocelyn.

"I don't know yet," replied her husband. "I'm only about a third of the way through the book, but already it's turning the lives of all who try it upside down."

"One of the Wright books I read is something like that," said Catharine. "It's called *That Printer of Udell's*."

"Do we have it?" asked Charles.

"It's over there," replied Catharine, pointing vaguely. "I've got five or six of his books."

"Well, now that I find myself branching out in the field of fiction whose foundation is built on spiritual principles, perhaps I shall try that next. Are you reading one of the Wright fellow's books at the moment?"

"Actually no," replied Catharine. "I'm reading *Ben-Hur*."

"Oh, right—the Roman story about the Lord and the galley slave, or something."

"I've been wanting to read it too," said Jocelyn. "Is it good?"

"It's different than a contemporary sort of story. But it's really making me think. And there's so much about Jewish customs and the history of that period—I'm learning a lot. Besides that, it's just a good story."

"It's been performed onstage in London I believe, hasn't it?" said her mother.

"I didn't know that," replied Catharine. "I would love to see it acted out!"

"It was a few years ago, as I recall," said Charles. "I've heard nothing about it recently.—By the way, what are you reading, George?"

"One of the Scotsman's."

"Which one?"

"*Warlock O'Glenwarlock.*"

"That's a spooky title!" said Catharine with a shudder.

"It's not that bad," laughed her brother. "Warlock is the family name, that's all."

"Ugh, but why did he pick a name like that?"

"Who knows—maybe he knew somebody called Warlock. But the story's great. Castle Warlock reminds me of Heathersleigh—hidden passages and ancient secrets. And I have the feeling there's a treasure somewhere, something about an old sea captain, but I'm not far enough into it to be sure. It's full of Scots dialect and spiritual truths—one of the best of his I've read so far."

"All right, Mother," said Catharine, turning toward Jocelyn, "you're the only one who hasn't told us what you're reading."

"I must confess," smiled Jocelyn, "that I am *not* reading a novel this evening. Not that I have anything against them, mind you. I love a good story. But tonight I was in the mood for something that made me think in a different way than fiction does."

"And what did you find?" asked her husband.

"I was in the mood for my *other* favorite Scotsman," replied Jocelyn.

"Ah yes—the good Professor Drummond. What of his are you reading?"

"I've read the love essay so many times, I thought I ought to branch out. And I found this that we had right here in the library, *The Ideal Life and Other Unpublished Addresses.*"

She lifted the book from her lap and showed it to Charles.

"It has addresses on salvation and God's will and a number of topics. I've been reading one whose title caught my fancy called 'The Man After God's Own Heart.'"

"Sounds intriguing. I presume he means *man* in the encompassing sense? We wouldn't want any feminist suffragettes crying prejudice."

Jocelyn laughed. "I took the liberty of including myself in his *man*," she replied. "I am quite sure Mr. Drummond intended it so. Listen to this."

Jocelyn glanced down again at her book, found her place, and began to read aloud.

"'We are going to ask,'" she read, "'What is the true plan of the Christian life? If you look you will see that the answer lies on the surface of our text. The general truth of the words of Acts 13:22 is simply this: that the end of life is to do God's will. Now that is a great and surprising revelation. It has been before the world these eighteen hundred years, yet few have even found it out today. One man will tell you the end of life is to be true. Another will tell you it is to deny self. Another will say it is to keep the Ten Commandments. A fourth will point you to the Beatitudes. One will tell you it is to do good, another that it is to get good, another that it is to be good.

"'But the end of life is in none of these things. It is more than all, and it includes them all. The end of life is not to deny self, nor to be true, nor to keep the Ten Commandments—it is simply to do God's will. It is not to get good nor be good, nor even to do good—it is just what God wills, whether that be working or waiting, or winning or losing, or suffering or recovering, or living or dying.

" 'But this conception is too great for us. It is the greatest conception of man that has ever been given to the world. The great philosophers, from Socrates and Plato to Kant and Mill, have given us their conception of the ideal human life. But none of them is at all so great as this. Each of them has constructed what they call a universal life, a life for all men and all time to copy. None of them is half so deep, so wonderful, so far-reaching, as this: *"I have found . . . a man after my own heart, who shall fulfill all my will."* ' "

It fell quiet for a few moments as they all contemplated the profound words of the renowned Edinburgh professor, dead now fourteen years. When Jocelyn next spoke, her words were not to the members of her family.

"Dear Father," she prayed quietly, *"with all my heart I do want to be a woman of whom you can say the same words you said of David, that you have found one after your own heart, who will fulfill your will. I thank you so much for loving me as I am, even for creating me as I am, that I might show forth your handiwork. It is my desire ever more fully to be your daughter, a daughter pleasing to you—one who does as you would have her do, who thinks as you would have her think, whose attitudes are ones you would have fill her being. Help me, Father, reflect you in all I do, in all I say, in all I am. Help me to ask what would Jesus do in everything that comes my way. Help me to walk in your will, do your will, and fulfill your will for me."*

"Amen," whispered Charles softly.

"That was a beautiful prayer, Mother," said Catharine, looking toward her mother with moist eyes. Her sweet smile was one of daughterly affection and a sister's mutual love for their common Lord.

Jocelyn returned the smile. After the deep expression of Jocelyn's heart, there seemed little more for anyone to say. Gradually each of the four returned to their books.

34

Suffragette or Society Belle?

*N*ever in her life had Amanda Rutherford been so busy. Balancing her exciting new social life with ongoing suffragette activities, every day was full from morning till night. Despite the brief awkwardness at the coronation reception, and the occasional annoyance of Geoffrey's presence, she had to admit it was a wonderful time. This is what she had always dreamed her life in London would be.

Even though she had been, as she saw it, deprived of a proper coming out at seventeen, and her family had never been part of the London scene, Amanda knew well enough what it all meant. She had read her Austen and Dickens, her Thackeray and Trollope. There was a surface gaiety to many of the gatherings. But she knew that fathers from throughout England came to London for the season to engage in the serious business of shopping their daughters around in what was rudely referred to as the "marriage market." She realized well enough that she was being "looked at."

Amanda was not anxious to marry. But she would play along, relish in the attention, and enjoy the round of concerts, parties, dances, dinner parties, and myriad other social occasions which the London season offered. Generally, if a girl did not get herself married within two or three seasons, she was in danger of being considered a failure altogether. But Amanda was enough of a modernist not to worry about such conventions. That she had started late did not make her the more anxious, but rather enabled her to take a more modest perspective of her future.

And she had come to admit, there was more to Cousin Martha than first met the eye. In her own way, Amanda admired her for being able to content herself in her marriage to Gifford Rutherford. Not that Amanda would ever be content with a man like her father's first cousin. But Martha managed to find purpose and meaning in her life in spite of it, and Amanda respected her for it.

Emmeline Pankhurst couldn't tolerate such women, and railed against exactly Martha's kind for contributing to the male domination of society.

Yet Amanda could not despise Cousin Martha. Maybe every woman couldn't fight for equality in the same way. Maybe what Cousin Martha had said to her on their first meeting was true, that there were different ways to exert one's influence, and she had chosen hers.

Amanda's supply of funds continued slowly to dwindle. She said nothing about it. Yet Martha seemed to understand and did what she could to make things easier for her.

There could not help but be awkwardness, of course, being involved with both Ramsay and Geoffrey, especially when both appeared at many of the same places. But as much as she would have loved to, Amanda could not ignore Geoffrey. The simple fact was, he was her ticket to society.

All the while, Amanda had not paused to reflect deeply concerning just what she really wanted, and why. Sooner or later she would no doubt be forced to choose between being a suffragette or a young lady of society. For the present, even Amanda herself did not understand what were her innermost driving passions.

So much of what she had become involved with had initially been a means to get away from home and express her individuality and independence. She *thought* she wanted to change the world and make it a better place. But did the suffragette cause really drive her as it did the Pankhursts? Amanda had not really stopped to ask.

She *thought* she wanted to be part of society. But did she really want to marry? Or did her motives spring merely from desiring to be the center of attention in what, on the surface at least, seemed an exciting and romantic world? Neither was this a query she had considered.

To ask herself such questions would have plunged Amanda into more self-analysis than she was prepared for. Thus she went along— her motives and activities and hopes filled with more contradictions than logic—doing what came to her to do, all the while trying to convince herself that it was the fun and fulfilling and independent life she had always longed for.

Meanwhile, by late 1911 it became apparent that the slippery Mr. Asquith had managed again to evade bringing the House of Commons to a resolution on the matter of women's suffrage. Several meetings were held between parliamentary leaders and the Pankhursts, without result.

One afternoon following such a meeting Emmeline was obviously upset. She calmed long enough as they sat down for afternoon tea to give a brief prayer of thanks, and to ask God's blessing on their activities. As Amanda bowed her head and listened, the curious fact did not strike her that the Pankhursts' religion did not grate on her like that of her father.

"Sylvia, would you pour?" said Emmeline as she passed the plate of breads to Christabel. The two daughters always took seats on either side of their mother, whether at the tea table, in a cab, or when standing before a crowd of women. Christabel spoke as she passed the plate on to Amanda.

"So what did you mean, Mother," she said, "when you came in a while ago, that today was the last straw?"

"I have tried to be patient," replied Emmeline, sipping at her tea but obviously still agitated. "We have tried to work through the system of government. But the House of Commons is intractable. It became obvious to me at today's meeting that they have no intention of granting us the vote. There is talk, talk, talk, all very soothing and placating. They pretend to be in agreement, but nothing is ever done."

"So what do you mean by the last straw?" asked Amanda.

"Just this—that it is time to take matters into our own hands. It is time to initiate our own tactics to show this country and its leaders that we will not be put off so easily."

As she listened to her mother speak, Christabel's eyes were alight. "What are we going to do, Mother?" she asked.

"We will begin with London's windows," replied Mrs. Pankhurst. "I am certain *that* will get Parliament's attention!"

And indeed, as soon as they could arrange it, a window-smashing raid was led against the home office, the war office, the foreign office, and at least a dozen other governmental buildings and men's clubs. Carrying rocks and hammers in their bags and under their coats, hundreds of women shattered thousands of windows. Over two hundred women were arrested, and a hundred and fifty sent to prison for varying sentences of up to a month.

Emmeline and Sylvia and Christabel thought nothing now of being arrested. Christabel, in fact, was slowly coming to replace her mother as the leader of the militant arm of the movement. At night, carloads of women drove out of the city to replenish their stores of rocks. Nor was jail a deterrent. For in prison the women could go on hunger strikes, which gained as much publicity for their cause as did riots, marches, and speeches.

Meanwhile, their magazine *Votes for Women* occupied more and more time and advocated more outlandish tactics. Telephone wires were cut, jam and tar were spread in mailboxes of notables who opposed them. Some fires in London and a few small bombs were attributed to the suffragettes.

By now all London was in an uproar, and public opinion was sharply divided.

Amanda, however, was no longer interested in being in jail or going on a hunger strike. And she certainly wasn't about to conceal a knife or hatchet in her coat at a rally! Even going to a ball on Cousin Geoffrey's arm was better than throwing a bomb, setting a fire, starving herself, or being arrested. Gradually it became more and more difficult for Amanda to identify herself with the Pankhursts and all they stood for.

35

The Chest

—— ♦ ♦ ♦ ——

As Amanda walked the tightrope between remaining a suffragette while living the life of a society debutante, and not really sure how much of either world she even wanted to be part of, her brother and sister were involved in an adventure of their own.

High in the garret portion of one wing of Heathersleigh Hall, still without benefit of electricity, George led Catharine, with an oil lantern in his hand, through a darkened and narrow passageway, then down a flight of stairs.

"Are you still frightened in here," said George as they went, "like you were the first time I showed it to you?"

"I wasn't afraid."

"You were too!" chided George playfully. "Don't you remember— you were worried about ghosts."

"Amanda put that into my head, but I knew there weren't any. And later, I only asked you about ghosts to make it more interesting for you so that you would *think* I was afraid."

"I must admit that to be an original explanation!"

"But what I have always been curious about," said Catharine, changing the subject, "is why all these funny passageways were built in the first place."

"That's why I brought you here today," said George. "I think I have finally discovered something to shed some light on that mystery."

"Really? George, that's great . . . what!"

"Well, maybe not *why* . . . but possibly *who*. And that might be the first step toward unraveling the why as well."

George led the way through various narrow passageways until they came at length to the storeroom on the second floor of the north wing from which he had first discovered the hidden labyrinth within the walls of the Hall. Up the narrow stairs through the floor of the room George climbed. He extinguished the lantern and set it on the floor, then reached down to lend Catharine a steadying hand as she climbed up. A minute later they were both in the room where only two weeks ago George and his father had completed the installation of an overhead light.

"Now we'll be able to see what we're doing," said George. "Isn't the light great?"

"But why does a storage room need electricity?"

"Father and I want to have current in every room of the Hall. And we almost have. But I want to show you what's in this old chest."

"Why did we come through the garret instead of just walking up the stairs and down the hall?" asked Catharine.

"It just seemed more fitting, since we were going to try to unravel the mystery."

"George, were you *trying* to see if you could frighten me!"

"I would never do that," he replied with a grin. "I was just getting us into the right frame of mind—you know, Sherlock Holmes and all that. Although now that you put the idea in my head, I'll have to see what kind of spookiness I might think up."

"It won't work. I'm too old for all that."

"What about some dark and stormy night, with the wind howling and the lightning flashing . . ."

"There's nothing spooky about that."

"Ah, but what if right at the stroke of midnight, you heard a wailing scream from somewhere behind the walls of your room?"

"You wouldn't dare!" laughed Catharine. Even as she tried to make light of it, however, her expression gave away the merest hint of anxiety that her brother might be serious.

"*Me* ... dare what?" replied George innocently. "I'm sure if something like that happened, I would be asleep in my bed. I was only asking what you would do in such a case?"

"Well it's not going to happen, because if it did, you would know that something worse just might come *your* way a few nights later ... so there!"

George smiled shrewdly. Catharine returned the look with a flash of her grey eyes. The challenge had been laid down, and both knew it.

"What I brought you here to show you was this," said George, now dragging the wooden container into the center of the room. "That's how I first discovered the stairway beneath the floorboards. I got curious about this chest—what was I, probably about sixteen at the time—and when I pulled it out, the boards underneath it were loose. I had been prowling around and exploring for years. But that's when I discovered how this room connected with the library, the garret, and the tower."

"How does all that tell us who was behind it?" asked his sister.

"It's in the chest," rejoined George. "The instant I found it I was curious what was inside it. But as soon as I discovered the passageway under the stairs, I forgot all about it. It was just full of papers anyway. But then when Father and I were working in here a week or two ago, I saw it still sitting there against the wall and was reminded of my earlier curiosity. And I thought to myself, 'What if there's something in those papers that might be interesting?' "

"Was there?"

"It's interesting to me. I'll show you. Father and I've been so busy with the wiring and putting in fixtures that I didn't get a chance to come back and dig into it until this morning..."

George paused and opened the lid of the chest.

"—that's when I found this."

36
The Ledger

——— ◆ ◆ ◆ ———

*C*atharine knelt down and bent forward to look inside the chest. It appeared about half full of notebooks, files, journals, various ships' logbooks, a dozen or so envelopes filled with records, receipts, and letters, and stacks of loose, miscellaneous papers.

George reached in and withdrew a thick brown leather journal, each of whose cover-boards was brittle and badly decayed but still holding together. Across the front, barely legible, were the words "Construction and Labor Accounts."

"What is it?" asked Catharine, her own curiosity now mounting.

"As far as I can tell it is the financial ledger for the original construction of Heathersleigh Hall, as well as for later building and remodeling and various other related construction projects about the estate."

George carefully opened back the cover.

"Look," exclaimed Catharine. "The first entry is dated 1629."

"That's when work on the Hall apparently began," said George, "because then follow pages and pages of accounts and references and expenditures—"

As he spoke George flipped through the yellowing pages at the front of the journal.

"—until you get here."

He stopped and pointed to the bottom of a page. Catharine followed his finger to the reference.

"Look . . . date, 1647," said George, "when it appears to me that the original structure, which would be the north wing, was completed. Then a second section begins a few years later, 1661, where you have the records for the east wing, which as far as I can tell was built between then and 1678. That's how the Hall must have looked for a couple of generations, an L-shaped building comprised of the north and east wings with the tower between them."

"I wish there were drawings," said Catharine.

"I'm sure there must be someplace in here," replied George. "I'm going to initiate a careful search of everything in this entire chest. I did run across a few entries that seem to refer to engineers' plans. No project of this size could have been completed without drawings."

"Can you really make heads or tails of all those entries?" asked Catharine, pointing to one of the pages.

"Not a lot," replied her brother. "But enough to get some idea how the construction progressed. This is mostly a financial account, so there's a limit to how interesting it can be. But it is a place to begin."

"To begin what?"

"Figuring out the history of the Hall. Can you imagine how fascinating it would be to unlock the Hall's secrets all the way back to the beginning?"

"A list of numbers and expenses can't do that, George."

"It might tell us when certain things happened. Already we've discovered when the different wings were built. We've learned quite a bit already from this ledger. Often it's finances that unlock doors in other areas."

"But it's the *people* who know the secrets. And our ancestors are all dead."

George recalled his experience staring at the face of Lord Henry.

"Have you ever spent much time in the portrait gallery?" he asked.

"I don't know. Not much," Catharine answered. "I mean I've walked through it a thousand times."

"Next time you do, stop and look into some of the faces. I mean, *really* look . . . gaze into their eyes. See if you don't start to imagine that they are trying to tell you something. Maybe they're not as dead as we think," he said.

"What is *that* supposed to mean!" laughed Catharine. "Now you *are* getting spooky."

"Only that maybe they left behind information, clues that point to those secrets. Perhaps even something on the surface as boring as a financial ledger might contain more than one thinks, *if* you know what to look for. Like how in old portraits people choose things to surround themselves with that are significant—a family jewel or hat or walking stick."

"So what do you think *this* ledger has to say?"

"What I found most interesting of all," said George enthusiastically, again flipping through the pages toward the latter portions of the book, "is the construction that went on during the time of Broughton Rutherford in the late 1700s."

"What kind of construction?" asked Catharine.

"Lord Broughton began—"

"Who is he?" interrupted Catharine. "I recognize the name, but I'm not sure of the connection."

"Let's see," replied George. "He would be our ... great ... no, our great-*great*-grandfather. He began work on the third and final wing of the Hall, which is the west wing. Also a gamekeeper's lodge was built between 1777 and 1779. But then Lord Broughton died suddenly at fifty-five."

"Did he have a son?"

"No, he was unmarried."

"What happened to the estate?"

"I've never really heard Father talk about it much, but it passed down to Henry Rutherford after Lord Broughton's death, who then became lord of the manor."

"Wasn't he a nephew or something?"

"Right—and young, too, as I recall, when he inherited. Eighteen, I think. He was father's grandfather, and I've heard both Father and Cousin Gifford say that they remember him from when they were boys."

"Who?"

"Lord Henry. In any event, from what I can tell from the records in this ledger, he carried forward his uncle's construction project, ultimately completing the west wing and bringing Heathersleigh Hall more or less to its present form. Moreover—"

George paused for dramatic effect.

"—I think I have may have found some cryptic entries pointing to the construction of these secret passages."

He scanned one of the pages, turned to the next—

"Here it is—look, Catharine. There are expenditures, both for lumber and labor, with only the single word 'garret' beside them."

"What do you think it means?"

"Like I said, I think it's got something to do with the hidden passageways of the house. The first 'garret' entries are dated 1799 alongside the name W. Kyrkwode."

"Who is that?"

"I assume a builder, laborer, stonemason, craftsman of some kind, I don't know . . . maybe a supplier of materials."

"The name rings a bell in my brain," said Catharine.

"I didn't know you were so up on your Milverscombe history. *I've* never heard the name. Where do you know it from?"

"I'm not sure. But I'm sure I've heard it . . . or seen it written somewhere."

"One thing's sure—whoever this W. Kyrkwode was, there are no Kyrkwodes in the area now. Otherwise we'd know it."

"The parish would have some record."

"If there was a birth or marriage or death or baptism or confirmation, or something like that. But what if this Kyrkwode was just an itinerant laborer of some kind whom old Lord Broughton—"

George stopped, puzzling over the page he had shown Catharine and that which followed.

"No," he said after a moment, "that could hardly be . . . because look—the Kyrkwode entries continue on after Broughton's death. Whatever project he had begun, Lord Henry obviously continued after he inherited, for he continued to employ Kyrkwode's services on and off all the way up until 1819."

"There's another name, too," said Catharine, pointing down to the same page. "Now that is one I *know* I recognize."

"Digges," said George, nodding. "I hadn't noticed it the first time. The family have been locksmiths in the village for generations. Some former ancestor of John Digges must have done some work at the Hall. I suppose it is hardly surprising. Most of the local craftsmen probably worked for the lord of the manor at one time or another."

Brother and sister fell silent for a time.

"This is really a mine of information," said Catharine at length. "Have you shown it to Father or Mother?"

George shook his head. "I just found it this morning, and Father's been out with Rune Blakeley all day."

"Mother's gone to the village too. But can we show it to them when they get back? They'll be excited."

George closed the ledger and rose, folding down the lid of the chest but keeping the old book of financial records in his hand. He helped Catharine to her feet.

"What do you say to a walk back through the passageway to the tower?" said George. "All this sleuthing in the ledger makes me curious to see if I can find something I've overlooked before. I'm sure there are clues about just waiting to be found."

"George, you *imagine* half the mysteries you try to solve," laughed Catharine. "What if they just built these passageways for *fun*, to give their children, and future generations like you, a place to romp and play?"

"You go look at the face of old Lord Henry in the portrait gallery," rejoined George, "and then tell me you see 'fun' in those eyes. No, Catharine—those eyes are trying to tell us *something*. I don't know what, but they've got a secret to tell, and these peculiar passageways have more to do with it than we've yet discovered."

"And *you're* determined to find out, even though it's more than a century old!"

"It might not be that old. But however old it is . . . yes, I am determined to get to the bottom of it."

"You always were the curious one of the family. Amanda and I could never understand your fascination with all the rusty old things you find."

George laughed. "I suppose you're right—once my brain sees something it doesn't understand, it can't rest. Come on, Catharine—let's go explore!"

37

Milverscombe and Its Secrets

*F*orty minutes later the two young people stood at the window of the tower which rose at the convergence of the north and east wings of Heathersleigh Hall, having little idea that the high empty room of stone walls and slab floor itself held some of the very secrets about their home which they sought. Unfortunately, however, its walls could not talk, and thus it would be some years before all would come to light.

The village of Milverscombe upon which their gaze fell sat roughly in the middle of Devonshire between the Bristol Channel to the north and the English Channel to the south. It was a peaceful landscape of gentle fields, green and flowered meadows, and occasional woodlands. Cattle and sheep grazed it, fox and deer and rabbit made its forests their homes, and potatoes, grain, and a variety of crops grew up from out of it. The people of this region thus derived from the land their sustenance, and enjoyed its unspoiled simplicity and beauty, each after his own fashion.

England was growing and its urbanization expanding. Yet thankfully for the people of this region, modernity had not quite yet stretched out its grasp to consume them. The railroad was here, it is true, and electricity was on the way. But though the telephone had made inroads, it would be years before it had quite taken them over. Thus, for now, the people of Devonshire yet had to meet one another face-to-face to express their thoughts and conduct their business. Humanity still ruled here, not invention nor technology.

But the pleasant setting hid the fact that a misdeed had altered the course of the history of this region. To a certain vicar and midwife long before had been entrusted the key to the mystery, each of whom dealt with the silence imposed upon them by the lord of the manor of Heathersleigh Hall in his own way. The vicar left the region, rose high in the church, became a bishop and did whatever bishops do. He returned to the country in his advancing years, when the fate of that night long past came back to bless him with the home in which he spent his final years. Happily they were years marked by the waking of his conscience and the discovery of that greatest of all secrets of the human race that so few ever find, the mysterious wonder that he was a child after all, and that a good and loving Father cared for him. The bishop's discovery of that central truth came late, but that it did come at last made a man of him.

The midwife, meanwhile, raised her own family in the village, and lived to see her grandchildren grow into fine, God-fearing girls and boys, though neither she nor her daughter's family enjoyed an easy time of it. She too was rewarded in the end, finding herself the recipient of the material benefit of the bishop's changed and humbled heart.

The village of Milverscombe had grown slightly since Victoria's time. The tall steeple of the parish church, where Charles and Jocelyn Rutherford had been married in 1884, rose above a cluster of homes and shops connected by a disorderly arrangement of dirt streets through which, on most days, a steady stream of horses, wagons, buggies, and pedestrians moved about their affairs. The Devon rail line had been built to pass the edge of the village some thirty years before, insuring that gradually the effects of advancing civilization would be felt here.

And now the fact that Sir Charles and Lady Jocelyn, whom everyone for miles around loved with all their hearts, had brought electricity to the Hall, and could be seen occasionally motoring through the village in the latest invention of the times, insured that Milverscombe would continue to grow and change with the times. Many Saturday afternoons saw Charles in the village, giving rides in his Peugeot to the children as a reward for their hard week at school, or else attempting to teach some of the more daring of the locals actually to sit behind the wheel and drive it. That its one bright red coat of paint had suffered a good number of scrapes and bruises in the process concerned Charles not in the least. He valued people more than things. If sheep farmers Mudgley and Bloxham, or Bob the station master, or Andrew Osborne, husband of the new village schoolteacher, drove his car into a tree, his only concern would be for their safety, not the damaged fender.

Even some of the more intrepid women of Milverscombe ventured into the backseat when it came time for their husband's turn at the wheel, usually to the accompaniment of much banter from the watching crowd and many shrieking wifely exhortations against haste once the ride was under way. Charles refused, however, to allow Mrs. Osborne, when it was rumored, according to Jocelyn, that she was in the early stages of pregnancy, to ride with her own eager husband.

The highlight of the entire year surely had to be the day when the red Peugeot appeared one Saturday afternoon in Milverscombe with Lady *Jocelyn* Rutherford behind the wheel in place of her husband. Immediately word spread. Within minutes twenty or thirty women were scrambling to climb in. The rest of the afternoon saw the Peugeot touring all about the countryside with load after load of ladies jammed inside, many of whom had never before ridden in an automobile. It was a day talked and laughed about for the rest of the year. The discussion on the ladies' part nearly always contained mention of the fact that not so much as a single scratch had been added to the already numerous dings, dents, and other alterations administered to Sir Charles' car by the *men*.

As brother and sister gazed outward from the tower, Catharine's eyes gradually came to rest upon the cottage in the woods between the Hall and the village by which bishop and midwife were linked. Her conversation with George put her in a reminiscent mood, which oddly turned her thoughts toward Maggie McFee.

"I think I'm in a mood to visit Grandma Maggie," said Catharine at length.

She and George turned and left the tower, this time by the stairway. George went back to the library, whereas the conversation had left him, on the other hand, in the mood for a good book. He and Catharine parted at the second-floor landing of the main stairway.

38
Curiously Disappeared Bible
◆◆◆

*C*atharine set out for her room to change into her riding habit. Her way took her back through the gallery. Like George, she had passed through it many times nearly every day of her life without giving any of the silent personalities a moment's thought. But today, with George's references to the portraits still fresh in her mind, her step slowed.

She gazed up at old Henry Rutherford. George was right—he seemed desirous of saying something. It certainly wasn't a happy face.

Slowly Catharine wandered about, gradually taking in face after face from the other portraits.

A certain family resemblance was clear enough—the lines of the face, the wide-set eyes, the high foreheads on most of the men. And as George had said, it was interesting to note what special items had been chosen as props for the various portraits. Two elderly women had been painted together, with a framed portrait sitting on an easel in the background. The brass plate on the frame identified the two subjects, but there was no way to tell who might be the woman whose portrait rested behind them. Catharine glanced about, but saw no earlier portrait hanging anywhere which might be the same picture.

Two other paintings featured a light cream-and-peach-colored marble pedestal beside the subjects. In one the pedestal held a potted plant. In the other it served as a base for what appeared to be an open family

Bible. Catharine recognized the pedestal as the same family heirloom that stood upstairs in their library right now with a small potted palm on it.

One of the largest portraits, a horizontal view, displayed a family grouping—a seated man and woman with their seven children standing gathered around and behind them. In the woman's lap lay the same large Bible.

Catharine moved as close as she could, though the painting hung higher than her head, to examine the mother's face. Yes . . . it was the same woman whose portrait stood on the background easel of the other painting.

Who are all these people? said Catharine to herself. *What might they tell me if only they could speak!*

As her eyes drifted about, she saw the Bible, variously placed, in a number of other portraits. Again her eyes came to rest on Henry Rutherford. There was the Bible beside him too, not being held but lying on a table beside him.

But . . . hmm, that was odd—none of the more recent portraits had the family Bible in them.

Catharine glanced about, looking at all the dates now. All the people who were painted posing with the Bible predated Henry Rutherford. His was the last portrait in which it appeared.

She would have to remember to ask her father about it, Catharine thought, then finally continued on the way to her room.

39
Catharine and Grandma Maggie

*C*atharine left the Hall in the direction of the stables. She saddled Black Fire and was soon on her way across the fields in the direction of the cottage where dwelt Robert and Margaret McFee, as close to spiritual parents to her own parents as two individuals can be. The old couple were thus affectionately known to George and Catharine as Grandma Maggie and Grandpa Bobby.

Their cottage stood at a point approximately between the Hall and the village, in the midst of a lightly forested region, about a mile and a half from the Hall. It had once been part of the lord of the manor's estate, constructed originally, as George had recently discovered, during the time of Broughton Rutherford as a gamekeeper's lodge. It had remained within the precincts of the lord of the manor's estate until the year 1847, when financial reversals and fear of scandal resulted in its ownership being transferred to a certain Arthur Crompton, bishop in the Church of England. When the repentant bishop died in the mid–1850s without heirs, his will stipulated that the cottage should go to a local peasant woman. No one ever knew why. It had been in Maggie's family ever since.

Catharine's conversation with George in the tower of Heathersleigh Hall put Catharine in a thoughtful mood of inquiry. As she set off across the fields northeastward toward the McFee place, her thoughts were on the history of the region. She had been to the cottage many times throughout her years, as had George, for their parents visited the wise and friendly couple weekly, if not more often.

Catharine rode up and saw Maggie behind the cottage taking her laundry down from the line. She dismounted, tied Black Fire's reins to a post, then went to greet her spiritual grandmother with a loving embrace.

"Catharine, my dear!" said Maggie. "You make my heart glad just to see your smiling face."

"How are you, Grandma Maggie?" said Catharine, reaching up to remove a towel and then working her way through the linens and shirts in the opposite direction.

"We're well indeed. But I declare you've grown another inch or two since I saw you last!"

"That was only last week, Grandma Maggie, when you and Grandpa Bobby were at the Hall for Mum's birthday. I can't have grown since then!"

"You know how old folks' eyes see years passing like they were days."

"You're not *that* old, Grandma Maggie."

"True enough, there's a world of difference between being old and thinking old. I hope I never start doing the one, but nothing man or woman does can stop the other from coming at its appointed time. I'll be seventy-four in a month's time.—There, that's the last of my Bobby's shirts. Thank you, lass!"

Catharine walked toward her and placed her load of sun-ripened laundry on top of Maggie's wicker basket, then picked it up with her two strong hands and began walking toward the cottage. Maggie opened the door and led the way inside and into the large sitting room.

"Set it there, Catharine dear," said Maggie, pointing to the couch.

Catharine did so. Of one accord both women began removing the topmost items, folding and setting them aside in two or three piles.

"Where's Grandpa Bobby?" asked Catharine.

"He's out to Mr. Mudgley's," answered Maggie. "One of his rams is ailing."

They continued about the task a minute or two in silence.

"What's this?" asked Catharine, holding up a piece of white lace.

"That's a bit of Irish handwork," answered Maggie. "Bobby's mother gave it to me."

"It doesn't look like tatting."

"It's not tatting exactly, like I've been teaching you, Catharine. But similar."

"This is beautiful. Can you show me how to do this too?"

"I'd be happy to, lass, if I knew it myself."

"Mrs. McFee didn't show you the stitch—did she make this herself?"

"That she did. But she was old when she passed on to me a chestful of her linens. This was in the box with the rest, but she never taught me the secret."

"We could figure it out!" said Catharine excitedly. "It looks enough like tatting. Let's try, Grandma Maggie!"

Maggie laughed. "You think we can, eh, lass?"

"Why not!"

Maggie rose from the couch and walked across the room to an oak secretary that appeared somewhat too ornate for the tastes of the humble couple dwelling in the cottage. But it was one of two ancient family heirlooms which Maggie treasured, fabricated by her own great-grandfather. From one of its front drawers facing the room Maggie withdrew two odd-looking clumps of white thread, to which were attached what appeared to be half-completed doilies, linked by single threads to two small contraptions known as tatting shuttles, one of carved whale bone, the other of solid ivory. Whenever Catharine came for a visit, they would sit on the couch together, working side by side as Maggie taught Catharine the little-known skill, and chatted together for hours. Maggie had done her best to interest Amanda in it as well, but to little avail. Catharine, however, had taken to it immediately. She and Maggie had worked on various tatting projects together for years, and the moments shared together in this way were among the most enjoyable and special in the memories of both.

As Maggie returned, Catharine's eyes followed her movements with an expression of curiosity.

"I've watched you open that drawer and take out our tatting a hundred times," she said. "But I never noticed the cabinet before. It's funny how your eyes see and grasp more as you get older."

"It's one of the facts of life, lass," replied Maggie. "Young people's eyes *think* they see everything clearly. But it takes years to begin seeing inside of things. What made you notice the old cabinet?"

"It looks just like one in the Hall," said Catharine.

"The one that's in your father's library, you'll be meaning, no doubt."

"How did you know!"

"I've seen it there, lass."

"Why are they so alike, Grandma Maggie?" As Catharine spoke, she rose and went across the sitting room to examine the secretary more closely. "They're practically identical."

"As to the why, I can't say," said Maggie. "But it might be explained by the fact that this particular cabinet was made by my very own great-grandfather."

"How does that explain it?"

"Because just maybe he did similar work for the lord of the manor. Back in those days, all the local tradesmen and craftsmen would have had occasion to work for him at one time or another."

"I still don't see how that explains it."

"No doubt he made one for the Hall that he liked so much he made another one for himself, or the other way round."

Full of thoughts, Catharine returned to the couch. Maggie had already moved the laundry aside. Catharine sat down beside her. As was their custom, their fingers unconsciously fell into the pattern of the tatting motion, Maggie's moving with such rapidity that an observer would have seen only a blur. She picked up the shuttle with her right hand, pulled out the thread, and deftly wrapped it around her left hand. The shuttle began to fly back and forth over and under the thread in the left hand, back and forth, back and forth, stopping every eighth time to make a picot. She repeated the pattern several times, then pulled the ring of thread tight and then began the next ring. She had taught Catharine and Jocelyn the skill years before, yet beside her, Catharine's fingers moved at only about half the speed.

Maggie now paused and picked up the piece of Irish lace her mother-in-law had given her to examine its knots and loops more closely. A few experimental movements of her wrist followed, which she then examined and compared with the old lace. She went to the cabinet to fetch another ball of thread. She tied the second thread to her first and began working a chain between the original rings.

The two worked together for another thirty minutes or so, combining the efforts of Maggie's skillful fingers with Catharine's youthful eyes to see if they could unravel the mystery of the ancient Irish lace.

"When I'm working like this," said Maggie, "I often wonder what kind of linens and lace it was that the Lord God instructed the old daughter of Israel to make for the priests' robes and the altar blankets and the cover for the ark. Can you imagine a lace pattern of God's own devising!"

"I'd like to know their patterns!" said Catharine. "But does it really mention linen and lace in the Bible?"

"It does indeed, dear—twined and fine linen, it's called. And lace there is too. And it talks about cord of fine linen, which is all we're making here, tiny cords. It's all in Exodus, somewhere around the thirty-eighth and thirty-ninth—well, let's look at it, lass, and see what it says."

Maggie set down her shuttle and clump of thread, rose, and again walked to the oak cabinet and picked up the Bible that had been in her family since before she herself was born, from where it lay on top of it. She carried it back to the couch with her and sat down beside her young friend.

The white-haired woman opened the ancient Bible and began flipping through it. But she did not come close to reaching the book of Exodus. Beside her on the couch, Catharine's eyes shot open wide as she turned back the cover and the first few pages.

"Wait!" she exclaimed. "I just saw something . . . a name."

Maggie turned back to the presentation page.

"There—that's it," said Catharine, pointing down. "*Kyrkwode*, I was right. I *knew* I'd seen it somewhere!"

"What do you mean, dear," said Maggie in surprise, "that you were right?"

"George and I just ran across it earlier today, in some old records at home. I thought I recognized it."

"You know the name?"

"I've heard it," replied Catharine. "But I know nothing about it. I must have seen this page sometime when I was here. Your Bible's always out, and I've looked through it many times. That must be why I knew I'd seen it. So who is Orelia Kyrkwode?"

"You know, dear," answered Maggie, "I must have told you more times than you can remember—this was my grandmother's Bible."

"I don't remember hearing her name before."

"That is my grandmother, Orelia Kyrkwode. She was a midwife—an honorable profession, despite what some people said back in those days. This Bible was given to her when she was confirmed. That was in 1797, as it says here. That was her name, of course, before she married. Then she became Orelia Moylan. The Bible passed to my mother, Grace Moylan, who became Grace Crawford, and then to me."

"That's . . . you, written there?" said Catharine, pointing farther down the page.

"That's my maiden name," answered Maggie, "—before I met Bobby.—There's my name written by my mother's hand—Margaret Crawford, 1837. Of course now everyone just knows me as Maggie. You see all the names here that have been added as the Bible's been passed down."

"And the Bible was given first to Orelia—"

"By her parents Mary and Webley Kyrkwode on her confirmation."

"Webley Kyrkwode," repeated Catharine.

"He's the same man I was telling you about before, my great-grand-father that made the two secretaries—the one I still have, and the one that's in the library at the Hall."

Webley Kyrkwode . . . *W. Kyrkwode*—the name in the ledger! What could it all mean?

The rest of the afternoon was taken up with halfhearted experimental attempts to copy old Mrs. McFee's tatting pattern. But Catharine's thoughts were far more taken up with the inscriptions in Orelia Kyrkwode's old Bible. She therefore continued to ply Maggie with questions about the history of her family's past and the cottage.

That evening she asked her father about the Bible she had noticed in the portraits.

"You know, that is a mystery, Catharine, my dear," replied Charles. "I don't think I've ever seen that Bible in my life. But now that you bring it up, it seems I recall my cousin Gifford expressing an interest in the same thing some years back."

"Didn't he say that his grandfather misplaced it?" asked Jocelyn.

"That's right, I remember now," added Charles. "I do begin to recall a vague rumor along such lines myself. It was also said by some that the London Rutherfords had stolen it."

"That could hardly be, Father," said George, "if Gifford knows nothing about it."

"I suppose you're right. But none of the conjectures get us any closer to knowing how so prominent an object could have disappeared without a trace."

40

Curious Gathering

As Charles greeted the other eight or ten individuals present at the Cambridge home of Hartwell Barclay, the man to whom he had been introduced at Green Park, the unmistakable impression came over him that this was *not* a government-sponsored gathering.

They were friendly enough. The food and drink and hospitality were lavish. He could not have asked for a warmer, more congenial environment. But Charles had been part of politics long enough to recognize parliamentarians and diplomatic types. And there weren't any here.

Charles' dealings with the secret service—Barclay's supposed background—had been minimal. He realized the intelligence community made use of individuals who weren't exactly your run-of-the-mill Whitehall crowd. That sometimes included foreigners. He supposed this *could* be some kind of preliminary recruiting attempt by an obscure branch of the foreign office, although that still wouldn't explain what they would want with him. There seemed to be three others here, too, who likewise didn't know the purpose of the meeting, and who had been invited, like him, under a certain cloud of mystery. Whatever was going on, it was an odd mix of unlikely individuals.

Many introductions were made all around as wine and hors d'oeuvres flowed freely.

"You remember Lord Burton's widow," said Redmond, greeting the tall, stately woman.

"Yes, of course," replied Charles. "I am sorry about your husband, Lady Halifax."

"Thank you, Sir Charles," replied the lady in measured tone. "Fortunately the shock of his passing is now over."

The woman held Charles' eye an instant or two longer than normal small talk would account for, though nothing in her placid countenance divulged so much as a hint of additional expression. Charles moved off with Redmond and was soon shaking hands with another of the newcomers, unaware that her eyes followed him for several moments more.

After having been served a sumptuous tea, and now with fresh cups of tea and coffee in their hands, all the participants took seats in the comfortable lounge.

"You several whom we have invited here this evening," Charles' naval associate Redmond began, speaking primarily toward Charles, but glancing at each of their other guests in turn, "have been chosen for very specific reasons. You are all men of impeccable reputation, experts in your various fields of endeavor, intelligent and skilled. You represent, as it were, our nation's finest, everything, indeed, that has made us great through the years. It is our sincere hope that you will want to dedicate the high level of your personal talents and resources to the future, to help us insure that the future is as bright, brighter, in fact, than has been the past."

As Redmond paused, a few *Here, heres!* and raisings of cups and glasses on the part of his colleagues affirmed their concurrence with his opening remarks.

"We are concerned for England, of course," he went on, "but even more for the entire future of Europe. . . ."

As Charles listened, he almost found himself wondering if someone had drugged his tea. The whole atmosphere was sleepily mesmerizing, yet try as he might he could not isolate a single point of specificity or substance in anything Redmond said. After ten or fifteen minutes he concluded, turning toward their host, who now began in much the same manner. Gradually, however, he became sufficiently specific as to finally attach a name to their organization, if organization it could be called.

"We represent an association," he said, "not known widely at present, but with adherents in all the nations of Europe. Our affiliates are devoted to a new order which we believe will emerge one day very soon out of, and even in the midst of many countries, nationalities, and races. It is called the Fountain of Light."

He paused to allow his words to sink in.

"Light and truth are our goals during these perilous times when most seek only their own ends," he went on. "As Morley has said, you whom we have invited are each influential in your own way and in your own circles. We believe you all will be very effective in helping us bring light and truth as the masses prepare for this new order which is to come."

"Are you talking about a new governmental order?" asked one of the guests. "What is it exactly—a United Europe, is that what you mean . . . something like the United States?"

"I think I can truthfully say that you are thinking along lines that are generally correct," replied Barclay. "Yet it will also transcend governmental systems altogether. It will not primarily be political in nature."

"What then? All governments are political."

"But the new order will be *new*," said Barclay softly but with intensity. "All will be clear as you know more."

As Barclay spoke, he gazed straight into the eyes of his questioner. Though his words conveyed nothing, his expression somehow seemed to alleviate any thought of further inquiry. The man slowly nodded his head in apparent understanding, though almost as a reflex action.

"I . . . I see," he mumbled, then sat back with a nearly glazed expression and said no more.

One by one the other newcomers raised various questions, each with the same eventual result. Barclay's voice was mesmerizing. A spell of acceptance was woven about his listeners by his very words, such that in the end everything made perfect sense. He spoke a while longer, then turned to Charles.

"You haven't spoken yet, Sir Charles," he said.

"I am listening," Charles replied.

"Do you have any questions you would like to raise?"

"I did find myself curious a few moments ago," said Charles, "whether you have any written literature, anything I might study that would shed more light on your organization."

"We prefer to discuss our precepts by word of mouth."

"But is anything written?"

"There are our *Annals*."

"Might I see a copy? I think it would help a great deal toward an understanding of your beliefs, motives, and goals."

Barclay glanced around. A few heads shook on the part of his colleagues.

"I'm afraid copies are scarce," he said, turning again toward Charles. "We do not seem to have one readily available."

Charles nodded. He had almost expected it.

As the exchange had proceeded, he was aware that Barclay was attempting to catch his eyes and hold them. Having seen the result on the part of the other guests, however, Charles prevented it by continuing to address his remarks about the entire room. He was now aware of a silent frustration beginning to set in on Barclay's part.

"Light and truth can be vague terms," said Charles. "Everyone believes in truth. I am all for light. But I cannot get involved in something without knowing specifics. Frankly, Mr. Barclay, I've heard nothing here—nothing of substance at all. Can you just tell me plainly, what does 'Fountain of Light' really mean?"

"Simply this, Sir Charles," replied Barclay, with great effort keeping his voice calm, "that one day very soon, a new order will spring up, will appear as a fountain bursting forth. Its characteristic feature will be light—pure light . . . light itself, and truth."

"But all that means nothing. It's more nebulous than air. Where did the name originate?"

"All these questions will be answered in time, Mr. Rutherford," answered Barclay in the smoothest tone possible. Again, with great determination he sought to lock on to Charles' eyes, but still was not successful. "I am sure you can understand that all revelations must come in their proper order, that precept must be built upon precept, as it were. If you choose to help your nation and join us as we spread light into the lives of our fellowman, I can assure you that you will be satisfied at all the points you have raised."

"I'm sorry to be importune about it, Mr. Barclay," said Charles, now at last summoning the strength to return the man's stare. Now *he* locked on to Hartwell Barclay's eyes and held them, "but it still sounds vague and nebulous. If you will forgive me, I have heard nothing here of substantive foundation. Therefore, I must tell you very clearly, my allegiance is not something that can be divided. I am looking for no cause, nor can I commit to any nebulous new order with man at its center. I am not merely a Christian, I hope I am a disciple as well—a follower. I have but one Master, and that is Jesus Christ. You talk about truth ... what you call a fountain of light. I believe in truth. I have committed my life to the one who *is* Truth. But at this point, I simply do not know what you mean by the term. I will have to have very direct answers to these questions," said Charles, "or I am afraid I will not be able to participate further."

"Our goal is truth. Our enemy is darkness," replied Barclay. "I can say most emphatically that you will have not the slightest difficulty incorporating your religious views in with everything our cause stands for. As to our name, I will say this much now—it was given as a revelation, as a glimpse into the future, as a picture of the new order which we have been shown and which we now desire to expand as we are given opportunity. For in the days to come, the light of this revelation shall indeed become as a fountain, from the heavenly realms as only light is capable of...."

As he listened, at last Charles found his resolve weakening. He glanced away. He could no longer hold Barclay's eyes. Gradually he felt himself being lulled into complacent acceptance, just as the others had been.

With great effort he rose, excused himself briefly, and sought the lavatory. He needed to dash some cold water on his face.

41

A Caller

◆ ◆ ◆

*H*ubert Powell drove up the driveway to Heathersleigh Hall feeling especially pleased with himself for having stumbled upon the information that the lord of the manor of this second-rate estate had left Devonshire for London the day before. How long he was going to be gone he didn't know, but he intended to take no chances and to strike quickly. This time he would bypass the old fool altogether and not allow himself to be humiliated with all that religious idiocy.

He rang the bell at the front door and waited. Half a minute later it was opened by Sarah Minsterly. She knew him instantly, though betrayed nothing on her face.

"Good morning," said Hubert, presenting his card, "I am calling to speak with Sir Charles."

"I am sorry, Mr. . . . er, Powell. Sir Charles is away from Heathersleigh at the moment."

"Oh, I see . . . hmm, that is a shame. I have driven some distance."

He paused as if thinking to himself.

"May I please, then, perhaps speak for a minute with Miss Catharine?"

Sarah hesitated briefly, then nodded and reentered the house. She went straight to Catharine's room, knocked, handed her the card, and related the brief encounter that had just taken place at the front door. Catharine thanked the housekeeper, thought to herself briefly, then left her room and descended to the ground floor. She found Hubert waiting patiently outside where Sarah had left him, looking every inch the gentleman and country squire.

"Hello, Mr. Powell," said Catharine without expression. "What may I do for you?"

"It is wonderful to see you again, Catharine," replied Hubert, smiling graciously. "I came to call on your father, just as you suggested."

He paused to allow a crestfallen expression to fill his face.

"I seem," he went on, "to have the misfortune to have timed my visit badly. So I thought, since I was here, you might enjoy a short ride in the country with me. As you can see I have my Opel, and it *is* a spectacular day for a drive."

"I am afraid I shall have to decline," said Catharine.

"Surely there can be no harm in a short ride in the middle of the day."

"I thought I had made it clear earlier," said Catharine, "that any further relationship between us must initially include my parents."

"Yes, but your father isn't here."

"Then you may call again, Mr. Powell.—Oh, wait . . . I have an idea!" she added excitedly. "I'll go get my mother. I'm sure she would love to go. The three of us can have a lovely ride together."

Catharine spun around and disappeared inside.

She walked up the stairs, not exactly hurrying, then paused and crept to the edge of the window and glanced outside. Already the Opel roadster was disappearing from sight down the driveway far more rapidly than was advisable.

Nearly as much smoke was coming from the ears of its driver as from the automobile's exhaust.

42

A More Welcome Visitor

When the front doorbell of Heathersleigh Hall rang a second time less than ten minutes after the first, good Sarah Minsterly strode toward it with lips pursed in resolve to send the young Powell fellow back where he came from without benefit of any extra kindness out of her mouth. She threw open the door and was on the verge of unleashing a most unpleasant verbal barrage, when her motion was arrested in its tracks by an unexpected visitor standing calmly before her. For a second or two she stood staring still as a statue.

"Mr. Diggorsfeld!" she exclaimed after a moment.

"Yes, Miss Minsterly," he laughed, "it is me, I assure you, not a ghost."

"My apologies, sir. It's just that I was expecting someone else—"

Unconsciously Timothy glanced behind him, beginning to put two and two together.

"—but come in, come in, please, sir," gushed Sarah, her hospitable nature returning as quickly as it had departed a few seconds earlier at the sound of the bell. "Come with me, Mr. Diggorsfeld. Lady Jocelyn is in the little garden outside the kitchen."

Timothy followed along the corridor to the left toward the west wing, then left again until they came to the kitchen, whose double glass doors stood open to the sunshine streaming down from the southwest. Sarah led the way through the room and outside, where Jocelyn sat with two other of the household staff, stringing and snapping green beans for canning. She looked up as they approached.

"Timothy!" she exclaimed in delight, leaping to her feet. Beans flew out of her apron in all directions onto the ground as she ran forward and warmly clasped his hands. "This is such a surprise—what on earth are you doing here!"

The man before her was not such as the world would consider imposing. He was of average height—perhaps even an inch or two less than average—and medium build. His hair, light and plentiful when first Charles Rutherford had walked into New Hope Chapel years before, was now thinning noticeably and gradually intermingling with white. Though he was younger than Charles, a stranger might have taken him for several years older. Yet his eyes sparkled with the vitality of life, love, and wisdom, which had made him for years a favorite with everyone at Heathersleigh.

"It is nearly as unexpected on my part," said the pastor. "I was summoned to perform a funeral in Exeter—"

"Oh, I am sorry," said Jocelyn. Her face grew serious.

"Think nothing of it," replied Timothy, shaking his head to alleviate her concern. "To tell you the truth, I hardly knew the woman—I believe we'd met once years ago. But she was a friend of my mother's and apparently had requested me. In any event, it was all very hastily arranged. I simply had no opportunity to let you know ahead of time I was coming."

"No matter—I am delighted you are here."

"I certainly couldn't be so close without seeing you.—By the way, who was the chap in the auto who almost ran me and my horse and buggy off your drive in a heap?"

Jocelyn returned his question with a blank stare.

"I'm afraid that would be my fault," said a voice behind them. They turned as Catharine, who had seen Timothy arrive from upstairs, now walked through the kitchen doors.

"Catharine, my dear!"

"Hello, Mr. Diggorsfeld," replied Catharine, who then proceeded to tell her mother of the visit from Hubert Powell and the state in which he had left. "I'm sorry, Mr. Diggorsfeld—I didn't mean for him to drive off so recklessly."

"No harm done."

"I am sorry too, Timothy," now said Jocelyn, "but Charles is away. He's up in Cambridge."

"Well then, I shall enjoy my visit with the rest of you all the more."

"Shall we go inside and have some lemonade . . . or would you like some tea?"

"Lemonade sounds wonderful," replied Timothy. "But to be perfectly honest, I'd rather stay out here. It's a lovely day, and I haven't snapped beans since I was a boy. You don't mind if I join you?"

"Mind . . . heavens no," laughed Jocelyn. "But do you really want to snap beans?"

"Of course. It will be fun." He glanced around for a chair, then hurried back into the kitchen to fetch one. In two or three minutes he and Catharine had joined the circle and were snapping and destringing like experts.

"You know, Sarah," said Jocelyn, "we'll have these finished in no time. Why don't you and Kate and Enid go inside and start boiling the water and getting the jars ready? Actually, come to think of it, two of you could go down to the garden and finish picking that last row."

Just then George came through the kitchen.

"I heard we had a visitor," he said. "Hello, Mr. Diggorsfeld!"

"George, my lad!" exclaimed Timothy, rising and shaking his hand. "You're looking fit and well."

"Thank you—so are you."

"How does it feel to have university life behind you?" said the minister, sitting down and resuming his task. "And by the way, congratulations on your degree—I haven't seen you since."

"Thank you very much. To answer your question, it feels good—

it's a relief actually. Not that there aren't aspects of it I miss, naturally. But it was hard work, and it's good to be home and working with Father again."

"Join us, George," said Jocelyn, pointing to the chair Kate had vacated.

"What—cutting up beans?"

"Come, George," added Timothy, "a little good honest women's labor never hurt any man that I knew of. Especially a bachelor like me. It's a matter of necessity. Although I am extremely thankful for my housekeeper."

George laughed but sat down. Within five minutes the beans were flying as rapidly from his hands into the tub in the center as from the others.

"Hubert Powell was just here," Catharine said to her brother.

"Where was I?"

"Out in the stables. He wasn't here long enough for you to know." Again Catharine recounted the incident.

"It sounds like you handled him fine without any assistance from me," said George.

"I really have to hand it to you," said Timothy, "for recognizing the need to let your father be your protector in such matters. More and more these days young people think such a thing is too old-fashioned. But believe me, I've conducted too many ill-advised marriages not to be concerned at how quickly and thoughtlessly marriage is rushed into."

"Why do you marry people, then?"

"I am an agent of the church. There are certain rules that young people must follow to receive the sanction of the church. If they do, I am bound to marry them. But often they are utterly unprepared."

43
Marriage and God's Will

*W*hy didn't you ever marry, Mr. Diggorsfeld?" asked Catharine after a moment.

Jocelyn glanced over quickly at Timothy, taken aback by the directness of her daughter's question. But the smile of humor on the minister's face showed plainly enough that he had taken no offense.

"I am not, as the saying goes, 'a confirmed bachelor,' if that is what you mean," he replied. "It is just that the right opportunity never came my way."

"You mean you would marry if it did?"

"Of course."

Catharine appeared almost shocked.

"We ministers in England are not celibate like Catholic priests," he said, smiling again. "No, I would happily marry if such was what God wanted for me."

"But you're—" she began.

Diggorsfeld laughed. "I'm *old* ... is that what you were going to say?"

Catharine's face turned red.

"I'm only forty-three, my dear. Do you think human feeling stops with the appearance of a few grey hairs?" he added, still chuckling.

Catharine sheepishly shook her head.

"As I said," the minister continued, "I would marry if it were God's will. But equally will I remain happily single all my life if that is what God wants for me. Whether married or single is immaterial, so long as I am in God's will."

"But how do you know God's will?"

"Ah, my dear Catharine—that is the question of the ages. I am more delighted than I can say that you are beginning to ask it at such an early age in your own pilgrimage. But its answer is one you will seek the rest of your days."

"You make it sound hopeless, as if the question is unanswerable."

"Oh, by no means! It *is* answerable, and it is full of hope and wonder. But that does not alter the fact that you will continue asking it, in ever more profound ways the deeper your faith grows."

"Are you saying we *can* know God's will?"

"I believe so," answered Diggorsfeld. "But it is a *process*, not an event. God's will is not comprised of a series of precise revelations that come singly and specifically, but is a style of life in which one walks with the heavenly Father."

"I don't think I follow you."

"Perhaps one day you and I shall sit down and have a long talk about it. Or maybe we shall go for a long ride together and discuss it."

"When you do, I'm coming along!" said George. "I want in on that discussion too."

"Wonderful!" rejoined Diggorsfeld. "We shall do it indeed. In the meantime, Catharine, I shall send you a little book called *Life at the Center*, which should help you think in a generally correct direction on the matter. Once you have read it, you will doubtless have even more questions. Then we shall go for that long ride!"

"How did you know it was God's will for you not to marry?" now asked George.

"My, but aren't you two curious about marriage!" laughed Timothy.

"Young people cannot help but think about it," replied George. "Catharine and I want to do the right thing."

"I commend you both for that," rejoined Diggorsfeld. "Let me answer your question about myself by saying that I did not *decide* to be single. There was no moment of revelation indicating bachelorhood to be some momentous thing called *God's will* for me. Such is simply the way my life went. Therefore, I say that up to this point that *is* God's will. My way has been committed to him, and that is what he has done with what I gave him. What his will might be for my future, I cannot say. But back to your question—when I was in my mid-twenties and fresh out of theological college and recently ordained, serving in my first parish as an assistant, there was a young lady in the congregation who had eyes for me."

"*Ah!*" said Catharine, drawing out the word with heightened interest. The beans immediately stopped falling from her fingers. "But you weren't interested in her?" she added.

"She was very attractive," answered Timothy. "I suppose in a manner of speaking I could not help being drawn to her. She lavished attention upon me, and did everything in her power to win my affections. No man is immune to the charms of such a young woman. I must admit there were times my soul was in danger. Yet I recognized that her heart and affections were not dedicated to the service of the Lord as were mine. She was forward and coquettish, in love with her own wiles, not the kind of woman who could ever have been a minister's wife. Her father was rich. I could have made myself what the world calls a very nice marriage indeed. I would probably now be preaching in one of London's large and fashionable pulpits. But I knew we would both be miserable in the long run for marrying for the wrong reasons. I would rather remain single all my life than to marry for the wrong reason."

"Have you ever regretted your decision?" asked George.

"Heavens—not for a second! I am happy as I am because I know I am in God's will. And if God sent a woman of like mind to the door of my study for me to marry tomorrow, I would be equally happy."

"I don't see how you can say that," said Catharine. "How can you be *equally* happy either way?"

"Because I content myself where God has put me—wherever that may be. In other words, to marry or not to marry, to paraphrase Shakespeare, is *not* the question—but to do God's will, and to be content in the way in which he brings that will about in your life. You see, working out the details of life according to such-and-such a pattern is not always something we can control. Things don't always happen by our choice.

"But contentment *is* a choice. Contentment is *always* a road any man or woman can walk at *any* time in *any* circumstance. And I happen to believe that contentment is one of the secret ingredients in that mystical and elusive thing we call God's will. Circumstances and events lie outside our control. Contentment does not. *We* control contentment but not circumstance. It's all in the book I will send you when I get back to London."

Throughout the conversation, Jocelyn had remained strangely quiet. Timothy now turned to her with a look of question on his face. "Is something troubling you, Jocelyn?"

Jocelyn glanced up and cast him a melancholy smile.

"I hadn't realized it, but perhaps there is," she said.

"Care to share it?"

"I don't know if it's worth talking about," she answered. "Somehow the talk of marriage and your sharing about your past . . . it all sent my thoughts back into my own—not a very good place for me to go sometimes. I couldn't help starting to think about my mother and what a heartache my appearance was to her."

Jocelyn paused reminiscently.

"Actually, I was thinking more about my younger sister," she went on. "I received a letter from her today—a belated birthday greeting, really. I don't know, it was so impersonal and cool—I suppose it brought back a lot of memories."

"You and your sister are not close, I take it?"

Jocelyn shook her head.

"We never have been. She is five years younger than I. She was still a girl when I left home for my nursing studies."

"But there is more to it than mere age?"

Again Jocelyn nodded. "My mother was so relieved when Edlyn was born," she said sadly. "Even at five, I could feel the joy that suddenly filled the home, a joy she had never felt or expressed in any way about me. The next five years were the most awful years of my life. My mother poured her whole life into my darling little baby sister. Sometimes I hardly saw her for days. Nurses and tutors—it was the only life I knew. I resented it for many years, as you know. It is still painful to recall, though I hope I have forgiven her. But as we grew, how could it be helped that my sister picked up some of my mother's disdain for me? As she got older, she would look at me with peculiar expressions. I still remember one such look when I was eleven and she was but six. At times I wondered if she even knew that I was part of the family. She had been kept so carefully shielded from me. Even now I occasionally detect hints of that same uncertainty from her, on the edge of a remark, in her tone, by a glance, in the rare instances when we see one another, or even in the occasional letter that comes."

"It's more Uncle Hugh than Aunt Edlyn, Mum," now commented George. "He doesn't go very far to hide it. The last time we stopped by to visit them, it made me angry."

"My sister's second husband," Jocelyn explained to Timothy. "—But I didn't know you were aware of it, George," said his mother.

"How could I not be? He treats Father the same way, with that little edge of superiority. I'm sorry to say it, but I don't like him."

"He sounds like an interesting man," said Timothy.

"He always has had something of a peculiar attitude about us," said Jocelyn. "I noticed it even at their wedding. I've wondered if Hugh secretly resents Charles for some reason. I can't imagine why. But there is a subtle undercurrent whenever we see each other, which isn't often. It puts an added strain on my relationship with Edlyn, which is none too warm in the first place."

"What does your brother-in-law do?" asked Timothy.

"He is a solicitor with some connection to shipping. I don't really know. He has money, that I do know, and my sister enjoys it. They're religious in their own way. I think perhaps that's one reason for the resentment, that Charles made what they consider a display of his faith by being so outspoken about it, when they had been good church people for years without making, what they would say, a big fuss about it."

"I know the type," rejoined Timothy. "Every church in the country is full of them. They consider religion respectable the more it is reserved for Sundays only, and its principles never thought about throughout the week. Men like Charles, who try to live their faith *every* day, they find worthy, not of their respect, but of their very quiet, dignified, and respectable resentment."

44

Evening at the Theater

The setting was not at all what Amanda had anticipated.

When Ramsay said the "theater," she had assumed they would be attending the opera. Puccini's *La Bohème* was all the rage right now and was playing at the Royal Opera House. Everybody was talking about it.

But the driver kept going right past Covent Garden toward the Strand. When he stopped in front of the Vaudeville Theatre, Amanda didn't know what to think. She had never even been to this part of the theater district, much less attended a performance here. And this particular theater was not one with the best of reputations!

The somewhat questionable reputation of the theater in general had, of course, improved noticeably since the middle of Queen Victoria's time. The Strand was now a respectable part of London. Yet Amanda could not help a momentary flutter in her stomach as Ramsay offered his hand and helped her down to the sidewalk. She strongly doubted she would see any of Cousin Martha's society friends here. The bawdy posters on the billboards did little to alleviate her anxiety.

She probably should have asked what Ramsay had planned for the evening at the time of his invitation.

On second thought . . . *why* should she have?

She was a progressive young lady. What was she worried about? They had enjoyed a lovely dinner at Rules Restaurant. There was nothing to be frightened of. She could partake of anything the world had to offer. Wasn't that why she had come to London in the first place, to escape the confining constrictions her parents had always placed upon her?

Amanda took Ramsay's arm, trying to squelch her flutter of nervousness, and they walked inside. Ramsay nodded to a few of the others in attendance as they walked through the lobby. Since only about ten minutes remained until curtain time, they went straight to their seats.

She relaxed as soon as the pit orchestra began to play. The music was lively and generated a festive and happy mood. In two or three minutes the curtain opened to a dimly lit pub scene.

The instant the drama began, Amanda found herself swept into the world being acted out on stage before her. Everything was so colorful, so loud, so boisterous, so much larger than reality.

Annie McPool, the lead character, burst loudly onstage singing a bawdy tavern ballad. She flirted sensually as much with the audience as with the bit characters clustered about her as props, half of them pretending to be drunk, the other half eyeing her with winks and grins and catcalls as she pranced and danced in and out among them. Annie's heavy makeup and painted eyes, low-cut dress, and seductive mannerisms conveyed clearly enough the nature of the establishment where she was employed.

Amanda's eyes widened in a mixture of horror and fascination. She was shocked, yet at the same time could not but be mesmerized by the risqué melodrama.

It did not take long for the men of the audience to follow the lead of the actors in the make-believe tavern. Actors and patrons alike were seduced by Annie's charms. Calls and whistles began to erupt all around, as was intended, accompanied by laughter from most of the women in attendance.

Amanda's fascination mounted. Along with it, however, came the inescapable sense that what she was being drawn into was anything but wholesome. She tried to tell herself nothing was wrong, that this was a respected theater, that she was among respectable people, and that Ramsay would never bring her anyplace she shouldn't be.

The song ended. Applause and whistles echoed. The men onstage returned to their tall foamy pints and conversation, while Annie sauntered to the front of the stage and, taking the audience into her confidence, complained:—

"You see what I have to put up with . . . a voice like mine in a pub full of blokes like this—"

A few calls and jeers from the men on stools behind her.

"You see," she added with significant expression, still addressing the audience, and a wave of her hand back toward her drinking customers, "they know it too—Annie McPool deserves better than the likes of them! I was born for the opera. But I waste away my days in a run-down dump like the Boar's Head."

She turned and returned to the bar to pour more drinks for her thirsty patrons.

From stage left a man approached. He had been onstage since the rise of the curtain, but obscure and unnoticed. Now the pace slowed and the mood changed as the well-dressed and obviously sophisticated man, out of place in such an environment, introduced himself to Annie, lavishing upon her praise for her multitude of talents.

"I could not help overhearing your comment a moment ago," said he, one Daniel Prentice by name, "that the longing of your heart is to sing in the opera. It may be that I can make that dream come true."

It did not take long for Annie to fall in love with the dashing Prentice.

From the opening curtain, the drama became much more than a mere story. It was real, but in a way yet *more* real than anything Amanda had ever experienced in her *own* life. Visually and emotionally, she found herself drawn into the life and hopes of Annie McPool.

The second act opened in Paris, where indeed Annie McPool's dream had come true. If she did not exactly occupy a leading role in Puccini's latest at the Théâtre du Châtelet, it could truthfully be said that she had been engaged as a professional opera singer. She was an understudy, it is true, and for one of the lesser-known touring companies. But there was hope of better roles, and the company was scheduled to travel throughout the Continent. With confident optimism, Annie sang happily of her future, and of her love for Daniel Prentice, who had rescued her from pub-singing oblivion and made her the future star of the European stage. But the subtle minor strains from the orchestra pit as Prentice made his next appearance signified to the audience what Annie herself could not yet know, that all did not bode so well as her present happiness indicated.

The curtain fell for intermission.

Ramsay and Amanda rose and began making their way out toward the lobby.

"Well, what do you think?" said Ramsay enthusiastically. "They're good, aren't they?"

"Uh . . . yes!" replied Amanda. "Yes . . . really great."

"She's from Austria, the actress—Sadie Greenfield . . . quite famous all over the Continent."

Throughout the intermission Amanda kept close to Ramsay while he visited and chatted with one person, then another. Everywhere they went he seemed to know everybody, though he introduced her to no one. Once or twice the conversations were hushed and guarded, though such occasions were brief. After ten or fifteen minutes they began moving back to their seats.

The curtain for the third act rose to reveal Annie McPool in a salon full of cheap furnishings. Her clothes were poor, her expression grim. It was obvious her circumstances had drastically changed. She was reading aloud a letter from a friend who was the only one who knew where she was. It told of the heartbreak of the woman's mother, ending with the suggestion that Annie return home.

Annie set the letter aside and rose. A tuneful lament followed, in which the audience learned that her former savior had taken all her money to feed his gambling habit. Annie had lost her job and was now alone and penniless and far from home. She sang that the only prospect left for her was to return to the only thing she knew, to paint her face and use her charms singing to drunks and bores and men who wanted from her what no woman should be willing to give.

As the song faded away, her lover was heard ascending the stairs to the pitiful flat. Prentice entered drunk. He had lost everything. His one-time smooth demeanor had turned coarse and rude. Annie pleaded with him to take her back where he found her. He was rough and cursed at her. Annie responded in kind. Bitter arguing ... a loud slap across his face. The women in the audience cheered. The fight continued, now with heckling and shouts from everywhere in the theater.

Amanda glanced to her side. Ramsay was laughing with delight at the comedic tragedy. Amanda looked back toward the stage. Why was everyone laughing? Didn't they ache for her? She wanted to *cry* for poor Annie McPool's desperate plight.

The fourth and final act opened to a bitterly cold winter in Paris. Food and warmth were scarce. Prentice had descended lower and lower, and finally had left Annie altogether. Annie came down with tuberculosis, never to return home or see her mother again. After a final doleful realization of what a fool she was to fall in love with such a cad about whom she knew nothing, Annie begged the audience, if they remembered nothing else, not to forget the voice that could have made her an opera star if only she had been discovered earlier.

Annie slumped to her ragged settee as the final notes of the song diminished to a scarcely audible level, slowly leaned her head back, then closed her eyes ... and died as the curtain fell.

A great ovation followed. Ramsay was on his feet in an instant, clapping vigorously along with everyone around them. Amanda rose at his side, but it was with difficulty that she prevented herself from bursting into tears. It had touched her too deeply to make light of. The performance pulled emotions from her depths she had not anticipated. What at first had shocked her, in the end overwhelmed her.

Rather than moving toward the lobby, Amanda now followed Ramsay forward along the crowded aisle, through the stage door and backstage. Still numb, Amanda gaped about in awe to see many of the actors and actresses suddenly so close. The actor who had played Prentice walked past. Amanda's eyes widened and she gazed at him with something like fascinated horror. With difficulty she pulled her look away and stumbled on after Ramsay.

They arrived at the dressing room of the leading actress. Ramsay knocked lightly twice, then opened the door and walked in.

"Ramsay!" Amanda heard a familiar voice exclaim from inside. She followed him in. There stood Annie McPool, alive and well and bigger than life. If it were possible, Amanda's eyes increased to yet greater diameter to see the woman so close ... her face, her eyes, the strong perfume, the dress which, even in the final scene from which she had just come, revealed a bit more of her chest than Amanda's cultured eyes were accustomed to.

"Sadie, you were wonderful!" said Ramsay, embracing the actress warmly. "As always, I must say."

"Thank you—you are a dear," she replied, kissing Ramsay lightly.

The two were obviously on familiar terms. Amanda could hardly believe her eyes. Here was a liberated woman indeed!

"I've brought you a little something from Paris," Greenfield said. "Our troupe just finished up there two weeks ago." She turned to her dressing table, picked up a plain brown packet, then turned around again and handed it to Ramsay.

Ramsay took the envelope without comment. "How long will you be performing in London?" he asked.

"Three weeks," she replied.

"And then?"

"On to Berlin, and after that Vienna."

"Well, then, perhaps I shall see you before you return to the Continent," said Ramsay. As he said the words, he caught the actress's eyes for the merest second. He then turned to Amanda with a nod, and led the way from the dressing room and out the side entrance of the theater onto the Strand.

The cool night air jolted Amanda awake. She breathed in deeply, still overwhelmed at the range of emotions through which the past several hours had taken her.

"I'll take you straight home," said Ramsay as they climbed into the cab. "I have a little business I must attend to before the night is over."

Amanda's emotions were too full to mind. When she arrived back at the Pankhursts' she could not keep the feeling away that she was still living in the fantasy world she had just left.

45
Planting Seeds

◆◆◆

*N*ight fell over the northeast coast of Yorkshire. An occasional flash from the rotating combination of reflective glasses sent a blinding ray from the top of the lighthouse out into the North Sea. No ships were in peril at the moment, for the night was clear and the sea calm. But the lighthouse on Hawsker Head must be ready with its signals when the need came. These were days of darkness when the Fountain must be prepared with its proclamations of Light.

Below, in the lounge of the house with the red roof on the plateau near the edge of a steep and jagged shoreline, an earnest discussion was in progress. Secret service liaison Hartwell Barclay was speaking.

"What do you hear from *Die Schwarze Hand*?" he had just asked a newcomer who had arrived from the Continent the day before.

"Only that their numbers grow daily. They have gained much support in Russia."

"And Austria?"

"Aehrenthal knows nothing of the ring's activities."

"What of the Serbian government?"

"Pashich suspects something but thus far has successfully been kept in the dark. His minister in Vienna, however, is in the society."

Barclay thought a few moments.

"It may become more and more difficult to play both sides. Meanwhile, we must keep our contacts strong both with *Die Schwarze Hand* and in Vienna."

"Don't forget Moscow," added a woman's voice.

Barclay turned. "Of course, Hildegard," he said, "we shall certainly not forget Moscow. We are relying on your contacts to make sure nothing is overlooked. Do you think the Bolsheviks will make their move before the Serbs?"

"Not unless Russia collapses suddenly from within," she replied. "I believe they will await the outcome of war, and strike when the tsar is most vulnerable."

"Then our forecasts must continue on the basis of Russia's existing framework. Thus," he added, now turning and glancing around at each of the others present, "we must have friends everywhere—as has been our goal from the beginning. It is impossible to predict which embassies, which parties, which coalitions, even which nations will be left standing. Nor can we predict where the holocaust will erupt. The order of Light will grow out of the collective ashes of them all. The Fountain's seeds must be planted everywhere, that out of the rubble, growth toward the Light will emerge simultaneously from England to the Urals. Then we will step forward to seize control."

Again it fell silent.

"And speaking of the seeds being planted in England," said Barclay, "I want this fellow Rutherford."

As he spoke he turned toward his colleague, Dr. Morley Redmond, with an obvious expression of annoyance.

"I said from the beginning that Charles was nobody's fool," replied the professor. "He always was a free thinker."

"All the more reason why we need him in our camp," remarked Lady Halifax.

A few nods went around the room. The Welshman took a long swallow from his glass of stout. The very fact that Charles Rutherford was proving to be his own man caused them to desire his allegiance all the more.

"I sense him wavering," said Barclay. "His expression and the questions he raised at Cambridge have concerned me. I felt an antagonism toward our cause. He was extremely persistent in resisting my gaze."

"He does not yet even know the cause. That is not fully divulged until initiation is complete."

Barclay nodded. "The Fountain's precepts appeal to those alienated from the status quo, individuals disconnected from countries and governments and their present courses, people looking for something, but they know not what. Such individuals are eager to give themselves to a cause, even if they are not aware of its subtleties. None of this I sense, however, in the man Rutherford. His loyalties will require more shrewdness to cultivate."

"Why are you so intent on recruiting him?"

"Because now that he is aware of the Fountain, he could be

dangerous if not one of us. He must be brought all the way in, or else destroyed. I see no middle ground in his case."

"What do you propose?"

"Have you considered an approach through the estranged daughter?"

"An intriguing possibility—anyone else in the family, relatives, skeletons in the closet . . . anything or anyone we might find useful in that regard?"

"He has a cousin, high-up banker in London."

"Finances are always useful."

"That might be too high profile for our purposes. Anyone else? The pressure on him must be subtle."

"I recently learned something interesting about the wife's younger sister," now said Redmond. "Actually, not the sister herself, but her husband."

"Anything we can use?" asked Barclay.

"Possibly. It's just that he and Rutherford aren't exactly on the closest of terms. The fellow is a solicitor, reasonably well thought of, and climbing rapidly."

"Practicing where?"

"Birmingham, if my information is correct."

"What are the man's politics, religion?"

"A good churchman, but makes no fuss of his convictions."

"And the wife . . . the sister?"

"Goes along with her husband on most things—they're progressive types."

"Close to Lady Rutherford?"

The man shook his head.

"Find out if either of them has any hidden grievance against Rutherford that we might exploit. What's the man's name?"

"Browne . . . well, *Wildecott*-Browne actually. He took on his wife's name. Hugh Wildecott-Browne."

46
A Talk

*H*ow are things progressing with your cousin?" Gifford Rutherford asked his son one evening as they enjoyed a brandy together after Martha had retired to her room.

Geoffrey shrugged and muttered a noncommittal reply.

"You do not sound hopeful," rejoined the father in a concerned tone. "It was my understanding she was gradually being drawn more closely into our family's life."

"She is," replied Geoffrey. "She and Mother are together often enough, I suppose."

"And you?"

"I see her when I can."

"You don't sound enthusiastic. Have you forgotten Heathersleigh? Now that you have succeeded in winning her confidence, it is time for you to seal her affections."

Geoffrey stared down, sloshing the amber liquid about in his glass.

"What is it, my boy?" persisted Gifford. "Something is obviously on your mind."

"It's that blasted Halifax fellow!" replied Geoffrey with a boyish whine.

"The journalist you told me about? I thought you said he and Amanda hardly knew one another."

"That was before. They more than know each other now, that's for sure. He hangs around everywhere—she's *always* with him."

"Hmm . . . I hadn't realized the situation had grown so precarious." Gifford took a sip of his brandy.

"What do you know about him?" he asked after a moment or two's reflection.

"Just what I told you earlier—that he works for the *Mail*."

"Well, we'll have to scuttle it somehow."

"How? I can't exactly go along with them when they're together."

"I'll see what I can learn about him."

"I don't see what good that will do."

"Everybody's got a skeleton in their closet," replied Geoffrey's father. "If we can find his, that might be all we need."

"And if he doesn't?"

"Everybody's got something. If we can't find one, we'll *put* a skeleton in his closet. In the meantime, do what you can to increase the girl's dependence on you."

"But how? I've tried everything, but she's always short with me. She doesn't like me, that's all there is to it."

"Have you taken her flowers?"

"Flowers!" exclaimed Geoffrey.

"Certainly—a guaranteed way to a woman's heart."

"She would laugh at me if I tried that. Or throw them back in my face."

"Don't be too sure, my boy. Talk to her—women like that."

"*Talk* to her . . . about what?"

"Serious things."

"Like what?"

"Ask her what she thinks about things. Act interested."

"That's not so easy to do with Amanda."

"You can do it, my boy. It's what must be done."

47

Nr. 42 Ebendorfer Strasse

$\mathcal{L}$ate in the seventeenth century the magnificent Austrian city of Vienna was besieged by the Turks and Hungarians under Turkish Grand Vizier Kara Mustafa. But with the aid of Polish forces, the Habsburg dynasty was saved. The defeat of the Turks began the slow process of driving back the powerful Ottoman Empire, and eventually ousting it from Europe altogether.

Not only was the city of Vienna preserved—events of the siege produced an unexpected result destined to alter the entire course of western civilization, at least insofar as concerned its morning routine.

A certain Pole by the name of Kolchitizky, a spy during the siege, managed to make off with a sack of coffee beans from Turkish soldiers. Inside the city, his boasting of the feat was laughed at by the Viennese, who, after one look at the contents of his bag, concluded it full of camel fodder. But Kolchitizky knew the secret of roasting and grinding the precious beans to create a strong, black, aromatic, and invigorating brew. Thus was coffee introduced to Vienna.

An Armenian immigrant, one Johann Diobato, immediately perceived the commercial possibilities. He obtained the first official right from Vienna's ruling council to prepare and serve "the Turkish beverage." The year was 1865, two years after the Turkish siege. Diobato's coffeehouse was followed by many others, and soon became an institution in the Austrian capital.

By the opening of the twentieth century a hundred or more Viennese cafés had become the center and focus of the city's early-morning social life. Every political or intellectual group frequented its own particular café—from the Café Griensteidl to the Herrenhof to the Café Central. Whatever one's preferred coffee mixture, whether *Kleiner Schwarzer, Einspänner, Melange,* or *Kapuziner,* and whether it was ordered with croissant or other pastry, coffee always came with a newspaper. For besides pleasant conversation, cigarettes, and pipes, the men of Vienna mostly frequented their favorite coffeehouse to pore over the day's news.

Students had their favorite cafés, old retired men had theirs, laborers had theirs, socialists had theirs. One or two had even begun catering specifically to women, where the thick haze of tobacco was replaced by talk of women's issues, news of which had now reached this far east.

Every café had its own specialty—from billiards, to cards, to chess. Certain coffeehouses were frequented by musicians, others by painters, others by journalists. Vienna's musical tradition had been well established since Haydn and Mozart, up to the days of Beethoven and Schubert. And now the ghosts of recent legends Johannes Brahms and Johann Strauss—not the only composer whose early melodies were scratched upon some scrap of paper on a coffeehouse table—were gradually giving way to the new peculiar harmonies of Arnold Schönberg and the Vienna School. Such developments in many other fields of discipline, besides music, were frequently discussed at various of the city's coffeehouses, for Vienna was for centuries one of the creative, intellectual, and artistic centers in all of Europe. One of Vienna's rising men of prominence, however, Dr. Sigmund Freud, whose house was situated not far from the university, was rarely to be seen in such establishments. He was too busily engaged in analyzing the human psyche to allow his own to be taken up with such a mundane affair as keeping up on the day's news.

In a small café in an out-of-the-way street two or three blocks from the university, several young men were engaged in an earnest conversation around a table filled with empty coffee cups. The subject usually under discussion these days at the *Kaffe Kellar* was not music or architecture, not women's suffrage, nor psychoanalysis . . . but revolution. Here gathered students, many of them Russian, and idealists and socialists from throughout Europe. One or two Serbs and a Bosnian were present, and the heated discussion had alternated between the tenets of communism and the future independence of the Balkan states.

"I tell you, the enemy to our future is Austria," one particularly passionate youth, who appeared no older than sixteen, was saying.

"Keep your voice down, Princip," said another in a thick Serbian accent, in scarcely more than a whisper.

"I don't care who hears me," rejoined the first, who had already had far too much to drink of a brew even stronger than the coffee. "You are right in what you say about our enemy, and I say it is the emperor Franz Joseph."

Sensing that the conversation might begin to get out of hand, one of the men seated around the table glanced at his watch, then nodded to a colleague. The two rose, excusing themselves, and left the café. The evening was already late and dusk was well advanced. They made their way along Alser Strasse, then right onto Ebendorfer Strasse. It was about a ten-minute walk from the Kaffe Kellar to the stone building which at last loomed before them. Guests were expected, and they should not be late.

The four-story grey stone building on Ebendorfer Strasse, whose side door they entered, gave no evidence to the passerby that it was any different from five hundred similar buildings in central Vienna constructed just prior to the neoclassical period sometime in the late eighteenth century. Situated as it was almost between the comparatively new and lavish Rathaus, or City Hall, and the buildings of Universität, it passed itself off as containing offices of some kind on the ground floor, and residential apartments on the three upper floors. From the third floor, looking west, the grounds of Rathaus Park were visible, and beyond them, from the windows on the fourth, the wide boulevard surrounding the Old City known as "The Ring," one of Europe's widest and most elegant thoroughfares.

Most assumed that whatever activities went on behind the stone walls of the unassuming edifice were in some way connected with the university. Several students and two or three professors did in fact reside at Nr. 42 Ebendorfer Strasse. But the comings and goings from the side door of the building that opened toward Grillparzer Strasse, often at night, as in the case of the two young men who had just entered, sometimes more resembled the activities of a hostel than an apartment building. Indeed, those who did make this their residence entertained frequent visitors from all over Europe. There were a half dozen guest rooms which were always prepared, along with a full kitchen and staff, whose duties were to accommodate the unseen business of the place.

As they unlocked the door and entered, the two newcomers nodded to a lady in her mid-forties seated in a small parlor adjacent to the outside door. Through its thin curtains the window at which she sat maintained a clear view of the street and approach to the building. Though she was sipping a cup of tea and nonchalantly browsing through a newspaper, the woman was in fact the doorkeeper. This parlor was occupied, and the private entrance thus attended to, twenty-four hours a day.

"Are they here?" asked one of the coffeehouse arrivals.

"About ten minutes ago," answered the lady. "They're waiting for you upstairs."

48

A Country Ride

◆◆◆

*W*hen the telephone call came to the Pankhurst home, Amanda assumed it to be Ramsay.

"Who is it?" she asked Sylvia.

"I don't know—a man. He didn't identify himself."

With reluctance Amanda went downstairs to answer the call. Something about the evening with Ramsay at the theater had left her inexplicably unsettled. After the hypnotic trance of the evening wore off, by the next afternoon the memory of it gave her a funny feeling, almost of defilement, of having been somewhere she shouldn't have been.

She didn't want to talk to Ramsay right now. Was the bawdiness of the theater and play bothering her? Or was it Ramsay's familiarity with the actress? Was she jealous of the woman's presumed friendship with Ramsay?

She . . . jealous? Amanda hated even the thought of admitting to such a weakness. The reminder of the evening made her feel strange, weak, vulnerable . . . and she did not like the sensation.

Was she perhaps closer to falling in love than she realized? If so, why these peculiar feelings of hesitation and reluctance . . . almost caution? Why wasn't she running down to the phone with heart pounding, *hoping* it was Ramsay!

She lifted the telephone receiver, sighed inwardly, then answered.

"Amanda . . . hello," said a voice that for an instant she did not recognize. "It's Geoffrey."

More inexplicable even than her hesitation to answer the phone when she thought it was Ramsay was the brief surge of relief which filled Amanda at the sound of her second cousin's voice.

"Good morning, Geoffrey," she replied, in as pleasant a tone as she had ever managed to generate toward him.

"It promises to be a beautiful Saturday afternoon," Geoffrey went on. "I wondered if you might like to go for a drive in the country."

"Your family is planning an outing?"

"No, just the two of us. Mother and Father are staying in the city."

A brief pause on the line followed. There was a suffragette march planned for the afternoon in which she knew she was expected to participate.

The next words out of her mouth surprised Amanda as much as they did Geoffrey.

"Yes . . . yes, I think I would," she said. "That sounds like it might be fun."

Two hours later, with Geoffrey at the wheel of his convertible, the two cousins motored their way along the Thames, finding themselves inwardly surprised at the relatively pleasant conversation they had enjoyed thus far.

"Tell me, Amanda," Geoffrey was saying, "do you really go along with all that suffragette business?"

"I believe that women ought to have the right to vote, if that's what you mean."

"I mean the wild antics, the violence?"

"I don't suppose I like it all," she answered. "But the Pankhursts think that's the only way to be heard, that the cause will be ignored otherwise."

"What do *you* believe?" he said.

Amanda glanced over across from where she sat. Geoffrey was looking forward, eyes on the road ahead, and did not see her momentarily probing his face. As she stared at his profile, the most peculiar sensation came over her, a feeling of familial bond, of relationship, almost of camaraderie by virtue of shared heritage and roots.

In the most obscure way, Geoffrey's nose and chin and jawbone reminded Amanda . . . of her father.

She glanced away. But then just as quickly she returned her gaze to his face. The faint similarity was still there—there could be no mistaking it. And why not? Their fathers were first cousins. They shared the same grandparents, she and Geoffrey the same great-grandparents. Why shouldn't there be a family resemblance? Why, then, did the look so startle her?

The silence lasted only a second or two.

"I suppose I think there might be other methods," Amanda replied to Geoffrey's question.

The uncharacteristically thoughtful exchange between the two—

whose conversations till then had been what might best be called an antagonistic verbal sparring, almost as if they were playing a game with each other, and both knew it—sobered both. They drove on for several miles in silence. What each was thinking, the other couldn't have remotely begun to guess.

"What's your father like, Geoffrey?" Amanda asked at length. Once again, the words out of her mouth surprised her. She had not anticipated the question. All of a sudden, there were the words hanging in the air between them.

"What do you mean, what is he like?" replied Geoffrey. "You know my father as well as I do."

"That can hardly be."

"You know what I mean."

"I'm not sure I do. But what I meant is, what kind of man is he? Is he your friend? Do you like him? What do you and your father talk about?"

"Of course I like him," replied Geoffrey. He could hardly tell Amanda the subject of their discussion the last time they spoke together! Reminded of his father's words upon that occasion, Geoffrey fumbled to heed his advice.

"But what about you, Amanda," he said. "What is *your* father like?"

"Now I might turn your own words back on you and say that you know him as well as I do. But I won't because that would be ridiculous."

"All right, then, tell me why you left Heathersleigh. Is it because you don't like your father?"

She paused and grew serious.

"I don't know that I ever thought about it in quite those words," Amanda said. "Maybe I *don't* like him, I don't know. It's just that he never understood me, or even tried to understand what I was thinking and feeling. He wanted me to be just like the rest of them and believe all the same things and act the same way. But I couldn't."

"What about your mother?" asked Geoffrey.

"I love my mother," replied Amanda. "But she went along with my father about everything. She would never side with me. And when she starting talking about the absurd idea of submitting to him as her *head*, as she called it, that's when I realized any hope I might have had of her understanding what I was thinking and feeling was gone. That's when I knew I had to get away from Heathersleigh eventually."

"But you like Heathersleigh, don't you?"

"I hate the very thought of Devonshire."

"But it's not so bad a place. Might you not someday want to get married and go back there to live, back to the old family estate, as it were?"

"What are you talking about? When and if I get married, I certainly wouldn't go back to Heathersleigh. Why would I do that?"

Geoffrey did not answer. He had inadvertently overplayed his hand. Best to change the subject.

"Uh . . . what do you think of the situation on the Continent?" he asked feebly.

"Oh, Geoffrey—heavens . . . who cares!"

"I don't know, I just thought maybe you'd be interested in all that, since your father used to be in politics."

"I used to be, not anymore."

"Actually, I'm not either. I was just trying to make conversation."

Amanda glanced over at him again with a curious expression.

"Why, Geoffrey," she said, "—why were you trying to make conversation?"

"I don't know . . . I suppose because it seems like we ought to be able to talk together intelligently, without always sniping at each other."

He glanced toward her uncertainly. She was still looking at him. Her expression caught him off guard, and he forced a somewhat nervous smile. She returned it with a smile and nod of her own.

"Perhaps you are right, Geoffrey," she said. "Perhaps we should."

The rest of the afternoon passed more pleasantly than either would have anticipated when the day began.

PART IV

— ✦✦✦ —

Divergences
1911–1912

49

A New First Lord of the Admiralty

*C*harles Rutherford took a sip of tea and continued in the magazine editorial he was reading concerning the state of the world.

It would hardly do for the French and Germans to rattle their sabres too violently along the banks of the Rhine or the Mosel, though their deepest grievances originate in these debated regions between them. Apparently they intend instead to allow their natural antipathy for one another to clash in parts of the world a little more removed from each of their homelands.

This antagonism grows steadily more pronounced in North Africa, especially Morocco, where German and French colonial and commercial interests have often collided. It was in Morocco that the major crisis erupted in 1905, which many European leaders now see as the foundational prelude to recent mounting tensions.

Great Britain, still trying to accustom herself to the strange notion of thinking about France in a friendly manner, sided on that occasion with her new ally against the ancient empire of the revered queen's people.

Kaiser Wilhelm II of Germany expressed shock and profound offence. Were not the royals of England of his own family? Was not Victoria, after all, a German? The British monarchy is German through and through. Had not the kaiser's own mother maintained apartments in Windsor Castle? How *could* Britain side with their longtime mutual enemy—the French frogs!

The crisis in Morocco gave dark portent of things to come. War in that instance was only averted by a conference of powers, in which President Theodore Roosevelt interceded from the United States for peace.

The Moroccan problem, however, was not solved, as we see now all too clearly.

What will be the result this time—another crisis averted, then another, and another? Or will hostilities eventually explode?

Charles set the magazine aside and sighed. That was the question on everyone's mind these days. With Germany and Austria increasingly belligerent, how long could war be put off?

Germany was more powerful than she had been in 1905. And with a new king on the throne, Kaiser Wilhelm had reason to be confident that England would not oppose him again. Edward the Encircler, as the kaiser had called the English king, was dead. A few days prior to the funeral, the German emperor had said to Theodore Roosevelt that the new English king George was "a very nice boy." With Edward out of the way, Wilhelm considered himself the supreme ruler in Europe.

Again France and Germany clashed in North Africa, this time even more seriously. Following a palace revolution in Morocco, French troops entered the capital city of Fez to protect Europeans living there. Germany protested, saying that France had violated the 1905 agreement. Not to be outdone, and feeling increasingly confident in its growing naval power, she sent the gunboat *Panther* to Agadir on July 1, stating that Germany must likewise protect *its* interests. The Panther was poised to open fire if the command came from Berlin.

But the alliance between England and France had deepened since 1905. Proximity and increasing common interests were thrusting the ancient enemies closer and closer together. Again Britain sided with France. Her threats to Germany were even more strongly worded than before.

Within days of this new crisis British Brigadier General Henry Wilson sailed to Paris. A hastily concluded agreement was reached with French leaders, which detailed how British and French divisions would conduct themselves against Germany if war came over the incident. The question in the diplomatic and military rooms in London during the summer of 1911 was a simple one: *Would* Germany go to war against France and England over its minimal holdings in Africa?

In late August, Prime Minister Asquith called an all-day secret meeting of the Imperial Defence Committee in order to clarify British strategy in case of war. Throughout the morning General Wilson laid out the army position according to the terms of his agreement with the French. All afternoon Admiral Arthur Wilson presented the navy's plans.

The army planned to land six divisions across the Channel in northern France and Belgium to aid the French forces in combatting the predicted swift German attempt to encircle Paris from the north. The navy, however, basing its strategy on an entirely opposite series of assumptions, told the prime minister of its plan to land an expeditionary force on the northern shores of Prussia six hundred miles away.

"Gentlemen," said Asquith, shaking his head almost in disbelief. "Your two strategies have nothing whatever in common. I am astonished. Have you even consulted together?"

A bitter argument ensued between the army and navy, each trying to convince the prime minister of the soundness of its plan. One of the most outspoken men in the meeting held no military post at all. His insights, however, were sound and his military acumen keen.

The home secretary, a young man of a mere thirty-seven years, now spoke up vigorously. He was especially critical of the navy, but dared confront generals and admirals alike, all old enough to be his father.

Eventually the army carried the day. Prime Minister Asquith sided with his generals over his admirals. Furthermore, as a result of their talk of a Prussian landing, his confidence in the leaders of the British navy was profoundly shaken.

Within weeks of the meeting, a wholesale restructuring of naval leadership had taken place. The knowledgeable home secretary was transferred to a post where Asquith felt he could be more valuable to the country in the critical days ahead—First Lordship of the Admiralty.

At thirty-seven, Winston Churchill was now in charge of the mightiest fleet in the world.

As the crisis in Morocco dragged on, Italy meanwhile decided that she too deserved a portion of the receding Ottoman Empire. Taking advantage of the preoccupation of Britain, France, and Germany with Morocco, Italy declared war on Turkey in September. Immediately she seized Tripoli and the Dodecanese Islands.

Further hostilities, it seemed, might be likely to break out anywhere.

50

Another Curious Invitation

•••

$\mathcal{S}$ir Charles Rutherford read for the third time the letter and invitation which had arrived earlier that day. He already had a pretty good idea what he intended to do. But the invitation was addressed to them both, so he needed to discuss it with Jocelyn. He rose and went downstairs.

> *Dear Charles,* the letter began.
>
> *I sincerely hope you and your dear wife will be able to accept the enclosed invitation. I am aware not all your concerns were satisfactorily addressed when we met previously. However, I am confident that the more you learn concerning our purposes, the more you will find yourself in agreement with our objectives. Others who share our concerns will be in attendance, and I believe you will find both the event itself and the discussions it affords to be most stimulating, as well as illuminating with regard to some of the questions you raised at our last gathering.*
>
> > *I am sincerely yours,*
> > *Dr. Morley Redmond*

The invitation itself was formal and disclosed few particulars other than time and place, which again, was located in Cambridgeshire:

> *3 October, 1911*
> *Sir Charles and Lady Rutherford*
>
> *H. Barclay, Esquire, and friends*
> *request the pleasure of your company at an Evening Party,*
> *Heathwood Green Estate,*
> *Little Wilbraham, Cambridgeshire,*
> *on Saturday, 14 September.*
>
> *An answer will oblige.*
> *Dancing.*

Jocelyn read the two communications and handed the sheets back to Charles.

"A formal ball is not exactly something I would look forward to," she said. "But I would go for your sake. It might even be fun to dress up and dance with you again. We probably wouldn't know anybody anyway."

"This is more than a social occasion, Jocie," said Charles. "I don't know what it is, but these people are up to something."

"Does it feel as strange to you as it does to me?" she asked.

"It is certainly beginning to."

"Do you really think they are trying to get you to join their group?"

"It seems that way. Whatever it is, they are doing all they can to win my confidence without divulging anything specific."

"And you still don't know why?"

"No," replied Charles, shaking his head. "I can't imagine why they are so intent about it. I am not an influential man. What could they possibly want with me? They are so vague about everything. It almost feels like a lodge or some secretive rite."

"I like the sound of it less and less," said Jocelyn with a shudder.

"But they're so hospitable. When you're actually with them, sitting talking informally, everything seems so normal."

"But wherever there are secrets, that is a warning sign that all is not as it should be."

Charles nodded his head. "But neither are they the kind of people you can ignore," he sighed. "It feels like they are trying to force me to take one side or the other, without divulging what their side is all about. Once they've set their sights on you, neutrality doesn't seem to be an option."

"What are you going to do?" Jocelyn asked. "Will you reply?"

"Only with polite regrets that we will not be attending," replied Charles.

51
Romantic Weekend

$\mathcal{A}$manda spent the entire afternoon getting ready!

She had been to many places with Ramsay Halifax—to lectures and plays, to horse races and on drives.

But *never* to a formal ball!

She had been to plenty of dances and balls, of course. But always with Geoffrey and Cousin Martha. This would be a weekend to remember—she just knew it.

Ramsay's words had been in her mind for two weeks:

◆ ◆ ◆

Amanda, I would like you to go with me for the weekend to a country estate up in Cambridgeshire."

"The weekend!" she had exclaimed.

"Relax," Ramsay laughed. "It is all very proper. My mother and some of her friends will be there. Your reputation will be perfectly secure. We will be guests of a diplomatic associate of Mum's. He is throwing a lavish ball on Saturday night at his country estate east of Cambridge. It is an enormous place, from what I understand—guest rooms by the score. Most will be staying over."

"What kind of ball?"

"I don't know. Lots of dignitaries and foreign types will be there, according to Mum."

Whatever discomfort Amanda had felt from the evening at the theater was quickly vanishing. If she had been so naïve as to be shocked by what she saw, then she was glad for the experience. Perhaps at last she was ready to be a woman of the world, and put all those silly inhibitions from childhood behind her for

good. A weekend in the country with Ramsay Halifax should succeed in accomplishing just that.

"You're sure you're not working on some secret spy story
you're not telling me about?" she said jokingly.

Ramsay laughed. "Purely social, I promise. Whatever the others may have in mind with their discussions and closed-door
meetings with cigars and brandy, I assure you I will have eyes only
for you."

"Then . . . I accept!"

———————— ◆ ◆ ◆ ————————

Amanda had made the mistake of blurting out news of Ramsay's
invitation at the very next meal. Sylvia had been noticeably cool ever
since. It wasn't the nature of the proposal itself. Sylvia didn't like men
at all. Her view was that no young woman in her right mind should
have anything to do with *any* man.

The awaited weekend finally came.

Mrs. Halifax immediately put all Amanda's anxieties to rest.
Quickly she took her under her wing during the train ride north. When
they arrived at the estate called Heathwood Green, Amanda shared a
room with dear old Mrs. Thorndike, who fussed over her as if she were
her own daughter.

They arrived just before tea on Friday evening. Neither Ramsay nor
his mother attended. Amanda and Mrs. Thorndike went downstairs to
the dining room alone, and afterward retired to their room for the
night.

Amanda did not see Ramsay all day Saturday, though his mother
was present most of the time. The two older women fussed with her
hair and dress and shoes and jewelry for half the afternoon, until every
hair was perfectly in place.

At last Ramsay called for her at half past seven. He wore formal
black trousers, black jacket, and black waistcoat with white tie and
shirt. He bowed slightly, allowing the faintest hint of a smile to come
to his lips as their eyes met. Amanda curtseyed, then walked out into
the corridor in her floor-length white gown, took his arm, and together
they descended to the ballroom. Around her neck hung a stunning

string of pearls belonging to Mrs. Thorndike, which the lady had insisted she wear.

"You look absolutely lovely, Amanda," Ramsay said as they went. "I don't think I've ever seen you so dazzling."

Amanda felt the redness rising in her neck and cheeks. She only hoped he wouldn't notice!

They entered the ballroom, and the sight took Amanda's breath away. Why did this occasion seem so much more glamorous than any before? Was it Ramsay himself? Was it the international flavor, the mix of many tongues all around her, the sense almost of danger and intrigue?

Music was already playing. Without a word, Ramsay took her in his arms and they glided off across the dance floor. It was a dream ... a fairy tale!

She and Ramsay danced and danced. By ten o'clock it was already a night Amanda would never forget. And the hour was still young!

The orchestra took a break from the music to relax and refresh themselves. Ramsay led Amanda outside to the veranda. They walked to the railing of a balcony overlooking the expansive gardens and stood for a few moments, gazing in silence out into the peaceful moonlit evening. The loveliest hint of a gentle breeze lifted fragrances of autumn grasses toward them. The setting could not have been more romantic.

"The moon is almost full," said Ramsay softly.

Amanda remained silent. With all her senses, she breathed deeply of the magical moment. Ramsay gently placed his hand on top of hers where it rested on the edge of the railing. At the touch, a momentary tingle went through her frame.

Was this really happening! Was she falling in love?

"Oh, Ramsay, sometimes I get so afraid," she all at once blurted out.

Where had the words come from? Even Amanda herself could not have said. For at this moment she could not have felt more dreamy and content.

"Afraid of what?" he asked.

"I don't know—what is to become of me, I suppose. Doesn't the future frighten you?"

"Never!" exclaimed Ramsay with easygoing laughter.

Amanda glanced toward him. His face wore the irrepressible smile she had grown so fond of. Was it Ramsay's confidence and buoyant optimism that made her like him? Or was there . . . *more?* As she looked, his eyes and teeth seemed to gleam in the glow of the moon.

"I wish I could be so confident," said Amanda. "You seem to have everything so—"

Amanda stopped. She didn't even know what she was trying to say.

"So *what?*" Ramsay said, smiling down at her.

"I don't know—so . . . figured out, I suppose."

Ramsay laughed good-naturedly. "Well, don't you worry, Amanda Rutherford, I'll figure things out for you too. I'll take care of you. I'll always be here for you. Whenever you get afraid, all you have to do is come to me."

He grasped her hand, lifted it from the railing, and turned her toward him. Amanda gazed up into Ramsay's moonlit face as he bent down and gently kissed her on the lips.

How long the moment lasted, she could not know . . . a second, five seconds.

It was an instant. It was an eternity.

Ramsay lifted his head, then took her in his arms and pulled her close. Amanda relaxed as never before in his embrace. She leaned her head against his great strong chest and sighed. If only she could feel this safe, this secure, every moment.

Yet the future was still out there, and still uncertain, and one wonderful evening like this couldn't change it.

Or could it?

52

Melancholy Memories

*C*harles Rutherford set the letter he had just read down on his desk and glanced about his office. So much of his life, his past, his family heritage, was here.

There had been another day when both past and future had been on his mind. With reminiscent fondness he recalled that time, when a very different sort of communication lay on his desk. The future he was now contemplating was now so very altered from what he thought it would look like back then.

That was fourteen years ago. It hardly seemed possible.

How much had happened since … yet how quickly the years had flown by.

Then he had all his life before him, or so he thought. He had been a mere thirty-eight, dubbed by the London *Times* one of England's top ten politicians to watch, a rising Liberal star in Parliament with a better-than-likely opportunity to become prime minister someday. Everything he had ever wanted had seemingly been laid before him on that day when the invitation with the royal seal lay on his desk from Queen Victoria's office, signifying the ceremony in London which would confirm his knighthood.

How far away that day seemed at this moment.

Now he was fifty-two. His hair contained more grey than brown. Though deep contentment resided in his heart, his eyes did not burn with the same fire of vision they once had. Though he still *felt* young and vigorous inside, he could sense age imperceptibly laying claim to his earthly vessel. He couldn't keep up with George now, either on the back of a horse or when wrestling on the lawn. He found he had to be more attentive to back and knees. Bobby McFee was now so stooped over he walked like a wizened little old gnome out of a fairy tale. Charles smiled at the thought. He wondered if the same fate awaited him thirty years from now.

The smile turned gradually melancholy, then disappeared. Why on some days did all thoughts return eventually to sad reminders of his middle daughter?

He had been made a Knight Grand Commander. But what did the *Sir* in front of his name really mean now? He would trade it all in an instant for …

Charles glanced away and drew in a deep breath. He had shed enough tears over her during the last three years. He didn't feel like crying again just now. The mood had to be right to allow tears to come, and he did not feel like enduring their pain on this day.

He turned and began pacing about his office, gazing absently at the da Vinci drawing, then the paintings of his father and grandfather, at the faded but still colorful Persian rugs on the floor, at two or three of his own small inventions. His little motor, for which he held the patent, had been overtaken by the rush of electrical technology such that it was outdated almost before he could begin putting it to use.

Everything changed so fast these days. It was hard to keep up with all the developments. The thought caused him to glance upward where light from Edison's invention illuminated the room.

Now his gaze fell to a quick scan of his bookshelves. Their contents had changed markedly in the last fourteen years. In place of Darwin, Wells, Shaw, and Huxley, now the spines of Henry, Schaff, Moody, Strong, Spurgeon, Jukes, and Symonds gazed back at him, along with more than two dozen of the Scotsman's novels. His tastes had changed. His whole outlook had changed. The autographed first edition of Darwin's *Origin* still sat on his desk between the ivory bookends, as a reminder of his past. But it had been joined by three well-worn Bibles—a copy of the Authorized Version, a Revised Version, and a copy of Dr. Weymouth's New Testament, published in 1903. Beside them on the desk sat a copy of the newly published *Tercentenary Commemoration Bible*, which he had not had a chance to investigate yet in any depth. He was more interested in the brown packet next to it, which contained proofs for the Gospel of Mark sent him for review and comment by Professor Moffatt from Oxford in preparation for the publication of his modern language New Testament. It was scheduled to be completed a year or two from now. It was the opportunity of a lifetime, to actually participate in some small way in the production of a new edition of the Scriptures.

Slowly Charles walked to the window and let his gaze drift about the Devonshire countryside he loved. Autumn was well advanced. Most of the trees had lost their leaves, except for the numerous beech scattered about the hillsides. A chill in the air signaled the approach of winter. Rain and storms would be upon them soon.

And Christmas. But the thought brought no surge of childlike anticipation. The holiday would forever after be incomplete until their family was whole again.

Today's paper carried news that Germany had finally backed down in Morocco in exchange for a relatively worthless portion of the French Congo. War had again been forestalled. He should be happy. Why was his heart so heavy?

Charles knew well enough.

Whatever surface smiles he wore, whatever laughter came from his lips, however much he and Jocelyn and Catharine and George enjoyed life with one another these days, in the midst of whatever business he was about, even in the midst of exciting opportunities that came his way like the Moffatt project, there remained a portion of his soul that was *always* heavy.

His heart could not but be sorely burdened for Amanda. How could he cease to care that one he loved so dearly was estranged from them?

Again Charles sought the window. Staring out upon the now solitary landscape where once had rung the happy laughter of three little children, somehow helped to keep the tears at bay. Gradually thoughts of electricity and knighthood, Leonardo and books and Bible translations faded. The father's mind filled with memories of those precious years that slip by so quickly, and whose promises and hopes and dreams so often seem to go unfulfilled.

He had tried to pour himself into all three of his children equally, though obviously in different ways. Each was uniquely special to his heart.

Yet Amanda's rejection of the training he had tried to give stung with particular pain. She it was who somehow had more deeply inherited his own outlook and way of looking at things. He had always considered that she and he were bonded together as father and daughter in an unusual and wonderfully special way. George and Catharine had grown into more blended expressions of both himself and Jocelyn. But Amanda had always been so much like him, her intellect and vision so like his.

Amanda was a questioner. He had helped fashion her so, and had so relished that aspect of her nature. And now that mental vigor and feisty spirit had actually been turned against him. Even after three years, Charles still could hardly believe it.

The grief over the loss of his daughter—whether temporary or permanent, how could he possibly know?—had by now gone down into the deep quiet places of his being, there to be cherished in his quiet inner sanctuary of painful worship with his Father.

Life went on. He could laugh and converse and work and function in all ways necessary, keeping the inner anguish from view. He knew Jocelyn did the same. Who but the two of them, or another parent who had suffered the same tearing between himself and son or daughter, could understand what they felt? He had accustomed himself to the pain. But that made reminders of it no less keen.

He knew there were those who would say he should not dwell on what was past, that he should look ahead, and let Amanda live her life as she chose.

But would he ever stop caring . . . *could* he ever stop? She was his daughter and he loved her. It *hurt* that she despised him. It would always hurt. It was not something he could pretend wasn't there. It wasn't something time alone would heal. Time made him able to endure it. But time couldn't heal the parental wound.

He missed Amanda. He missed her vibrant personality and their vigorous exchanges. And no matter what wonderful times he still enjoyed with George and Catharine, nothing could altogether assuage the ache of knowing a piece of his own flesh, his very nature, had been severed from him. It was sometimes a grief he thought too painful to bear.

Yes, thought Charles, he would trade all he had ever done and been, he would even give up Heathersleigh itself, to be reunited with his daughter, to feel her arms of trust around him, to see her embrace Jocelyn, content again to be their daughter.

53

Light ... Or Darkness?

*C*harles turned from the window and picked up and scanned again the letter which had arrived in today's post.

Today's communication from Hartwell Barclay was quite different than the invitation to his ball in Cambridge several weeks earlier. This was no invitation. In these words Charles could feel more of what was perhaps the man's true nature than he had previously allowed himself to reveal.

My dear Mr. Rutherford, it began.

I confess to deep disappointment that you neither attended the gathering last month at Heathwood Green, nor felt the courtesy of explaining your decision to be appropriate. No doubt you had your reasons. However, our cause moves forward. Times are dangerous. The future we seek approaches, and dedicated individuals such as yourself are needed. We must know whether you are with us. Opportunity will not last forever. The future of your nation is at stake. Consider your course well. Opportunity is always double-edged. A new order of Light will soon emerge. Will you be part of it?

Earnestly,
H. Barclay

The words were couched in cordiality and friendliness, but an unmistakable message lay hidden between the lines.

It almost seemed to carry the ring of an ultimatum. Who was Hartwell Barclay anyway? Was he truly about their nation's business ... or his own?

As on that day fourteen years ago, though in an entirely different way, Charles felt again that his future lay before him, that much depended on his response to this letter, more even than he was aware.

"Lord, show me what you would have me do," he whispered.

For several more minutes Charles sat thinking. If he wrote and expressed what was on his heart, and his words were misconstrued ... who could tell what might be the consequence? Perhaps that was a chance he must take in order to stand for light and truth. Not Mr. Barclay's version of so-called "light" but for *true* truth.

He went downstairs to seek Jocelyn. He showed the paper to her. She read it through twice, then glanced up with puzzled expression.

"What do you think, Jocie?"

"I haven't even met the man," she said, "but he would frighten me. I see why you felt reluctance before. Something strange is at work here. I would very strongly urge you not to become involved further."

Charles nodded seriously as she spoke, weighing her words carefully.

"Something is wrong," Jocelyn continued. "I can sense it. It feels like some kind of political factionalism is involved here, almost conspiratorial."

"That is a strong statement."

"Secret objectives they are reluctant to share, taking offense when questioned or opposed, which I read so clearly in Mr. Barclay's letter—those are classic symptoms of schism groups. Such movements are always dangerous."

Charles nodded, took the letter, and returned to his office. Jocelyn's confirmation was all he needed. Her instincts were usually sound on such matters. He should have asked her advice more directly before allowing himself to become involved even to the limited extent he had.

He sat down at his desk, took out a sheet of paper with his letterhead, and began to write. Thirty minutes later he again returned downstairs and handed a single sheet to his wife.

Dear Mr. Barclay, she read.

As much as I appreciate the interest you have shown and the apparent confidence you have in me, I must say that none of the questions which have concerned me about further involvement with you have been satisfactorily addressed. I love my country, and I am concerned for its future. It has been my experience, however, that truth, as you claim to love so highly, is rarely produced by methods of stealth and secrecy. I have attempted to be straightforward, direct, honest, and sincere with you. But I have not found such open disclosure concerning your goals and objectives and background to have been reciprocated. I am sorry to be so blunt, but I cannot help feeling you are hiding something, hoping to win my loyalties before revealing exactly what you envision for the so-called new order. I must therefore decline any further contact with what you call the Fountain of Light.

I am, Mr. Barclay, respectfully yours,
Sir Charles Rutherford,
Heathersleigh Hall, Devonshire

Jocelyn looked up, then nodded slowly.

"It's direct," she said, "but I think you are doing the right thing."

54

Hugh Wildecott-Browne

───── ◆ ◆ ◆ ─────

*H*artwell Barclay read the letter he had just received for a second time.

Anger rose up within him. Not violent anger, but of the quiet, seething variety. Of the sort compelled to exact revenge.

He was not used to being rebuffed by individuals he had gone to such lengths to befriend. And spurning his kindness with such pointed and openly critical words!

This was no longer a matter of mere recruitment. Rather than joining them, by the words of this letter Rutherford had pitted himself *against* them. Such an outright challenge could not be allowed to stand.

"Redmond," he said across the room, "it is time I had a personal chat with the relative we were speaking of before—the brother-in-law."

"Browne . . . er, *Wildecott*-Browne?"

"Right, the wife's sister's husband. It may be we will have to get to the man through his wife."

"What do you want me to do?"

"Make contact, however seems most appropriate. Divulge nothing concerning our motives. If he is a solicitor, we may need more information about him before telling him of the Fountain. But we can see how he is disposed toward the family. In the meantime, get me all the information we have about the estranged daughter."

♦♦♦

When Hugh Wildecott-Browne walked into the comfortable lounge a few weeks later, he did not expect to find six or eight individuals awaiting him. The invitation from the professor who said he was a friend of the Rutherfords had said only that a matter would be discussed about which he might be able to help.

Introductions, pleasant food, expensive wine, and stimulating, though vague, political conversation followed. By the time the discussion at last arrived at that for which the invitation had been sent, Jocelyn Rutherford's brother-in-law, warmed and relaxed by the wine, and his ego and receptivities skillfully massaged by a lounge full of experienced experts, was in a congenial and responsive frame of mind.

"You are, as we understand it," said Barclay at the appropriate moment of opening, "a man of religious feeling."

"I am of high standing in my church," replied the guest.

"You care about right and wrong, and know the difference?"

"Of course."

"What we have to tell you, Hugh," continued the lean white-haired gentleman, "is an extremely sad story. You are well familiar with the individuals involved. I speak primarily of your niece Amanda, daughter of your wife's sister. You know Amanda is not with her parents at present?"

"I am aware of something to that effect."

"Do you know the reason?"

"I'm afraid I do not. I have never been close to Jocelyn's family. They are—"

Wildecott-Browne cleared his throat briefly.

"—I suppose it would be said that they are not exactly *our* kind of people. I don't go in for that business of making a public show of your religion, as if you're better than everyone else."

"We understand perfectly," nodded Barclay somberly. "You couldn't have expressed our sentiments more precisely."

"Religion is a good thing," went on Jocelyn's brother-in-law, warmed by the approval, "but if you ask me, it belongs in the church. I am a man who prefers his religion not made so much of, if you know what I mean."

Again Barclay nodded. "We do indeed. I am happy to know that we have not misjudged you," he went on. "You are clearly a man of conscience and moral decency."

Barclay paused and grew serious. "What you are about to hear may shock you, Hugh," he continued. "For a public man such as Charles Rutherford, or *Sir* Charles as he prefers to be called—though if ever a man was *less* deserving of the honor I do not know of him—for such a man to be lauded by the public, when behind the doors of his own home nothing short of such insensitivity and meanness toward his own family went on for years."

"Meanness . . . I am afraid I do not understand."

"Even cruelty, though it is admittedly a strong word, Hugh."

"*Cruelty* . . . to what specifically do you refer?"

"You cannot be unaware, Hugh . . . that is to say, there *are* some things it is impossible to hide . . ."

Barclay allowed his voice to trail off, leaving Wildecott-Browne to draw his own inference. In the absence of fact, the doubt of innuendo will serve almost as well.

"You don't mean . . . the scar on his wife's face?"

"No, of course not, Hugh," rejoined Barclay. Even in the denial, he had achieved his end, which was to place suspicion and mistrust in the man's mind. "I speak of far more subtle things. I would not like to spread rumors. All I can say is that the poor woman has suffered beyond what any woman should have to endure from a man. Suffered psychologically, I mean, not physically. No doubt she convinces herself that such is her religious duty. But no woman should have to put up with it. Yet what poor Amanda has suffered, which finally left her with no alternative but to leave home when she was old enough to be able, truly is a dreadful indictment against a man who prides himself on being virtuous above his peers."

"They have always seemed a bit high and mighty for my tastes," nodded Hugh. "But I did not know the girl had actually been *forced* to leave home."

"There is nothing else to call it. Of course, they paint a different picture. No doubt your wife has been told another side of it altogether so as to lay the blame on Amanda."

Barclay paused, shaking his head sadly.

"The poor girl, it is all I can say," he went on. "Her father was so overbearing, even dictatorial, so as to suffocate any possibility for free expression in his home."

The room fell quiet for a moment. Wildecott-Browne was not exactly shocked by what he heard, though it was all new to him. The lower side of his nature eagerly lapped up the news, as most unconsciously do, just because it was negative. Already his attorney's brain was revolving the different sides to the situation.

"Tell me," he asked, "is my wife's sister involved? You say she too has been abused by the man, but what is her relation to her daughter? Is she culpable as well? She always struck me as a gentle and reasonable woman. Surely—"

"Ah, there is the doubly sad aspect of the case. Your poor wife's sister is trapped by the situation, yet is unable, like her daughter, to escape it. Poor Lady Rutherford is the one we feel sorry for. Yet she has deluded herself into thinking her husband a great man and that, however glaring his faults, she must stand faithfully by him. Thus we hardly see what can be done for her."

By now the eyes of Jocelyn's brother-in-law were wide and his ears even more than normally receptive. Like Charles' cousin Gifford and many relatives generally, he was all too willing to accept unsubstantiated reports about one whom, though he had not spoken twelve words to him in the last twelve years, he had always harbored a bit of a secret annoyance.

By the time the evening was well advanced, with the information added by Mrs. Halifax, Hugh Wildecott-Browne was well on his way to becoming a loyal initiate into the Fountain of Light, though he had never heard the phrase, nor possessed the faintest inkling of what these new seeming friends stood for. He convinced himself that what he felt was familial responsibility, and inwardly determined to do his best for his niece and his sister-in-law. Without knowing it, the intelligent but foolish man had become the worst kind of pawn, one who believed what he was told with no attempt to substantiate it.

"What can I do to help?" he asked at length.

"You will have to determine that for yourself, Hugh," replied Barclay with great humility. "It might be that you will want to contact your niece. She may need an understanding ear, or even a place of refuge."

"Of course, of course," he replied, "I will do whatever I can."

55

A Skeleton

♦ ♦ ♦

*G*ifford Rutherford could hardly believe his good fortune. Whether the report was true or not hardly mattered—it was so deliciously certain to ruin the man!

At least in that vixen Amanda's eyes, which was all that mattered.

Struggling to keep a smile from breaking out over his face, Gifford nodded soberly, as if the information contained in the brief communication were all but worthless, then folded it, paid the man whose services he had made use of, and closed the door.

Now he could give vent to his delight. *Ha, ha!* he laughed loudly as he walked upstairs to his study, pulling out the sheet and reading its opening line again.

RAMSAY HALIFAX, 27, EMPLOYER THE DAILY MAIL, STEPSON OF LORD BURTON WYCKHAM HALIFAX (D. 1908), WAS SEEN IN MOROCCO. . . .

Ha, ha, ha! Just wait till that fool Amanda learns of this!

It would probably be best to keep his son from knowing the *full* truth of what he had discovered, which was that there might not be a grain of truth in it. That *some* people believed it was good enough for him.

Now all he had to do was put the skeleton in the man's closet, and that would be the end of Ramsay Halifax.

Ha, ha, ha! It was really too good to be true. Heathersleigh would be in the bag after this.

Gifford calmed and fell to thinking.

What was the best way to proceed—leak the information to the *Times*? No, they would probably never print it without substantiation of the source.

One of the rags would be best. The *Sun* . . . the *Mirror* . . . it hardly mattered, as long as it found its way into print.

He'd take it to Elmer Farmon. After the loan he'd approved for him, his solicitor would probably do anything he asked.

Two hours later the attorney and financier discussed the communiqué the former had received behind the closed doors of the latter's office.

"They'll want to know where it came from," said Farmon.

"Make something up," replied Gifford. "You solicitors are good at that."

"I can't *lie* . . . even for you. I would be disbarred if it were discovered."

"You would likewise be disbarred if your financial affairs were closely examined, my friend," said Gifford. "Don't make me remind you that you owe your reputation at present to my signature on your loan documents."

Farmon squirmed slightly in his chair. The fact that every word the banker spoke was true only made him hate him the more.

"My financial difficulties won't alter the fact that they will want to know where this came from," he said, lifting the sheet of paper and holding it toward the banker.

"Then be creative," said Gifford, turning to go. "Frankly, I don't care how you do it, but I want to see this in print. Otherwise, the bank is going to find your file at the top of the stack when the time comes for its next loan audit. I presume I make myself clear."

56
Stormy Birth

A blustery wind blew out of the north over Devonshire early one evening during the first weeks of 1912, picking up force as the night advanced. By the time the residents of houses large and small took to their beds, they fell asleep hoping their roofs would still be above them when they woke in the morning. Rain was likely.

George Rutherford carted cot and blankets up to the little room in the garret which he had gradually converted into his own private work-room, office, and laboratory. Now that it was supplied with electric light and power for his experiments, he spent a good deal of his time in the lofty perch above the three inhabited floors of Heathersleigh. On nights of heavenly commotion such as this, he always slept here. If the roof blew off, he wanted to witness the event!

Below him, sister and parents slept comfortably in their own beds, secure in the knowledge that this was not the first wintry storm to blow over Devon, nor would it be the last, and that the walls of Heathers-leigh would not budge from the fierce blast.

When the galloping sound of horse and rider approached, none heard the sound amid the tumult. A minute or two later Sarah Min-sterly, who never slept well during a storm, jumped out of her bed with heart pounding in answer to the sound of the urgent fist upon the door.

With candle in hand, for she was not yet accustomed to the ease of flipping a switch to produce light, she made her way up the stairs to her master and mistress's quarters.

She knocked lightly on the door.

"Lady Jocelyn . . . Lady Jocelyn," she called out as loud as she dared while continuing to knock. She timidly opened the door the slightest crack. "Lady Jocelyn," she called inside.

A moment later Jocelyn was at the door in her dressing gown.

"I am so sorry, Lady Jocelyn," said Sarah, "but it's Mr. Osborne . . .

he's downstairs, mum—he's afraid for his wife."

Already Jocelyn was hurrying along the corridor and toward the stairs with the housekeeper at her side. With the benefit of light, she flew down the main staircase. She found their midnight caller at the door where Sarah had left him.

"Andrew . . ." she said as she hurried toward him.

"It's Sally, Lady Jocelyn," the frightened man replied. "It's her time, mum, but Doc Cecil's away from the village for two days."

"Is she—"

"Yes, my lady, that's what I'm telling you—'bout half an hour ago. I didn't know who else to turn to."

"You did just the right thing, Andrew," replied Jocelyn, wide awake and already making hurried plans. "You get back to her and make her as comfortable as you can. Build a fire and boil water. I'll be there in ten minutes."

"Thank you, mum!" replied Osborne, already disappearing back outside into the blackness.

"Sarah," said Jocelyn, turning to her housekeeper, "go wake Hector."

Sarah turned toward the servants' quarters while Jocelyn ran back upstairs, turned on the light, and woke her husband.

"Charles . . . Charles," she said, "Sally Osborne's baby is coming and Cecil's away. I need to get to her right away."

"A nurse's duties never stop," said Charles groggily as he sat up. Jocelyn was dressing as she spoke.

"Would you ride over and get Maggie and bring her to me?" Jocelyn was saying. "Sally's larger than I've ever seen. I have the feeling it might be twins, and I've never delivered twins on my own."

By now Charles was out of bed and looking for his trousers.

"How are you going?"

"I'll have Hector hitch the buggy. No, come to think of it," she said, pausing a moment, "you'll need the buggy for Maggie. I'll just ride over."

"Take the car," said Charles. "It will be faster."

"I've never driven at night."

"It's no different than daytime. Just turn on the headlights, and watch for rabbit and deer."

"All right, I suppose that's best." Already she was disappearing from the room.

"I'll be there as soon as I can!" called Charles after her.

✦✦✦

Forty minutes later, though it was approaching two o'clock in the morning, the small cottage of Andrew and Sally Osborne on the eastern edge of Milverscombe had turned into a beehive of activity. Thankfully the rain had not yet begun. All the newcomers, as well as Sally's husband, who had been out in the approaching storm, were dry.

Maggie and Jocelyn were busily engaged in the business which women of all eras have performed since time began—with boiling water and hot rags and soothing words, doing their best to ease new life into the world with as little of the inevitable pain as possible. Catharine, who had been awakened by the commotion and come with her father, and who shared her mother's gifts of ministry and compassion, tenderly sat at the head of the bed keeping Sally's forehead and cheeks cool with a moist cloth and dry towel. Maggie and Jocelyn held each of Sally's two hands, watching progress, applying new hotpacks as needed, with Jocelyn gently encouraging and giving Sally instructions alternately to breathe, then push, then relax.

In the only other room of the cottage, meanwhile, Charles kept the fire blazing and the water hot. For his purposes the kettle was required not for rags and towels, but for the brewing of strong tea to settle the nerves of poor Andrew, who paced the floor nervously awaiting the birth of his firstborn.

A knock on the door sounded. Charles went to answer it. There stood Agatha Blakeley who lived but two or three cottages away.

"I heard there was a birthin'," she said. "I came to see if I could help."

"Come in, come in, Mrs. Blakeley," said Charles, smiling warmly. "The women are in the bedroom with Sally now. They will be grateful for your company."

Returning his smile with more feeling than it would have been possible for her to express—for she owed her husband's sobriety and dawning interest in life to Sir Charles, not to mention her son's education—Rune Blakeley's wife hurried through the room to join the women.

The ordeal of the new mother and the anxious waiting of her man lasted about another hour.

Suddenly from the bedroom a cry was heard. Andrew Osborne leapt to his feet in a panic of eager terror. He began pacing in earnest, waiting for the door to open and expecting an announcement. When several minutes passed without news, he began to worry. He was almost on the verge of entering the sacred chamber when suddenly he heard another cry.

Jocelyn appeared at the door a minute or two later, ragged and perspiring, hair flowing off her head in every direction, but breathing obvious happy sighs of relief. A great smile was on her lips.

"Congratulations, Mr. Osborne," she said, "you are the father of *two* strapping young sons!"

A *whoop* of delight followed from Charles, who clapped his hands together, then offered a vigorous handshake to Andrew, who then slumped into the nearest chair with exhaustion.

Within minutes the wind died down, and soon the rain began to fall upon Devonshire. It was the happiest, most welcome rain any of the rejoicing gathered in the Osborne home remembered in years.

57

Milverscombe Parish

◆ ◆ ◆

The final strains of the morning's closing hymn reverberated up and around through the parish church of Milverscombe, and echoed out into the village and faintly into the surrounding countryside. The zeal of the voices creating the music was heightened, it is true, by the celebration on this day of the healthy new lives recently arrived in the village. Yet celebration of worship was heard nearly every week at this time, a vibrancy which resulted in the difficulty of finding an empty seat when services began.

It could hardly be said that everyone in the community attended the services of the Church of England every Sunday morning. Yet the spiritual life of the parish had certainly deepened and widened its impact in the years since Sir Charles and Lady Jocelyn had become such visible and active participants in it.

This husband and wife, the leading man and woman in the community, could not have been more loved by its people. The reason was simple. They sought to follow their Master's example. They had begun late in life to learn of spiritual things. But once begun, they learned quickly and well the practicalities embodied in chapters five, six, and seven of the Gospel of Matthew, because they sought to *do* them. And despite the personal trials which were part of that life, they sought always to spread that which they had been given.

They had allowed God to make of them that most unusual breed of man and woman to be found upon the earth—great in both the kingdom of God *and* in the kingdom of man. Usually the one form of greatness excludes the other. How precious must it be in the Lord's sight when that one form of greatness *includes* the other.

They were called Sir Charles and Lady Jocelyn by the common folk of the region who had for generations looked up to the lord of the manor with the reverence, respect, and esteem the people of Great Britain had for their landed nobility. But these two had become great in that eternal kingdom, not because of the *Sir* or the *Lady*, but because they had made themselves both servants and friends to every man, woman, and child within reach of their hands of ministration.

Such feeling could not have been in more evidence on this particular Sunday in February of the new year. For young Hadwin and Gildan Osborne had just been christened and, by permission, their godparents named Charles and Jocelyn Rutherford. If this man and wife had only three children of their own, one of whom at present disavowed that relationship, they were being blessed by a rapidly expanding family of godsons and goddaughters throughout the community.

Out the open doors of the church, past the busy hand of vicar Stuart Coleridge, streamed the good folk of Milverscombe. Now came the highlight of the week, standing in front of the church for a *second* hour visiting with everyone in attendance. Such custom had begun quietly, as Charles and Jocelyn had determined together that they would shake the hand of every villager each Sunday before leaving for home.

"Where can have originated the practice, Jocie," Charles had said one day two years earlier on their way home from Sunday worship, "of glumly shaking the hand of vicar or priest, then silently filing out of the church, glancing neither to the right nor the left at one's neighbors, and moving as if drawn by some invisible force immediately and irre-sistibly toward home."

Jocelyn had laughed at his portrayal, though the words could not have given a more accurate representation to the reality.

"What we are going to do next Sunday," Charles had continued, "is sit in the very back pew, and get outside before anyone has a chance to walk away. We shall be there waiting for them . . . and I am going to shake every man's and woman's hand and at least say 'hello' or 'the Lord bless you' before they scamper off!"

What had thus begun almost as a challenge, in the two years since had become a village tradition.

On most Sundays the crowded hubbub of happy faces clustered around Charles and Jocelyn at its core. Yet the informal time of visi-tation had drawn and bonded the whole community together in many unpredictable ways, such that a spirit of camaraderie existed even be-tween individuals and families who had scarcely known one another before.

Sunday mornings became the agency whereby news, friendship, in-vitations, and unity were spread throughout the village and commu-nity. No occasion for gossip was this, but for prayer requests and answers to prayer, and mostly simple friendship. Not a Sunday went by without numerous dinner and tea invitations circulating through-out the crowd. Thus was the fabric of the community woven into a beautiful garment of hospitality, service, and caring.

To miss "church and fellowship," as it came to be called, required almost a bedridden state. And even in such cases, when news of a sick-ness or injury was reported, half the congregation usually made their way to whatever home was involved, taking the fellowship of the day with them. Truly the life of the parish had burst out from the walls of the church building, to be carried by lips and hands and hearts throughout the paths and byways of the region.

"Jocie," Charles called amidst a sea of heads and boisterous con-versation and laughter, "I'm going out to Mudgley's for an hour or so. You take the car—I'll walk home later."

"That's good," she replied, jostling little Hadwin Osborne in her arms. "Maggie, Agatha, Catharine, and I, and a few of the others are going over to Sally's for a bit."

Next to her, the proud mother of the newborns held Gildan, the other half of the pair, while every woman of the community pushed and pressed and clustered about to see and poke at and babble a few unintelligible words into the two pink little faces.

"It looks like you may be joined by about fifty others," rejoined Charles, laughing. "Maybe I should take Andrew with me."

"I'd be sorely grateful!" now came the father's voice from somewhere amid the mob of women.

Everyone nearby laughed.

Gradually a portion of the throng began separating into two groups separated along lines of gender, twenty or more of the women beginning to move in the direction of the Osborne house. Jocelyn loaded her car with the new mother and Maggie and the two babies, while Catharine joined the other women on foot. An equal number of men followed Charles in the direction of Gresham Mudgley's sheep farm to observe the progress toward full electrical power in his barn, and what wonders might lie in store for their own homes one day. Some, meanwhile, continued to visit outside the church, while yet others began slowly making their way toward their own homes.

"What do you think, Sir Charles," said Mudgley as they went, "is the crisis past now that the Germans have withdrawn?"

That a simple man like Mudgley was both interested and knowledgeable concerning current affairs in the world was not so remarkable considering that the lord of the manor had been holding lectures at the Hall for several years for the men of the community, on topics ranging from politics and the scriptural duties of a husband, to technology and the Gospel of Mark. Indeed, Milverscombe parish was changing in more ways as a result of Charles and Jocelyn Rutherford's influence than the camaraderie evidenced after services on Sunday mornings. In addition to drawing the men of the region into more of a tight-knit social bond, the men's gatherings had greatly increased the general cultural and societal literacy of the entire community. At the same time, Jocelyn met with the men's wives in another portion of the Hall, where many things emerging out of her nurse's training were discussed, including sanitation and hygiene, infant care, as well as encouraging Maggie to add scriptural teaching about marriage for women. It could truthfully be said that the lower classes were being brought into the modern century at a rate easily four times more rapidly in and around Milverscombe than in the rest of the country. And the scriptural injunction for the older women to teach the younger made lives much easier and more fulfilling for the newer brides and mothers.

"I don't know, Gresham," answered Charles as they walked along, the other men crowding about to hear. "To tell you the truth, I fear the world has not seen the end of such displays of power. Eventually one of them could become dangerous."

"You sound worried, Sir Charles," said Rune Blakeley.

"I do not think it unlikely, Rune, that there will arise a crisis one day from which neither side will back down. Can you not envision Russia and Germany eye to eye, neither willing to admit it has made a mistake?"

A few of the men nodded.

"These are indeed worrisome times," Charles went on. "Yes, I think it is accurate to say that I am worried."

"But Germany and Russia, Sir Charles," said the man called Bloxham, "that's got nothing to do with us here."

"Don't be too sure, John," replied Charles. "I read in the *Times* just yesterday evening that the Germans are infiltrating more and more of the waters off our coastline."

A serious look passed across his face. When he spoke again, the men could sense that these were things he had been thinking about deeply. "It's a different world now, as I've been telling you," Charles said. "The nations of Europe are more interconnected. I think we may have to face the fact that change may be coming to all of us—change we cannot predict."

"Even here, Sir Charles—to Devonshire?"

"We may yet have to consider what is our duty as loyal Englishmen," nodded Charles. "Yes, even in Devonshire. Change may be coming to our lives sooner than we think. Many of our sons may be called upon to protect our waters and colonial interests. Remember how the wars in Africa and in the Crimea drew so much out of England fifty years ago. Our whole economy was affected and we lost many good men. I have the feeling this could be even worse."

A good many questions followed, such that by the time they reached their destination, the discussion continued for another forty minutes about the current state of the world rather than the electrical progress being made at the Mudgley farm.

58

Father and Son

$\mathcal{C}$harles and George were busy stringing wire from Heathersleigh to an electrical transfer station they were building on the outskirts of Milverscombe, from which plans were already being laid for bringing electricity to some of the local businesses and homes. Their own small generator could not light the town, but they hoped to bring in an electrical source large enough to do so.

The Electric Lighting Act of 1909 had established laws and regulations for local agencies desiring to supply electricity to rural areas. But little was being done yet in a widespread way for the connecting of transmission networks. The two Rutherfords, father and son, hoped successfully to demonstrate that such could be accomplished in a practical and cost-efficient manner.

Toward that end Charles had put up a large portion of Rutherford capital, with which he had purchased materials and supplies and hired as many men as he could afford and keep busy. Only a few months earlier he had succeeded in gaining a government grant of ten thousand pounds for the project to supplement his own resources. This had enabled him to bring even more men from the area into his plans.

Rune Blakeley and his nineteen-year-old son Stirling had already been working with Charles and George for about a year, both being instructed in the rudiments of electricity. Plans were also being made for Stirling to attend university the following fall, where he would follow George to Oxford.

As they worked together, father and son fell to talking about not only the future of Stirling Blakeley and electricity, but about their own.

"What do you want to do, George, my boy?" asked Charles. "What about *your* future? Surely you don't intend to string wire with me forever."

"Why not, Father? I'm perfectly happy here. I find electricity so fascinating, an opportunity on which to build a livelihood."

"But don't you have mountains you want to climb, vistas to cross, horizons to conquer—youthful ambition and all that?"

"This is exciting work, bringing electricity to Devonshire," replied George. "What we're doing will follow all through the country one day. And we're doing it here first. I almost feel like we're exploring something altogether new."

Charles laughed. "Right you are. I feel the same way."

"Maybe I'm not the ambitious sort. I hope it's not a weakness, Father, but for now I'm content with what I am doing."

"What about more education, as we've talked about once or twice before?"

"I want to work with you as much as I can. Being at university was fine. I love to study, and I might one day like to continue my education. If I could live here and go on with higher studies at the same time, that would be different."

"You really like it at home?"

"Are you kidding! I love Heathersleigh."

"You know that we're only too happy to help with the cost of further schooling?"

"I know that. You've told me so before. I appreciate your generosity, Father, but—"

George stopped.

"Are you trying to get rid of me, Father?" he said with a smile.

"You know better than that, George, my boy. Your mother and I love having you with us. Heathersleigh will always be your home. It's only that—"

Charles paused. A momentary look of pain crossed his face.

The smile from George's intended humor disappeared. He could tell that his father had been reminded of something that was none too pleasant. "What is it, Father?" he asked.

Charles sighed and glanced away. The wire went limp in his hands. George waited.

"I suppose ever since Amanda left," said Charles at length, "with all her talk of parental control and my forcing my ways and ideas on the rest of you . . . maybe I've been especially reluctant to do anything resembling that with you."

"Oh, Father, don't even *think* that about me!"

"I just want to make sure I give you every opportunity to get out on your own, to think for yourself—"

"Father, please," interrupted George. "I don't even want to hear you say such things. Amanda had it all mixed up. I love her, but she never saw things as they really were. Surely *you* realize that."

Charles nodded. "The accusations of a child go deep into a parent's heart," he sighed, "whether true or not. Her leaving has really shaken my confidence, not only as a father, but as a person. It has caused self-doubts to surface that I've never had to face before."

"I don't suppose I can really understand what it has been like for you, never having been a parent," replied George. "But when I think of some of the things Amanda said to you and Mother, it angers me even after all this time. You've not only given me every advantage, you've given me complete freedom to develop as my own person, to think independently, to personalize my faith without you forcing it on me. When I was at Cambridge I saw young men making all sorts of choices once they were away from home. And I knew what choices I wanted to make."

"You can honestly say that your beliefs are entirely *yours*?"

"Absolutely. That doesn't mean you haven't been influential in my life. You *have* been, in every way. You taught me, trained me, introduced me to the principles of God. You taught us about the Bible. You pointed me in certain directions, and gave me intellectual and spiritual shoves, I suppose you could say. But I had to keep the momentum going on my own, and decide on my own ultimate destinations."

"You didn't resent the changes I tried to make in our family when you were still a boy?"

"Resent them—what would give you an idea like that?"

"Amanda did."

"Amanda was ... well, Amanda was Amanda. I certainly did not share her resentments."

George paused momentarily.

"I've never tried to put it in words before," he said at length. "Perhaps I should have. Perhaps I should have expressed to you how I admired that you changed your perspective on the world, how I admired your withdrawal from Parliament."

"Why *admire* it?"

"It showed me you were willing to stand up for what you believed," replied George. "That influenced me in probably deeper ways than I may even have realized myself. I found myself wanting to be the same kind of man that you were. I saw you making decisions based on conviction and belief, not from pressures of society or peers."

"That's a pretty remarkable thing for a son to say to his father."

"You *forced* nothing on me," George went on. "You taught me to think, Father! What more priceless gift can a man pass on to a son? You can't let Amanda's distorted perspective keep you from seeing the whole picture. Don't let her leaving obscure your vision from how much Catharine and I love you and respect you. You were the best father I could imagine. Especially after being at University and talking with others. I met lots of people at Oxford. No one had a father like you. So many complained that they were being forced into one career or another or into one field of study or another, or in some other way pushed in directions against their will. I always found the saddest cases the young men being pressured into the ministry and priesthood by their fathers. The more people I met, the more unusual I realized my own upbringing was. You instructed us, taught us, trained us, but always encouraged us to think for ourselves, even occasionally to oppose what you thought, taking different sides of different arguments just so that we would look at some particular issue we were discussing from every possible angle. I still remember a discussion we had once riding through the woods when we were talking about changing times and the various classes of people in England. You intentionally kept changing sides in the discussion, always trying to get us to look at the question from different angles. You were *always* doing that," he added, laughing.

"I'm not sure I remember the incident as well as you seem to."

"You wouldn't, because you did that a thousand times. Every time we discussed something, you were shifting positions, asking questions, shining light on the topic in a slightly different way, just so that we *would* think for ourselves. Amanda's saying that you forced your views on us is just exactly upside down from what really happened. You cannot imagine, Father, how thankful I am for the way you instilled curiosity, thought, question, and mental vigor into me as I grew."

Long before George was through speaking, Charles' eyes were full of tears. Now suddenly he broke down altogether and began weeping freely. The wire he had been holding fell to the ground. Unconsciously he turned away.

It was silent for a minute or two as the tears continued to flow.

Softly Charles felt a hand on his shoulder. He turned. The next moment he found himself wrapped in the strong embrace of the son who was now the taller of the two. He returned George's embrace. They stood for another minute in silence.

Gradually the two men, who loved one another as only a true father and son can, parted.

"Thank you, George," said Charles in a quavering voice. "You cannot know what a burden you have lifted from my heart."

It was silent for several minutes. Gradually they resumed their work. After some time had passed George spoke again.

"I do have some things I would like to do, Father," he said. "You taught me to think, and you taught me well. I would like to travel someday, to see more of the world. I might even like to go to America. And maybe I will want to continue learning, possibly at the university again. I don't know. I appreciate the opportunities you've given me, both past and future. But what I was trying to say before is that I'm in no hurry. I have my whole life ahead of me. It's not every son who has the chance to work side by side with his father as I do. I want to make the most of it."

"Not many young people would say such a thing."

"Not many young people realize that their parents can also be their friends. I am beginning to realize it more now than when I was younger."

Again tears welled up in Charles' eyes. This was a day of healing he would not soon forget.

"Wherever I go, whatever I do, whatever I become," George went on, "I will always first of all be your son."

"You make me proud, George."

"No, Father, it is I who am proud to say such a thing. I am proud to be your son, not because you used to be an M.P. or because you are lord of the manor or a Knight Grand Commander, but because of who you are . . . the man you are. You helped make me who I am. And I am more grateful than I've probably ever told you before today."

In the distance they saw Rune and Stirling Blakeley riding up to join them.

59

The British Museum

With the coming of the year 1912, the suffragette movement stepped up to a new level of militancy. By now the movement was taking in over £30,000 annually and had thousands of loyal soldiers to carry out the Pankhursts' orders. That men were also involved was evidenced by the fact that Mr. Pethick-Lawrence had not only taken his wife's name, but was now actively involved helping to run the organization, and spent most of his own inheritance paying suffragette fines.

At a dinner held for some of their released prisoners in February, Mrs. Pankhurst laid out her agenda for the next month. "The argument of the broken windowpane," she said, "is the most valuable argument in modern politics."

Two weeks later, on the first of March, Christabel announced to Amanda at breakfast, "Today we're going to the British Museum—have you ever been, Amanda?"

"Once or twice when I was younger. What's the occasion?"

"To show the world we suffragettes are interested in culture too," added Emmeline.

Around midday, Mrs. Cobden-Sanderson, Mrs. Pethick-Lawrence, Mrs. Tuke, and a number of other women began to arrive, among them wild-eyed Emily Davison. By one o'clock fifteen women in all had gathered, women whom Amanda recognized as the most committed and radical of Mrs. Pankhurst's inner circle in the movement. She could hardly imagine *this* gathering of women coming together for a sedate and cultural visit to the British Museum! Some of them carried large bags. Most wore large winter coats.

At two o'clock they set out, in five separate automobiles. By this time Amanda realized they were *not* all going to the museum, for as they left the house, Emmeline said to all the others, "We shall meet back here for tea. Good luck. Be brave. Remember the cause!"

"What is going on, Sylvia?" she asked as they walked to the car.

"You will see, Amanda," replied Sylvia with a smile. "The whole world will know of our cause after today!"

Amanda did not reply. She began to grow restless as they rode into the heart of the city.

She saw none of the others until evening. As it turned out only Sylvia and Christabel, Amanda herself, and the two other women riding with them went to the British Museum. The other cars obviously had different destinations in the city . . . and other business.

The five of them entered the museum and began strolling about casually. Sylvia and Christabel appeared distracted, glancing around as they went, paying more attention to the guards, it seemed, than to the exhibits.

"There is a new display of porcelain up on the third floor," said Christabel.

"It's not open to the public," said one of the others. "It requires a special pass. Some of the pieces are priceless."

"I want to see it," she said determinedly. "We will get in." She turned and walked toward the stairs.

The others followed. Ten minutes later they approached the exhibit room. A uniformed guard stopped them.

"Pass, miss," he said to Christabel.

"We don't have a pass. But we very much wanted to see the exhibit."

"Can't let you in without a pass."

"This is the daughter of Sir Charles Rutherford," said Christabel, gently pulling Amanda forward. "She came today just to see the porcelain exhibit. Surely you would not deny Miss Rutherford the opportunity to see these treasures she has heard so much about."

"Is that true, miss?" said the guard to Amanda. "Are you who she says?"

"Yes . . . yes, I am."

"You don't sound too sure of yourself, miss."

"I am Amanda Rutherford," said Amanda. She tried to summon her courage, though she had a bad feeling about what was happening. The guard glanced her over, then nodded to himself.

"All right, then," he said. "Can't see there'd be any harm. You ladies enjoy yourselves."

He stood aside and let them through the wide doorway. Christabel led the way into the exhibit hall. Amanda and the others followed. Amanda detected a glint in Christabel's eye. Other things than ancient porcelain were apparently on her mind. A subtle motion of her head gave a signal to her sister and the others.

The five immediately spread out through the room.

As the strange tour of the porcelain exhibit was in progress, in another part of London little groups of women, all carrying oversized purses and bags, nonchalantly drifted along Piccadilly and the Haymarket. Suddenly out came hammers and stones. Within seconds the whole area resounded with the tinkling and smashing of broken plate-glass windows. No sooner had the police rushed to the scene and rounded up the expensively dressed hoodlums than a similar outbreak began against the glass in the Strand and along Regent Street. Once more arrests were made. Then along Bond Street and in Oxford Circus dozens more windows came falling in.

Still not divining her danger, Amanda strolled casually about the exhibit, looking at the unusual shapes and designs and the exquisitely colorfully painted displays.

Suddenly a crash sounded behind her.

Amanda's heart leapt into her throat. All at once the horror closed in upon her of what she had not wanted to allow herself to suspect. She turned to see Christabel standing beside an empty pedestal, whose former contents now lay on the tile floor shattered in a thousand pieces. Her eyes shone with the fire of triumph.

"Christabel, be careful!" cried Amanda. "We'll be—"

Whatever words had been on Amanda's lips never left them. The next instant another great shattering crash echoed from the opposite side of the room. Amanda spun around, this time to see Sylvia, face aglow, with the fragments of a large vase still bouncing and sliding across the floor where she had thrown it.

Suddenly the purpose of the entire affair was clear!

Throughout the room now echoed the shattering of a dozen priceless artifacts, mingled with the guard's angry voice as he ran into the room.

Shouts of "Votes for women!" and "End male domination!" sounded along with continuing wreckage.

"Stop," cried Amanda in horror. "Sylvia, Christabel—"

But her voice could not be heard in the pandemonium. "Suffrage for women!" screamed one of the women, amid continuous crashing and breakage.

Whistles filled the air. The pounding feet of more guards hurried to the scene.

At the opposite side of the room from the two Pankhursts, Amanda crept behind a huge oak display case and hid.

Three more guards now ran in, then two more. Lumbering across to join their colleague in his attempts to subdue the wild women, none saw Amanda where she had taken refuge.

Suddenly the way to the door was clear. She darted from behind the case and slipped noiselessly from the room.

She glanced back and forth. All the guards seemed to be in the exhibit hall. Shouting and yelling and arguing came from inside.

Suddenly she was running ... running down the corridor away from the scene, terrified that any moment she would hear sounds of pursuit behind her.

Amanda flew down the stairs, reaching the landing of the floor below.

She slowed and took in two or three deep breaths, then continued toward the right, then along the wide entryway into a hall of tapestries, where people were milling about.

A guard ... he must be looking at her! She walked slowly through the room, trying to blend in, pretending to be interested in the priceless hangings.

Her eye spotted a washroom.

She walked toward it, forcing herself to move slowly. A minute later she was safely inside. She moistened a handkerchief with cold water and wiped her face and neck, trying to compose herself.

But she couldn't delay. She had to get out and away before the search from upstairs involved the entire museum.

Amanda exited the washroom, glancing about, then left the room of tapestries. She found the next stairway, continued down to the ground floor, and made her way as quickly as she dared outside.

The cool afternoon breeze felt wonderful on her face!

She drew deep breaths into her lungs, trying to steady her nerves, then walked along the street away from the museum as quickly as seemed safe. When she was far enough that she dared, she broke into a run.

Amanda ran and ran until exhaustion compelled her to stop. In the distance she heard the sound of police sirens and whistles.

She stopped and turned into an alley. There she waited in the cool darkness of the shadow of the great brick building. The sounds grew louder. Three police cars screamed past. She waited several minutes more, then crept out of the shadows and made her way again along the sidewalk.

Turning several more corners, when she was certain she was out of danger, she began running again. She ran for several blocks, until she came to a small wooded park. She turned in, found a bench, and sat down.

At last fatigue overtook her. She would wait here awhile, until she could decide what to do. She had been involved with the Pankhursts for over three years now. Why she was so shocked by what had just happened she didn't know exactly. Was it because this went further than anything they had done till now?

Even as Amanda sat reflective and alone, throughout the West End of London the cost of the destruction was mounting into the multiple thousands of pounds. The well-known business establishments of Swears and Wells, Hope Brothers, Cooks, Swan and Edgar, Marshall and Snelgrove, and many others were assaulted by the hammers and stones of the suffragettes. Emmeline Pankhurst herself, with two of her associates, had managed to hurl four stones from a taxi through the prime minister's windows in Downing Street, before making a temporary getaway.

60

Argument

When Amanda Rutherford approached the Pankhurst house, still her home in London, a few minutes before six, it was with a cautious step. She had paid the cab and had been let out three blocks away in case trouble might have followed them from the museum. As she approached, however, she saw no sign of the police.

She walked inside. Most of the women from that morning had gathered again. All were obviously in high and exuberant spirits.

"Amanda!" she heard her name called out. "You're safe . . . Amanda dear, we were worried about you!—Amanda's back, everyone!"

A general hubbub broke out as the women clustered about, asking a dozen questions at once. It soon became clear that she was the only one to yet return from the museum. Briefly she recounted what had happened.

"A triumph!" exclaimed Emmeline. "After everything else—to disrupt the prized new exhibit at the British Museum. The day could not have gone off more perfectly according to our plans!"

"What plans?" said Amanda. "Do you mean there was *more*?"

"More! Why, Amanda dear, the whole city is in an uproar over what we have achieved today.—Is that not right, ladies?"

Laughter and general celebration broke out again.

"The police will no doubt be here for me within the hour," continued Mrs. Pankhurst. "Once again it seems I will join my daughters on a new hunger strike for the cause!"

She laughed, as if anticipating the experience as an adventure.

"Why—what did you do that will bring the police?" asked Amanda.

"Nothing more than set off a small bomb in the middle of Trafalgar Square," laughed Emmeline.

"You should have seen the people running for their lives!" cried one. "There were cries of being attacked by the Austrians!"

"And I only returned a few minutes ago from Downing Street," laughed Emmeline.

"You had a meeting with the prime minister?"

"Not exactly, my dear. I sent four rocks through his window!"

Now the rest of the women began boasting of their various exploits of the day throughout the many parts of the city.

"We cut the main telephone wires between the city and Chelsea!" cried Mrs. Tuke. "It will be weeks before the telephones are all working again!"

"We incited a crowd of women in Westminster to throw stones over the fence toward the Houses of Parliament!" added Mrs. Cobden-Sanderson. "Several windows were broken."

Amanda suddenly felt as though a nightmare was closing in around her. Was *this* what she had come to London for, breaking the law, violence, and bombs!

"But, Emmeline," Amanda cried, "this is all horrifying! What kind of people would do such things?"

"Amanda, dear—what do you mean? There is no other way to make people listen. Our speeches and leaflets have changed nothing. The Conciliation Bill is going nowhere. We must *force* them to stand up and take notice."

"But ... *bombs*, Emmeline! Destruction of property. These things are criminal. I thought we were trying to get the vote for the good of the country, for the good of society, for the good of *women*. What does it accomplish if we have to break the law to achieve that good?"

"We will do whatever it takes," rejoined Mrs. Pankhurst, suddenly sounding very determined. It was obvious she was not appreciative of Amanda's challenging words in front of her troops.

The room grew suddenly quiet. The other women listened to the argument between the renowned leader of the women's movement and one of her protégées, grown suddenly full of hostile questions.

"What about people? What about loyalty?" said Amanda. "Where do they come into your plans?"

"I have no idea what you mean, Amanda."

"Don't you understand—they lied. They used me."

"Who?"

"Sylvia and Christabel."

"Men have been using us for centuries, Amanda. It is time the women of the world redressed that."

"But I am not a man. I thought we were friends. They *used* me and lied to the guard at the museum."

"Whatever is necessary for the cause, that we will do."

"I did not intend to be a pawn in your game!" shouted Amanda.

"It is no game, Amanda. It is a cause."

"I have been willing to help. But you left me in the dark, and then just used my name."

"It is your cause as well as ours."

"Suddenly I'm not so sure it is!"

Frustrated, angry, confused, Amanda turned and ran from the house, slamming the door behind her.

61

Confusion

◆ ◆ ◆

*D*own the sidewalk and away from the Pankhursts Amanda ran, heedless of how disheveled she looked, heedless of direction, heedless even of the hot tears running down her face.

How could everything have gone wrong so suddenly? It was a nightmare come true.

Where she ran, where her steps took her over the next hour, she could never recall. She vaguely remembered taking a cab to Cousin Martha's house, thinking to seek refuge there. But as she approached the gate, something checked her steps. Somehow she could not endure the humiliation of facing them. Perhaps it was the realization that word of her predicament could not help but get back to her parents.

She turned and walked away, and again walked and walked, where she did not know. It was getting late, but she was not paying attention to time.

When next she came to herself, she found herself standing in front of the *Daily Mail* building. Whether she had arrived on foot or had hired a cab, she did not know. She stood several moments staring up at the imposing structure, then walked into the building. By now she did not care what people thought. Let them stare. She had nowhere else to go.

She asked the receptionist if Mr. Halifax was still here at the late hour. The woman replied that she thought he was, then pointed Amanda toward the stairs where, up two flights, she would find the world editorial department.

The moment Halifax saw her he knew something was seriously wrong. Amanda had determined to maintain her composure and not cry, but he could see trouble written over every inch of her face. Quickly he excused himself from conversation and led Amanda to a room where they could be alone.

"Amanda, what in the world has happened?" he said the moment the door was closed. He gestured toward a chair. "You haven't been involved in what's been going on all over London?"

Amanda nodded as she sat down.

Ramsay sighed, and now sat down opposite her with serious expression.

Amanda took a breath and tried to be stoic. "I'm sorry to bother you here, Ramsay," she said, "but . . . but I didn't know where to turn."

"No trouble, Amanda," replied Ramsay. "You should have come to me. Tell me what happened."

Briefly she recounted the day's events at the museum, followed by her blow-up with Mrs. Pankhurst.

The journalist took the information in with interest. His expression grew yet more somber.

"What are you going to do?" he asked.

"I don't know. I hardly think I will be welcome at the Pankhursts again. Although they will probably all be in jail before tonight, if what Mrs. Pankhurst said is true."

"Believe me, it is true," replied Halifax. "The whole city's abuzz. Our tomorrow's edition will have the Pankhursts and their dirty tricks all over the front page. That's why everyone's here so late. The police are looking for her now. They're reported to have Sylvia and Christabel in custody, but I've heard nothing to confirm it."

"I suppose I could go back to the house," said Amanda. "I have a key, and who knows, maybe by now there is no one there but a servant or two."

The journalist was silent another moment, thinking to himself.

"From what you've told me," he said at length, "you may not be safe there. Your name has come up a time or two around here today, although I let on nothing."

"*Come up*—how do you mean?" said Amanda.

"The police are looking for you too. That's big news that the daughter of Sir Charles Rutherford was involved in the museum incident, and was the only one to escape without apprehension."

"Oh, Ramsay, what am I going to do!"

"I thought jail was an honor for you suffragettes."

"The rest may think it so, but I've about had my fill of jail and the whole movement altogether. I'm frightened, Ramsay. What they did today was the worst by far."

"That's why the news is full of it. Your colleagues upped the stakes considerably today."

"What am I going to do?"

Again he thought.

"Hmm ... it's a risk," he said, "but I think she'll go along. It will give us overnight to think of what should be done."

"Go along—who?"

"You go back downstairs, Amanda," he said. "I just need to wrap something up here briefly. I'll meet you down on the street. I'm taking you to my mother's for the night."

62

What to Do

◆◆◆

It was not until she arrived at the home of Ramsay's mother that Amanda began to grow conscious of her appearance. Mrs. Halifax and Mrs. Thorndike were seated in the drawing room. They rose when the two young people entered.

Ramsay explained briefly what had happened, that Amanda had had a falling out with the Pankhursts and needed a place to stay for the night.

"Heavens ... such a frightful business," said Mrs. Thorndike, shocked to learn that Amanda was involved with such people as the Pankhursts.

"Don't you worry about a thing," said Mrs. Halifax. "We will have you bathed and in a fresh dress, and you will feel much better before you know it."

Amanda was not inclined to argue. She was too exhausted mentally and physically. After what she had been through today, she was willing to do whatever anyone told her.

"Amanda," said Ramsay, "I'm going to go back to the office, then maybe down to the police station. I want to see if I can find out anything."

He saw the look of alarm that passed across Amanda's face.

"Don't worry," he went on quickly. "I won't tell anyone you're with me. But we have to be careful. I want to learn how serious is the situation. It may be that you will have to turn yourself in tomorrow."

"You cannot be serious, Ramsay," interposed his mother.

"I simply want to know where things stand," he replied. "We cannot turn your house into a refuge for suffragette fugitives, or the police would be around here just like they are the Pankhurst place."

Mrs. Halifax nodded soberly. She knew the necessity for avoiding such a development even better than her son.

"Don't worry," Ramsay went on, "I have no intention of placing Amanda in harm. We simply must be prudent."

He turned and left the house. The moment he was gone, the two ladies busied themselves getting Amanda bathed, dressed, and fed.

As the evening progressed and dusk began to fall, Amanda could not prevent misgivings creeping in. She had never noticed it before now, but being in Mrs. Halifax's home made her realize that she was a little afraid of Ramsay's mother.

This arrangement wasn't really proper anyway, staying in the home of an unmarried man. It would be far more seemly to go to Cousin Martha's.

And yet . . . she might be in trouble with the police—serious trouble. And Ramsay was the only one who could help her. She *had* to stay here.

What am I worried about? she said to herself. She could trust Ramsay. He would let no danger come to her.

Ramsay returned at half past nine. The four sat down at the table, and as he partook of a modest tea, Ramsay gave his report.

"The situation is serious, as I suspected," he said. "Besides the incident at the museum and the bomb at Trafalgar Square, there were telephone lines cut, hundreds of windows broken in the business districts, and tar put in the mailboxes of many M.P.s. It is clear to the police that Mrs. Pankhurst has changed her tactics."

"What about Amanda—is she in danger?" asked Mrs. Thorndike.

"To a degree—yes," replied Ramsay. "The guard at the museum reported what happened and that he let the women into the exhibit on the basis of Miss Rutherford's request. They *are* looking for Amanda. But it has not yet come to the point of a warrant being issued for her arrest. The bomb at Trafalgar is more serious, though no one was injured. The fact that they presently have Mrs. Pankhurst in custody makes the police less inclined to press the matter with Amanda."

"What about the others?" asked Amanda.

"Somehow Christabel and Sylvia managed to slip out of the grasp of the police," replied Ramsay. "I don't know how. A warrant has been issued for Christabel. Meanwhile, a raid took place at the Pankhurst home two hours ago. Mrs. Pankhurst, Mrs. Tuke, and both Mr. and Mrs. Pethick-Lawrence are now behind bars in Cannon Row police station."

"What am I going to do, Ramsay?" asked Amanda. "I don't want to go to jail."

"I doubt it will come to that," replied Ramsay.

He paused a moment and sipped his tea.

"As I was driving back," he said, "I had an idea. But let me ask you a question first, Amanda—what is your future with the Pankhursts?"

"I don't know," answered Amanda with a forlorn expression.

"How long do you anticipate continuing to be part of the suffragette movement?"

"Everything happened so fast today that I've hardly had the chance to think about it."

"Do you plan to return to live with the Pankhursts?"

"After what I said today, I am not sure I would be welcome. Besides, didn't you say Emmeline was in jail?"

"At present. And Christabel and Sylvia in hiding."

"Whatever I decide, it would seem that after today, everything is bound to change."

"Do you *want* to go back?" asked Ramsay.

"I don't know," sighed Amanda. The truth of the matter was that she didn't know what else she could do. Her bank account had dwindled to something less than three hundred pounds, which would not be enough to support herself for more than another year, if that. She might be able to afford a flat of her own, but then what would she do a year from now? If only she hadn't spent her money so foolishly!

Mrs. Halifax astutely observed the expression on Amanda's face. "Is it a matter of finances?" she asked.

"I'm afraid that is partially the case," replied Amanda, nodding her head.

"Amanda dear—worry yourself no more about it," she said. "We have plenty of room in this huge old house since my husband died. It is just the three of us—Ramsay, Mrs. Thorndike, and myself, along with two servants. You will stay with us as long as you like."

"I couldn't impose—" began Amanda.

"Nonsense, dear. The matter is settled."

"What do you think, Amanda?" said Ramsay. "If you indeed are through with the Pankhursts after today, I could arrange to have your things picked up. Or, as you said earlier, you have a key and you could return for them."

"I will think about it tomorrow," sighed Amanda. "What about the police?"

"I may have an idea that will help," answered Ramsay. "I will write an article. We will get it into day after tomorrow's edition—an exclusive interview with Amanda Rutherford about the incident at the British Museum."

"What!" exclaimed Amanda.

"Don't you see—it would give you a chance to explain publicly what happened, and, if you like, say that the incident caused a falling out between you and Mrs. Pankhurst and that you are leaving the movement. That is why I asked what your plans were."

Amanda thoughtfully took in his words. Such a step could not help but affect many things about her future.

"Such an interview would prejudice the police in your favor. I do not think they would press the matter further. You could make a public apology for your complicity in the affair, and even go so far as to turn yourself in. I realize the risk such a course would involve. But at this stage, the authorities would gain so much positive publicity by having a defector, as it were, speak out against the movement, I am certain they would not arrest you."

It fell silent around the table. Amanda was the first to break it.

"It's so ironic . . ." she said in a softly melancholy tone, then paused and smiled a sad smile. "I came to London thinking that I was joining a great cause. For as long as I can remember I wanted to make a difference in the world. I wanted to have an impact. I wanted my life to count for something of significance. I was so angry with my father when he resigned from the House of Commons. I thought that he was reneging on his duty to change the world for good. I determined that I would never shirk that responsibility to help my fellow man."

As she spoke, Mrs. Halifax listened with keener interest than she allowed her Teutonic features to reveal. The wheels of her mind were turning over many possibilities which she had only been considering vaguely until then. For the time being, however, she would keep her own counsel and see what developed.

"And now here I am," Amanda continued, "trying to figure out a way to keep from being arrested. And for what? For a cause that sets bombs and cuts telephone wires and destroys priceless antiques. What has it all been for? How do such things make the world a better place? What good has it done anyone?"

Amanda laughed lightly. But there was no joy in her voice, only the bitter realization that her life was not turning out as she had hoped.

"Your Mrs. Pankhurst would say that such means are justifiable if the end is gained," suggested Ramsay.

"I might have said the same thing two years ago," rejoined Amanda. "But their tactics have changed since then." She smiled ironically. "Perhaps I have changed too," she added.

Again it was silent, this time for several minutes.

"Well, what do you say?" said Ramsay at length.

"About what?" asked Amanda.

"The interview. Shall I write the story, saying that you were duped and knew nothing of their plans to damage the exhibit at the museum, and expressing your horror at what happened?"

Amanda sighed deeply.

"Yes, write the story. I will consent to an interview for your paper. And then tomorrow—that is, Mrs. Halifax," she added, turning to Ramsay's mother, "—if you were serious with your offer—"

"Indeed I was, dear."

"—then tomorrow I shall return to the Pankhurst home and gather up my things."

63

New Shock

After a restless night, Amanda returned to the Pankhursts' not knowing what to expect when she arrived. Ramsay drove her once or twice past the house, surveying the neighborhood for police activity. As there seemed to be none, he stopped to let her out.

"If anything comes up," he said, "if there is any trouble or if you need help, call me at the paper." He reached across the seat and took her hand, giving it a reassuring squeeze. "Don't worry about a thing," said Ramsay. "Remember what I told you before—I'll take care of you."

Amanda nodded and got out.

"In the meantime, I'll get started on the article," added Ramsay, then smiled and drove off.

Amanda watched the car disappear. She turned and walked nervously toward the house she had called home for three years, unaware that the newspaper article destined dramatically to change her future was not the one Ramsay planned to write about her, but rather the one planted about *him* which had made its appearance in the *Sun* only a few hours earlier.

At least Emmeline wouldn't be home, thought Amanda as she approached. Maybe no one would be here who had witnessed her outburst yesterday evening.

Amanda let herself cautiously in through the front door, then glanced about. The house was quiet. There was no sign even of the housekeeper. She walked through the entry hallway and began to ascend the stairs to her room.

"Amanda!" she heard behind her.

Startled, she nearly jumped out of her skin. Amanda spun around to see Sylvia entering from the drawing room, a newspaper in her hand.

"I didn't know what had become of you! I never saw you after the museum."

"I slipped out when the guards came in," said Amanda. "But how did you and Christabel—"

"There were two carloads of women waiting outside. As soon as they saw our trouble, they distracted the guards with a volley of stones at the museum windows. We ran for it, and managed to get out of sight before the police arrived. But now Mother's in jail."

"I heard. And Christabel?"

"She is hiding at a friend's house. I decided to sneak home to see if it was safe. I arrived in the middle of the night. The place was deserted, except for Edna, who's upstairs in her room."

"Everyone must have thought the police would be watching. That's what I assumed. I was afraid to come back too."

"We've got to get in touch with everyone," said Sylvia. "We have a big demonstration planned for Parliament Square the day after tomorrow."

"More . . . after what happened yesterday!"

"We have to seize the initiative."

"Well I am here to pick up my things. I just don't know if I can be part of it anymore."

"Amanda, what are you saying?"

"I don't want to get into it now, Sylvia," replied Amanda. "I already had an argument with your mother last night. I just need some time to think."

A peculiar expression came over Sylvia's face, but she seemed to realize it would not be a good time to press their differences.

"I assume your being upset has something to do with this," she said, holding up the newspaper.

Amanda stared back at her with a blank expression.

"The article about Ramsay Halifax."

Momentarily confused, Amanda did not stop to consider the impossibility of it so soon, but replied, "You mean *by* Ramsay Halifax . . . about me?"

"It's got nothing to do with *you*—it's an article about Ramsay Halifax. And none too favorable."

"I don't know what you're talking about," said Amanda.

"I was looking for the news about us and yesterday's events. Then I saw this about your friend. It insinuates that he might be a spy."

"What! That's the most absurd—"

Already Amanda had grabbed the newspaper from Sylvia's hand and had begun to read the account under the heading: MAIL REPORTER IMPLICATED IN PHONY MOROCCAN STORY.

She had only read half the article when she was out the door, all thought of retrieving her belongings and moving in to the Halifax home instantly gone.

64
Denial

───── ♦♦♦ ─────

*A*manda hurried up to Ramsay's office in the *Daily Mail* building, this time not pausing for an interview with the receptionist. Her confusion and disbelief had hardly cooled during the ten-minute cab ride.

Ramsay, who had only been shown a copy of the libelous account not more than ten minutes earlier, was still reeling from the blow when he saw Amanda, red-faced, walking toward him. That she carried in her hand a crumpled copy of the same issue which had been handed to him indicated clearly enough what was on her mind.

Before she managed to say anything, he quickly ushered her into one of the small editorial offices and closed the door behind them.

"What is this all about!" she demanded, nearly throwing the paper in his face.

"Amanda, believe me," he replied, "I know as little about it as you do. I only saw it myself a few minutes ago."

"Falsified stories . . . that you were seen on the *Panther*, that you—"

Amanda stopped and glanced away. *That* part of the article was too painful.

"It's not true, Amanda," said Ramsay softly.

Amanda turned back toward him, determined not to cry.

"I thought we—" she began, but she could not bring herself to say it.

"We do, Amanda—we have something very special. Please believe me, I know nothing about her."

"But it says you and she . . . that you were seen . . ."

Ramsay looked down at the floor, shaking his head. "It was as painful for me to read as it was for you, Amanda. My first thought was for you—how it would hurt you if you saw it, and then for my mother, and what pain this would cause her as well."

A heavy silence filled the small room.

"Oh, Ramsay," Amanda exclaimed at length, "I just don't know what to think. What good will your article be able to do me now? Who will believe it if you say I am innocent? I might as well march down to Cannon Row and put the handcuffs on myself!"

Ramsay sensed from her tone that the moment had arrived when her fury could be turned to sympathy.

"Aren't you being just a little selfish, Amanda," he said. "I could go to jail too—and not for a day or two, but for treason, for the rest of my life . . . that is if I'm not shot! Not to mention the fact that I will be fired before today is out and my career ruined unless I am able to disprove this ridiculous report. They accuse me of being a spy."

His words had a calming, even a sobering effect on Amanda. She glanced away.

"Amanda, I tell you," Ramsay went on, "not a word of this is true."

"Where did it come from, then?" she asked. "Allegations like this don't just appear out of thin air."

"I haven't an idea. Go out there on the floor," he said, gesturing toward the door, "and ask the men I work with. We all just found out about it a few minutes ago. We're on it already, trying to find where it originated. There's not a grain of truth in it."

"What about the woman?"

"I tell you, Amanda, there was no such incident. I haven't the slightest idea who they're talking about."

"*Were* you in Morocco?"

Ramsay nodded. "You remember, when I was away last October—right after the weekend up in Cambridge. My editor sent me down to Africa to report on the situation, and I filed a story which ran in November. Believe me, I had nothing to do with the Germans there . . . or any woman named Adriane Grünsfeld."

Amanda shook her head in frustration.

"I just don't know what to believe."

Ramsay approached to embrace her. Amanda stiffened slightly, then backed away. She could not so easily forget the words about Ramsay she had read, true or not. She didn't want his arms around her right now.

She turned and left the office. As she walked through the editorial room, she was aware of every eye upon her. The walls of the room were not so thick as to prevent a good deal of the conversation from reaching the ears of Ramsay's colleagues. She half expected to hear footsteps behind her and for Ramsay's voice to make one final appeal. But no sound attempted to stop her.

A few minutes later she was back on the street, tears now flowing in earnest.

Why hadn't Ramsay's repeated denials helped? She was confused and didn't know what to do.

The police were probably looking for her. She had burned her bridges with the Pankhursts. Ramsay was her only hope. Yet suddenly she didn't know whether or not she could trust him.

What could she do ... where could she go?

65

Geoffrey

 ⊙he house on Curzon Street had lost much of its luster in Amanda's eyes during the winter months since the end of last year's season. There had been no parties, no balls, no new dresses, no invitations. Only a few months had passed. But all that now seemed so long ago.

She was in trouble and she knew it. At a time like this, the mere fact of familial relation was somehow comforting. Who else did she have to turn to other than Cousin Martha?

She walked up the steps onto the porch and rang the bell. A moment or two later the housekeeper opened it.

"Hello, Louisa," said Amanda.

"Come in, Miss Amanda," said Louisa, then turned and disappeared upstairs. Amanda walked into the nearby drawing room to wait, as she had many times before.

Two or three minutes later Geoffrey appeared. Amanda heard his step and turned around in surprise.

"Is your mother here?" she asked.

"I'm sorry, she's not," replied Geoffrey with a smile. His tone was pleasant, but something about his expression reminded Amanda of the old Geoffrey.

"I need to talk to her," she said.

"You may talk to me."

"Thank you, Geoffrey, but I am in some trouble and I really need to talk to her."

"*Trouble?*" he repeated with significance, drawing out the word.

"Yes, trouble," Amanda returned with a slight edge to her voice.

"Perhaps *I* could help," he said, moving closer and reaching out toward her.

"Get away, Geoffrey!" she snapped, taking a step back. "I don't need *that* kind of help."

"What kind, then?"

"Oh, never mind! When is your mother going to be back?"

"I really couldn't say. How do you know I couldn't help, Amanda?" he said. "You never give me a chance. I'm not really such a bad person."

Amanda glanced away. His voice reminded her of when he used to whine as a boy.

"Your trouble, I take it," Geoffrey continued, an annoying tone creeping into his voice that indicated he was in on some secret, "might have something to do with your friend Halifax?"

"What do *you* know about Ramsay Halifax?" returned Amanda.

"Just that he is in a lot of hot water at the minute. As I hear it, his arrest might not be far away."

"His arrest—don't be ridiculous. The story in the *Sun* is pure fiction. It is being investigated."

"That's not the way I hear it."

Amanda looked up, suddenly alert to the implication of his statement. She tried to find his eyes.

"*What* have you heard, Geoffrey?" she asked pointedly.

"Oh ... nothing," he replied evasively, "—just what the paper reported, that's all." Geoffrey realized he had been careless.

But Amanda detected something more in his voice. She might not like her second cousin, but she *knew* him. And right now she was sure he knew more than he was telling.

"What do you know, Geoffrey?" she demanded.

"Nothing, I tell you!"

"I don't believe it. You know something more about this than you're letting on."

"No I don't," he retorted. "Even if I did, I wouldn't tell you."

Forgetting that she had come here to seek refuge, Amanda was quickly getting angry. She sighed and glanced briefly away. Geoffrey always had been capable of arousing the most profound irritation within her. Now he was at it again!

Misreading her hesitation as a sign she was weakening, again Geoffrey stepped forward. This time he attempted to take her in his arms.

"Geoffrey, what are you doing!" cried Amanda, half stepping, half leaping backward as if she had touched a snake.

"Just trying to comfort you in your time of distress." He did his best to make his voice sound smooth and suave, as he perceived was called for by the situation. He succeeded, however, only in making himself seem all the more oily and conniving.

"Comfort me!" repeated Amanda, almost laughing. "Since when have you ever tried to comfort me?"

"I have always cared about you, Amanda. Why won't you let me help you?"

"Why should I?"

"Because . . . because we are—"

"Because we are *what*, Geoffrey?" Even as the words came out of her mouth, Amanda wasn't sure she wanted to hear the answer.

"Can't you let me offer you a moment's consolation—"

Geoffrey paused and removed something from his pocket.

"—for old times' sake, Amanda dear," he said, now jingling a small set of old-fashioned keys in front of her.

Amanda's eyes narrowed as she gazed forward. Suddenly recognition dawned.

"Those are the keys from the tower room at Heathersleigh!" she cried. "How did *you* get them?"

"Don't you remember the day a long time ago when a very naughty little girl locked her cousin in that tower?"

"I can't believe . . . do you mean—"

Amanda could hardly get the words out for her renewed rage at her weasel of a cousin. Whatever Geoffrey's motives for showing her the keys at this precise moment, if he thought doing so would win her sympathy or endear her affections, he was seriously mistaken.

"No wonder they've been missing all these years," she cried. "Give them back, Geoffrey! They're mine!"

She reached forward. But Geoffrey was too quick for her and jumped back. A look of glee spread over his face. Quickly he repocketed the keys.

"We'll see whose they are in the end!"

"Give them to me!"

"I might consider doing so . . . *after* you and I are married."

"Ugh!" Amanda shrieked. "That's disgusting. Never!"

"You think you'll do better?"

"*Anything* would be better!"

"Ha—no one would marry you!"

Amanda turned and ran from the room. Behind her she could hear Geoffrey's voice laughing. The mischievous boy had briefly gained the upper hand over the wealthy financier, the debonair suitor, and as he viewed himself, the handsome winner of women's hearts.

As soon as Amanda was out the front door, however, her cousin calmed. The smirk on his face disappeared. He stole to the window and probed at the edge of the curtain with his fingers, opening a crack to peep at her as she walked down the street away from the house and out of sight.

It was a good thing his father wasn't home, Geoffrey reflected, or he would be furious. He may have just loused the whole thing up.

Well, one thing was certain. Amanda would never tell anyone what had just happened. And he still had the keys. And now that Halifax had shown himself the cad Geoffrey had always known him to be, Amanda was certain to come to her senses eventually.

Maybe it wouldn't turn out so bad after all.

Having no idea that Geoffrey's eyes were glued on her back, before Amanda was half a block down Curzon Street her eyes burned with tears. What was happening to her? It seemed that in just a few hours all her life had crumbled at her feet.

What should she do? Now she really had no place to go! In a few short hours she had succeeded in alienating herself from every possible source of refuge.

66
Happy Day

$\mathcal{A}$s Amanda tearfully wandered along Curzon Street, across Park Lane and into Hyde Park, confused, angry, filled with a hopelessness and despair she had never before felt in her life, her mother and sister were busily engaged in the kitchen of Heathersleigh Hall with plans that would culminate late that same afternoon. It was Charles' fifty-third birthday. The Blakeleys and McFees, and, they hoped, Timothy Diggorsfeld, would be on hand for a magnificent high tea scheduled for five o'clock.

At the moment Sarah Minsterly was vigorously sifting flour and sugar in preparation for fruit scones, Catharine was checking what promised to be a delectable mint pork loin roast, which had been in the oven for some time, while Jocelyn beat up the eggs for a lemon pound cake. The other two servant girls were occupied cleaning up-stairs and in the dining room. The guest of honor himself, who was not about to take a day off from the labors he loved for something so insignificant as his own birthday, was at present occupied with George, Rune, and Stirling on the other side of Milverscombe attempting to repair a malfunctioning generator, which was a key component of their local electrical network.

"George and Father are going to love this!" said Catharine. "I can't wait to see their faces light up."

"There's nothing so much fun," remarked Jocelyn, "as cooking for hungry men who enjoy their food."

"I just hope no mice show their heads," laughed Sarah.

"Why would you think that?" asked Catharine.

"Don't you remember when the three mice came scampering out of the meat grinder?" said Jocelyn. "No . . . of course you don't remember! What am I thinking—you were only three at the time."

"Tell me about it, Mother."

Jocelyn did so, and a great deal of laughter followed.

"I haven't made paté since!"

Within an hour, the whole west wing of the house had begun to fill with the pleasant and festive aromas of baking. Sarah left to supervise Kate and Enid at their duties, then to attend to the day's washing. Mother and daughter were left alone in the kitchen to finish up the preliminaries for that afternoon.

"What would you think, Mother," said Catharine as she worked, "if I was to say I would like to go to university?"

"I would say . . . wonderful! My, but you are becoming a modernist, just like your sister."

"Not a modernist, Mother. But learning is one of the most valuable things in life. It seems I ought to pursue it if I have the opportunity. Maybe I am getting a late start, but I'm coming to enjoy learning and reading as never before. I might even write a book someday."

"Ambitious too! But isn't this from out of the blue?"

"I've been thinking about it for a year or two. Maybe I am a little like Amanda in wanting to do something permanent and significant. And I love books and learning."

"University is still a man's institution. Have you thought of the difficulties you would face?"

"Oxford has four women's colleges. Times are changing."

"Which college would be your preference?"

"Probably Somerville or Lady Margaret Hall."

"Do you have any *other* big dreams you haven't told me about?" laughed Jocelyn.

"Only one—to sail around the world."

"What!" exclaimed her mother. "I can't believe it. Now that *is* ambitious. According to the paper there are still tickets left for that huge new ship that is sailing from Southampton to New York next month. That would be a good start."

"The *Titanic*—no, that's too big," replied Catharine. "I read about it too—more than two thousand passengers. I was thinking of something much smaller and more exciting."

"Well, I'm not certain of *that*, but let's at least talk to your father about educational possibilities. I'm sure he will be delighted."

"Do you really think so?"

"Of course. There's nothing that gives him more pleasure than helping another person reach his dreams and potential. That's one of your father's greatest ambitions in life."

"Wouldn't Amanda say he *kept* her from her potential?"

"She might," replied Jocelyn. "But her perceptions were backwards. We wanted ... we *still* want the best for her, and for her to reach her potential and achieve her dreams, just as we do for you and George. But that doesn't mean we support *selfish* dreams and ambitions, which Amanda's were at the time she left. A parent isn't supposed to give a child anything and everything he wants, but those things that genuinely contribute to the reaching of the potential that God has in mind for him."

"Do you think university might be that for me?"

"It well could. We will pray, and talk to your father, and then see in what direction the Lord leads. But I have to admit ... I would miss you!"

"I would be back," replied Catharine, setting down the spoon, wiping her hands on the apron tied around her waist, then giving Jocelyn a warm daughterly embrace.

"Promise?"

"I promise," said Catharine, returning to her work.

"You might go away and fall in love and that will be the last we shall ever see of you."

Catharine laughed. "That will never happen," she said. "Remember what I told Hubert Powell. And even if I do someday fall in love, I will bring my husband back *here* to live."

Now her mother laughed. "It doesn't work that way."

"Otherwise I won't get married at all."

"It sounds like *you* ought to be the suffragette. Modern, ambitious ... and stubborn!"

"Mother!"

"I'm only teasing. I think your idea sounds delightful. Whether you will ever find a man to go along, now that is another matter! But how does coming back here to live fit in with sailing around the world?"

"This will always be *home*—but that doesn't mean I can't have adventures too!"

Mother and daughter continued to talk and laugh as they worked side by side for the rest of the morning.

George and Charles arrived back about three o'clock to clean up and relax before their guests arrived. Rune and Agatha Blakeley, along with their son Stirling, drove up to the Hall in their carriage about twenty minutes before five.

"Look who we found at the station," said Rune as they greeted Jocelyn at the door.

"Timo—" Jocelyn began to exclaim.

"Shh!" interposed Diggorsfeld, quickly bringing his finger to his lips. "I want to surprise Charles! Where is he?"

"Up in his study," replied Jocelyn.

Diggorsfeld hurried inside and up the stairs on tiptoe. Two minutes later a great shout of surprise erupted overhead in Charles' voice, and they all knew the minister's surprise had been successful.

Bobby and Maggie arrived at the front door ten minutes after that, Bobby puffing heartily from the walk through the wood and across the fields.

"I'm gettin' a mite old for this sort o' thing, Lady Jocelyn," he sighed, his red face and bald head perspiring freely. He sat down briefly in a nearby chair.

"I told you we would have been happy to fetch you in the buggy."

"Ay, but I thought the wee walk would do me good," replied Bobby, coughing once or twice and still struggling to catch his breath. "I haven't been feelin' quite me same spry self lately, and I was determined t' get some good o' the fresh air and the exercise."

"*Determined!*" repeated Maggie. "*Stubborn* is more like what he is. Bobby, I keep telling you, we're old folks now, and we've got to let the young ones give us a helping hand now and then."

"*Young ones* ... did I hear someone talking about me?" laughed Charles, now descending the stairs to welcome the new arrivals, his minister friend a few steps behind. "I'm fifty-three today, and are you still calling me young!"

"You will always be young in our eyes, Sir Charles," said Maggie.

"I don't suppose that can be helped.—But come in and join the others."

Fifteen minutes later, the Blakeleys, the McFees, the Rutherfords less one, Timothy Diggorsfeld, along with Sarah, Hector, Kate, and Enid all sat around the large oak table in Heathersleigh's formal dining room.

Ever since their conversion, both master and mistress of Heathersleigh Hall had been training themselves to see things differently than was their custom before the divine imperative of childship had been infused into them. This self-training had by no means always been easy or pleasant, for it involved death to their own right of self-rule. One principle Charles had learned, however, was that the last shall be first and the first last, and that he who would be great must be last of all and servant of all. Moreover, Charles Rutherford had discovered the daily joy of living in the midst of this great truth. This being Charles' birthday, therefore, he would not be waited on by servant, wife, or daughter, but would *himself* serve family and guests. He had just finished setting everyone's plates before them, pouring each a small glass of birthday wine, and then taken his own seat at the head of the table.

"Do ye mind, Master Charles," said Bobby, "if an old Irishman offers a wee toast in honor of his host?"

Charles roared with laughter.

"No, Bobby," he answered. "I heartily give my consent, so long as you keep any kindnesses you might be inspired to utter ... that you keep them short and not unreasonably laudatory!"

"I'm not ay certain I can oblige ye in that, Master Charles," replied Bobby with a twinkle in his eye, "but I'll keep yer caution in mind."

"Then proceed, Bobby! I might as well face the music."

The table fell silent as Bobby rose to his ancient, and on this particular day, weary feet. He picked up his glass and lifted it toward Charles.

"Master Charles," he began, "ye've been a man for everyone in all Devonshire to respect an' admire. And we who're privileged t' be sittin' around this table with ye today are especially proud to know ye and t' call ourselves yer friends. Ye're a man worthy o' praise because ye've made yerself the servant of all who cross yer path ... and we're honored t' be here t' celebrate this day with yer family. God bless ye, Master Charles!"

He lifted the glass once more in Charles' direction, then to his lips. A few *Here, heres!* followed, and sips around the table, as Bobby resumed his seat.

Now Charles stood.

"Thank you, Bobby," he said reflectively and seriously. "Your words are humbling indeed. I don't know what to say other than to thank you one and all." He glanced about the table. "I don't feel I deserve what Bobby has just said, but I am deeply appreciative nevertheless."

A pause followed.

"It seems there is nothing left to do," Charles went on, "but offer thanks to God. So I suggest we do just that."

He paused again briefly, then began to pray.

"Father in heaven, you are indeed good to us. We thank you for life, for health, for provision, for friends, and for days such as this to help remind us of the bountiful blessings you bestow. I thank you for these fifty-three years you have given me, and for your watching over me and bringing me into life as your child. We remember, too, our dear Amanda on this day. Keep her in your care, and bring her back to us—and to you . . . in your time. We thank you. Amen."

67

Refuge

By the time Amanda found herself on the street walking toward the familiar house she had left that morning, she was in nearly as bad a state as the day before. She had been wandering about the West End all afternoon.

Amanda knocked at the door of the Halifax home just before tea-time.

Mrs. Halifax, who had been more than half expecting her, answered it.

"Come in . . . come in, my dear," she said, in words that sounded more soothing and comforting than any Amanda had heard all day. "Don't you worry about a thing," she added. "We have your room all ready for you."

Ramsay appeared behind his mother a moment later. The mere sight of his face caused Amanda to break into tears.

"I . . . I didn't know where else to go," she sobbed.

He approached and took her in his arms. She cried a minute as he held her, stroking her hair gently and whispering soft, comforting words into her ear. As he did so, he glanced with an imperceptible nod toward his mother. She closed the door, then turned and left them alone.

"I'm so sorry, Ramsay," blubbered Amanda. "I'm sorry for the dreadful things I said. Can you ever forgive me?"

"Of course," he whispered tenderly. "We will not speak of it again."

"I'm so sorry I doubted you."

"You were upset and confused."

"I can't imagine what I was thinking."

"I understand . . . don't worry, everything will be fine now."

They stood another moment or two in silence. Ramsay stepped away. With his arm around her shoulder, he led her into the dining room, where Ramsay's mother awaited them along with a well-spread tea. By the time Amanda lay down two hours later—after a satisfying meal, another relaxing bath, and many reassurances on the part of Ramsay and his mother—in the same bed she had slept in the night before, it seemed as if a week had passed.

Physically and emotionally exhausted from the ordeal, Amanda remained in bed most of the next day. On the day following that, the activities of her sister-colleagues in the fight for women's rights proceeded without her.

When news of it reached her, Amanda could scarcely believe she had so recently been part of such outlandish activities. In light of the continued escalation of suffragette tactics, aided in no small measure by Ramsay's article, published later in the week *without* his temporarily tarnished byline, police interest in the apprehension of Amanda Rutherford quickly disappeared.

Midway through the afternoon of Amanda's second day in the Halifax home, Amanda, Mrs. Thorndike, and Ramsay's mother sat down to enjoy a leisurely cup of tea. Amanda had sent for her things from the Pankhurst home, thinking no one but the servants would be home because of a scheduled demonstration before the Houses of Parliament. Her two or three bags arrived save and sound. The demonstration, however, turned out to be a ruse. News of the event had been so widely publicized that thousands of spectators gathered throughout the day about the square and along the nearby streets. By afternoon as many as three thousand policemen were on hand to prevent a riot.

Everyone waited. But no suffragette appeared, and no demonstration took place. Again they had outwitted the government. For while the crowd waited, more than a hundred women strolled along Knightsbridge, where not a policeman was to be seen, smashing the windows of every shop for blocks, then made good their escape. Not a single arrest took place.

Two weeks later, Emmeline Pankhurst, Mrs. Tuke, and both Mr. and Mrs. Pethick-Lawrence all appeared before the Bow Street magistrate. He released Mrs. Tuke, but committed the others for trial at the

Old Bailey. The charge was straightforward enough: "Conspiring to incite certain persons to commit malicious damage to property." In the meantime, led on by false trail after false trail planted by the suffragettes, the police continued to comb London for Christabel Pankhurst. Within days, however, she had fled to Paris.

The trial date arrived. Mrs. Pankhurst and the Pethick-Lawrences were sentenced to nine months, the two women in Holloway prison, Mr. Pethick-Lawrence in Pentonville. A hunger strike followed, which spread throughout to the other suffragettes in Brixton and Aylesbury jails. Christabel Pankhurst, living in Paris under the name Miss Amy Johnson, sent orders to the troops across the Channel.

In the various prisons where suffragettes were being held, the authorities now had no choice but to release their prisoners or resort to force-feeding. The first option would admit defeat. They therefore embarked upon a program to employ the second.

To get food into the belly of an unwilling prisoner required that several wardresses—however many were required, two, perhaps, at the feet, and at least two or three keeping the writhing head and shoulders motionless—held the prisoner down on her bed. Medical personnel forced the jaws open to insert wood or metal gags in place to hold them. This process cut the gums dreadfully, insuring that whatever food eventually found its way into the system was mingled with a good deal of blood. The feeding tube was then thrust down with extreme difficulty, doing the throat no more good than the gags did the lacerated gums. Through it was passed liquid nourishment, most of which was almost immediately vomited back up. It reportedly took nine women to subdue Mrs. Pethick-Lawrence—a large and extremely strong-willed lady. The ordeal left her in such bad condition that she was soon released on medical grounds.

Meanwhile, from Paris, Christabel urged the battle forward. Nothing in England was safe. Britain's golfing enthusiasts now felt the suffragette wrath, discovering the words VOTES FOR WOMEN burned in acid across their greens, and teeing up to discover the flags on the pins replaced by purple suffragette banners.

Government officials were harrassed, accosted, heckled, even attacked. Incidents of arson increased everywhere. At first the women found empty houses in the country to burn, but gradually the tactics grew more dangerous and disturbing, with far-reaching effects everywhere.

Somehow the prison personnel managed to keep their captives alive, though the women who resisted with most determination were reduced to a dreadful state of nerves and health. But the hunger strikes continued.

One of the doctors in Holloway was so brutal in his application of feeding techniques that Emily Davison, already of nerves none too reliable, shrieked in horror at the mere sight of him and threw herself from the corridor into which her cell door opened onto the floor one story below.

If she had been trying to kill herself, she did not succeed. A wire screen broke her fall.

PART V

❖❖❖

Hostilities Loom

1912–1914

68

Out of the Frying Pan

*C*harles and Jocelyn Rutherford sat in their private sitting room on the first floor of the east wing of Heathersleigh Hall staring numbly at the walls surrounding them.

Two newspapers lay in their laps, which coincidentally had both arrived today. Husband and wife had each read the article in the *Mail*, though Charles had only moments before stumbled by accident upon the account in the *Sun*. He was the only one of the two with basis to feel its potential import concerning their lives. He had only moments before set it down, shaking his head in perplexity.

The heading above the *Daily Mail* account had been nearly enough to send them into shock: DAUGHTER OF FORMER MP RUTHERFORD EX-ONERATED IN MUSEUM ATTACK.

They had read on in disbelief.

Police are reportedly about to call off their search for suffragette Amanda Rutherford. A source close to the movement has confirmed to the *Daily Mail* that a statement will soon be released repudiating recent tactics of the W.S.P.U. and disavowing foreknowledge of the incident two days ago at the Porcelain Exhibit in the British Museum. It was on the basis of Miss Rutherford's request that she, Sylvia and Christabel Pankhurst, and two other suffragettes were admitted to the exhibit, which resulted in the reckless breakage of a number of priceless objects on display.

Miss Rutherford, however, immediately broke off her affiliation with the Women's Social and Political Union. She expressed outrage over the incident, claiming to have been used against her will, and agreed to an in-depth interview with this paper to set the record straight. She has stated that she will at that time outline her reasons for leaving the movement after a close association with the Pankhursts for three years. "Suffrage is one thing," Miss Rutherford is quoted as saying, "violence and illegalities are another. I believe in the former, but I cannot endorse the latter. I only hope the public can forgive my part in what happened at the museum, which I deeply regret." Miss Rutherford, it may be recalled, is the daughter of former Liberal M.P. . . .

Jocelyn put the paper down after perusing the account a second time, her horror at first reading moderated by a pride in her daughter that she hadn't felt for some time.

"It is so odd to read about our own daughter in the newspaper, and have no idea where she is even living or what she is doing," she sighed. "But at least we can be glad Amanda is finally distancing herself from those dreadful Pankhursts."

Charles did not reply. His suspicions had only deepened as he reflected on the implications of the two articles.

Again he picked up the *Sun* and read through the strange account, looking to see if there was anything between the lines he had missed the first time through.

Daily Mail journalist, Ramsay Halifax, Esq., stepson of the late Lord Burton Wyckham Halifax, has been implicated in a plan to falsify news stories. His future journalistic career is in serious jeopardy as a result of a piece published last October in the *Mail* concerning the state of French troops in Fez. It has been learned that most of the individuals quoted are fictitious, and the accounts altogether made up to embellish the story.

The *Mail* has not yet issued a formal response to the charges, though rumors indicate that Halifax will soon be relieved of his duties.

Moreover, the reporter's allegiances have come under close scrutiny. According to high-placed anonymous sources at the Bank of London, Halifax was seen aboard the German gunboat *Panther* during last fall's tense stand-off in Morocco, raising even more serious allegations than falsification of a news account. He was seen with a German woman reported to be his mistress, Adriane Grünsfeld, leaving the Moroccan nightclub Chez Roi for the Hotel Ritz, from which, after spending the night together, they disappeared the following morning, apparently again to the *Panther*.

Halifax could not be reached for comment; however,

sources close to the *Sun* indicate that these incriminating find-
ings have been turned over to Scotland Yard for investigation.

A full report is expected from the *Mail* this week.

Charles was not the only individual to take note of the potential
import of these developments. Three weeks later, midway through the
afternoon, the telephone rang. The call was from London.

"Sir Charles," he heard on the line, "it's Admiral Wellington Snow."

"Hello, Admiral," replied Charles, sitting down at his desk in his
study where he took the call.

"I am sorry to bother you, Commander," the admiral went on, "especially on a matter involving your daughter. I understand it is a painful subject for you. However, there may be national security at stake,
and therefore I really have no choice."

"National security," repeated Charles in alarm, "involving my
daughter?"

"We doubt she is involved directly," replied Snow. "But the Lord of
the Admiralty suggested I ring you up and talk the matter over with
you. Actually, we don't know who is involved—it's all a bit of a mystery
at this point, which is the reason for my call."

"I can't imagine what I can to do help," said Charles. "I've been out
of London for years."

"It's not you, Commander, it's your daughter we're interested in at
the moment."

"Of course I'll do anything I can."

"You were aware of her suffragette activity?"

"Only vaguely. She has, I believe, given it up, has she not?"

"As far as we know. You saw the article in the *Mail*, and the sub-
sequent interview?"

"We did."

"It is her activity since then that is of concern."

"Of concern to the *navy*?" asked Charles, still bewildered as to why
Winston Churchill and one of his admirals would be interested in
Amanda.

"The navy is *not* part of the inquiry. I am acting as sort of an un-
official, and may I say private, liaison with the foreign office. Mr.
Churchill is involved, discreetly of course, as well. It's on the hush,
hush—we're not really sure who we can trust. No more than six individuals know of our inquiry. We are trying to keep it that way."

"It sounds serious. But I can't imagine what Amanda—"

"Are you aware that she is now living with Lord Halifax's widow?"

"No . . . no, I wasn't aware of that," replied Charles, mounting concern clearly evident in his tone.

"Apparently the move took place after her break with the Pankhursts."

The news sent a chill down Charles' spine.

"She is apparently close, shall we say, to young Halifax, Lord Burton's stepson. It was he who conducted the published interview given by your daughter."

"Hmm . . . I see—the same Halifax implicated by the *Sun* article in all that business down in Morocco?"

"The same. Although in the meantime that report's been proven to be rubbish."

"I suppose that's a relief."

"We haven't a clue how it fits in. We're trying to track down the source but have no leads," Snow went on. "In any event, it's not Halifax himself we're interested in, but his mother. That's where your daughter comes in. She was involved with the Pankhursts for three years, and now Lady Halifax. She seems to have gotten herself mixed up in both things at once. We're trying to discover if there's a connection, to find out what she knows. That's why we came to you."

"We have scarcely heard from Amanda in three years. Mixed up in what?"

The phone was silent for several moments.

"Have you heard of the Source of Illumination?" asked Snow after a moment.

"I've heard of something that goes by the name Fountain of Light."

"Hmm . . . the term is new to me—might be the same. Our information was intercepted and translated from German, so that could account for the difference. What about something called the Black Hand?"

"No, that phrase is new to me. Are they connected?"

"We don't know. The Black Hand is an underground Serbian organization. Tell me what you know about this Fountain, as you call it."

"I could never get any information from the people involved other than an extremely vague and, I must say, peculiar-sounding kind of almost pious nationalism. What is the group you are looking into?"

"We're not sure," answered the admiral. "We suspect they have connections with the east, and have a headquarters somewhere in England. Our sources suspect the east coast, perhaps Scotland, but we haven't been able to penetrate the network. We hoped you might know something."

Charles briefly told about the peculiar meeting he had attended in Cambridge.

"It sounds more a theosophical fraternity than sedition," remarked the admiral. "Although the comments you say they made about people from other countries being involved—that worries me. As does the emphasis on secrecy."

"It concerned me too, Admiral," replied Charles. "There were definitely peculiar overtones."

"What exactly do you mean?"

"I felt that spiritually things were not right, out of order, if you know what I mean."

"I am not sure I do."

"Actually, my wife was probably more in tune with it," added Charles, "even though she spent far less time with the people than I did. I must admit, their smooth talk lulled me to sleep at first. It was very enigmatic, like a mystical society of sorts."

"Interesting . . . hmm—I think I begin to get the picture."

"Is the son involved, the journalist?" asked Charles.

"Not that we know of. He does travel abroad a good deal. But then he writes for the international desk of the *Mail*, and his reputation, except for this Moroccan business, is unsullied. Nothing in his history gives us reason for suspicion."

"What about the secret service?"

"What about it?"

"I would think they would keep tabs on all such fringe groups."

"They try, but there are hundreds . . . thousands—from full-fledged spy networks to little queer cult groups to the communists to the W.S.P.U. Keeping them all straight is impossible."

"The spokesman at the meeting I told you about was a fellow by the name of Hartwell Barclay, who apparently works for the secret service. That's why I wasn't concerned at first."

"Barclay, hmm? I'll look into it—don't know him personally. There are some, however, whose loyalties have come under scrutiny, which is why the investigation is being handled outside normal channels."

"I know nothing more than that he and Lady Halifax are involved together."

"We suspected as much. Have they tried to involve you?"

"Actually, yes, they have. That was apparently the purpose of my being invited to Cambridge. But that was last year—I've heard nothing since."

"What did you tell them?"

"That I wasn't interested. But there was certainly nothing treasonous in anything they said. In fact, it was love for the country which they kept talking about. In fact, I first met Barclay through an old navy acquaintance, now a professor of economics as I understand it—Morley Redmond."

Again the line went quiet.

"I know Morley," said Snow. "We were stationed together during my early naval days. Where did you and he see duty together?"

"Only a brief training stint at Portsmouth."

"Well, I had no idea Morley was involved."

"Now that I recall the afternoon at the coronation," remarked Charles. "Dr. Redmond arrived with my old friend Chalmondley Beauchamp. Perhaps he knows something."

"Beauchamp—this thing points in new directions all the time . . . now toward Parliament!"

"This . . . *thing*," repeated Charles. "What exactly do you mean?"

"I don't know, Sir Charles . . . none of us knows. I just pray to God our suspicions are wrong."

Charles did not pursue the matter further.

"Is this . . . this *thing* you speak of," Charles asked after a moment, "is it connected with the suffragettes?"

"Not that we know of. But then there's your daughter, as I say, who shows up right in the middle of both. And with Christabel Pankhurst off in Paris, who knows what quirky people she's mixed up with?"

When Charles hung up the phone, he knew instantly that he and Jocelyn needed to talk and pray.

69
Serious Talk With the McFees

———— ♦ ♦ ♦ ————

*C*harles left his office and immediately sought his wife.

"Jocie," said Charles, "let's go for a walk."

She rose and they left the house together, wandering first toward the heather garden. He filled her in as they went.

"You know," said Charles, "come to think of it, let's go see Maggie and Bobby. We need some good sage advice."

As they went, Charles explained what had come to him almost immediately after getting off the phone with Admiral Snow—to write Amanda a letter.

"What would be your purpose?" asked Jocelyn.

"To warn her—I honestly believe she is in danger."

"Danger! Charles . . . surely—"

"I don't necessarily mean physical danger. Good heavens, three years with the Pankhursts—I shudder to think what she might have been involved in. But with this change, I don't know . . . somehow I feel a turning point may be coming in her life, and I am not sure we ought to continue being silent."

"But do you think it would do any good, Charles?"

Charles sighed. "That I don't know. In a way, I suppose I am doubtful. Yet I almost feel we must say something, whether she heeds it or not. We are her parents, after all. We still have a responsibility to her before God. That's why we need to talk and pray with Maggie and Bobby—I don't *know* what is the right course."

They arrived at the cottage. Maggie greeted them, though a look of concern was visible on her face. They saw the reason soon enough. They entered the large sitting room and found Bobby seated inside, an unheard-of state of affairs during the middle of the day. His aging face lit up as they entered. He attempted to rise, but thought better of it and settled back down into the couch.

"Master Charles, Lady Jocelyn—good of ye t' come by!" he said. His voice sounded tired.

"Are you ill, Bobby?" asked Jocelyn.

"Just weary," he replied. "Don't know what it is, but my energy's up and left me. But ye didn't come t' hear me complain about my old bones, I'm sure o' that."

Charles laughed and sat down beside Bobby. Jocelyn also took a seat while Maggie busied herself in the kitchen with preparations for tea.

"You're right, Bobby," said Charles. "But I am concerned. You look rather worn out."

"Ay, that I be."

"The favor we have to ask requires only your brain, and your years of wisdom."

"Whatever wisdom the Lord might have blessed me with along the way, it'll be his doing and none o' me own. But the thinkin' part o' me is still working as well as ever. You're welcome t' what ye can learn from it."

"I am happy to hear that," rejoined Charles, "and grateful. We would like to talk and pray with you about Amanda again."

"Has there been some word from the lass?" asked Maggie from the kitchen.

"Not from her," answered Jocelyn, "but *about* her."

"What kind o' news?" asked Bobby.

A brief silence fell, interrupted only by the sounds of cups and water, spoons and saucers, from Maggie's hands. Charles waited until all four held steaming cups of tea in their hands, then briefly filled the old couple in on the reason for the visit.

"Maggie, Bobby," he concluded, "I know you're not parents your-selves. But I'm not sure it takes a parent to give good advice, and we need some. These people Amanda has apparently become involved with do not, I believe, have her best interests in mind."

Charles went on to explain that he was thinking of contacting Amanda.

"What does a parent do," he said, "when he sees danger ahead to which a young person is altogether oblivious, yet knows his headstrong son or daughter is almost determined to go down the slippery slope right into it? How hard should a parent fight when they see something their son or daughter either cannot or will not see?"

"So you're thinking of writing to her?" said Maggie.

"That is the idea that came to me—should I write and warn her? Sometimes it even crosses my mind to go to London and forcibly bring her home with me. But almost as soon as I think it, I realize I cannot do that."

"The prodigal's got t' say, 'I will arise an' go t' my father,' because he wants to," put in Bobby. "The good father the Master spoke of waited patiently."

"It is the most difficult thing I have ever faced!" groaned Charles. "Especially when you can't see what the future holds. Is the danger I perceive really all that bad? Do I sacrifice the posture of patient waiting in order to warn her?—I don't know. I've never wanted to force Amanda. Even now, it seems that we must leave her free to make her own decisions. Yet what if they are simply bad decisions? Where does a parent's responsibility begin and end?"

"How old would the lass be now?" asked Bobby.

"Twenty-two," answered Jocelyn.

"Ay . . .'tis an awkward age fer a parent."

"Why do you say that, Bobby?"

"Because the young person's nearly grown, and *thinks* he's completely grown, but is in many ways still lookin' at the world through the eyes o' self as he did at fifteen."

Charles and Jocelyn glanced at each other and sighed. The description could not be more fitting of their daughter.

"What should we do?" asked Charles.

"Warnin' folks is a tricky thing," Bobby went on. "Them that's most in need o' good strong words o' counsel is oftentimes the least willin' t' listen."

"And it's worse yet when sons and daughters have some grievance against their parents," added Maggie. "Nothing falls quite so unwelcome upon the heart and mind of an independent youth as *advice.*"

"But wisdom and sound judgment in such a case are often clouded by factors which only years of experience can recognize," added Charles. "I know that I had my own moments of foolishness when I was young. I suppose it's natural. But now that I am older, I am finding it more and more difficult to understand why the voice of experience is so unwelcome. I would say the same of myself when I was younger— *why* was I reluctant to listen?"

"Why is it," added Jocelyn, echoing the same frustration, "that at the times when they *most* need the sober judgment of parental insight to guide them into the fullness of adulthood, so many young people find the input of mother and father odious and insulting to the elevated sense of their own maturity?"

"Is it because they want to think that adulthood is complete before it actually is?" suggested Charles.

"I suppose we've all been guilty of that," laughed Jocelyn. "It is difficult to recognize that wisdom comes with years."

"Heedin' the advice and counsel of an experienced parent or mentor," now put in Bobby, "—especially when that advice goes *against* the natural inclination o' the flesh—'tis one of the chief indications of a mature and growin' character. 'Course age of itself doesn't always bring wisdom. There's foolish and crotchety old folks as well as young ones. But years are one of the best teachers life has."

"It's such a strange thing," said Jocelyn. "If ever there was a time of life when you would think people would *want* advice, it would be during the years when they are young. I would love to have had the kind of relationship with my parents where they prayed and sought God on my behalf."

"Ah," said Bobby, "but young people approaching the season o' manhood and womanhood convince themselves that they possess the *right* t' make every decision without parental influence. An' the worst of it is that they think they possess the *wisdom* t' make those decisions wisely and prudently. The sad fact is, most o' the time they're workin' against their own ultimate good and happiness."

"I don't understand it at all," said Jocelyn.

"Ye can't be too hard on them fer their foolishness," said Bobby. "I say that speakin' as one perhaps a wee more knowledgeable o' what the lass might be goin' through than yerself. I *can* understand it because I was such a youth meself—hotheaded and foolish. I didn't want anyone tellin' *me* what t' do. If I do have any sense in this thick head o' mine now," he added, chuckling momentarily but then turning serious again, "'tis not as much as the Lord could've given me had I been more trustin' o' my elders a wee sooner in my life."

"I can hardly believe that about you, Bobby," said Jocelyn.

"Ay, 'tis true. I was a thickheaded lout when I was a lad. I'm only grateful the Lord got hold o' me and eventually shook some sense into me."

A brief silence fell.

"Maybe this is an opportunity the Lord wants to give Amanda, Charles," suggested Jocelyn after a minute or two. "If what you said when we were walking over here is true, and a turning point is approaching in her life, perhaps the Lord wants her to be confronted with a hard decision, so that she has to face what kind of character she wants for herself."

Charles nodded. "You may be right," he said. "I do have the feeling this is such a time. But for someone like her, doing what Bobby said and taking advice when it goes against your own will . . . that is one of the most difficult things for a person to do."

He sighed at the seeming impossibility of the situation, then turned to their host.

"Well, then, Bobby," he said, "what do you think? If you can sympathize with Amanda, and were of similar inclination yourself at one time, what is your counsel? You know that we've tried to give her the freedom to figure all this out on her own. But does a time come when a parent *has* to speak out? And yet . . . would a letter perhaps risk alienating her yet more?"

"Ay, it might. 'Tis a chance ye take."

"You don't sound very hopeful."

"The predicament's an ancient one, Master Charles," said Bobby, "the struggle between one's *own* judgment—an' we always trust that, just because it *is* our own—an' the judgment of *another*. The mature young man or woman is capable o' layin' pride aside, recognizing that age an' experience *may* give extra weight t' the perspective o' someone older. But immaturity, on the other hand, rejects such counsel, assumin' his own judgment is all he needs. This latter 'tis aye the great folly o' youth, as I well know. But it may be Lady Jocelyn's right, that now is the lass Amanda's time t' be faced with the two ways o' respondin' an' havin' t' decide which kind o' person she wants t' be."

Charles thoughtfully took in Bobby's words.

"It is still difficult for me to see," he sighed at length, "how this resistance to our input could have become so extreme in Amanda's case, when we worked strenuously to instill positive and godly values in our family."

"Sometimes the rebellion is most vigorous in such cases, Master Charles. 'Tis one o' the great mysteries o' parenthood. But in the end of it, I don't see that ye have any choice. The Lord obviously put the

idea into yer head. If ye're right and there is genuine danger involved
. . . ye must write her."

"And if she doesn't hear and rejects our counsel?"

"Like I said before . . .'tis a chance ye take. If yer heart's motivated
out o' love fer the lass, whatever may come of it now, good has t' come
of it in the end."

70

Unwelcome Letter

When the letter arrived for Amanda at the Halifax home, she had
been enjoying a happily pleasant day. The last thing she was thinking
of was her family. With scarcely a moment's thought as to what could
be its contents, and taking no note of the hand which had penned her
name, she saw nothing of the return address. Still talking gaily with
Ramsay, she slit the envelope and pulled out the two sheets inside.

Whether she would have opened it at all had she known of its origin
or purpose would be impossible to say. As it was, by the time the truth
dawned on her, she was several lines into it. By then some unknown
force—whether curiosity or anger, perhaps wondering if after all this
time her father might have had a change of heart, or merely the ina-
bility to lay it aside once she had begun—compelled her to continue.

Ramsay saw the expression on her face turn serious, then ashen.
Gently he led her to a chair, eased her back into it even as she read,
then left her alone.

The words she read, in her father's hand, were the following:

My dear Amanda,

*I pray this finds you healthy and well. Such we pray for you daily, for
you are in our thoughts constantly. Even more in our hearts.*

*Admittedly I made many mistakes as your father, which I regret and
for which I have tried to express my apologies. However, I tried always to
give you the freedom to think and question and be your own person. I know
it has not seemed that way in your eyes. Yet such was always my goal and
my hope as your father.*

Except for the objections your mother and I raised at the time of your leaving, we have subsequently kept silent concerning your going to the city to join the Pankhursts with their political fight for women's suffrage, even though we felt the cause a temporal one which would leave you empty and unfulfilled in the end. We have maintained that silence till now. We knew that you had to make such a discovery for yourself, and that no amount of expostulation on our part would change your mind.

As I am occasionally in the city, it cannot have escaped my attention that you have entered certain social circles and become a part of London society generally. This also has been an exercise which, though I am grateful to cousin Martha for the love she obviously has for you, in the end, I have known this will not satisfy the hunger for fulfillment which lies in the soul of every man and woman. Yet I judged it best to maintain my observations from a distance, and to limit my involvement on your behalf to prayer.

Now, however, I have recently become aware of your new boarding situation at the Halifax home, and at last I feel I ought to speak. There are factors concerning your friend Mr. Halifax and his mother, as well as some of their associates, which are of grave concern to me. I do not think I over-state the case to say that I consider you in no small danger in thus affiliating yourself with them in this way. I urge you most strongly to reconsider, and to seek other lodging arrangements.

I know my words may grate against your ears. I hope you will be able to look for the truth in what I say. My dear Amanda, errors and mistakes in judgment can be made. The eyes of experience are often able to perceive rocky shoals ahead more clearly than those of youth. This is a plea that you will listen to the counsel of one who cares for your well-being, and knows something of circumstances and loyalties of which you may be unaware. Please, for your good not my own, listen to my cautions.

These people you have become involved with are simply not what they seem.

You are an adult now. I urge you to stand tall and mature and to exercise sober adult judgment. Recognize that my years, my experience, and the mere fact that I am your father may indeed lend a validity to my words of greater weight than what might be your own perspective on this situation. Whatever you may still think of me for what I have done or not done, for your own sake, please heed my words.

To do this will take great humility and maturity on your part. Such is the most difficult thing a young man or young woman can face. You desire so strongly to manage your own affairs without counsel or oversight. Yet it is a time more than any other in life when you need wise guidance. I call upon you, therefore, to approach the matter with maturity and wisdom.

No doubt you think you see all things clearly, and consider yourself strong enough not to be swayed. But I repeat, these people are not all they seem. They are more powerful than you have any idea—powerful over minds, over loyalties, even over hearts. You will be a mere pawn in their hands.

Oh, Amanda, my dear, dear daughter—I love you more than you can possibly know. You will know, as do most young people, when you have children of your own. Only then, it seems, does the depth of parental affection break in upon the mind of son or daughter. To fulfill itself, parental love seems required to extend in two generational directions at once.

Your mother and I love you, and pray for you daily. For we know that one day you will—

Amanda threw down the letter in disgust. She would not listen to another word. How dare her father insult her friends, and insult her in the process! She did not need him to preach to her.

She jumped up, face glowing in rage, and stormed from the house.

71

Curious Eyes

Hearing the front door slam, Mrs. Halifax entered from an adjoining room.

"Did you and Amanda have an argument?" she asked.

"No—she received a letter from her father," Ramsay replied.

"Oh..."

"That was the result," Ramsay added, nodding toward the half-crumpled sheets on the floor.

Mrs. Halifax took in the information with interest, then walked to the window where Amanda's back was still visible as she retreated with haste along the sidewalk.

"Go after her, Ramsay. She is in obvious distress."

Ramsay left the house and followed Amanda. The instant he was gone, his mother hastened from the window, picked up the letter, and quickly began scanning it for any useful information. Her eyes slowed and absorbed the content with great care when she came to the portions which had unmistakably been written concerning her.

A very different reaction than Amanda's rose within her at the words from Sir Charles Rutherford. She could hardly be justified in feeling anger, for the words were true enough.

Her brow creased in dark reflection.

They had underestimated Rutherford. He could prove a more troublesome adversary than they had thought. Yet knowing exactly where he stood was a valuable thing to have learned, as well as just how volatile remained the relationship with his daughter. Both pieces of information could prove useful.

Carefully she laid the two sheets back precisely as they had fallen from Amanda's hand, then retreated to her boudoir. This development warranted careful thought.

72

Shifting Loyalties

♦♦♦

*T*he next eighteen months signaled an era of slow internal change for Amanda Rutherford. The transformation in outlook came by such infinitesimal degrees, however, that Amanda herself hardly perceived the shifts that were taking place.

To have called it a period of *growth* would imply that the changes were wholesome and toward the betterment of her character. Unfortunately, it was too soon to know whether such would be the ultimate outcome of her response to those circumstances in which she found herself.

All that could be said at this point was that the mental and spiritual ground was being tilled. The fact that she had not yet resolved the foundational wrongness at the core of her own being, however, kept whatever thinking she did from yet doing her much good. She was still thinking mostly of *herself*, not the best focus for the inward eyes of one seeking maturity of character. Indeed, her reflections during these months distanced her yet further from those places the Holy Hound of heaven must chase her in the end.

Infuriated by her father's letter, rather than heed his warnings she instead did what so many foolish young persons do when confronted by unwelcome counsel—she rushed headlong toward the very dangers wiser eyes than her own were able to recognize.

As her loyalties shifted away from the Pankhursts, she now came all the more to depend on Ramsay Halifax and his mother. At the same time, however, in her deepest heart Amanda could not quite rid her memory of the article about Ramsay. Once sown, the seed of doubt was difficult to dislodge. The tension of being pulled two ways at once was sobering, making her less apt to commit her feelings one way or the other. On the surface she tried to maintain her gaiety. But deep in her heart she began slowly to retreat into a shell of self-protection.

The mere fact that her father mentioned Cousin Martha in a favorable light, augmented by Geoffrey's hideous display at a moment of her own vulnerability, for a time prejudiced Amanda against further approach to the home of the London Rutherfords on Curzon Street. She did not visit Martha again for several months, nor reply to the numerous invitations that came for her from Cousin Gifford's wife.

Whatever guilt or pangs of conscience she may at one time have felt from such a posture toward one who had shown her such kindness, Amanda now did her best to squelch. The disillusionment of recent events steeled her heart against such feelings. Slowly a coldness became apparent if one looked deeply enough into her eyes. The onetime smile did not spring as quickly to her lips. The exuberance of the child who had once been thrilled by sight of a simple daisy and the excitement of the big city would now look upon the same sight with hardly a flutter of interest. What did daisies and dreams matter anymore . . . what did *anything* matter?

Whether she was growing it would be difficult to say. But she was certainly growing *up*. The hardness of toughened adulthood gradually could be seen in her visage. A few lines gradually etched themselves around the edges of her eyes. Whatever fragments of the innocence of her childhood that might have remained had been dashed to the ground and swept away along with the bits of porcelain on the British Museum floor.

Doubts assailed her about many things, though she kept them to herself. As yet she refused to look squarely at them and inquire what they might be trying to tell her about her values, her outlook, and where she was going in life. She only began to feel a gradual unrightness about things which she could not rationalize with the romanticism that had driven her to London in the first place.

When word of the *Titanic's* sinking reached London in mid-April, Amanda took in the dreadful news with placid expression, turned without a word, walked upstairs to her room, lay down on her bed, and inexplicably cried for the next hour. She could not even have said why. What unknown place in her heart had been struck, she hadn't an idea. She knew not a soul aboard. No disaster had affected her so before. Now suddenly she found herself devastated, nearly unable to eat for two days.

Another shattering of innocence had intruded unbidden into her life. What was wrong with the world when such things could happen? What did her former ideals amount to in a world where the best ship in the world sunk on its maiden voyage? What was there left to depend on?

Such questions set off a chain of further reactions to the most unrelated of occurrences, causing Amanda to reflect yet the more deeply and personally on the militancy advocated by Emmeline and Christabel Pankhurst. She had wanted to do good, to change the world. She had hated her father for not trying to do so.

Yet what good had *she* done for the past three years? Bombs were being set and houses burned down and businesses ruined and the government disrupted, all in the name of right and truth.

Right, truth . . . bombs and arson and destruction! It was all upside down and wrong.

Two months after the *Titanic*, Amanda read a brief notice in one of the papers about a bombing incident reportedly instigated by the W.S.P.U. in which an innocent ten-year-old boy had been blinded and lost his leg. This news was even more devastating than the sinking of the great vessel. This was close, personal. She had been part of the W.S.P.U. She had spoken on its behalf, and thrown her own share of stones.

Again Amanda sought her bed, this time sobbing for two hours. *The poor boy . . . the poor boy!* she cried to herself, over and over. Never in all her life had Amanda Rutherford felt such feelings as on that day. She felt as if she herself had ignited the fuse.

As she lay weeping, the image came back to her of Rune Blakeley's drunken cruelty to his son Stirling that day so many years before in

Milverscombe. The vision was followed by shouts of her own voice, lashing out at her mother in cruel accusation. It still made her angry knowing her parents cared nothing for poor Stirling. What good were money and title if you didn't use them? She had been so furious that her mother would do nothing. Yet now the very cause in which she had been involved had *created* even greater suffering in the life of another innocent boy.

How could her own ideals have slipped so far? She had been part of *causing* the very thing she once had hated. She came to London to change the world—what had the city made of her? What kind of way was *this* to help anyone?

When Amanda rose from her bed that afternoon and at last dried her tears, the cold pessimism had penetrated yet deeper. The idealism that had brought her to London was dead. And no more fertile soil than disillusionment exists in which can grow new loyalties, allegiances, and perspectives.

Aware of the tensions and doubts within their houseguest, Mrs. Halifax shrewdly planted subtle seed after subtle seed, to grow and bear fruit in their due season. Amanda never recognized them as such—a stray remark at breakfast, a chance comment to Mrs. Thorndike, which their hostess was careful that Amanda should overhear, certain periodicals and papers left open for Amanda to stumble upon.

Amanda never realized the imperceptible ways in which her former desire to change the world, leavened by disillusionment, now slowly shifted in socialist directions. As she continued to express doubts and frustrations, her points of view and ways of looking at things were skillfully manipulated without her slightest awareness. At the very center of this process continued to sit the division with her parents, which Mrs. Halifax was only too happy to exploit along with the rest. For no disillusionment is so powerful as that in the forming of alternate loyalties, and in making attractive the kinds of new ideas to which Amanda was now exposed. Doubt sows its seeds, mistrust provides the sun, disillusionment sends its rains, and thus do many spiritual weeds flourish in the fertile soil of a discontented soul.

The first time she overheard Amanda speak of the Halifax house as her *home*, Ramsay's mother quietly smiled to herself.

The girl was nearly turned, she thought. All that was left now was for Amanda to begin calling her *Mum*.

73

A Visit and a Conversation

• • •

*W*hen the invitation from her aunt and uncle Wildecott-Browne arrived, Amanda took it in stride, not pausing more than a fleeting moment to reflect upon how they came to know her whereabouts or what might be their purpose in suddenly contacting her out of the blue. She took it, as she did most things these days, as a matter of course. At Mrs. Halifax's urging, she accepted.

It was neither a particularly pleasant but neither an unpleasant evening. Amanda did her best to enjoy herself, though she scarcely knew her mother's sister and almost did not remember her husband Hugh at all.

Aunt Edlyn and Uncle Hugh were full of questions about her present life, and what it had been like growing up at Heathersleigh. They were especially inquisitive about her parents. Amanda gradually warmed as her aunt and uncle seemed sympathetically inclined toward the annoyances and grievances which she was only too willing to freely share.

They parted, if not exactly kindred spirits, certainly on amiable terms, with many promises to see one another more in the future now that Amanda was residing in London.

Mrs. Halifax was more than ordinarily interested in what had transpired, and Amanda recounted her recollection of the evening the next afternoon at tea.

"Is your uncle—what is his name, dear?"

"Hugh."

"Yes, your uncle Hugh," Mrs. Halifax went on, "is he an influential man?"

"I don't know how influential he is—he's a solicitor."

"What are his . . . *views* on things?"

"On what?"

"The world, government, politics, religion."

"I don't know. He didn't strike me as overly interested in any of that. We really didn't talk about it."

"Is he the sort of man who is interested in making the world a better place?"

"I don't know—better in what way?"

"Throwing out old outmoded systems," replied Mrs. Halifax, probing a little more directly than she had previously with Amanda. "Equality for everyone."

"I'm beginning to doubt there's any such thing," laughed Amanda cynically.

"But, Amanda dear," said Mrs. Halifax, "the fact that the world has its injustices does not mean we should not do our part to change it."

"What's the use? How *can* we change it? I tried. It didn't do any good."

"There are other ways, my dear. There *are* groups and political systems which are inherently based on the very sort of equality your suffragette friends are striving for."

"Such as?"

"Such as systems where all men and women are equal, where no one lords it over another."

"I don't see any of that in England."

"Change is coming, Amanda. This is not only a new century, but a new era. The light of true equality will dawn one day very soon. We will be part of it . . . you can be part of it too."

And thus, by many vague comments and indistinct conversations, did Amanda's mind come gradually to be filled with new ideas and lured in leftist directions. Though she did not recognize them, doubts toward the English system of government were dropped as well, invisible seeds cunningly sown into her consciousness, which silently sprouted in the soil of Amanda's general spirit of alienation.

Amanda did not know she was being brainwashed. She considered the occasional new thought that popped into her head from time to time entirely her own. Perhaps, she convinced herself, she was at last growing up and starting to see the world in more of its true perspective.

It was in measure a sardonic outlook, to be sure. But better, she told herself, a cynical realism than idealistic fancies of someday becoming the first woman prime minister.

74

Another Letter

*C*harles found Jocelyn late one afternoon sitting in the sun-room quietly weeping. Two sheets of paper lay in her lap. He sat down beside her.

"What is it?" asked Charles.

"A letter from my sister's husband," she replied softly.

"Hugh?" said Charles with a look of question.

Jocelyn nodded.

"What can he have said that is so painful?"

"He and my sister have spoken with Amanda. This is the result."
She began to cry again as she handed Charles the letter.

Dear Jocelyn, he read,

Edlyn and I have had the opportunity to spend some time recently with your daughter. I must say Amanda is a delightful young woman whom I have every confidence will grow and mature into a wonderful lady.

I know enough from things I have heard and from what Amanda has told me to realize the method you employed in raising your children was a complete failure. The control you imposed upon Amanda, I can think of nothing else to call than parental cruelty. You know in your heart and mind what the truth and facts are. God will not protect you just because you are obeying your husband's demands. God never intended for a wife to live under the authoritative and controlling conditions that you have had to put up with these last twenty-five years. You will certainly not gain a loftier place in heaven because you have endured his persecution.

Amanda explained to us of your continual lies to bolster your husband's reputation. Edlyn was shocked, as am I, to learn of your refusal to face what must, in everyone's eyes but your own, be his very obvious faults.

We both honestly think you should leave your husband. But from what Amanda says, you worship the ground he walks on, so I doubt you will heed our advice. I speak for us both—Edlyn finds this whole thing too painful even to write you about. You are my wife's sister and therefore I feel it my

287

duty to speak up and hope that you will listen. I feel sorry for you, and for your whole family and hope that someday you will come to your senses and do what you know is right.

I remain, my dear sister, your loving but disappointed brother-in-law,
Hugh Wildecott-Browne

Charles threw down the letter, not knowing whether to be furious or heartbroken, rose, and walked straight to his office. Five minutes later he was talking on his telephone with Timothy Diggorsfeld in London.

"Timothy," said Charles, "would it be possible for you to come for a visit after the weekend? Jocelyn and I need a friend."

"Of course," replied the pastor. "What is it?"

"It continues to be very difficult," replied Charles. "I'm afraid we've had a bit of a setback today about Amanda. We need your perspective."

"I will see you in a few days."

75

Another Conversation

-------◆◆◆-------

*J*ocelyn had been subdued ever since the painful letter from her sister's husband. She and Charles had not spoken much of it, desiring to wait until Timothy was with them to let out their feelings on the matter. He arrived late the following Monday afternoon.

It did not take long for the three friends to get around to the subject which had prompted the invitation. Charles showed Timothy the letter from Hugh Wildecott-Browne.

The pastor read it, then set it aside with a pained sigh.

"It is remarkable to me," he said after a moment, "that people can be so oblivious to the true signs of character. I don't know the man, so forgive me, Jocelyn, if I seem a bit harsh toward your brother-in-law. But it is abundantly clear that he knows neither of you further than I could throw those two sheets which he tries to pass off as brotherly concern. His suggestion is so ludicrous it merits no response. What does he mean, 'come to your senses and do what you know is right'?"

"I can't imagine what he means," answered Jocelyn. "Amanda's been gone three years. We've had almost no contact with her whatever. I shudder to think what she has told him."

"*Leave* a man like Charles," exclaimed Diggorsfeld, "—who is your brother-in-law, anyway? I take it he is not a Christian."

"Actually, he is a devout churchman."

"It gets worse and worse. What kind of mockery to truth is that! And coming from a Christian!"

"Charles is the best thing that ever happened to me," said Jocelyn, first to Diggorsfeld, then glancing with a smile toward her husband. "Were it not for Charles, I cannot imagine where I would be. He's the one who helped me accept myself. I could never have learned to accept God's love had he not helped me come to terms with who I am first. Charles' love for me is—"

Jocelyn glanced away, tears rising in her eyes. Charles placed a gentle hand on her arm. It was silent a moment.

"You haven't answered this letter, have you, Jocelyn?" asked Diggorsfeld.

She shook her head.

"Don't. It is not worth it. His ears are closed, at the moment at least, to anything you might say. What does he have against you, Charles?" Timothy asked, turning toward his friend. "What in the world can account for such a bitter attitude?"

"Honestly, Timothy," sighed Charles, "I haven't an idea. Until this came, I assumed that Hugh and I were on friendly enough terms. It isn't as if we are close, or see one another with any frequency. In fact, we rarely see each other and have never had a serious and personal conversation."

"Ah, perhaps that partially explains it, then."

"How so?"

"Accusations are often easier to make the less you know about someone. Facts tend not to get in the way."

"Perhaps you're right," sighed Charles. "But I am still shocked by his words. I always took Hugh for a decently reasonable man."

"An angry son or daughter who blames mother and father for every ill and inconvenience visited upon them is hardly the paradigm of balanced perspective and truth. This Wildecott-Browne is a grown man and I would assume reasonably intelligent—what is his profession, by the way?"

"He's a solicitor."

"Worse still!" exclaimed the minister. "A man who earns his bread sifting truth from falsehood. Why cannot he see Amanda's bitterness in an instant? I return to my original question—how are some people oblivious to the signs of character?"

"That is why I called you, Timothy," laughed Charles. "You're supposed to be giving us perspective to understand this."

"I am sorry," replied Diggorsfeld, shaking his head, now disgusted with himself rather than the sender of the letter. "Forgive me—this kind of thing has the tendency to anger me. But," he went on, still trying to make sense of it, "he must know you, Jocelyn—how can he say such things of you?"

Jocelyn laughed lightly. "To tell you the truth, Timothy, it actually feels good to have someone else be angry on our behalf. Up until now I thought this pain in my head, not to mention in my heart, would never subside. And to respond to what you said, no, I would say my brother-in-law doesn't know me in the least. Nor does he know Charles. He hasn't spent ten minutes with Charles in twenty years."

"Yet he is willing to pass judgment on the basis of Amanda's skewed accusations." Timothy shook his head in irritated bewilderment. Again it fell silent.

"Why is Amanda doing this to us, Timothy?" asked Jocelyn at length. "Why does she tell people such things when we tried to do our best for her?"

"Doing your best for people is not always what they want," replied the pastor. "In Amanda's case, she resented what you tried to do. She didn't want your *best*. Most people don't. They want what is comfortable. The best means growth, change, personal development. None of that comes about without a recognition and a facing of our personal weaknesses. How can we mature if we don't come to grips with our problems so that we can overcome them? Such is the essence of growth. You both have been down that road, and it was painful at times."

Charles and Jocelyn both nodded and smiled. They remembered all too well their own struggles early in their mutual walk of faith.

"When an individual doesn't want to look at his or her problems, they do all kinds of things to try to cover them up and hide them," Diggorsfeld went on. "It is a way to pretend they don't exist. If they do admit their shortcomings, they blame others for them. Parental accusation is a convenient means for refusing to look yourself in the eye. Saying that your parents caused your selfish habits, blaming them for everything that is wrong in your life, is the easiest way in the world to avoid facing who you really are."

"But we tried to help Amanda face herself realistically and see her self-centeredness, just as we were rooting out problem attitudes within ourselves."

"Exactly. You were doing your best to help Amanda face her own self and learn personal accountability. You wouldn't let her hide from her problems. And she despises you for attempting to carry out that function in her life—exactly as God ordained that you should. Those who look to accountability, and try to make other people do so, will always be blamed and accused."

"But why, Timothy?" asked Jocelyn.

"Because accountability is uncomfortable. We'll squirm out of it any way we can. It's human nature. But the only way to grow and mature is to *face* what you are, what you have made of yourself, what has been the result of your choices. There's no one to blame, no one to point the finger of accusation at but yourself. As uncomfortable as we find it, personal accountability is the straightest and quickest road to maturity."

"That is why Amanda resented me, all right," sighed Charles, "almost from the first moment I tried to impose an accountability to scriptural principles in our home."

"But why is Hugh so hostile?" said Jocelyn. "At least Amanda's resentments make some sense. But this letter from Hugh utterly bewilders me."

"There will always be those who will encourage blame of others, as your brother-in-law has done," replied Timothy. "I doubt he understands the basic principles of accountability and authority, otherwise he would have encouraged Amanda to get her own heart right. How he cannot understand them, being a lawyer, is a puzzle. But the world functions according to different principles. I do not know the man, but the fact that he offered such a willing ear to a young person's complaints tells me that he does not grasp some basic and essential principles about the proper ordering of relationships. He had an opportunity to help Amanda, to turn her heart in the only direction where help is to be found, back toward you. Instead, he has justified her anger and done her the gravest disservice possible. I am sorry to say it, but your brother-in-law is not Amanda's friend."

"Oh . . . I feel so bad for Amanda!" Jocelyn sighed.

"It is her own *self* that she has never faced," said Timothy. You tried to help her see herself clearly, as it is a parent's duty to do. You did not coddle her self-will, you exposed it. Thus you are temporarily seen as the enemy to her independence."

"Will she ever come back to us, Timothy?"

"I cannot say, Jocelyn. Such is certainly my prayer. But there are two kinds of responses prodigals make. The one, when the knock of personal accountability comes at his heart's door, answers it and begins to look at himself or herself honestly and realistically. Suddenly the blame and accusation of others falls away, and he sees his condition for what it is—of his *own* making. Such a one is at that moment ready to arise and go to his father, and say, 'I am at last ready to be a true man, because I am at last ready to be a son.' Or, if we are to be fair in this age of equality, 'I am at last ready to be a true *woman*, because I am at last ready to be a *daughter*.' "

"And the other?" said Charles.

"Sadly, there is another kind of prodigal," replied Timothy, "who, when that same knock comes at his or her heart's door, turns *away* from the call of accountability, and retreats yet deeper into the self-imposed dungeon of blame and accusation toward others. It is at such times when they need wise friends and mentors and elders who will speak the truth to them of their need to come out and into the light of self-examination and personal accountability. Unfortunately, there are many who will feed such attitudes of self, for reasons and motives of their own."

"How do you know which kind someone like Amanda is?"

"One cannot know," answered Timothy. "All you can do is pray for light, for an opening of the eyes . . . and wait."

76
Derby Disaster

—— ◆◆◆ ——

$\mathscr{N}$otwithstanding Amanda's disenchantment with the suffragette cause, she remained moderately interested in the general theme of women's rights and voting in particular, and continued to follow developments in the news throughout the next year.

Aware that the militancy and violence which had forced her away had also driven a wedge between the two older Pankhursts and the younger, she was not altogether surprised when the telephone call came from Sylvia.

"I don't know if you are aware, Amanda," said Sylvia, "that I have left the W.S.P.U."

"I read something about it in the paper," replied Amanda.

"I want to carry the cause of women's suffrage forward with less violence than my mother and sister," Sylvia went on. "I am attempting to organize lower- and middle-class women. I am starting a new federation and wondered if you might consider joining me?"

The call resulted in a resumption of their relationship, and once again Amanda became involved for a brief time around the fringes of the movement. The boredom which had begun to set in—for Mrs. Halifax was away a good deal, Ramsay was at the paper night and day, and she was left to while away most afternoons with Mrs. Thorndike—Amanda thus relieved in the former baker's shop which Sylvia had rented on Bow Road down in the middle of the East End. The setting was not the most glamorous—grimy and with the stench of soap factories and tanneries filling the air. But mingling with working slum women who sweated and slaved plucking chickens and packing biscuits and weaving ropes at least kept the face of humanity before her, to carry out its own special work of compassion in the due course of Amanda's destiny.

In May of 1913 Ramsay reminded Amanda of their first days of acquaintance.

"What would you think," he said, "of attending the Derby again this year? A celebration of the second anniversary of our first formal outing together?"

Amanda happily accepted.

"I should say," added Ramsay, "that the invitation applies only to *you* this time. Now that you are involved with Sylvia again, I don't want any surprise tagalongs."

"Don't worry," laughed Amanda. "I haven't seen or heard from Emily in I don't know how long. The last I heard she was in jail."

"Oh, right, tried to kill herself, wasn't it?"

"That sounds like her!"

"But didn't they release them all?" asked Ramsay.

"I don't know. In any event, I promise she will not be along."

Derby Day arrived on June 4. Ramsay and Amanda—not knowing that the ill-fated Miss Davison, who had accompanied them on the previous occasion as a preliminary to what she planned to do, had, the evening before, calmly placed a wreath at the foot of Joan of Arc's statue, then drove to Epsom Downs happily alone.

No sooner had they taken their seats for the beginning of the race than Amanda gave a little start.

"I don't believe my eyes!" she exclaimed. "There is Emily Davison after all!"

"Where?" asked Ramsay, following Amanda's pointing hand.

"Yes . . . I do see her," he said, "there in the crowd at the rail along the track, just as the curve of Tattenham Corner begins. She is wild eyed even from this distance! I must say she is the worst dresser I have ever seen."

Amanda's onetime colleague was wearing an unfashionable pale yellow dress which came down not far below the knees. On her feet were laced what appeared to be a pair of men's boots as if she intended to be off for a romp across the countryside. No hat covered her head of unkempt red hair.

"She is a sight," agreed Amanda.

"It doesn't look like the stint in Holloway did her constitution much good," laughed Ramsay, "—thin as a rail. But enough of her— let's look at the program."

Their eyes were soon distracted by the pre-race activity, and trying to see the king, whose colt was one of the favorites.

"All right, we've got Whitey's Dream, Irish Pride, Aboyeur, Highlander, Centennion, Craganour . . . who do you like, Amanda?"

"I think I'll root for Medusa Lady—I like the name."

"A fifteen-to-one shot—not a chance," laughed Ramsay. "My money's on Craganour."

The race was soon off.

Down the backstretch galloped the tight cluster of horses. As Amanda and Ramsay watched with the rest of the crowd, they did not see Amanda's former colleague inching closer and closer through the spectators toward the edge of the track.

Gradually the field separated into two clusters.

"Go, Medusa Lady!" yelled Amanda.

Leading the way sprinted the favorite Craganour, but with 100-to-one Aboyeur hanging surprisingly close. George V's horse led the following pack several lengths behind.

The field now raced through Tattenham Corner.

Suddenly a great unison gasp of panic went up from the crowd. The slight figure of a woman jumped the railing and now rushed into the middle of the track.

The lead pack thundered past. Into the gap between the two packs of horses ran the deranged red-haired suffragette. The king's horse and jockey crumbled into a heap. Those close behind pounded into them and crashed and fell across the track.

Shouts and screams sounded everywhere. Pandemonium erupted.

Dust flew amid shrieking whinnying. Horses tumbled over one another. Several jockeys flew through the air. At the bottom of the heap lay Emily Davison, crushed and beaten by powerful hooves and falling, struggling, kicking horseflesh.

Ramsay cast one quick glance toward Amanda. Her eyes were wide, her face ashen. She sat stunned as in a trance of horror at what she had just seen.

Ramsay leapt from his seat and ran toward the track. Stretchers and doctors hurried toward the scene. A few of the excitable horses jumped back to their feet and were led away. Others lay with broken legs. Moans, yells, and innumerable horse sounds came from the scene.

Unaware of the tremendous accident, the lead pack of horses raced on to the post. Shoving Aboyeur momentarily into the rails, Craganour managed to hold his lead and win the race. All eyes, however, were on the site back in the final curve where two horses, a jockey, and Emily Davison lay on the dirt. The horses and jockey were alive, though badly injured. The woman lay motionless, awaiting ambulance transport to a hospital.

When Ramsay returned for Amanda, she still sat where he had left her. Her face was pale, her eyes staring forward at the scene. He took her hand and led her away.

As they returned to Ramsay's car the announcement came over the speaker that Craganour had been disqualified. Long-shot Aboyeur was declared the winner. In light of what they had just witnessed, and since Ramsay had laid his own bet on neither of them, the news hardly seemed to matter.

77

Confusion
◆ ◆ ◆

The drive back to London was quiet and somber.

Amanda stared out the windows unseeing. Her shock was not so much from what she had witnessed, horrifying as it had been, but in the realization that she had been an integral part of a cause that had now taken such a bizarre turn. Both she and Ramsay could not prevent themselves thinking of the Derby two years earlier, when unbalanced Emily Davison sat in this very automobile accompanying *them* to the race. Amanda did not exactly feel responsible, but somehow she knew she had been *involved*.

Again feelings of horror rose up within her of betrayal, of having been used by the Pankhursts. Slowly her horror was replaced by anger. What right did the Pankhursts have to use everyone else for their own ends? They had used her. They had used Emily. How much did any of them really care, deep down, for Emily Davison? Had they perhaps encouraged her to do what none of the rest of them had the courage to do? Now Emily's body lay crushed and broken because of them.

They would all express words of sorrow at what had happened. But Amanda *knew* Christabel. She would secretly be delighted at the publicity this turn of events would bring the cause.

They drove on into the city. Gradually Amanda's agitation

mounted. She had to get out of here.

"Stop the car, Ramsay," said Amanda abruptly at length.

"What?" he said, glancing over at her.

"Stop . . . please—I'm sorry, I need to get out . . . I need to walk. I'm confused and upset and angry and I don't want to start crying . . . please, just let me out."

Ramsay slowed. They were by now driving through Brompton and only two or three miles from home.

"If you need to talk, Amanda, I'll—"

"Please, Ramsay, I just need some time alone. I can find my way back. I'll walk or get a taxi . . . please."

Ramsay said no more, pulled over, and stopped. Amanda got out and walked away without another word.

For the rest of the day Amanda walked and walked, heedless of direction, keeping mostly to smaller streets and parks, working her way along King's Road and through Belgravia into the middle of the city where so many of her activities with the Pankhursts had been located. She spent an hour in St. James's Park, then crossed the Mall, through some of the business district, and into the western edges of Holborn.

As she went, confused thoughts and angry questions kept her brain stirred in turmoil. Every street, it seemed, reminded her of a rally, a protest, a march . . . then later dirty tricks and fires and broken windows.

What had it all been about, these years in London? What had anything accomplished if it was going to end like this—a young lady probably no older than herself being trampled under dozens of pounding hooves at a horse race?

It was all so wrong!

Everyone was selfish. Everyone was out for their own gain. Emily Davison was just as selfish as the rest—she had killed a horse or two . . . if not a jockey . . . if not herself.

The cause . . . the cause . . . everyone spoke of the cause!

But what was *the cause* but an accumulation of selfish people all seeking their own selfish ends, using whoever it suited them? Where was the ultimate *good* . . . good to humanity, to the country . . . good to individual men and women?

Hadn't she come here to accomplish something, to do good?

And now this!

Was there any *good* to be found in the world? If so where?

As she turned along Bloomsbury Way, she began to encounter more people, reminding her that she probably ought to be heading back.

Everyone had been nice to her, she thought, but for what? For their *own* ends?

The Pankhursts ... what did she really mean to them? Nothing.

Cousin Gifford could pour on the charm, but she knew his type. Geoffrey hadn't yet mastered the art of his father's oily ways, but he was just the same. They wanted her for something—she could see it in their eyes. What, she wasn't exactly sure. How much did even Cousin Martha really care about *her* ... suddenly Amanda wasn't sure.

Ramsay ... Mrs. Halifax ... what did *they* want from her?

Everyone wanted something ... everyone was out for himself. Had she ever in her life met a single person who—

Suddenly Amanda stopped.

A face in the middle of the crowded sidewalk ahead arrested her attention. She stared for a moment in perplexity.

Why did she seem to recognize that face? Who could it possibly—

Had full knowing come in time, it is hard to say what Amanda might have done. She probably would have made a quick about-face and walked the other way without completing the encounter. As it was, though she had changed far more than he since the last time either one had laid eyes on the other, it was the man walking toward her upon whom recognition first dawned.

He broke into a slight run, and was standing in front of her before she could even complete the thought that had been poised on her lips.

"*Amanda!*" he said, with a broad smile, in the tone of mingled exclamation and question.

Amanda began to nod, still with a look of uncertainty on her face.

"Timothy," he said, "—it's Timothy Diggorsfeld."

The words brought with them a flood of confused and mingled sensations into Amanda's brain, reminders of her past, of Heathersleigh, of her parents. Had she possessed leisure to rationally analyze the unexpected meeting, she would probably have turned a cold shoulder and walked away. Was not this the man who had started all the religious trouble in the first place!

But she did not have time to think about it. In the first instant she did not even remember that he was a minister. He was not quite so tall as she remembered him, and had lost a little hair since. But his smile was so infectious—a result that genuine smiles usually produce—she could not help reflecting it right back to him.

"Hello, Mr. . . . uh, Mr. Diggorsfeld," she said, smiling pleasantly, shaking his outstretched hand.

"It is so wonderful to run into you like this, Amanda," said Timothy. "You have indeed grown up since I last saw you."

Already, however, with recognition were coming into Amanda's consciousness hints of the man's profession, his visits to Heathersleigh, and his friendship with her parents. Reminders of her father's letter of the previous year were not far behind.

"I had heard you were in London," he said exuberantly. "I am so happy to have run into you."

"Thank you," she replied. "It is . . . uh, nice to see you again too," she added, though more as a reflex than because of the sincerity of her words.

Aware that the smile was already beginning to fade from her lips, and desiring to keep the interview a friendly one, Diggorsfeld brought it to a conclusion as quickly as possible.

"I don't want to detain you," he went on. "I must be going anyway. If there is ever something I can do for you, or if you need a friend's ear, I hope you will call on me. Here is my card," he said, removing a card from his vest pocket and handing it to her. "My church is right up the street—"

He pointed along Bloomsbury.

"—its steeple is just visible there."

He turned and took a couple of steps away. "Call me anytime, Amanda. The Lord bless you . . . good day."

And then he was gone. The entire episode had taken no more than twenty seconds, and was over before she could think what she might even have wanted to say.

Amanda watched the minister disappear in the direction of his church, then continued on her way, sobered, thoughtful, yet at the same time inexplicably warmed inside from the friendly encounter.

He had wanted nothing from her . . . not wanted to *use* her . . . not tried to gain anything for himself from her. It had just been a friendly, *nice* exchange.

She had already forgotten the question she had been about to ask when Diggorsfeld's face had suddenly interrupted her step. Unbidden, however, out of her subconscious now came its answer.

She *did* know someone who didn't try to take from everyone he met.

His name was Charles Rutherford. Her own father was such a man. Was he the only person who had allowed her freedom to be herself, to think and express herself without strings attached?

Stunned that such a conclusion would find its way into her brain, instantly she tried to stop it in its tracks.

No, she said to herself. There *were* strings attached! All his religious strings! It wasn't freedom at all, it was slavery . . . slavery to his ideals, his control, his trying to make her be just like he was.

Even as she tried to force them from her brain, she knew her counterarguments couldn't stand up. Her father *had* allowed her to be herself. He had even paid for her transportation to get here. He had *not* stopped her from coming to London. He could have, or at least made it very difficult for her.

But he hadn't.

Though he had objected to her decision, he had actually given her the money to come. He had expressed his opinion, but then had done nothing to coerce or force her. What else could it be called but giving her the freedom to direct her own course?

He had sent his ridiculous letter a year ago about the Halifaxes, yet the fact was, he had done nothing to prevent her from making her own decision in the matter. She had hated and resented him for years, yet had not her father actually been the only one who *hadn't* tried to use her or get something from her?

She had only been deluding herself that the Pankhursts loved and accepted her. She now saw so clearly that they had never cared about her. Had she been just as wrong about—

No! she screamed silently to herself. She would *not* listen to such thoughts! They weren't true.

Her father was manipulating and controlling. Nothing could change that. She remembered what it was like living under his roof. It was tyranny. She would not go back! She hated it . . . she hated him!

Amanda was running now, bumping her way through people . . . hands clamped over her ears as if to stop the voices trying to tell her she was wrong about her father. Battling them as if these inner cries were bombarding her as she ran, she shook her head and pressed her hands against the sides of her head more tightly.

No, no! she cried. *I won't listen. I won't . . . I won't! He doesn't trust me to be mature enough to see dangers for myself. I'm old and wise enough to handle it . . . I can take care of myself . . . how dare him write me a letter like that . . . it's an insult—I'm twenty-three years old. Who does he think he is! I won't listen . . . I won't. It's all lies. . . .*

78

Difficult Question

◆◆◆

*O*n June 8, 1913, four days after the Derby, Emily Davison died without regaining consciousness. Front pages throughout the country were full of the incident. Six thousand women marched in solemn procession through the street accompanying the body to its final resting place of glory. The suffragette movement at last had a full-fledged martyr.

Charles and Jocelyn's anxiety over their daughter deepened. Yet they knew they could do nothing for Amanda now. They must only wait and allow accountability to come.

Reading of the Derby tragedy in the *Times*, though it was not directly related either to Amanda or the Fountain of Light, somehow triggered a series of thoughts in Charles' mind that caused him to think that the danger he had written Amanda about was increasing.

How exactly Charles arrived at the conclusion he could not have said. But within three weeks the conviction had grown upon him that it was time to speak out more directly, that what had briefly involved him—or tried to—had more widespread implications that could no longer be ignored.

Later that same month, he traveled to London and arranged to see the First Lord of the Admiralty Winston Churchill.

"Winston," said Charles when they were alone in Churchill's office, "I don't want to be an alarmist, but I am very concerned about this Fountain of Light business. I've found myself thinking more and more about some of the things I've heard, about the implications of some of their statements. It sounded innocuous enough to begin with, but now I'm not so sure. There were undercurrents I missed at first. Now I must tell you, I am extremely concerned about what might be their underlying motives. Has anything more been learned since Admiral Snow contacted me?"

"We've learned a little more, but not much. The people involved are extremely evasive."

"I am convinced that danger is afoot," Charles went on, "that whatever it is, the so-called Fountain of Light is not what it would like people to think. There's something involved . . . again, I don't mean to be alarmist, but I think it may be a plot, a spy ring of some kind that may have even infiltrated the government itself."

"You're serious, aren't you, Sir Charles?"

"Very serious. What about Hartwell Barclay—is anything more known about him?"

"I'm afraid I've never heard of him."

"I thought this was your investigation."

"Not really. I asked Admiral Snow to keep tabs on developments."

"I see," nodded Charles.

"So who is this Barclay?"

"He works for the secret service. Admiral Snow and I discussed him."

"Hmm . . . I'll get the admiral on the phone immediately and get an update."

Churchill made the call. In answer to his questions an anxious look came over his face. He set down the telephone and looked up at Charles.

"It seems Hartwell Barclay has disappeared," he said. "Admiral Snow was about to notify me. He thinks something may be up as well. There are reports of heightened activity in Serbia. It's a powder keg. Last year's war between the Balkan states and Turkey solved nothing. It looks like it's going to explode all over again. It would appear that your timing is on the mark."

Churchill grew thoughtful.

"Would you consider going public?" he asked at length.

"What do you mean?" asked Charles.

"A brief statement for one of the papers, issuing a sound and reasonable warning against anything connected with the Fountain of Light."

"Why make it public? What would be the purpose?"

"Because if it is a spy network, then the security of Great Britain may be at stake. Exposure is the surest means to insure that others are not ensnared. We cannot afford to take any chances."

"That's a difficult question," sighed Charles. "Why me?"

"Because even though you were not a part of it exactly, you at least attended one of their meetings. You saw firsthand what went on. A formal document would accomplish little. But you can offer an eye-witness account of what you actually saw and heard. Nothing is so convincing."

"I see what you mean. I suppose I will consider it," said Charles seriously.

He paused a moment. "I've got to tell you, Winston," he said. "I'm not a whistle-blower. And I haven't been involved all that deeply in their activities. What if I don't see it all clearly?"

"Do you trust your instincts, your sense of things, your gut reaction?"

"Yes . . . yes, I would say I do."

"As do I. I trust *you*, Sir Charles. Therefore, the qualms you feel in your gut have credibility in my eyes."

"But what if I am wrong? What if it is *not* a spy network and nothing sinister is going on at all?"

"Their response will tell the story," replied Churchill. "If they are innocent of the charges, they will come forth with specific evidence about their purpose, and explain themselves in a reasonable way. You may wind up with some egg on your face. But I'm asking you to take that risk for the sake of your country. On the other hand, if they become enraged and accusatory, if they lash out vindictively at you personally, and all the while if they further try to hide and shield their motives and activities with secrecy rather than making a full public disclosure, then we may be pretty certain your perspectives are on the mark. The venom with which a man denies a charge against him is very often in exact proportion to the likelihood of its being true."

"I see what you mean. In other words, you are convinced I am right in this, but since we don't know for certain, their response will tip the scale one way or the other. If they are innocent, they will respond accordingly. But if they go on a vicious counterattack, it will prove our suspicions."

"I couldn't have said it better myself. But don't worry, Sir Charles. From what Admiral Snow just told me, there is much corroborating evidence piling up from other sources to back up what you are feeling."

A week later, in the first week of July, Churchill's predictions proved correct. Serbia declared war on its neighbor Bulgaria.

79

Mounting Tensions

◆◆◆

The tension which gradually mounted between the nations of Europe, large and small, during the second decade of the twentieth century was about a single idea: freedom.

What did freedom mean, who possessed the inherent right to be free, and which nations had the right to rule themselves?

At the heart of these fundamental questions flowed the Sava and Danube rivers, circuitously noting the division between Serbia and Austria, a border marked across the landscape between the Dinaric and Transylvanian Alps with hatred.

Events had heated up on and off in the Balkans for half a century. But now they were reaching the boiling point.

A revolution in Turkey led Bulgaria in 1908 to proclaim her independence. Fearing some similar move in Serbia, Austria seized the opportunity to formally annex the Turkish provinces of Bosnia and Herzegovina. These regions, however, were mostly occupied by Slavic Serbs, and Russia threatened to intervene on their behalf. Germany made it known that she would support Austria if Russia declared war.

The crisis was averted when Russia backed down. Austria was allowed to keep her new provinces. The stage for future conflict was set. The major players had taken their sides.

Swallowing their hatred of Austria, the Serbs of Bosnia and Herzegovina vowed to get even another day. A time would come for the throwing off of the Austrian yoke, and when that day came, they would act. In the meantime, Serbian unrest went underground.

Serbs not only in Serbia itself but cooperating with their ethnic brothers and sisters in provinces under Austrian rule began establishing secret organizations directed toward the overthrow of Austrian tyranny, which had now replaced that of the crumbling Ottoman Empire. Their goal was simple: the unification and independence of *all* Serbian peoples.

At the vanguard of this conspiracy was the terrorist society called the Black Hand, made up chiefly of students, Serbian army officers, and other Serbian officials. New members were secretly recruited and support sought throughout Europe. Intrigue, plots, rumors, and spying between the various factions, stirred by fierce nationalism and passionate century-old ethnic and religious hatreds, kept tension in the region at such a pitch that anything could set it off into full-scale conflict.

Encouraged by the continued weakening of the Turks, and in order to exert their own independence as a show against any Austrian intentions, in 1912 the three Balkan states of Serbia, Bulgaria, and Montenegro banded together with Greece to form the Balkan League of Christian States, which then declared war on Turkey in an attempt to complete the expulsion of the Turks from Europe. Hostilities in this First Balkan War continued until mid–1913.

But the peace proved short-lived. Now the four members of the Balkan League fell to fighting among themselves over the spoils they had gained from their victories against Turkey. The Second Balkan War between Serbia and Bulgaria lasted but a month. Atrocities, however, were widespread and the region remained tense.

Prompted by these events, Germany added more than 100,000 troops to its standing army. Uneasiness in the international community resulted everywhere. France responded by voting large financial increases to bolster its *own* army. Russia followed suit.

None of the conflicts involving the powers of Europe during the previous two decades in themselves were serious enough to lead to widespread conflict. All had proved local and containable. Yet each successive incident wore away at the general patience and resolve of the European community. And as Germany, Austria, and Russia grew in power and stature alongside the two powerhouses, Great Britain and France, they also grew more belligerent and less inclined to back down in the future.

With every successive incident war was forestalled. Yet each new threat left these three principal players more irritable and antagonistic. How long would they continue to show restraint?

Meanwhile, Germany's military muscle continued to strengthen. And Serbian passion to free Bosnia and Herzegovina from Austrian rule grew still more feverish.

80
Stealthy Escape

A thick fog settled over the east coast of England during the night. As dawn now broke, nothing but grey whiteness was visible anywhere. The North Sea was calm. If the fog lifted, even for an hour, all should go well.

Doyle McCrogher awoke at dawn. He put on the teakettle, then took a brief walk out to the edge of the Hawsker bluff and peered into the dim nothingness. He loved thick misty mornings like this! The moist air felt so good in his lungs he could almost taste it along with the sweet scent of the sea. The sounds of a few gulls in search of breakfast, and the waves lapping against the rocks below met his ears. But he could see nothing. He drew in another full and contented draught, then ambled back to the house with the red roof to enjoy his tea.

His employer had arrived the night before. There was no need to wake him yet. He wasn't going anywhere in this muck.

Hartwell Barclay arose an hour later.

"Any word yet?" was his first utterance to the Irish keeper of the lighthouse.

"Havena been up there yet, guv," replied McCrogher. "Can't see a thing."

"Get up the tower, McCrogher," the white-haired Englishman snapped back. "I don't pay you to be impertinent."

"Won't do no good, Mr. Barclay."

"I've got to get out of here! I don't want to miss my opportunity."

"Ay, but I can't send the signal till it clears."

"I want to know the instant the fog breaks up, do you understand? For all I know, they've picked up my movements and are on the way here even as we speak!"

"Won't be afore eleven, if it lifts a'tall."

"Don't argue with me, McCrogher! Get up there, I tell you, and get the light on."

The Irishman turned, stopping at the kitchen for his tea on his way, and left the house to do as he was told. With a cup of tea, the company of the gulls and the fog up in the lighthouse would be preferable to this anyway, given his employer's present mood.

Midway through the morning, as Barclay was still grumbling about the fog, and as Doyle McCrogher sat up in the midst of it in the lighthouse whose beacon was not even visible from the ground much less the sea, the sound of an automobile approached up the lonely road along the bluff. Barclay went out to meet his expected colleague.

"You weren't followed?" he said by way of greeting.

"Of course not," answered Lady Halifax, climbing out of the Mercedes. "I'm no amateur. No one suspects me." Her tone was a little brusque at Barclay's manner. "Frankly, I'm not at all sure you're in as much danger as you think," she added as they walked toward the house.

"There were enough suspicious questions floating about concerning the secret service," rejoined Barclay. "I didn't intend to take any chances. From here on, you and the others will have to carry the work forward. I'll be safe with our friends in the east.—But what was so important that you had to make a trip all the way up here to see me in person before my departure?"

"Do you have water for tea?"

"There on the stove."

Lady Halifax proceeded to prepare a pot. When it had brewed, she poured out a cup for each of them and they adjourned to the lounge to continue their discussion.

"Carrying the work forward, as you say, may prove more difficult than we had hoped," she said, sitting down and taking a sip from her cup.

"What do you mean?"

"A letter came for the Rutherford girl some time ago."

"What is that to me?"

"I took the liberty of writing out a copy when she was away," she answered, holding a sheet of paper toward him. "*This* is the reason for my visit. I think you may find that it concerns you very much."

Barclay read it, his expression clouding.

"This Rutherford is proving more trouble than I anticipated. I am beginning to rue the day Redmond mentioned his name to us. You don't suppose he learned of our contact with Wildecott-Browne?"

"Not that I am aware. Unfortunately, this is not all," Lady Halifax went on. "A father writing to his daughter with advice is one thing, but it may escalate beyond this."

"What on earth do you mean?"

"I learned from my son that an article is about to go to press in several of the major newspapers, an interview with Charles Rutherford. Ramsay has seen the article and says Rutherford speaks of the Fountain by name and warns people against involvement."

"What! That's impossible—he wouldn't dare!" cried Barclay, leaping to his feet. His cup of tea nearly fell to the floor as he began to pace about the room in white fury.

"Does your son know of your connection?" he asked at length.

"Not yet. He only shared the news because it concerned Amanda's father."

"It may be time he is brought in."

Lady Halifax nodded.

"In any event, Rutherford has to be silenced!" added Barclay. "I simply cannot believe he would go on the attack like this. What possible motive can he have against us? What harm have we ever done him? Is there any way to stop the interview?"

"My son said it is as good as on the press, and that it would be impossible to stop."

Barclay stewed as he took in the news.

"What about Beauchamp?" he asked.

"I have not heard from him in weeks. I fear he is exactly the kind that could waver as a result of this Rutherford development. How many others in the network might this affect—it could have devastating results."

"Exactly why Rutherford must be discredited!" rejoined Barclay. "If we cannot stop him, then we must invalidate whatever he might say about us."

"It is our only possible response."

"It was a serious mistake to try to bring him in. We should have seen him for too independent a thinker from the beginning. We have to ruin him before he ruins us. We'll have to taint Rutherford somehow so that his article does us no ultimate harm."

"What do you suggest?"

"We must get something in print about him."

"And the girl?"

"This makes her all the more important to us. We had hoped to use her to get him to join us. Now we will have to use her *against* him."

"How will we make her go along?"

"That is your concern. She's in your home—I shouldn't think it would be difficult."

"You are probably right, given the tension that already exists between them."

"If we cannot have him as one of us, we must have her. She must be all ours. Once her allegiance is gained, we will get *her* to speak against him. There is no more powerful and effective way to discredit a man than from the lips of his own children."

"She has been gradually coming around. She may be nearly ready to speak on our behalf."

The lady paused briefly. "And I have another idea," she added, "which could solidify her loyalties yet further."

Lady Halifax then explained what had come to her on the trip north from London.

Barclay smiled. "I like it," he said. "Very shrewd, Hildegard. Would the old woman go along?"

"The timing could not be better. She has been talking of a voyage. I will make sure that she thinks it is her idea."

"And the girl?"

"I don't think there is a great deal to keep her here. There are also financial considerations which may play into our hand."

A few minutes later Doyle McCrogher burst into the room.

"The fog's lifted an' I've reached them, Mr. Barclay," he said excitedly.

"She's there?" Barclay exclaimed rising, turning to glance out the window. Indeed the fog had almost completely lifted as they had been talking.

"She's sittin' about a mile offshore," said the Irishman. "I returned their signal with the message that ye'd be along within the hour."

"Good—excellent. Good work, Doyle. Is the dinghy ready?" Already Barclay had sprung into action.

"I'll check it while ye're gettin' yer duds, Mr. Barclay."

"Well, Hildegard, it looks like I am off," said Barclay. "I will handle affairs from the Continent. Keep me apprised concerning the two women. We'll keep in touch through the usual channels. And I'll meet you back here at the lighthouse as events warrant."

Ten minutes later, the thin, white-haired man made his way down the steep rocky steps to the sea, carrying a single bag, to the concealed little dock beneath the bluff. Doyle McCrogher already had the engine of the dinghy's motor running in readiness for the voyage out to meet his employer's hidden transport south toward a warmer port.

In reality the so-called dinghy was a good-sized seaworthy craft of thirty feet, which would be capable of transporting a good many people—for whom more public modes of transport would not be advisable—onto and off Britain's shores safely when the time came. This particular location had not been chosen by accident. Far enough away from any large cities or military installations to avoid detection, the sea channel here was deep enough near shore to allow the approach of certain vessels it would be well were not detected by the First Lord of the Admiralty.

Into such a vessel, about thirty minutes later, one Hartwell Barclay, formerly of the British secret service and now carrying secrets of his own away from his homeland, climbed steeply down. Even as he was shown to his quarters for the cramped voyage, the captain had begun the dive.

81

An Offer

*L*ady Halifax did not remain in the north once her colleague was out of sight and McCrogher safely back on the rocky shore of the protected inlet. Immediately upon her return to London, she cunningly set in motion a new series of events which resulted in a conversation between her two houseguests.

Within the week, Mrs. Thorndike sat down for a little talk with Amanda over tea. It was only the two of them, as their hostess had contrived it should be.

"Amanda dear," began Mrs. Thorndike. "I have been terribly bored of late, and I simply do not feel up to the season this year. I need to get away for a while, have an adventure. Lady Halifax and I have been talking about a voyage, perhaps to the Mediterranean, then to the Continent."

Amanda took the information in with polite interest, though she had no idea why the good woman was confiding in her with such plans.

"Unfortunately," Mrs. Thorndike went on, "Lady Halifax is unable to leave London for several months. But now that the idea has come to me I don't think I can bear to postpone it. This winter cold has just been too dreadful. I must get away. But I need a companion. A woman such as myself cannot undertake a journey like this alone. So, my dear, what would you think of accompanying me?"

"Me?" said Amanda in surprise. "I could never afford such a trip."

"You misunderstand me, dear," replied Mrs. Thorndike. "I didn't dream that you should have to pay. I mean for you to accompany me as my companion—you would keep me company and help me dress and make tea for us. You are young and would be a great help to me, as well as being a lovely companion. I would of course pay for all your expenses. Lady Halifax would meet us in the spring."

Amanda took in this new information with a flicker of heightened interest. She did not have many prospects. There could be no denying that her life had become tedious. And if both women left London, she could not remain in the Halifax home. Her funds were almost gone. She couldn't support herself for long. Like it or not she was to the point of being dependent on Ramsay's mother. If she didn't accept Mrs. Thorndike's offer, what was left her?

"Where will you be going?" asked Amanda.

"I don't know—everywhere . . . Paris, Vienna, perhaps Rome."

The mere names of such cities sparked more interest in Amanda's ears than anything had for a long time. Maybe an adventure on the Continent was just what she needed.

On the other hand, what about Ramsay . . . and Sylvia . . . and her own future? Had she sunk to this, that from balls and dances and parties, the only option before her now was to become a lady's maid to a dull old lady like Mrs. Thorndike?

"I . . . I will—thank you for the offer, Mrs. Thorndike," she said at length. Her voice did not sound very enthusiastic. "I will think about it."

Momentarily her father's letter crossed her mind. But the next instant she dismissed his warnings. Dear innocent old Mrs. Thorndike had nothing to do with any of those things he had been talking about.

For that matter, neither did Ramsay or his mother. They had all been wonderful to her.

82

Another Offer

$\mathcal{M}$arch 1914 arrived. Mrs. Thorndike was scheduled to sail in two and a half weeks. Amanda still had not made up her mind what to do.

An invitation came. The return address read Curzon Street. Amanda opened it to find a formal dinner invitation in celebration of her twenty-fourth birthday.

She smiled to herself. No one at the Halifax home even knew she had a birthday approaching. Leave it to Cousin Martha to remember.

Amanda sat down and, still holding the invitation, looked quietly out the window. She had gradually come to that lonely point in her life where another birthday only served as opportunity for melancholy reflections. She had done her best to put it out of her mind. But she could hardly prevent awareness of what another birthday signified. Unthinking Mrs. Thorndike, who probably thought she was nineteen or twenty, had blurted out the other day, "I would have died not to be married at twenty-five. Dear Mr. Thorndike came along when I was twenty-one, just in time to prevent me from a spinster's fate."

It wasn't as if Amanda was anxious to marry, or terrified of spinsterhood for that matter. Still, it would be nice, she thought, to have people around when the day came, even if it was Cousin Gifford's family. She sent back a return acceptance that same day.

Her thoughts still full of Mrs. Thorndike's offer, as well as her own diminishing prospects for the future, four evenings later Amanda walked up to the familiar stone house on Curzon Street. Martha had offered to send a car, but the day was warm for this time of year and the streets were well lit. She paused briefly on the walk, glancing up at the structure. This had once practically been her second home. She had to admit those were happy days. But now it looked foreign and forbidding. What had happened? she thought to herself.

Martha had tried so hard to be her friend . . . why had she allowed that friendship to slip away? This past year or so she had spurned Martha's every advance, and had not seen her more than a half dozen times. Where had the time gone? She thought of all the meaningless drives, shopping excursions, luncheons and teas, and even more meaningless conversation. How could she have filled her days with so much emptiness?

Suddenly Amanda felt very, very lonely.

Why had she allowed so many things to slip away? London had certainly not turned out to be all that she had hoped.

But enough of that! It was her birthday.

She drew in a breath of resolve and walked the rest of the way to the front door. Slowly she lifted the iron knocker and let it clang the announcement of her arrival.

Martha herself opened the door.

"Oh, Amanda dear," she syruped in gushy exuberance, "how beautiful you look . . . come in!"

"Show her to the formal sitting room," Amanda heard Gifford's voice from somewhere in the house. "I'll be in momentarily."

Martha led the way and Amanda followed. No sooner had they entered the room, however, than Gifford's voice sounded again, this time beckoning his wife.

"Do wait just a moment, dear," said Martha. "We shall be in quickly."

Martha disappeared. Amanda began to stroll absently about the sitting room, which she had been in but once before. She knew it was used only on the most special of occasions. Her eyes fell disinterestedly upon an ornate oak side-by-side secretary, whose top shelf was cluttered with Martha-ish trinkets. A portrait of Gifford and Martha hung on the wall behind it, the images presenting the distinguished couple to notably better advantage than their living counterparts. A childhood portrait of Geoffrey beside it was hardly recognizable as the fat little boy Amanda had known.

Amanda turned back into the room, her eyes now falling upon a folded and yellowed newspaper sitting on one of the low tea tables in front of the couch, curiously out of place in the midst of such expensive decor.

Amanda could not prevent her eyes from wandering to it as she approached, then sat down on the couch.

Why—

She could hardly believe her eyes!

—it was the issue of the *Sun* which had caused Ramsay such trouble ... opened and folded back to the very page of the article!

For an instant Amanda was confused. What a remarkable coincidence. That *this* newspaper with *this* article would be here at such a time. And two years old!

Gradually the incongruity of its being displayed in such a prominent place began to dawn on her ... in the very room to which she had been ushered and left with nothing to do.

Amanda glanced about. Not a book, not a magazine was in sight.

There could be no other explanation but that it had been *purposefully* put here, knowing she would eventually see it.

Cousin Gifford always had a motive. But why now, why tonight ... why on her birthday?

Or maybe, she thought, it was Geoffrey's doing. It would be just like him to try to rub her nose in Ramsay's past difficulties. She knew Geoffrey was jealous of him.

Absently she picked up the newspaper and read through the brief article again. A momentary reminder surged through her of the pain it had first caused to read of Ramsay's alleged illicit liaison with a German mistress.

She heard footsteps approaching. Quickly she set the account back down on the table. She did not want to be caught having taken the bait. She rose as Gifford and Martha entered.

"Ah, Amanda, my dear," said Gifford, "how lovely you look. A wonderful birthday to you!"

"Yes, happy birthday, Amanda!" echoed Martha.

"Thank you ... thank you both," replied Amanda. "It was very thoughtful of you to remember me."

"I can't imagine what's keeping—" began Gifford.

"—ah, here he is now!" he added as Geoffrey now entered the room, appearing oddly out of sorts, almost nervous.

"Hello, Amanda," he said. "Happy birthday."

From behind his back, he pulled a single red rose. A bit woodenly he shuffled forward and handed it to her.

Shuddering inside, though doing her best not to show it, Amanda smiled and took it from him, then retreated a step.

"That's lovely!" sighed Martha.

"Let us adjourn to the dining room, shall we?" said Gifford as the effusive, benevolent host. He offered Martha his arm. She took it and they led the way. A bit awkwardly, Geoffrey again closed the gap between them and likewise offered his arm. Reluctantly Amanda took it, and they followed the parental couple out of the room.

Dinner proved a stiff and formal affair. It had been obvious from the moment of her arrival that each of the family had dressed up for the event. Amanda could hardly believe all this was merely for the benefit of her birthday. Two bottles of expensive wine stood uncorked and ready. From the kitchen came the aroma of *duck à l'orange*.

"Amanda dear," said Martha as Louisa began serving the first of several courses, "we haven't seen much of you. I've missed you."

Even as Amanda did her best to blandly reply with untruths about being busy and time flying, suddenly Martha appeared old and pathetic in her eyes. Had Martha aged so much in a few short months? Or were her own eyes seeing things that much differently? She had almost been part of this family for a while, going everywhere, doing everything, with them. But she was twenty-four today. No more thoughts filled her dreams of coming out and attending society functions, of being the debutante, the belle of the ball. If she went around now, people would talk behind her back—twenty-four and unmarried, just as Mrs. Thorndike had said, one step from spinsterhood. Who had she been trying to fool with all that activity? London society hadn't been her world any more then than now.

"How is your father these days?" asked Gifford.

"I really couldn't say," replied Amanda.

"I see in the paper that he is to be in London next week—something about that electrical commission he is involved with. Do you plan to see him?"

"I doubt that will be possible."

Across the table, Geoffrey kept staring at her with an expression Amanda wasn't sure she liked. But he said little. At least that was a relief.

Dinner endured, they retired again to the formal sitting room. The newspaper had miraculously disappeared from the tea table. Tea and small cakes were served. Martha babbled. Gifford waxed ponderous, chiefly on the many difficulties facing young people in these difficult times, and the necessity of marrying well, with sufficient financial stability to ward off hardship. Geoffrey continued to remain silent.

After about thirty minutes Gifford shifted in his chair and cleared his throat significantly.

"Come, my dear," he said to Martha, "the young people want to be alone."

Amanda could feel her skin beginning to crawl. Gifford and Martha rose and left the room with many additional birthday wishes. Amanda wondered if she caught a brief wink from father to son. If so, Geoffrey gave no indication of response.

Geoffrey sat silent, the effects of the pre-dinner brandy and pep talk from his father both wearing off, and the dinner wine serving to subdue rather than invigorate him. But if he didn't do it, his father would berate him. Slowly he rose and paced about a bit. With his back still toward her, he finally began to speak.

"Amanda," he said in quavering voice, "I know I haven't always been as kind as I ought to have been . . ."

As she sat listening, Amanda was beginning to feel a distinctly strange and horrible sensation.

" . . . was a positive cad when we were young," Geoffrey went on, his voice growing more smooth but no less detestable in her ears as he turned to face her.

" . . . realize it now . . . but I hope you will be able to . . ."

Amanda was trapped and knew it. She could do nothing but sit and listen, though the terror of what she was afraid she had gotten herself into prevented her from remembering a fraction of his words.

"What I am trying to say—"

Geoffrey paused, obviously frustrated with himself for being so nervous. His sweaty hand now began fishing about the outside pocket of his coat.

"Well . . . I will let this say it for me—" he added.

He now withdrew his hand, clutching some small object. He held it toward her. It was a tiny black box. Geoffrey opened it.

Amanda's horrified gaze fell upon a monstrous two-carat diamond ring.

"—I am trying to say," struggled Geoffrey, "that I want you . . . to be my wife."

The words stunned Amanda with such force that her face went immediately white. All she could do was sit in abject disbelief. Had she actually heard what she thought she heard!

She returned Geoffrey's gaze as if mute. He *couldn't* mean it! It wasn't possible. After several long and excruciating seconds, Amanda found what little remained of her voice.

"Geoffrey . . . are you actually *proposing* to me?" she stammered.

"Yes, of course—what else could you call it when a man asks a woman to marry him? I am asking you to be my wife."

Again Amanda returned his words by staring back in a renewed trancelike stupor.

Geoffrey, while one side managed to convince himself that she *had* to accept, another side was almost shocked that she seemed to be taking it so well. He half expected her to fly off the handle. But she was sitting there very calmly. That mere fact, notwithstanding her ashen look and non-reply, encouraged him to heightened boldness.

"Here," he said, "try it on."

He removed the ring from the box and took a step forward as if to take her hand in his and slip it on the dainty white finger himself.

In no more than an instant or two of time, now slowly the words from the *Sun* article began to filter back into Amanda's brain.

. . . reporter's allegiances have come under close scrutiny. According to high-placed anonymous sources at the Bank of London, Halifax was seen aboard the German gunboat—

Wait, of course . . . sources at *the Bank of London*!

How could she have not noticed it before? Suddenly it dawned on her that it wasn't only the paper that had been planted for her to find tonight to make Ramsay look bad, the whole article had been planted in the first place! No doubt planted by Geoffrey, who was the high-placed Bank of London source! Had he been scheming toward this end all along?

Amanda pulled her hand back and deposited it safely in some fold of her attire, then looked up and for the first time this evening took hold of Geoffrey's eyes. He stopped dead in the tracks of his approach, his hand stretched forward, the huge diamond clutched between two fingers at the end of it.

"You planted the article about Ramsay, didn't you?" she said. Her voice was calm, not accusatory or angry, merely the expression of one stating an obvious conclusion.

"I don't know what you're talking about," Geoffrey replied.

For some reason, the look on his face momentarily confused her. His expression was one of genuine shock at mention of something so long past, almost as if he had completely forgotten it. The conviction immediately possessed Amanda that he was actually telling the truth.

"Then your father did," she said. "It was a setup, wasn't it, to make Ramsay look bad in my eyes? And then this tonight . . . what was it, to soften me up so you could move in for the kill?"

"I honestly haven't the slightest idea what you mean," Geoffrey replied.

Amanda eyed him without expression. An ironic smile slowly came to her lips. It was all beginning to make sense. Geoffrey's father was the prime mover in this little plot—perhaps Geoffrey was as much a victim as she.

"Aren't you going to try on the ring?"

"I don't think so, Geoffrey," Amanda replied. "I don't intend to take a diamond like that until I'm sure."

"Don't you at least want to see how it feels?"

"No, I'm afraid I don't . . . not yet."

"So what's the answer to my question?"

Amanda again smiled with the same ironic expression. A long silence hung in the air.

"I will think about it, Geoffrey," she said at length.

Amanda rose. There was no use prolonging the evening.

"Tell your parents thank you for the dinner," she said. "It was delightful, and I am appreciative that you all remembered me on my birthday. And thank you for the rose—it was very thoughtful of you."

She turned, left the room, and walked unescorted to the front door and let herself out.

83

Acceptance

───── ◆◆◆ ─────

*A*manda walked away from the house in a somber mood.

The taxi ride through the dark streets of Mayfair was quiet . . . melancholy . . . depressing. The evening's events slowly replayed themselves over in her mind, every word of every conversation now in retrospect tinged with new subtleties of meaning in light of what had transpired.

That ring must have cost two or three hundred pounds—more money than she had left to her name. No young woman who wanted to marry for money could do better than to marry into the family of Gifford Rutherford!

How could she have sunk so low, that it would come to this—a marriage proposal from Geoffrey Rutherford, her second cousin? It was not the way she imagined her life progressing.

Thoughts of the future unconsciously stimulated thoughts of the past. A brief fit of nostalgia swept through her. Her mother's face, with a great smile upon it, rose in her mind's eye.

At the thought of her mother a lump rose in Amanda's throat. She wanted to cry.

What in the world had she done with her life!

She had just been proposed to. Shouldn't she be happy? And by a wealthy young man who could give her everything any young woman could possibly want.

She was almost out of money, and now here was—

Her own words came back into her mind. *I will think about it, Geoffrey.*

Suddenly she realized what she had said. What could have come over her?

Think about it!

Think about marrying *Geoffrey*!

The very idea was positively disgusting!

By the time she arrived back at the Halifax house, Amanda had made up her mind what to do. And it was definitely *not* to marry Geoffrey.

The following morning she told Mrs. Thorndike that she would accept her kind offer to accompany her as lady's companion.

"That is wonderful, dear!" exclaimed Mrs. Thorndike. Mrs. Halifax smiled at the development. She had been certain Amanda would come around.

The next day or two around the house were ones of great enthusiastic planning and preparation. Mrs. Thorndike was almost beside herself. Amanda, however, seemed noticeably subdued. A voyage to the Mediterranean did not excite her. Nothing excited her.

Almost the moment the decision was made, Amanda found herself thinking of Devonshire. And now as she recalled them, a certain quiet melancholic nostalgia drew itself around her thoughts.

As on the ride back from her birthday dinner, it made her want to cry, though she did not know why. Did she actually . . . miss the country?

The fits of nostalgia increased over the coming days. Perhaps she ought to go back for a visit to Heathersleigh before leaving. She really ought to see her mother one last time.

That same evening she told Mrs. Halifax that she would be leaving for a few days.

"Where are you going, dear?"

"I want to see my mother before I leave."

Mrs. Halifax took in the information with inward frown.

"Do you think that is such a good idea, Amanda?" she said. "As things presently stand between you and your parents, it seems that such contact might be too painful for you."

"I just think it is something I should do," replied Amanda.

"I see," nodded Mrs. Halifax. She did not like the idea. Parental involvement at this stage could prove dangerous to their plans. There must be no reconciliation, no creeping in of past fondnesses. The distance and alienation must be preserved.

But there appeared nothing she could do at present. She would just have to make sure nothing came of it, and that Amanda returned to them unscathed.

84

The Black Hand

◆ ◆ ◆

The grimy tavern in Belgrade was a far cry from the upscale coffeehouses of Vienna, where the man who had just entered would have preferred to be right now. But important business had brought him here.

He had spent some of the fondest times of his student years in two or three of Vienna's fine cafés, and had loved the city ever since.

Unfortunately, the Serbian capital of Belgrade was not Vienna. The city had felt the effects of centuries of Turkish, Hungarian, and Austrian overlordship as well as the recent years of strife from the two recent Balkan wars. Its Moorish name, *Darol-i-Jehad*—the home of wars of the faith—was not altogether inappropriate.

He glanced up from the dark corner where he sat with his second cup. At least the coffee here was tolerable, a lingering legacy to the Turks, who, whatever else might be said of them, could still finesse the world's strongest brew from the energy-giving aromatic beans.

His dealings with the underground organization had begun during those heady days in Vienna when socialism, talk of revolution and independence, and new alignments in the world were all new and exciting. There was no such thing as Die Schwarze Hand then. But his contacts and friends from those days, among them several Serbian nationals, had later become involved in its inception after the Bosnian crisis of 1908.

He had kept contact with them through the years. And now with tensions rising between Serbia and Austria-Hungary, gradually he found himself drawn into the activities of the terrorist organization.

It was not so much that he believed in what they were doing—certainly not with their ethnic fanaticism. It began merely to help a friend. But the danger possessed a seductiveness of its own and could not but draw him. The politics of the different sides were less interesting to him than that they were exciting, dangerous . . . and lucrative. He had nothing against the Austrian government any more than he did the Russians or anyone else.

Actually, had he reflected on it to any depth, he probably didn't have many good reasons for involvement other than the chance to travel and the secret thrill of playing both sides of the fence with his double life, coming and going respectably in society, no one knowing what he did when he was away. Sometimes he thought of himself as a modern-day Scarlet Pimpernel, even though he knew he was but a minor player in a vast network he knew little about, and without quite such a noble cause to fight for as the legendary English dandy. But these were modern times. All so-called causes now had strings attached.

He glanced at his watch and took another sip from his cup, its contents growing lukewarm as he waited.

A minute later two figures entered. He raised a single black-gloved hand slightly to signal his friend from the shadows. The two approached. The Serb and the Englishman greeted one another.

"This is Princip," said the Serb. The young newcomer nodded at the coffee drinker.

They sat down and ordered two pints of dark ale.

The Englishman did not like the look of his friend's accomplice. The bulge under his coat likely concealed a gun. He appeared unbalanced, although, he sometimes thought, so did half the people in this country.

"My friend may need transport out of the country," said the Serb.

"It can be arranged," replied the Englishman. "When?"

"That is yet to be determined. We are awaiting the right opportunity."

"For what?"

"You will know when that moment comes."

"It was my understanding the house in Vienna was the safest retreat."

"If all goes well, perhaps. But that could only bring added danger. Our kind are increasingly at risk in Austria."

He paused and chuckled lightly.

"Besides," he added, "during our last visit, my young friend here was a bit more vocal than is sometimes advisable. I fear he may have given some offense."

"I see," replied the Englishman. "If you do require my services, it may not be possible for me to attend to it personally. My movements are more closely watched these days . . . since the trouble in—"

"Don't mention it, my friend. If you can assist us with arrangements, we will see that you are not compromised."

"But your friend Princip here . . . what is his game?"

"No game, but deadly serious business," rejoined the other. "We intend to bring down the entire Austrian government."

The Englishman eyed his friend, then let his gaze drift toward the fellow called Princip. He looked more like a madman than a politico.

"Well," he laughed, not more than half believing his friend, whose bold ideas he had been listening to for ten years, since their first meeting in the Kaffe Kellar. "At least when you do, I will have rights to the inside story."

"The whole world will know it then."

"How do you mean?"

"We are watching the movements of certain Austrian nobles. A trip is planned through Sarajevo in a few months. Can the arrangements be made from there?"

The Englishman took in the question thoughtfully, not sure what to make of it.

"I never know what to think of you hot-blooded revolutionaries in this part of the world," he laughed after a moment. "But yes, I have friends in the region."

"Good. It will not be long now."

The Englishman rose, downed the dregs from his cup, grimaced slightly, then set the cup down on the table.

"You know how to contact me," he said, then left. He had to get back to the official business which he had arranged for to bring him here.

85

Return

As the carriage wheels crunched along the gravel approach to Heathersleigh Hall, the sound seemed too loud, as if it were disturbing a peculiar sense of quiet that had descended over the whole region. No words were passed between Amanda and the coachman she had hired from the village, a man relatively new to Milverscombe who knew nothing of who she was.

In another minute or two they drew up in front of the stately stone mansion.

Only a moment Amanda waited, glancing back and forth with the strangely altered vision that adulthood brings. She did not want to be pensive just now. She took the man's hand, stepped down, paid, thanked, and dismissed him, then walked toward the front of the house.

She could not help but be nervous. She had struggled the entire train ride with many conflicting emotions, having no idea what most of them even meant. But she had determined not to let them show.

She was certainly not so nervous as she would have been had she been thinking any moment to encounter her father. She probably wouldn't have come at all had he been here. But she had Cousin Gifford to thank for the tidbit of information that he would be in London all week. By the time he returned, she would be gone. That fact could not eliminate the nervousness, but at least she could relax in knowing she didn't have to face him.

No sign of life was apparent. Where was everyone? she wondered.

The inner hush deepened as she approached the front door. She felt that she was reliving some dream from far away, in a scene hazily familiar yet unreal. Mingled memories of childhood rushed in upon her, along with the peculiar sensation that she had never been here before, but that the girl in her mind's eye had actually been someone else.

Amanda reached the front door, paused only briefly wondering if she should knock, then set her hand to the latch. It opened to her touch, swinging silently back on well-oiled hinges.

The simple motion of the door brought an involuntary smile to her lips. She had never thought consciously of it in her life, but suddenly she was reminded of her father's penchant for keeping things operating efficiently.

The entry into Heathersleigh Hall was not the only door that opened in that moment. An invisible but momentous change began to grind into motion, though Amanda did not perceive its import. It was the first infinitesimal movement *toward* rather than *away* from the one whose being was the most important doorway through which she herself would have to walk in order to discover the Fatherhood of God.

He was always trying to make things the best he could, she thought to herself.

The realization followed that such had also been the case with people. Whatever might be done to make someone's life more pleasant, even in some trivial way, that would her father do.

Though not for her. She shook her head to dispel the warm thoughts of her father that were trying to intrude. But she could not prevent them, and subtly smiled again.

She had never noticed the fact before now. As she grew she had become preoccupied with, as she thought, his inattention to her needs and those of his fellow man in the community and the world. But now dozens of incidents involuntarily sprang up in her memory, including one time many, many years before when she had seen him, oil can in hand, lubricating these very hinges.

With such insights about her father came a few drops to loosen the rust from the doors of Amanda's own heart. Years of character direction had silently, invisibly begun to reverse, though Amanda scarcely knew it. Nor did it dawn on her that it was the first memory in years of the man she had called father not accompanied by a rousing of angry emotions.

Her own inner door would not swing back and forth quite so freely as this at which she stood for some time yet. But a good beginning is the most important step toward all eternal objectives, and that beginning had just been made.

Still smiling, and unaware of the deeper implications of the memory, Amanda walked inside.

The sound of her footstep on the tile floor of the entryway brought a figure to the landing above.

The eyes of mother and daughter met. A moment—a second, an eternity—followed. What words could convey the tidal wave of emotions which struggled to gush forth in each, yet which were kept back behind gigantic dikes of uncertain reticence.

"Amanda!" said Jocelyn at length, in questioning, fearful, joyous disbelief.

"Hello, Mother," said Amanda.

Jocelyn was already on the stairs, not exactly running but hurrying briskly down them. Her pounding mother's heart twisted in a hundred directions before she reached the bottom. Her eyes were already filled with tears and the tidal wave was about to burst forth.

But at the last instant, lingering uncertainty prevented it.

She could not quite overcome the strain of previous encounters, nor forget Amanda's harsh words. Her arms ached to throw themselves around her daughter in that most natural of all human impulses—the urge toward *oneness* with our fellows. Yet she was not able to risk the fear of being rebuffed yet again. She slowed her step, then approached indecisively, arms clinging unwillingly to her side.

Amanda saw the hesitation. She was no more prepared than Jocelyn for intimacy right yet, and tried to ease the awkwardness with a light comment.

"I'm sorry I didn't write ahead," she said.

The words finally unlocked the mother's heart, even if the tidal wave was still kept at bay, and she gave Amanda as much a hug as she dared. Amanda returned the embrace somewhat stiffly, but with genuine affection.

"Oh, Amanda," said Jocelyn stepping back, "you are welcome *any* time. I'm just sorry George and your father aren't here. They would love to see you!"

"Where is George?" asked Amanda.

"In Exeter, and your father is in London. How long will you be here? He is due back on Friday."

"Only for a day or two—"

Jocelyn winced but did her best not to show it. The hope had already burst to life within her that possibly Amanda's appearance signified something more than a mere visit.

"—I have to get back."

"I am glad you came, Amanda. It is so good to see you!"

Just then another form appeared on the stairway. Amanda glanced up.

"Hello, Catharine!" said Amanda, smiling and taking a few steps toward her. "Goodness, you have changed since I saw you last—you're beautiful!"

Her twenty-year-old sister, rarely at a loss for words, did not reply immediately.

Catharine stood, hand on the balustrade, displaying the same awkward indecisiveness as had her mother. She made an attempt at a smile at this unexpected guest whom she remembered so well, yet hardly knew. The big sister of her memory was confused with images of her own childhood. Now before her stood a young lady appearing so much older and refined. Catharine's *eyes* told her it was Amanda, and the *voice* was the same. But her feet, brain, and voice all balked together.

Amanda observed the look on her sister's face and it puzzled her. The confusion lasted only an instant. For the first time in all her twenty-four years, Amanda Rutherford suddenly realized they were *afraid* of her. Her own mother and sister!

The stunning revelation stung her to the quick. The power it might have caused her to feel at another time in her life now felt positively dreadful. She didn't want to be fearsome . . . she only wanted to be herself.

Within seconds Catharine recovered her shock, confusion, and reticence all at once and bounded down the stairs. She did not hesitate a moment, but immediately confronted Amanda with her outstretched arms and embraced her as if they were children. From the momentary observation of fear on her face, Amanda now found herself smothered in loving sisterly delight, swallowed up in the presence of one whom she had always considered, and whom she had continued to remember, as such a little girl.

Lo and behold, her younger sister was now at least four inches taller and twenty pounds heavier than she! She herself had become the smallest member of the family. Catharine's physical appearance reminded her of how long she had been away.

"Amanda! I can't believe it!" exclaimed Catharine in girlish laughter. "You look so nice! And you're here—I didn't know if I'd ever see you again."

"What about you?" rejoined Amanda, caught up in Catharine's good spirits and laughing with her. "You're so—"

"Big?" said Catharine.

"That's not what I was going to say—but . . . grown up."

"It's all right if you say big—I don't mind."

"We were just about to have lunch," said Jocelyn, feeling great relief at how easily Catharine had broken the ice. "Won't you—that is . . . you can stay long enough to join us?"

"Yes . . . yes, of course, Mother. If it is all right, as I said, I would like to stay for a day or two."

"Oh, Amanda," said her mother, some of her pent-up emotion now escaping, "of course." Her eyes flooded as she spoke. "That would be wonderful! This will always be your home."

Amanda did not reply. The word sounded strange in her ears. *Home.*

This hadn't been her home for years. But neither was there anyplace else she would call by that name.

Then the question struck her: Did she even have a home at all?

"I'll ring Hector to take your bag up to your room," Jocelyn was saying as Amanda tried to shake off the momentary reflection. They began making their way toward the kitchen.

"Why can't you stay longer?" asked Catharine. "Why can't you just . . . *stay*?"

"I'm leaving for the Continent next week," replied Amanda.

"The Continent!" exclaimed Jocelyn.

Amanda explained the offer. "I am no longer involved with the Pankhursts, you see, and it is the opportunity of a lifetime." As she spoke the words, Amanda did not divulge her own ambivalence.

Jocelyn's heart sank. She had hoped perhaps Amanda's coming signaled something else.

"Yes ... yes, I see," she replied, doing her best to sound positive. "That does sound like a wonderful opportunity."

They entered the kitchen. Sarah Minsterly, who had heard the voices but hadn't imagined who might be their guest, nearly dropped the tray of biscuits in her hand onto the floor.

"Miss Amanda!" she said.

"Yes, Sarah, it is me," replied Amanda. "How are you?"

"Very well, miss—thank you."

She turned, set down the tray, and began flustering about nervously to set another place on the table.

86

Strange Sensations

*O*nce initial pleasantries, greetings, and exclamations were past, the conversation languished. It was not for lack of trying, but were it not for Catharine, it would have proved awkward indeed. There were just at present too few connecting points in all their lives.

The two sisters and mother did their best to keep up the conversation, but had succeeded mostly in exchanging a series of superficial questions and answers. None of the three knew how to find a place to link with the deepest parts of the others they had never known. They had all grown in six years. Catharine and Jocelyn had become best friends, and sad to say, Amanda was no longer part of their lives.

Catharine and Jocelyn were full of questions. But many of them involved subjects and individuals Amanda knew they would be uncomfortable hearing about. She did speak freely about Cousin Gifford's family—omitting mention of the most recent exchange with Geoffrey. And she and Catharine enjoyed a laugh about Hubert Powell's casanovian attempts to woo both their affections. But mention of his name brought to the minds of both Amanda and her mother the argument which came on the heels of Amanda's seventeenth birthday and her leaving Heathersleigh for London. A period of strained silence followed.

Jocelyn's and Catharine's hearts both ached as they all sat in the kitchen together an hour after Amanda's arrival, prolonging the meal with an extra cup or two of tea, yet it was obvious to both that in many ways Amanda was now a stranger. That Amanda was herself aware of the awkwardness made the timid exchanges all the more clumsy.

When lunch was over, after an unsettling attempt by mother and sister to make Amanda comfortable in her former room—which was exactly as she remembered it, and yet so changed to the eyes of her adulthood—Amanda wandered outside.

The emotional homecoming followed by an admittedly awkward meal had put her in a thoughtfully receptive mood.

A peacefulness hung in the air. Devon was certainly different from London—much different. She used to hate it so. But she had to admit . . . it was nice here.

But quiet.

So quiet. . . . She heard birds chirping somewhere off in the trees.

As Amanda strolled about the lawn near the house, she realized that the stillness was not just because she was in the country. There was something missing, an energy, a vitality—voices, laughter, things going on, projects and discussions, questions and banter. And she knew what it was that was absent.

Or rather . . . *who* it was.

She had always resented her father's overpowering influence. And yet she realized as she walked that his absence was responsible for the giant hush that seemed to have descended over everything. She had always considered him drab and lifeless.

Had he in fact been the spirit and soul of Heathersleigh all along?

But she was glad he wasn't here just now. She couldn't bear to see him.

Amanda hardly knew what to make of the questions that rose and fell within her consciousness like a quietly bubbling sea of inner reflection. She could *feel* that there was a difference about the place with her father gone. Everything *looked* the same, but nothing *was* the same.

Had it all been worth it, she wondered, doing the things she thought she'd wanted to do when she left here? What had her efforts accomplished in the end? Had she really made any difference about anything? Now she was back at Heathersleigh, and, except for the remarkable change in Catharine, everything was the same. What had it all been for?

She came upon what had once been but a small plot of heather between the east wing of the house and the wood at the edge of the lawn. She paused to gaze out over what had now become an expansively cultivated garden area. She remembered her father and mother working here, but had had no idea into what a magnificent little world they had transformed it.

More thoughts of her father slowly infiltrated her memory. She recalled hearing him talk about wanting some particular species of heather in bloom year round. It was all nicely trimmed too. She had despised any memory of him until this day. But as she thought about him, and imagined what it would be like if he chanced to walk up right now, she realized he would have a great smile of love on his face, and would speak kindly and warmly to her.

The thought stung. He *did* love her. Was that really such a terrible thing for a man to feel about his daughter?

Why had she resented so deeply just the fact that he *loved* her and wanted the *best* for her, just like he wanted the best for everything and everyone? Was that really such a terrible thing for a man to want? But, she argued with herself, he had such a way of controlling everything, always trying to make everybody be like him.

Amanda turned away and began walking again. These were unwelcome questions. Her thoughts had become suddenly far more personal and uncomfortable than she had bargained for. She was not ready for them. Yet she could do nothing to prevent them.

She continued walking, more hurriedly now, as if the mere movement of her legs and arms would rescue her from the unsought introspection. Leaving the trimmed lawn north of the Hall, she found herself walking across the open fields with no particular destination in mind. Activity was what she needed right now, anything to keep her mind from dwelling on unpleasant thoughts and melancholy memories.

Behind her, in a second-floor window, the silent silhouette of her mother watched Amanda recede toward the rolling hills in the distance.

Moisture again slowly filled Jocelyn's eyes, and she blinked it back, watching now through blurred vision the back of the girl who had made herself a stranger to her heart. How she longed to hold the daughter who had always resisted her embrace. How could the precious child she had carried in her womb . . . how could those happy times and optimistic hopes have . . .

She could not complete the thought. Her eyes flooded with tears and she turned away from the window. Thoughts like these were not what she had anticipated on that joyful day of Amanda's birth when first she held the tiny, wonderful, helpless form in her arms.

Jocelyn sought her bed, lay down upon it, and wept.

There were no answers to such questions. At least tears would temporarily wash away their sting, and soothe the ache of her heart with their sad balm.

In her own room, Catharine too had been observing Amanda. She was not quite yet ready to cry for her—a sister's ache could not extend so deep as a mother's. But her thoughts were quiet and her heart sad. She too eventually lay upon her bed, and likewise tried to pray for Amanda, though she hardly knew how.

Meanwhile, as her mother grieved and her sister prayed, Amanda found herself standing quietly in the middle of her father's prayer wood. She had not even realized this to be her destination until she was here. She remembered the day she secretly followed him here. She had not even thought of the place since.

But she could not remain more than a few seconds. A strong sense of Presence filled the silence, and she was not prepared to encounter it.

Amanda turned and left the private sanctuary.

Maggie and Bobby McFee came to her mind. She would go visit them. They would take her mind off her father. . . .

◆ ◆ ◆

Two days later, after a generally hospitable yet nonetheless awkwardly formal visit, Amanda Rutherford returned to London.

87

Departure

◆ ◆ ◆

*W*ith thoughts of the *Titanic* in her mind, and trembling just slightly as a result, Amanda followed an exuberant Mrs. Thorndike up the steep gangway onto the deck of the luxury Greek cruise ship *Ianthina.*

They found a place along the crowded rail, among many hundreds doing likewise to see their friends and loved ones, and after waving one last time down to Mrs. Halifax onshore, went to find their stateroom.

The two days back at Heathersleigh had thrown Amanda into an odd state of perplexity concerning her future. It was obvious after the visit that she did not belong there.

Yet London too had grown strange, cold, and unfamiliar. Even as she arrived back in the great metropolis, it seemed different.

She was glad for the upcoming cruise. She had nothing else to look forward to.

At Mrs. Halifax's suggestion she had withdrawn the final £107 from her account. She didn't exactly like the idea of having nothing to come back to. But she had gone along with the idea. If friends of Mrs. Halifax's were going to put them up in Vienna, she wanted to do nothing to ripple the waters of the friendship now. She would watch herself and make sure she didn't foolishly spend so much as a shilling.

And maybe it was time to cast caution to the wind. She was either about to have the adventure of her life, or end up a pauper! Perhaps both, Amanda thought mordantly.

Two hours later the *Ianthina* was steaming out of Portsmouth, bound for Lisbon, her first port of call. From there they would pass through the Strait of Gibraltar, with stops to follow in Algiers, Marseilles, Naples, Malta, and Crete, before entering the Aegean Sea and the islands of Greece. Three weeks from today they would be in Athens.

After that, Mrs. Thorndike's plans were indefinite. Mrs. Halifax was to meet them in Vienna for the summer, at the home of her hospitable friends. They planned a thorough visit in the Austrian capital and talked of taking the Orient Express back across the Continent to Paris, or else traveling the southern route from Belgrade to Venice and Rome and then north to France, before returning to England.

She would probably have to think about her future then ... but at least for now she could put it out of her mind and try to enjoy herself.

PART VI

◆◆◆

War!
1914

88

Churchill and Rutherford

*T*he First Lord of the Admiralty for the United Kingdom of Great Britain and Ireland walked thoughtfully along Downing Street where he had just left a meeting with the prime minister and his top military advisors.

Confidential documents seized less than forty-eight hours earlier indicated that the situation in the east was more grave than they had realized. A plot appeared afoot to assassinate a major world leader.

The only question was . . . *which* leader?

Tsar Nicholas II of Russia was the most likely. The Bolsheviks were growing increasingly restless, and it was only a matter of time before the whole country exploded. The Russian colossus to the east was a huge mysterious unknown, whose private inner workings were as shadowy as its military might was fearsome. The military planners of Europe usually looked to Russia first, and internal unrest threw a great unknown into the equation of potential war.

Threats had also been made against Emperor Franz Joseph of Austria by Serbian nationalists, and against Greek Prime Minister Venizelos. The king of Greece, George I, had been assassinated only a year before during the First Balkan War. Factions in that country seemed intent on adding a second murder to the list.

But what if the threats pointed elsewhere . . . to Paris, even London? There were those who feared that the lives of England's Prime Minister Asquith, or even George V, might likewise be in danger.

Nor was this all. The documents hinted at a clandestine operation, planned for years but only recently put into effect, whereby foreign agents were being moved in and out of England without detection.

Churchill and other British leaders had been aware of the danger posed by internal sabotage, espionage, and counterespionage for years. The Agadir crisis had prompted frank discussions concerning German spies and agents in many British ports. Further investigation had uncovered an extensive system of British men and women on Berlin's payroll. Lists began to be compiled for the War Book.

Coded language concerning this new discovery apparently pointed to some Irish connection, though they had not been able to fully decipher it. Immediately upon learning of it, Churchill had ordered a thorough combing of the Irish coast, especially between Dublin and Cork, which seemed the most likely, as well as updated intelligence files on the region.

This was serious news indeed. If spies were able to move freely throughout England without detection after all the attempts to root out their identities and organizations, what security was left them? Churchill had been issuing warnings for years. Now it seemed his worst fears were being realized.

Churchill's thoughts drifted to Charles Rutherford. Could any of these developments have to do with the suspicious group that had tried to recruit him? Perhaps he ought to talk to Sir Charles again.

Several days later the two men were speaking in confidential tones in a London hotel room. After the alarming communiqué, Churchill did not even want to trust this conversation to his office. News of an active spy network had everyone in the government on edge.

"Do you actually think all this is connected to that business with Hartwell Barclay?" Charles asked.

"We have no way of knowing for certain," replied Churchill. "But after his disappearance, the secret service uncovered several disturbing connections about his background that were completely unknown. You haven't heard any more from them?"

"No, although attacks are now being leveled at me."

Churchill nodded. "I saw that piece in the *Sun*—totally spurious. I am sorry it has come to this, Sir Charles—one of the hazards of being in the public eye, I suppose. You're not worried about it?"

"Not for my own sake. I ceased being concerned for my reputation long ago. If they want to discredit me in the public eye because I would not go along with their scheme, whatever it is, I will lose no sleep over it. The only thing I worry about is my family, and how the controversy will affect them. My greatest fear is that they will try to use one of my family to get at me."

"Do you consider that possible?"

"I have a daughter who is not with us, and . . . well, let me just say it is a troublesome situation."

"I am sorry to hear that," said Churchill sincerely. "But you don't think she has some connection with this fellow Barclay and his clique?"

"None that I'm aware of. But she is on the Continent, and that fact alone concerns me. But she had been living with Halifax's widow, and she was present at that one Fountain meeting I attended."

"Hmm . . . yes, I see," nodded Churchill.

A lengthy and thoughtful silence followed.

"The situation is not looking good, Sir Charles," said Churchill at length. "Once again events in Greece and elsewhere in the Balkans are growing hot. No sooner has the dust settled on the Second Balkan War but that a third appears imminent. Thus far, Germany has remained quiet . . . but for how long?"

Charles nodded, taking in Churchill's words seriously, knowing full well what they meant.

"If worse comes to worst, Sir Charles," the First Lord of the Admiralty went on, "it might be that I shall call on you."

"I am available anytime."

"I mean in an *active* role, Sir Charles."

"You don't actually mean—"

Churchill nodded.

"I may ask you to take up your commission again," he said. "I will need men of your caliber and leadership commanding my fleet—men I can trust."

Charles returned Churchill's penetrating gaze in disbelief. It was clear the words he had just heard were deadly serious.

"By the way," Churchill added, "have you heard from Chalmondley Beauchamp lately?"

"No, why?"

"It seems he has disappeared as well. There are some strange rumors circulating that he may be part of this thing."

89

The City of Mozart

*A*manda awoke, sun streaming through the window of her room, and tried to remember where she was.

She had not lain down at night in the same place more than two or three nights in a row for the last month. Most of those nights had been spent on board the *Ianthina*. The cruise had been relaxing, but tedious after a while. She read quite a bit, and some of the sights were fascinating, though after a while they all looked the same. A mysterious Greek man had shown more than a passing interest in her, which had added intrigue to the final stages of the voyage.

A week earlier they had finally arrived in Athens. After a tour of the ancient land so recently besieged by the conflict of the Balkan wars, she and Mrs. Thorndike had taken the southern Orient line north through Belgrade and Budapest, arriving in Vienna the day before. Amanda was glad to get out of the wartorn Balkans. Everyone there was unfriendly and suspicious and seemed angry. She was afraid fighting might break out again anytime. At least now they were in a city of culture and refinement.

Her money was dwindling faster than she liked. But they were now safe in Austria with friends, and on their way back west.

Amanda rose and dressed, then knocked on Mrs. Thorndike's door. She took a more careful look at their surroundings as they went down the stairs to breakfast a few minutes later. This was an odd place, she had to admit. From everything Mrs. Halifax had said, she expected to be staying with a family, but this was more like a boardinghouse. They had been let in by a side entrance last evening by the most peculiar woman who made not the slightest effort to make them feel welcome. She showed them their rooms without fanfare and, with scarce more than a half dozen words, told them when and where they could find breakfast, then immediately returned to her chair looking out on an uninteresting side street. Whether she knew who they were or had been expecting them was not discernible from her countenance.

After breakfast she and Mrs. Thorndike went out, this time through the front door, for their first look at Vienna. Amanda was too tired to do much sightseeing, but they would walk to the Ring and back, and maybe stop at one of the famous coffeehouses.

As they began walking down the sidewalk, Amanda glanced back. She wanted to be certain of the address and street to make sure she didn't get lost. The number was displayed on the side of the stone building, in small letters. It read Number 42. The street they were on was called Ebendorfer.

"I have always wanted to visit Vienna!" said Mrs. Thorndike with bubbly enthusiasm, thumbing through her guidebook as they walked. Her handbag was stuffed with city maps and various paraphernalia. "I am going to see if I can get tickets for us to the Mozart concert later in the week."

The great Ring was only two or three long blocks away and within ten or twelve minutes they approached it. Completed in 1865, the sixty-yard wide, two-and-a-half-mile diameter street encircled the Old City of Vienna, the imperial center of the ancient Habsburg dynasty. Around its circumference a magnificent display of new buildings had been under construction for the previous fifty years, from the State Opera House to several modern art academies to the parliament and other city government buildings—all of which made Vienna, the fourth largest city of Europe, also one of its most beautiful and stunning.

For all her enthusiasm, Mrs. Thorndike soon tired of the walk. They caught a cab into the center of the Old City, where they got out at St. Stephen's Cathedral. After an hour inside its majestic nave, both women needed a rest. Vienna would take weeks to see!

As they gradually recovered from the rigors of their month of travel, Mrs. Thorndike arranged for them to attend a performance of the Vienna Boys' Choir, as well as performances of Mozart, Beethoven, and Strauss. There was, of course, a tour of the Imperial Palace, called the Hofburg, and shopping at the Graben.

And music was everywhere. In nothing was Vienna so famous as for its music. Gradually the charms of the city of Mozart began to infect Amanda. All the sights so ancient and romantic that the boredom she had begun to feel on the voyage for a time disappeared. She found herself thinking again more fondly of home, remembering both her parents' passion for Mozart. After a few days she was enthusiastically helping Mrs. Thorndike plan what they would do and see, and what day excursions they would take.

In the midst of the history and culture and music and beautiful architecture, however, Amanda could not but be aware of an underlying militaristic atmosphere pervading the city. Not only were soldiers everywhere—she had almost grown accustomed to that after traveling through Greece and Serbia—they seemed on edge, wary, watchful, suspicious of everyone who passed. Sometimes she even thought they were looking at her.

Nor could she keep from being suspicious herself. Once leaving the *Ianthina*, the entire atmosphere changed. The very air was charged with tension.

And in the peculiar house on Ebendorfer Strasse where they were staying, with its unusual mix of ages and nationalities, she could never tell what anyone was thinking.

90

Subtle Shift in Loyalty

*A*manda and Mrs. Thorndike had now been in Vienna a week and a half.

For her part, Amanda considered it more fascinating—though sightseeing with Mrs. Thorndike *was* tiring!—than sailing about through Greek islands with little do to but sit and watch the water go by. They had visited so many buildings and museums and parks and churches and art galleries in the past ten days that they were all beginning to run together in her brain.

Still the peculiarity of this house struck her, with its strange comings and goings—often in the middle of the night—and the strange assortment of individuals who somehow seemed associated with the place.

A tall, thin, white-haired gentleman seemed to be loosely in charge, and had gradually become more and more friendly toward them. He was apparently an Englishman living in Vienna. By now he was the closest they had to what might be called a host, sharing most of their meals, inquiring as to their needs, and in every way deporting himself with friendly and gentlemanly manner. Mrs. Thorndike, Amanda thought to herself, was in danger of becoming smitten with him.

One morning, wondering what prospects the day would hold, Amanda sat at breakfast with several student types, one young man with dark skin and a fanatical look in his eyes whom she had not seen before. The look in his eyes reminded her of Emily Davison. Mrs. Thorndike had not yet made her appearance.

"Are you connected with the university?" she asked the white-haired Englishman.

"Many of us are. But it is much wider than that."

"What is?"

"Our organization."

"What organization?" asked Amanda.

"That to which we in this house are connected."

"I assumed it was associated with the university," she said casually, sipping her tea.

"Our affiliations extend throughout Europe, even to England," said the white-haired gentleman.

"But what kind of group is it?"

"We are trying to help people understand that war and conflict is not the way to truth, and to see that there must be brotherhood between all," he replied, his voice growing soft and hypnotic. As he spoke his eyes penetrated deeply into hers across the table.

"I certainly believe that," said Amanda, fidgeting slightly and trying to look away. The lure of his eyes, however, was too much to resist.

"I am sure you would find yourself in agreement with most of our ideas," he said. "But, sad to say, many in England are closed to our purposes."

"Why?"

"They do not see the light," he replied. "They think themselves enlightened, but actually are in the darkness about the new order that is to come."

"Is that why you left England?" asked Amanda, her interest in his strange words curiously aroused.

"One of the reasons. I felt my services were needed to bring light to those who would listen."

"Why don't you tell them back home?"

"We have tried. But they do not listen. They consider voices such as ours a foreign influence. They even call us dangerous."

"Surely they would not say that about an Englishman like you."

The man nodded with sad expression. "Because some of my views are out of the ordinary, I am considered an extremist and eccentric. There are those who would warn people against affiliating with me."

"But that is absurd," said Amanda, some of her old zealot's blood beginning to run at the thought of anyone criticizing this man. "You are a perfectly nice and normal man, and are only speaking what should be obvious to everyone. I see nothing the least bit dangerous about you."

"Perhaps you could tell them," he suggested in a soft and innocently beguiling voice.

"Why me?"

"You are one of them. You are English yourself. Did I not hear that your father was once an M.P.?"

Amanda nodded, not realizing at the moment that she had not uttered a word concerning her father to anyone here.

"You see," he went on, "yours is a voice that would be listened to and would carry far the purpose of light and truth."

"You are English and they did not listen."

"But yours would be a more sympathetic voice because you are the daughter of a respected man."

"I see what you mean," replied Amanda, her voice now growing soft under the spell of the eyes which bored into her. The next words out of her mouth were ones she hardly realized she was speaking. An unseen impulse, as it were, compelled her to speak them. "What should I do?" she said.

They were exactly the words the man with white hair had wanted to hear.

"Perhaps," he said softly, "you could write something denouncing the present English course against Germany and Austria."

"Denounce . . . but why?" asked Amanda. Her voice was softer yet, and the question lacked emotion.

"The English government is preparing for war."

"Oh, of course . . . I see."

"Only by denouncing its ways can you then use your influence to tell the people of England of light, and of the new order which is to come."

Amanda nodded, beginning now to feel drowsy. Why did this man have such an effect on her? She felt mesmerized by his voice.

"I am sorry to have to tell you," he now went on, "but actually your own father is one who has spoken against our cause."

"My father?"

"Yes—it is sad but true. He is one of those many in England who is deceived." Barclay went on. "He has in fact spoken damaging words about some of our very people and our organization."

He showed her the interview in which her father had spoken out, then looked away to remove the spell of his eyes from hers. Something in Amanda immediately awoke. Unfortunately, it was a rekindling of the anger against her father. He saw the blood rise in her cheeks. This had been easier than he had anticipated. She was indeed a confused young lady, with severely vacillating and unsteady loyalties. She was already nearly theirs.

"I am sorry to say it," he went on, now pressing his advantage to the objective toward which he had been aiming all along, "but your father does not love truth. That much is clear from what he says here. He professes, I believe, to be a religious man. Is that correct?"

"Professes is *all* it is!" replied Amanda angrily.

"There are many like him, whose religion is so self-motivated it takes them away from truth. Would you say your father is such a man?"

"He is exactly such a man."

"I see . . . that must have been very hard for you," he added sympathetically.

Amanda nodded but did not reply further in that direction.

"You have talked about your organization several times," she said after a moment. "Does it have a name?"

A brief silence followed.

"It is called the Fountain of Light," he replied. "We desire that people see the truth. That is why we call ourselves the Fountain of Light."

"Is this its headquarters?"

"We have people everywhere."

"In England?"

"Yes, in England as well."

Amanda glanced up at that moment to see Ramsay's mother walking into the room.

"Mrs. Halifax!" she exclaimed.

"Hello, Amanda dear."

"When did you get here?"

"I arrived late last night."

"Is Ramsay with you?"

"No, dear—I'm sorry to disappoint you," she answered, sitting down at the table. "I could not help overhearing part of your conversation as I came down the stairs," she said as she poured herself a cup of coffee. "My friend Mr. Barclay is absolutely correct in everything he has told you."

"Do you belong to their organization?" asked Amanda.

"I do. We are all devoted to the proclamation of truth and bringing light to the world. That is why I think your speaking out could do the world much good in these perilous times."

The conversation gradually drifted into other channels. Soon Mrs. Thorndike joined them and began to talk about plans for the day.

Now that Mrs. Halifax had arrived, she and Mr. Barclay often accompanied Amanda and Mrs. Thorndike. Another week or two passed, at a more leisurely pace, with more and more attention given to discussion. Mrs. Thorndike grew bored with the long talks about change and new orders, and often retired to her room. Her fascination with Mr. Barclay waned.

Amanda, however, was intrigued. It felt good to think and discuss again—an activity she had missed, though without realizing it, since leaving home. More and more she came to adopt the views of the older man and woman.

Gradually they became her mentors in the principles of the Fountain.

91

A Fall

◆◆◆

Maggie McFee, husbandwoman of God's blooms, wife, and woman of God, first became aware she was not alone in her garden by forceful puffs of a great moist breathiness sounding close to her ear.

She had been weeding, cultivating, and plucking on her hands and knees for an hour in absolute solitude. She had fallen into a prayerful reverie without thought of another living soul. Startled nearly out of her wits, she rose off her hands and spun around just in time to see the black-and-white face of their aging, faithful cow take a huge mouthful of tasty yellow-and-orange nasturtiums.

"Flora!" she exclaimed. "What on earth . . . I heard nothing of your footsteps."

Momentarily confused, thinking perhaps she had lost track of time, Maggie glanced up at the sun. "But it's not time for you to be coming back—"

Suddenly she saw the tether hanging loose from the great neck onto the ground.

Anxiety at once replaced her confusion.

"Flora," she said, rising and quickly glancing all around the garden and house toward the barn, "where's my Bobby?"

Having discovered a treat more flavorful than her oats, and busily engaged in gulping down as much of the patch as she could, Flora did not answer.

"Bobby . . . Bobby!" cried Maggie, "—where are you, my man . . . Bobby?"

Already Flora felt the tug at her neck indicating that the serendipitous dessert was over. As quickly as she was able, Maggie urged the animal's huge phlegmatic bulk into motion and led her to the barn, calling and looking out frantically as she went.

The moment Flora was safe in her stall—it was obvious from a quick shout and glance about that Bobby was nowhere to be seen— Maggie flew to the house.

"Bobby, Bobby," she cried, "please be here . . . where are you, Bobby!"

But the house was as empty as the barn and the yard.

She hurried back outside as fast as she was able. But Maggie herself was seventy-six, and though in perfect health was already tiring from the exertion and mounting anxiety.

Now she made for the little pasture between the cottage and the village where on most days of the spring and summer Flora could be found grazing on Devonshire grass rather than nasturtiums.

The way was not hard to find. A well-worn dirt path led from the back of the barn, through a light wooded region for about half a mile, emerging into an open series of pastures and fields, at the edge of one of which sat Bobby's two fenced acres.

Nor did she have to seek long for her husband. Reaching a narrow wood footbridge, without railings over the small stream which also provided Flora's pasture its water, she heard a dull moan from somewhere below.

"Bobby . . . Bobby, is that you!" she cried, stopping midway across it.

Again the moan sounded, this time a little louder.

Maggie glanced frantically about, then down below where she stood on the bridge. There was Bobby lying half in the middle of the stream!

She ran back off the bridge, then scrambled down the embankment, which thankfully was not particularly steep or rugged, to Bobby's prostrate form.

"Bobby, my dear man," she cried, kneeling beside him and smothering his face in kisses,—"what ails you?"

" 'Tis aye good t' see ye, lass," he breathed, closing his eyes in relief at sight of another human face.

"But, Bobby, how on earth did you wind up down here!"

"Flora gave me a wee bump as I was leadin' her across, an' the next thing I knew I was tumblin' down an' couldn't stop meself." His voice was weak and came in short puffs.

"Well, you dear man—let me help you to your feet," said Maggie, placing an arm under one of his shoulders and trying to lift his frail form.

"Nay, nay, lass," he said, " 'tis no use. If the leg isn't broke, 'tis jist as useless t' me now as if it were."

For the first time Maggie noticed how pale his face was. His skin was cold and clammy.

"Oh, Bobby, Bobby . . . what can we do!"

"Go fer Master Charles an' Lady Jocelyn. They'll know what t' do."

"But I can't leave you."

"Ye got no choice, lass. At least the leg's in the cool o' the stream. Now go, lass. But give me one last kiss t' sustain me."

Maggie's only disobedience was in that she gave ten instead of one, then turned and scrambled up the bank and ran for the Hall as fast as her old heart and tired legs would take her.

92
Gavrilo Princip
◆◆◆

𝒯he young Bosnian student whom Amanda had seen around the house began eyeing her more regularly at meals and speaking to her whenever he chanced to find her alone. This Gavrilo Princip was younger than Amanda by four or five years and his English was not the best. And though he had a certain wild and frightening look, she did not think to be afraid, since he was one of the apparent regulars of the place. His dark skin, perpetually stubbly face—as if he had always shaved about five days before—and deep-set narrow black eyes might have caused some young women alarm. But thus far he had kept mostly to himself and she had not taken much notice of him. Everyone else seemed to know him, although he only had one close friend, a Herzegovinian Muslim by the name of Muhamed Mehmedbasic.

One afternoon when the others were away, Princip approached her. Would she like to go out with him for a visit to the coffeehouse where all the communists gathered?

The mere word struck mystery in her heart. He observed her reaction.

"These are exciting times," he added. "This is where the revolution in Russia is being planned—right here in Vienna."

"Revolution!" she repeated in shock.

"Of course. Surely you cannot be so naïve in England as not to know it is coming."

Amanda shrugged noncommittally. She and the Pankhursts had spoken of such things, but they had always seemed to her remote and far removed from her actual life. Now here she was in eastern Europe where everything she had only *heard* about was actually happening. It was both exciting and frightening.

"And some things even closer to Vienna than that," he added mysteriously. "Come . . . see for yourself," pressed Princip. "This is *real* socialism, not just the women's rights you suffragettes think of."

"How do you know of my connections with the suffragettes?"

"Ah, Princip knows all!" laughed the Bosnian. "Come!" He tried to take Amanda's hand to lead her out of the house. She pulled it back, yet nodded with a smile.

Thirty minutes later they were seated at the Kaffe Kellar sipping strong cups of Kapuziner. Amanda gazed around with wide-eyed fascination. It was exactly as Princip had described. A thin haze of blue smoke hung over the dimly lit room, where no less than five languages could be heard in heated debate around various of the tables. Amanda took it all in with the captivation of having entered a dark and shadowy political underworld. Princip seemed to know many of those present, and several came up to him and spoke in languages and dialects Amanda could not understand.

"How would you like to see even more of the country?" Princip asked after several minutes.

"I don't know . . . how do you mean?" replied Amanda.

"Come with me. I am going to Sarajevo where I have business with some associates. We are then going on to Moscow."

"Moscow!"

"I can tell you want to go with me."

"But why are you going there?"

"In Russia we will achieve more than mere votes. We will turn society upside down. Come with me—it is your chance to make history."

"Make history?"

"Yes—don't you want to be known, to be famous, to change the course of history? Your name will be remembered alongside mine for all time."

The words rung a faint familiar chord in Amanda's brain, reminding her of a time long ago and a small girl's dreams. But from the mouth of Gavrilo Princip, it all sounded wrong.

"Will there be others?" she asked. "I couldn't go with you . . . alone."

"Why not?"

"It wouldn't be proper."

Princip laughed. "You English with all your rules. It will not matter much longer anyway."

"What do you mean?"

"Because everything will be changed."

Amanda took in the Bosnian's words in light of all she had learned recently about the Fountain and its new order. Was Gavrilo Princip talking about the same thing? As he looked across the table, the fire in his eyes showed at least that whatever his ultimate intent, there could be no doubt that he was deadly serious.

93

Bedside

*B*obby McFee was resting comfortably in his bed in Heathersleigh Cottage.

Charles sat beside him, spooning tiny bits of water into his mouth, though whether Bobby himself was conscious of the operation it would be difficult to tell. As weak as he was, transporting him home, then setting the leg had been difficult procedures. Besides being in obvious pain, Bobby was utterly exhausted. He now lay limp, pale, and motionless. Catharine had gone for the surgeon, though it was doubtful he would do more than commend Jocelyn's work and pronounce extended bed rest as the most needful restorative.

Jocelyn and Maggie had just left the room and walked slowly into the sitting room.

"His body has had a dreadful shock," said Jocelyn in a low voice. "More than anything now, Maggie, he needs rest and nourishment."

"I'll get as much liquid down him as he'll take ... hot soup, tea, broth, whatever I can. How serious do you think it is?"

"His leg is badly broken," said Jocelyn. "With the wooden splint we made, and keeping it well wrapped and still, the bones will heal. But it will be slow. He will not walk for three months or more."

"My poor Bobby."

"The worst of the pain is over," said Jocelyn, trying to reassure her. "The swelling is not as bad as it might have been because of the stream. He was fortunate for the leg to land submerged as it did. He is only weak, but not suffering."

Maggie sighed. Jocelyn's words gave some comfort. But her heart was torn for the poor man she had loved so many years, who had always been so lively and vigorous.

"The doctor will be here shortly," added Jocelyn, "and we will see what he says. You know about these things as well as I do. But one of us will come and sit with you so that you will not be alone through it. One of the four of us will be with you until Bobby is at least recovered from the exhaustion and shock."

"How can I thank you, Jocelyn, my dear?" said Maggie, her eyes filling with tears. "You are so good to us."

"You and Bobby have been the best friends and neighbors ever a family could have," replied Jocelyn.

The two women embraced warmly and long without further words, then set about together making a pot of soup.

94

Alone and Far From Home
◆◆◆

$\mathcal{A}$s to the question of whether or not Princip was connected with the Fountain, Amanda did not have long to wait for an answer. Later that same evening she overheard the Englishman talking in angry tones with Mehmedbasic.

"Get rid of your friend, Muhamed," Barclay was saying. "I do not like his look."

"Princip is harmless."

"Harmless is the last word I would use to describe him."

"Besides, he is with *Die Schwarze Hand*."

"Yes, and the Black Hand is rapidly getting out of control," insisted Barclay. "Our involvement with them is nearly at an end. We cannot afford to have either of you here any longer. You bring danger to us all. I mean what I say—I want him gone. I know more about some of your activities than you may realize. We cannot afford to provide sanctuary for hotheads."

"I will talk to him," replied the Muslim.

The following morning Mrs. Thorndike announced that she would be leaving Vienna at week's end.

Unconsciously, Amanda sensed several sets of eyes around the large wooden table subtly turn in her direction.

Mrs. Halifax spoke up before anyone else had a chance to reply.

"You *will* be staying on with us here, won't you, Amanda?" she said. Her tone of voice suggested that it was already a foregone conclusion. "I've already spoken with Mrs. Thorndike about returning to England without you . . . now that you are involved with our cause."

"I . . . I don't know," said Amanda, taken momentarily by surprise. She knew Hartwell Barclay's eyes were upon her. She shrank from glancing in his direction.

"Please stay, my dear," went on Mrs. Halifax. "The Fountain needs you. Mr. Barclay has told me that you plan to begin writing leaflets and articles enlightening people back home."

"We . . . we only spoke of it a time or two—possibly, I suppose." Amanda began to feel drowsy again. It always happened when Mr. Barclay looked at her that way.

What did she have to go home to anyway? Where would she live? What would she do? And with just forty-three pounds left to her name . . . what other choice did she have?

By week's end Mrs. Thorndike was gone.

Amanda awoke the following morning feeling more isolated and alone than ever before in her life. But for better or worse she had cast her lot with these people. There was no going back on her decision now.

Within the week Amanda Rutherford was busily engaged in writing an anti-English leaflet on which Hartwell Barclay placed great hopes for the swaying of public opinion in Great Britain against the man who had spoken out against the Fountain.

95

Attempted Abduction

*F*our nights after Mrs. Thorndike's departure, Amanda awoke suddenly.

It was the middle of the night. A sound had startled her out of a deep sleep.

Now came a shuffling footstep. She froze in terror where she lay. Someone was in her room!

"Amanda," came a muffled voice in the dark . . . a man's voice.

"What . . . who's there!"

"Gavrilo."

"Gavrilo . . . what on earth!" she exclaimed, suddenly afraid and drawing the feather comforter tight around her.

"I am leaving Vienna," he said.

"What do you—what are you doing in my room?"

"Come with me," he said. She felt his voice drawing nearer.

"I can't go *with* you, good heavens!" she replied. "Please . . . please go away. It's the middle of the night."

"I want you to come with me." The Bosnian's voice was urgent, agitated.

Suddenly Amanda felt a cold hand clamp over her mouth.

"I *want* you to come with me, do you understand!"

Amanda tried to scream. A sharp pain jabbed into her side. She felt herself being pulled from the bed.

"Now get up!" said Princip. "Get dressed. You are coming with me."

Amanda nodded in mute terror. She felt the hand relax. Slowly she groped toward the edge of the bed. She saw the figure in the dark and now smelled that he had been drinking.

"Go away while I dress," she said.

"I am staying here," he rejoined angrily. "It's dark—just get dressed . . . hurry."

Amanda tried to obey, but her hands were trembling such that she could hardly find her clothes. Several long, agonizing seconds passed. She located her dress and began to slip it over her head on top of her nightgown.

Suddenly overhead the light flashed on. Amanda spun around.

In the doorway of her room stood the towering form of Hartwell Barclay.

"Princip, get out!" he ordered, undaunted by the gun the Bosnian was holding on Amanda. The eyes of the two men locked. The encounter lasted but a second or two. Then Princip turned with a curse of hatred and left the room.

"I am very sorry, Miss Rutherford," said Barclay. "Are you all right? Shall I call one of the ladies to attend to you?"

"No . . . no, thank you, Mr. Barclay—I will be fine," replied Amanda.

"Thank you—I was terrified for my life."

"He will not bother you again."

Amanda returned to bed, tried in vain to read herself to sleep, and passed the rest of the night in fitful dozing.

In the morning Princip had disappeared along with his friend Mehmedbasic. Amanda saw neither of them again.

Shortly after breakfast two mornings later Mrs. Halifax was glancing through the newspaper. "Look," she said, "a photograph of Franz Ferdinand. He and Sophie are arriving in Vienna today from Chlumetz."

"Who is he?" asked Amanda.

"The emperor's nephew and heir to the Austrian throne. They are traveling south to Sarajevo, the Bosnian capital."

Hearing the name of the city again reminded Amanda what Princip had said to her at the Kaffe Kellar. She wondered if that's where the two strange young men had gone.

"Why are they going to Bosnia?" asked Barclay.

"It says that General Potiorek has invited Franz Ferdinand to maneuvers of the Fifteenth and Sixteenth Army Corps."

"I can't imagine why he would go to Bosnia at a time like this."

"A goodwill gesture, I suppose—let the heir to the throne be seen in the provinces."

"Perhaps ... yet it sounds a bit foolhardy as well."

96

Assassination

———— ◆◆◆ ————

𝒜 message arrived in Vienna from Serbian premier Pashich to his minister in the Austrian capital.

Archduke Franz Ferdinand, nephew of Austro-Hungarian emperor Franz Joseph and heir to his throne, must be warned, Pashich urged. He must cancel his planned visit to Sarajevo. A plot was brewing. His life could be in danger.

The minister in Vienna, however, himself a Serbian nationalist, did not deliver the premier's message.

Thus, the trip went on as planned. With his wife, Sophie, the duchess Chotek of Hohenberg, Archduke Franz Ferdinand traveled south to the province of Bosnia for the ceremonial visit to view the military maneuvers.

The provinces of Bosnia and Herzegovina were far more Serbian than Austrian. Their inclusion in the empire of the Austro-Hungarian dual monarchy had been a matter of bitter resentment in Serbia for years. Most Serbs cherished the dream of a Greater Serbia, which would one day unify all Serbian peoples.

When the fifty-one-year-old archduke stepped from his train onto the platform of the Sarajevo station on June 28, 1914, therefore, he stepped into the middle of a city where he represented the accumulated hatred of the entire Serbian race against the Habsburg dynasty.

General Potiorek was at the station to meet the royal party. A brief stop followed at the Philipovic army camp. Franz Ferdinand reviewed the troops. Everything seemed calm and orderly.

The party got into six waiting cars for the drive along the Appel Quay to the City Hall. There they would be received by Sarajevo's mayor. Franz Ferdinand and Sophie rode in the backseat of a grey touring car, whose fabric top had been rolled back so that they might be seen by the people along the route. The day was warm and sunny.

The streets were crowded. Among the spectators, mingling unnoticed, moved seven young men who had long trained for this moment. Their backgrounds and nationalities were diverse, but their purpose was one. Each of the seven carried a vial of cyanide wrapped in cotton to swallow when their business was done. None planned to live beyond this fateful morning.

Near the Austro-Hungarian Bank next to the Cumurja Bridge stood Muhamed Mehmedbasic.

A few steps away stood Nedjelko Cabrinovic.

Farther toward City Hall were positioned Vaso Cubrilovic and Cvijetko Popovic.

Still farther on, near Lateiner Bridge, stood Gavrilo Princip, whose friend Trifko Grabez paced impatiently along the street nearby.

Their organizer, Danilo Ilic, moved about between the others.

As the automobile bearing the royal couple moved in the direction of City Hall, Mehmedbasic's hand went to the bomb inside his coat.

But as the second car of the processional drew even, a policeman stepped up behind him.

Mehmedbasic froze. To make a move now, and be immediately apprehended by the policeman, would undo the whole plot.

He continued to hesitate.

Within seconds it was too late. The car passed. As it continued along the thoroughfare, so too passed Mehmedbasic's chance for immortality.

The procession now approached Cabrinovic's position. This time there was no hesitation. Cabrinovic removed the bomb from his own tightly buttoned coat, struck its percussion cap on a lantern post, and hurled it straight for Franz Ferdinand's green-feathered helmet.

But the alert driver heard the pop of the cap. Instinctively his head spun and he detected something flying through the air!

He jammed his foot to the floor. The car lurched forward with sudden acceleration.

At the last instant, the archduke also saw the object flying toward them. His hand jerked up to protect his wife. The bomb struck his arm, fell behind them against the folded roof of the car, and bounced into the street.

A deafening explosion followed.

Within seconds pandemonium broke loose. Smoke billowed up from the blast. Screams erupted everywhere.

The two lead cars drove on. But those behind were forced to stop. As the archduke's car sped away Franz Ferdinand glanced back at the commotion.

"Stop the car!" he cried. "Sophie's face has a cut. I want to know if anyone else has been hurt."

The car lurched to a halt. As the archduke tended to his wife and then inquired about other injuries, the driver jumped out to inspect the car. A few flying fragments had struck it, but the damage was not severe.

A number of spectators had been hurt from the blast. No one was dead, but some injuries were serious. Several of those in the following car were bleeding badly.

Cabrinovic, meanwhile, swallowed his cyanide and leapt into the river Miljacka. But by now he had been seen. Several spectators jumped in after him, pulled him out and back onto the quay, then proceeded to beat him severely. The police arrived in time to prevent his being killed on the spot. They took him to the station, sick but still alive.

Back at the scene, once the wounded and injured were attended to, the badly shaken archducal party continued on toward City Hall.

When Gavrilo Princip heard the explosion from his own vantage point, and saw the smoke and confusion, he thought the mission had been completed before it reached him. But then after the delay the procession continued on. Now his position was all wrong. He could not see the archduke anywhere.

At City Hall, Mayor Fehim Effendi Curcic attempted to launch into his welcoming speech. But before he could utter a word, Archduke Franz Ferdinand burst forth with an angry rebuke against his city's lax security measures. Apologies and assurances followed. Again the mayor began to speak.

"Your Royal and Imperial Highness, and Your Highness," he said, turning briefly toward Sophie, altering not a word of his planned remarks as a result of what had just transpired, "our hearts are full of happiness over the most gracious visit with which Your Highnesses are pleased to honor our capital city. All the citizens of Sarajevo find that their souls are filled with happiness and they most enthusiastically greet Your Highnesses' most illustrious visit with the most cordial of welcomes. . . ."

The lengthy speech continued, serving at least the purpose of calming everyone's nerves. When the mayor was finished, Franz Ferdinand gave his planned reply.

The official delegation turned and entered City Hall. Several telephone calls were placed to the hospital. The rest of the day's plans were discussed.

Perhaps, someone suggested, they should remain at City Hall until troops could be brought in. There may be more conspirators.

No, insisted Mayor Curcic, the troops were not in proper dress for the occasion. There could not possibly be a second attempt on the same day. Plans would proceed, but along a different route. They must stop first at the hospital, insisted the archduke, to visit the wounded of their party.

When plans were finalized, and when Sophie's reception with a delegation of Muslim ladies was completed, once again the royal party and dignitaries climbed into their cars.

The drivers of the first two cars, however, had not been informed of the change of plans. According to the route originally mapped out, they mistakenly turned onto Franz Joseph Street.

"Wait ... stop!" cried General Potiorek. "We're going to the hospital. Turn around. Back to Appel Quay."

The driver obeyed the command, stopped, backed up, and began to turn and retrace the way back to the main boulevard.

◆◆◆

During the goings-on at City Hall, Gavrilo Princip had wandered aimlessly from Lateiner Bridge down to Franz Joseph Street. Here there were not so many people gathered about. He still carried a bomb and a pistol, but assumed he would not see the procession again.

All at once, about half an hour after Cabrinovic's arrest, suddenly he saw the two lead cars of the archduke's procession stopping and turning around right in front of him!

Gavrilo Princip's moment of destiny had come. He did not hesitate.

He ran straight toward the stopped touring car. He pulled out his pistol as he went and fired several times into the open backseat.

The following cars had also stopped. Seeing a man running and hearing the report of gunfire, the cars instantly emptied.

Two or three men rushed Princip. They threw themselves upon him. Screaming and yelling, the assassin now attempted to shoot himself. But they were on him before he could pull the trigger.

Screams and shouts and confusion were everywhere. Someone pulled a sword and struck at Princip's head. As he scuffled with those beating him and holding him down, somehow Princip managed to get his cyanide out of his pocket and into his mouth. But it proved as ineffective as Cabrinovic's.

When they were able, the cars sped off in the direction of the governor's residence across the river. Still no one realized that Franz Ferdinand and Sophie had been hit, he through the neck, she in her abdomen. Sophie's face was white, and blood gushed from her husband's mouth.

"What has happened to you!" cried Sophie. Her head fell to the archduke's knees.

"Sophie, Sophie," said Franz Ferdinand weakly. "*Sterbe nicht ... bleibe am Leben für unsere Kinder.*—Don't die ... stay alive for our children."

They arrived at the governor's. Doctors were waiting. A dozen people ran out and converged on the car. Hurriedly they carried the archduke and his wife inside.

But Sophie's wound had split her stomach artery. She was already dead.

Four regimental doctors performed what emergency aid they could on her husband. But Franz Ferdinand was bleeding badly from neck and mouth.

Within fifteen minutes, the archduke had gone to join his wife.

97

Ultimatum

*W*ithin days all the conspirators but Muhamed Mehmedbasic had been captured and were in police custody.

Word of the murder spread like wildfire. The entire world was outraged.

Austria had long been hoping for some pretext to invade and annex Serbia as she had Bosnia and Herzegovina in 1908. Austrian officials suspected the complicity of the Serbian government in the plot. The assassination was greeted by rejoicing in Belgrade. Official condolences were offered, but no one was really fooled. The Serbian press hailed Gavrilo Princip as a national hero.

All Europe anticipated that Austria would now invade Serbia. Many expected war.

Days passed, however, then weeks. Still Austria took no action. Tensions slowly eased.

Perhaps the brief crisis would blow over, as had all others of the previous decade.

But all was not so quiet as it seemed. German Kaiser Wilhelm II and Austro-Hungarian ambassador Count Szögyény-Marich met on July 5. Wilhelm pledged Austria his "full support." Szögyény-Marich understood his meaning well enough—if Austria took action and Russia declared war, Germany would back her action.

Thus assured by the kaiser's blank cheque of support, Austria considered its options carefully on how best to exact its revenge against Serbia.

An ultimatum followed on July 23.

———————— ♦ ♦ ♦ ————————

With heavy heart Timothy Diggorsfeld sat down in his study with the afternoon edition of the July 27 *London Times* in front of him.

The headline across the front page read: ENGLAND'S APPEALS REJECTED, MOBILIZATIONS LOOM. He went on to scan the article under the frightening words.

The demands of Austria-Hungary's July 23 ultimatum to Serbia—requiring: suppression of all nationalist propaganda and of all conspiratorial societies against Austria, the removal of all officials in the Serbian government suspected of complicity in the assassination, or of anti-Austrian propaganda, that Austrian representatives be allowed to collaborate with Serbian police investigations to root out such subversive activities against Austria, the cessation of arms trade across the Austrian border, and a formal apology for the assassination by the Serbian government—appeared to have been met by Serbian compliance.

Within five minutes of the 48-hour deadline, Serbian premier Pashich delivered in person to the Austrian minister in Belgrade Serbia's capitulation on all but minor details.

The Austrian minister, whose instructions were to accept full compliance or nothing, rejected Serbia's reply. Immediately he left Belgrade for Vienna. Both Serbia and Austria began military mobilizations.

The capitals of Europe were shocked by Austria's belligerent posture, for Serbia had gone further than anyone thought she would.

The day following these developments, yesterday, British foreign secretary Sir Edward Grey proposed a conference of mediation involving Germany, France, Italy, and Britain. The proposal was rejected by Germany, who pled with Britain and France to keep their ally Russia from aggression. Russia, however, declared a pre-mobilization of her military forces, stating that if Austria crosses the Serbian border, she would defend her brother Serbs and have no choice but to declare war on Austria.

This morning, England made another appeal to Austria, Serbia, and Russia to suspend their military preparations, pleading again for a conference of powers to mediate the crisis. At press time, however, there has been no reply to these requests. Mobilizations apparently continue throughout the region.

It is feared that the crisis, though localized, may produce a ripple effect. For if Austria invades Serbia, Russia has already declared that it will fight in support of its Serbian ally.

If Russia fights, however, Germany will step in to defend her ally Austria.

In that event, Russia's ally France would no doubt enter the conflict against Germany.

If Austria continues determined to punish Serbia for the assassination of Archduke Franz Ferdinand, the only hope against what appears a disastrous potential chain of events is for the powers of Europe to lay aside their ultimatums long enough to gather around a table of mediation. Intelligence sources, however, report only increasing rumors of military preparations in all the nations involved. . . .

Diggorsfeld set down the paper with a sigh and closed his eyes.

"Oh, God," he prayed, *"have mercy on us that we have not learned to love one another as you taught us!"*

He thought of his friend Charles Rutherford, wondering how a former naval officer would react to such developments. And young George. How would these events affect him?

Again Diggorsfeld fell to praying, this time for the Devonshire family he loved, and for the entire nation.

◆ ◆ ◆

Though all Britain's newspapers carried detailed accounts of the summer's events, few in Britain even now recognized the peril. There yet remained a sense of isolation from events so far to the east on the Continent. Average men and women vaguely knew that Luxembourg and Belgium had perpetually been neutral. But they did not recognize the extent to which that neutrality had been guaranteed by Great Britain. Within the country, and within the cabinet itself, there were strong isolationist and pacifist elements. Few even in the government thought the Austrian-Serbian conflict worth going to war over, despite Britain's guarantees to Belgium and Luxembourg.

Newspaper editorials, leaflets, and pamphlets circulated through the country in favor of one position or another, though the number of those who took the military posturing on the Continent seriously remained a minority.

Winston Churchill, as he had done as long as Charles had known him, continued to declare the danger imminent, and to sound a clear voice of preparation. Even as Timothy Diggorsfeld prayed in his office with the newspaper on his lap, in his office in the Admiralty, the first lord of the British fleet considered a grave course of action which was certain to upset those of his cabinet colleagues still determined not to be drawn into a European quarrel unless Great Britain herself were attacked.

But First Lord of the Admiralty Churchill knew this hope of many in the government for British neutrality was illusory. After Serbia's acceptance of Austria's ultimatum, he too had briefly hoped the whole crisis might blow over. Or at least be confined to the east.

But then came the news that Austria was not satisfied with the Serbian acceptance. The temperature of events continued to rise. The plan Churchill now revolved in his mind would insure Britain's best chance of success on the seas if the worst indeed came.

The navy was fully mobilized for the Royal Naval Review at Portland on the south coast of England on July 26. Though it had been scheduled to disperse following the maneuvers, Churchill had held the fleet together.

But even that might not be enough. To be ready for war, the main battle fleet must be gotten secretly north to its war station at Scapa Flow in the Orkneys, Scotland. Moreover, it must move there quickly and secretly. They must not arouse German suspicion.

It would be an obvious act of readiness for war. But Winston Churchill did not intend to be caught unprepared.

It did not take long for the first lord of the admiralty to make the decision.

He would give the secret order for the entire fleet to steam north by the most direct route, passing the Strait of Dover during the hours of darkness, eighteen miles of warships running at high speed and without lights. He would not even bring the matter before the cabinet. He would only inform the prime minister.

Churchill went to his desk and immediately began to draft the order to the commander-in-chief for the home fleets.

Tomorrow, he wrote, *Wednesday, the First Fleet is to leave Portland for Scapa Flow. Destination is to be kept secret except to flag and commanding officers. As you are required at the Admiralty, Vice-Admiral 2nd Battle Squadron is to take command. Course from Portland is to be shaped to southward, then a middle Channel course to the Strait of Dover. The squadrons are to pass through the strait without lights during the night and to pass outside the shoals on their way north.* Agamemnon *is to remain at Portland, where the Second Fleet will assemble.**

98

A Sleeper Awakes

It was not quite so far north here as to remain perpetual dusk during these summer months as in the Orkneys or especially the Shetlands. But it was far enough north that the sun set late and rose early across the North Sea.

The newcomer had not been here long enough altogether to accustom himself to the sound of quiet. His world had been London for so long that the peaceful rhythmic waves slapping against the rocky shore still kept him awake at night.

But London was behind him. His days in the Commons were over. That was another life. He had cast his fate with the future. There was no turning back now.

He had arisen early, as he did on most days since he had arrived, unable to sleep. It was the morning of July 29.

---

*Adapted from Churchill's own recollection of events, some of the thoughts in Churchill's own words, as told in *The World Crisis,* vol. 1, pp. 208–225. The dispatch to the fleet commander is verbatim as delivered.

A grey light of predawn vaguely shone through his window. He looked at his clock.

Three-twenty. He lay back and closed his eyes.

A faint sound protruded into his consciousness. At first it registered no mark. Then gradually he remembered it was not in London. He was miles from anywhere. What could account for the dull, distant sounds of engines . . . of machinery amid the waves striking the shoals?

A few more minutes he lay, thinking his mind was playing tricks on him.

No, something was out there.

He rose and peered out the window but saw nothing. But wait, there seemed some vague shape off in the distance. He squinted eastward. It was a clear morning, thankfully, with no fog. But it was still too dark to make it out.

Genuinely curious now, and more than a little concerned, he dressed quickly and went outside. Still gazing toward the horizon, he walked toward the bluff.

There was no mistaking it now—there was something out there, outlined above the black of the sea against the thin light of dawn. Wait, now he saw two ships . . . no, three.

He turned and hurried back into the house. A minute later he returned with binoculars. He sprinted for the lighthouse. From its tower he should be able to see what this was all about.

Five minutes later the onetime loyal parliamentarian was staring dumbfounded at a seemingly unceasing convoy of giant warships, squadron after squadron, hundreds of ships of varying sizes, the British First Fleet, steaming northward along the coast.

Whatever was going on, it was top secret. He had heard nothing about it.

He must notify their people at once!

He flew down the lighthouse stairs and again made for the house.

"McCrogher . . . McCrogher!" he cried, running inside. "Get up. We've got to get a message off!"

Groggily the Irishman came to himself to see his new guest standing at his bedside.

"Get up—we must send a message!"

"Ay, Mr. Bee'ch'm. I'll be with ye in a moment," said McCrogher, climbing to his feet and glancing about for his trowsers. "What kind o' message?"

"The whole English fleet's on the move, man—we've got to get word to the Continent."

"I'll get the light burnin' right away, Mr. Bee'ch'm."

"No, you fool—not till they've all passed. We can't risk the wrong people seeing the signal. Just get up there and be ready. I'll come up directly to tell you what to report as soon as the last ship is out of sight."

McCrogher ambled off, thinking to himself that a few minutes more in his bed might be turned to better advantage than sitting waiting at the top of the cold lighthouse tower. He for one certainly had no trouble sleeping with the sound of the waves in his ears.

99

War and a Witness

*C*harles Rutherford was in London on the fateful day of August 14. He and Timothy Diggorsfeld spent the morning together, a good part of it praying for the fate of their nation, and the world.

Now he was on his way to see the first lord of the admiralty.

The previous two weeks had seen the perilous dominoes fall one by one, all, many would say, unnecessary, all equally inevitable.

Ignoring Serbia's virtual agreement to the terms of its ultimatum, on July 28, Austria declared war on Serbia. The following day she bombarded Belgrade. At the same time, Germany demanded that Russia cease its military preparations, reiterating that the Austrian-Serbian conflict was isolated, and that Austria had every right to take punitive action. But it was to no avail.

On July 30, both Austria and Russia ordered general mobilizations.

On July 31, Germany delivered an ultimatum to France to stay out of the conflict.

On August 1, Germany declared war on Russia. In honor of its treaty with Russia, France ordered mobilization of its troops.

On August 2, Germany invaded Luxembourg and sent an ultimatum to Belgium. Belgium immediately appealed to England, France, and Russia to guarantee its neutrality.

On August 3, Germany declared war on France and entered Belgium. Great Britain ordered the mobilization of its fleet.

On August 4, Great Britain sent an ultimatum to Germany demanding respect of Belgian neutrality. At the same time it ordered mobilization of its army. Germany, however, attacked Liège. An hour before midnight, Great Britain was at war with Germany.

On August 6, Austria declared war on Russia.

On August 9, Serbia declared war on Germany.

On August 13, Great Britain and France declared war on Austria.

Within two fateful weeks in August of 1914, all of Europe had been drawn into what would soon be called "The Great War." Never had its like been seen in the history of man. Never before had so much of the earth's soil been at war with itself. By the end of the month, as declarations of war continued to multiply and spread to the Far East, one billion of the world's population of 1.7 billion was technically in a state of war.

An hour after leaving New Hope Chapel, Charles Rutherford was walking with Winston Churchill quietly above the banks of the Thames. London was yet peaceful, though British troops were already on the Continent, and the fighting had well begun. Churchill had managed to escape for a brief respite from meetings to visit with his friend.

"I presume you've seen this," said Churchill, handing him a small leaflet. Charles read the title: WHY THE BRITISH MUST NOT GO TO WAR. His eyes shot open as below it he read the words, "by Amanda Rutherford, daughter of Sir Charles Rutherford, Devonshire."

"Oh, Winston, I am sorry! No, I knew nothing of it."

"They're being circulated throughout London. We don't know where it originated or how it got into the country in such numbers."

Charles groaned in despair.

"How bad is it?" he said.

"It paints none too pleasant a picture of you, I'm afraid. But otherwise it's mostly rubbish. No one will pay the slightest attention to it. But it does show that there is a public relations war being waged and that we *may* not have everyone in the country behind us in this conflict."

Churchill sighed. "But it's too late for all that anyway. Once the people read the belligerent words of the German ultimatum to Belgium, public opinion swung decidedly our way. In any event, we are at war, and nothing can stop it now."

Churchill sighed and smiled sardonically.

"I doubt there has ever been a week like it in our nation's history, Charles," he said, "that week between July 31 and August 4. I lived the week entirely in the official circle, seeing scarcely anyone but my colleagues of the cabinet or of the admiralty."

"It must have tired you out."

"Long hours are part of a politician's life—you know that. On Saturday evening I dined alone at the admiralty. Telegrams were coming in seemingly every minute. So far no shot had been fired between the Great Powers. I found myself wondering whether armies and fleets could remain mobilized for a time without fighting, and then demobilize."

"You were still having doubts?" asked Charles.

"Hopes would perhaps better describe it," replied Churchill. "I *hoped* it could be avoided. But almost the moment this thought came to me, another telegram came in. It read, *Germany has declared war on Russia*. There was no more to be said."

"What did you do?"

"I immediately walked across the Horse Guards Parade to Ten Downing Street, by the garden gate. I found the prime minister upstairs in his drawing room."

"Was anyone else there?"

Churchill nodded. "Sir Edward Grey, Lord Haldane, and Lord Crewe, and a few other ministers. I said that I intended instantly to mobilize the British fleet, notwithstanding the cabinet decision, and that I would take full personal responsibility to the cabinet the next morning."

"How did they take the news?"

"There was a little discussion. But they all knew it was the right course of action. I left the meeting a short time later with Mr. Grey and went back to the admiralty and gave the order to mobilize."

"And then the cabinet sat most of Sunday, as I understand it," said Charles.

"All day," replied Churchill. "Once we were informed of Germany's ultimatum to Belgium and invasion of Luxembourg, then we knew that we were as good as at war. By Monday it was clear the majority of Mr. Asquith's colleagues finally regarded war as inevitable."

"Surely not everyone could have been in agreement, even then."

"You're right, Charles. I knew well enough that some of the cabinet would resign if we declared war. On Monday afternoon the foreign secretary addressed the House of Commons. That night he sent the ultimatum to Germany demanding that the invasion of Belgium cease within twenty-four hours."

The two men walked on thoughtfully.

"It was like waiting for an election result," Churchill went on at length, "as those twenty-four hours passed, though few of us doubted what would be the response."

"When was the deadline, exactly, when the ultimatum expired?" asked Charles.

"Eleven o'clock the following night—midnight by German time."

"Where were you?"

"At the admiralty. I threw the windows wide open. The night air was warm. Under the roof where Nelson had received his orders were gathered a small group of admirals and captains and a cluster of clerks, pencils in hand. Some sat; some milled about. We were all just waiting. Along the Mall from the direction of the palace the sound of an immense concourse singing 'God save the King' floated in."

Churchill paused reflectively, then smiled.

"All at once," he continued, "on this deep wave there broke the chimes of Big Ben. It was a remarkable moment, Charles—the people singing, then those ominous tones from the clock tower. I'll never forget it as long as I live. And, as the first stroke of the hour boomed out, a rustle of movement swept across the room. That was it. The moment had come and gone. I gave the order for the war telegram, which meant 'Commence hostilities against Germany,' to be flashed to the ships and establishments under the white ensign all over the world."

The silence which followed this time as they continued to walk side by side was long and somber. Again Churchill spoke.

"Then I walked across the Horse Guards Parade to the cabinet room," he said, "and reported to the prime minister and the ministers who were assembled there that the deed was done.* We're at war, Charles . . . God help us all."

Another long silence followed as they now began slowly making their way back toward the admiralty.

---

*This conversation adapted from Churchill's own recollection of events, some of the thoughts and quotes in Churchill's own words, as told in *The World Crisis*, vol. 1, pp. 228–246.

"I hope you've been thinking about my earlier request," said Churchill at length.

"I've been doing the best, the only *complete*, kind of thinking about it," replied Charles, "—that is, *praying* about it."

"I admire your faith, Sir Charles," said Churchill, "especially at a time like this."

"It is not only *my* faith, Winston."

"How do you mean?"

"It is a faith available to any man or woman—even a man such as yourself. You did say, God help us all. What is that if it is not a prayer?"

"A figure of speech, I suppose—a cry of human helplessness."

"It is that, no doubt, but invoking of the Lord's name ought always to be more than a mere figure of speech."

A low chuckle sounded from somewhere deep in the big man's throat. "Are you trying to convert me, Sir Charles?"

"It never hurts to try," smiled Charles. "You have asked me to consider something which could change the course of my life. Now I am asking you to do the same. A little *quid pro quo* doesn't seem out of order."

"You are a shrewd one," replied Churchill. "But it has always seemed to me that the life of faith is more suited to some individuals than others. You are such a one. I am not."

"In other words, for priests and clerics, with a few misfits like me thrown in, is that it?"

"I said no such thing. No one who knows you would dare call you a misfit. You are one of the sanest men I know."

"Yet still you say living in friendship with our Creator is more suited to me than to you?"

Churchill nodded.

"A common misperception, Winston. But the only thing that makes some men and women more or less suited for faith, as you say, is that they *make* themselves suited for it by their acceptance of it. You cannot have forgotten that I myself was a modern and liberal in every way prior to my conversion. I *changed* my outlook."

"Perhaps," conceded Churchill. "But I would add that you were disposed in such a direction all along."

"I don't believe that for an instant."

"To what *do* you attribute the change in your perception, then?"

"I was confronted with the reality of God's claim upon me as one of his creatures. At that point the decision was entirely mine."

"What decision?"

"Whether to acknowledge that claim, and order my life accordingly, or whether to ignore it and continue to order my life by my *own* will."

"But what if an individual such as myself has not been confronted, as you say, with the reality of God's existence? I certainly have had no such experience."

"His claim upon you is no less because he perhaps has chosen to speak to you in whispers rather than shouts."

"But that's just it—I have heard no such whispers."

"Perhaps that is because you have not attuned your ear in the directions he is speaking. He speaks to everyone, Winston."

"I have the feeling you would stake your life on that."

"I would. He speaks, of that you may be sure. Some hear, some do not. One must learn to *listen*."

Again Churchill chuckled.

"You present a very persuasive case, Sir Charles," he said. "But I am afraid I have no time to think about all that at present. We are back at my office, and unfortunately I have a war to fight."

"When *will* you think about it, Winston?"

"Talk to me about it again in six months, after we have beaten back the Germans and Austrians. Then my brain will not be so cluttered with other matters."

100

Haze

✦✦✦

𝒯he months between June and August passed almost like a blur for Amanda. She and Mrs. Halifax and Mr. Barclay had traveled throughout Austria, though it was mostly uninteresting. They always had people to see, to whom they spoke in hushed tones.

Once she had written the leaflet, Mr. Barclay seemed to take less interest in her, though encouraged her with more of the same. She never heard what became of what she had written, and didn't ask. A discomfort over what she had said about her father began to set in. The best medicine for her uneasiness at present was not to think about it.

All the people she met now, and those who came and went through the house at Nr. 42 Ebendorfer Strasse, were connected in some way with the Fountain of Light and engaged in its activities, most of which Amanda knew very little about.

Mrs. Halifax spoke to Amanda as if she were an intrinsic aspect of the organization and their future plans, even as if Amanda would one day be one of its leaders. Amanda took everything in with a certain hazy interest, though she did not thoroughly understand much of what was said. Nor did she have the faintest grasp during those summer months where events were leading. She saw no English newspaper all summer, and had no idea that war loomed on the world's horizon and very, very close to where she happened to be.

Her brain lay in a fog. Slowly memories of her past grew fuzzy and indistinct. Sometimes she could hardly remember her previous life at Heathersleigh at all. Especially when Mr. Barclay looked into her eyes, she occasionally found herself unable clearly even to visualize her mother's face. The past faded into a blur. A trance of mental numbness came over her. She could do nothing but what he told her to do.

Yet it was a mental apathy Amanda had herself allowed, by her acceptance of influences contrary to the truth. Likewise, the fog that comes upon many is self-induced, and can lift at any moment a man or woman chooses to bring out the sun and blow it away. Mental vigor is a chosen possession available to any, no matter what his or her innate level of what is commonly called intelligence. Raw intellect itself is a vastly overrated commodity in its power over human character development. Such mental vitality is responsible for more growth a million times over than is intelligence, for it is the root of decision and will.

Amanda was presently asleep because she had let herself heed influences intended to stop her from thinking for herself.

But her waking was not far off. Deception is sure to overplay its hand in the end.

101

Courage to Look It in the Face

◆ ◆ ◆

*W*hen Charles returned from London, his heart heavy knowing that now all Europe was at war, and well knowing what that fact could mean to George, his firstborn, his first business even before returning to the Hall was to stop at the McFee cottage.

Bobby had remained in bed since the accident. Though the bones in his leg gradually healed themselves, his body's zip did not return. His strength seemed rather slowly to be ebbing away. The doctor pronounced him as fit as one of his age could be, perplexed that he was not back up on his feet.

It was clear Maggie was afraid the lonely trial of the aging wife was about to visit her.

The moment Charles walked in he knew from Maggie's face that Bobby had taken a turn for the worse.

"Oh, Master Charles," she said, tears falling down her wrinkled cheek, "I don't know what to do for my poor Bobby!"

Already Charles was striding toward the sickroom.

Bobby lay there, a frail form under the single sheet, for the afternoon was warm, looking as though he were wasting away, and would soon become part of the bed itself. A thin white arm lay outside it yet was nearly indistinguishable for whiteness from the sheet itself. His face was more drawn and thin, it seemed, than even since Charles had last seen him three days before.

The thin slits of his eyes opened a crack.

"Ay, 'tis Master Charles, my old friend," croaked a thin wisp of a voice.

"Yes, it's me, Bobby," replied Charles cheerfully, sitting down beside him and taking the limp hand at the end of the white arm. "How are you?"

"Weary, Master Charles . . . weary indeed. I don't doubt the time's about cum fer this old pilgrim t' lay aside his travelin' shoes."

"Nonsense, Bobby. You'll be up and out of here in no time."

"Master Charles . . . I would have ay thought that ye'd be above all that. We know some's got t' pretend t' themselves that there's no such thing as death, with their talk o' gettin' better. An' we can ay forgive them fer it, fer they don't have the strength t' look the thing in the face, or else their hearts'd fail them fer pure sorrow. But such men like me an' yerself, Master Charles, the Master's given us the courage t' look fear in the face an' say, 'Do yer worst, ye shallna conquer me.' Am I not right, Master Charles?"

What a joyous sorrow is the contented approach toward death of a childlike man with the clear conscience which comes of a life well lived in service to his Master and his fellows.

Tears rose in Charles' eyes from the dear man's honest speech. It was all he could do to get the words out past the lump in his throat.

"You're right, Bobby," he whispered. "Forgive me my foolishness."

"Forgive ye—now ye're talkin' foolish. I love ye, Master Charles. I love ye like a son—perhaps better'n a son. I can't say, fer I never had one. But ye been like a son t' me, God bless ye, an' I'm more proud o' ye than I can tell ye. I'm sore gonna miss ye."

At last the tears overflowed and streamed down Charles' face.

"But ye can't say a word o' this t' me dear Maggie, bless the dear lass," Bobby went on. "Let her talk t' me about when I'm back and up and takin' Flora back t' pasture, though she knows as well as I that Flora's seen the last o' me back. But the lass loves me so much, she can't bring herself t' look at the truth of it."

Bobby paused. For several long minutes the room was deathly silent. Charles thought he had fallen asleep, but then the ancient voice sounded again.

"Take care of her, Master Charles," he whispered.

"I will . . . I will, Bobby," nodded Charles.

"I'm sore gonna miss me Maggie doo. I love her, Master Charles. She's a good an' fine woman, the best friend I ever had, a woman after God's heart, that's me Maggie."

Tiptoes sped across the sitting-room floor, through the kitchen, and outside the cottage, where at last Maggie broke into great heaving sobs. Standing at the bedroom door, she had heard every word.

When Charles returned home, he knew he had no choice but to show Jocelyn the leaflet purported to be written by their daughter.

"Oh, Charles," she said as she began to weep, "when she came home for those few days, I thought there was hope. And now this! It is such a devastating turn. Here the country is at war and we don't even know where our daughter is. I am so afraid for her!"

"The Lord is with her, even if we are not."

"But what if something happens to her, Charles? What if—"

"We're not going to think about that," interrupted Charles. "This is the hardest thing we have ever faced. But we gave our family to the Lord long ago, and if we haven't forgotten, surely he hasn't."

"I know you're right," sniffed Jocelyn. "But it is so hard! She's my daughter."

Charles took her in his arms, and they stood another minute in silence as Jocelyn's tears spent themselves.

102

Trapped

On the morning of August 19, as Amanda lay drowsily in bed, strange sounds came in through her open window from somewhere in the distance outside—rumbling machinery and marching troops.

She rose and looked out. Toward the Old City, marching through the Ring, she beheld endless lines of soldiers and military vehicles. The sight struck awe, but also fear, into her heart.

All at once she felt very close to danger. Was Vienna about to be invaded!

She dressed and hurried downstairs.

Mr. Barclay sat with a cup of tea in the breakfast room, calmly glancing through a newspaper as though nothing whatever were out of the ordinary.

"What is all that commotion outside?" asked Amanda.

"What commotion?" he asked.

"The army, the troops—guns and cannons and trucks in the Ring?"

"We're at war, Amanda—surely you knew that?"

"Who's at war?"

"Everyone—every country in Europe!"

"England?"

"Of course. England declared war on Austria a few days ago."

"But . . . but is the fighting coming *here?*"

"It may, Amanda. Russia is already invading to the east. Serbia is invading Bosnia. Austria has invaded Poland."

"But . . . but are we safe?"

"I think so. I doubt Vienna is in danger."

"What about England? What is happening in England?"

"English troops have landed on the Continent and are fighting the Germans in Belgium."

For the moment Amanda asked no more questions. With wide eyes, stunned by what she had heard, in a daze she slowly returned to her room. The news had not altogether awakened her from mental languor, but had certainly jolted her senses. She stood at her window again, staring at the long columns of troops, then sat down on the edge of her bed and tried to think. But she was out of practice and the exercise proved difficult. She had too easily drifted into the habit of letting others do her thinking for her.

At breakfast with Mrs. Halifax thirty minutes later, Amanda again brought up the war and the potential danger.

"Shouldn't we return to England?" she said.

"Why, dear?" asked Mrs. Halifax.

"Well . . . because, I don't know—because if there is a war, we ought to be at home."

"This is my home."

"What do you mean?"

"I am Hungarian, dear," replied Mrs. Halifax. "My homeland is at war with England. I cannot go back now."

"But England is *my* home."

"Where *is* your home, Amanda dear? I thought all that was decided. Your home is with me now."

"But this house is not—"

"This house is mine, Amanda dear. *This* is my home."

"But what about your home in London?"

"I was merely visiting, dear. This is my home. Now it is your home."

"Oh, I am so confused," said Amanda, starting to cry. "I don't know what to think anymore."

She paused, blinking back the tears. Footsteps approached in the hallway outside.

"All I know," Amanda added, "is that I want to go back to England."

"I am afraid that will be impossible," sounded a voice behind them.

Amanda turned. Hartwell Barclay had just entered the room. She tried to return his statement with another question but found herself silenced by his eyes. Suddenly his tone, which always before now seemed calm, frightened her.

"But . . . I don't want to be here during a war," she whimpered.

"You are here, Amanda—that cannot be helped," he said in a voice of command. "Your life in England is past now. You are one of us. You cannot go back. You would only be shot as a spy."

"A spy! Why . . . why me?"

"Because of the anti-English pamphlet you wrote."

"You told me to write it."

"I told you to speak the truth. I wanted to insure your loyalty to our cause by making sure you could not go back."

"But . . . but Austria is at war with England, and I am English. I cannot stay here."

"You will be safe . . . as long as you remain loyal to us."

Amanda shuddered again at the threat. Barclay's eyes silenced her, and she said no more. For the first time in her life, suddenly she was really scared.

103

Muhamed Mehmedbasic

◆ ◆ ◆

*I*n fear and uncertainty, Amanda said little for the next two days. She hardly ate.

In the early-morning hours three nights later she was awakened by sounds from below. Someone had just entered by the side-street door and an argument was in progress in the small parlor adjacent to the entry.

Amanda rose, threw a robe around her, stole from her room, and crept silently along the corridor toward the stairway, up which she heard the voices clearly enough. She knew them immediately. It was

Hartwell Barclay and Gavrilo Princip's friend, the Herzegovinian Muslim Muhamed Mehmedbasic.

"Mehmedbasic, are you crazy, coming here like this!" Barclay had just said. He was trying to keep his voice low, but he was clearly angry. "You cannot stay here. We can offer you no refuge. Every Austrian policeman in the country is looking for you. If they find you, we will all be shot."

"Relax, they're not going to find me. They think I am still in Montenegro."

"News of your escape reached us. How did you manage it?"

"The guards allowed me to escape," laughed the Muslim. "They did not want to extradite me to Vienna."

"Yes, you fool, and you are in Vienna now!"

"Precisely where they will never think of looking for me—under the very noses of the Austrian dogs."

"Watch your tongue, Mehmedbasic. What do you want? You cannot stay here."

"I only need a place to stay for two or three days. All the others are in jail."

"You cannot remain here," insisted Barclay.

"I want passage to England."

"Do others know of us?" said Barclay, ignoring his statement. "Have you been so free with your tongue about us as I hear you were about the conspiracy?"

"Only those who are friends."

"You fool—you have placed us all in danger."

"You were well known to be in support of Mlada Bosna."

"You are an imbecile—we supported no assassination!"

"You try to play both sides, Barclay—you and your kind. You hoped to precipitate an event so that Austria would go to war without dirtying your own hands. I know your game."

"That's nonsense, Mehmedbasic. We never had anything to do with madmen like you."

"Nevertheless, I want passage to England. I can disappear there."

"That's insane. How do you expect me to arrange something like that? Haven't you heard—your little affair in Sarajevo started a war."

"You can arrange it, Barclay."

"I have no contacts left. I burned my bridges. They know about me."

"Yes, and I know about your Lighthouse."

"What lighthouse?" Barclay shot back.

"Don't play games with me, Barclay. I know about the whole scheme, about your network to move people in and out of England. They're closing the net on us all. I'm the only one left. I'll blow your secret little operation wide open if you don't get me on one of your tubs."

"All right, all right, you win. I'll see what I can do."

The voices went silent. A minute later Amanda heard their steps coming her way below the landing. Quickly she retreated toward her room.

"Stay in your room," Barclay was saying. "You must not be seen. Everything you need will be brought to you. I will see what might be arranged."

104

Coming of Life

────── ♦♦♦ ──────

*C*harles sat at the bedside of his lifelong friend and neighbor and spiritual mentor, dozing intermittently in the chair he and others of the vigil had shared at Bobby's side every minute of the past two or three days.

Catharine, Jocelyn, and Maggie were in the other room. Catharine had arrived a few minutes before to take her morning shift with Maggie so that Jocelyn, who had been at the cottage most of the night, could return to the Hall for a few hours sleep.

A sound came. Charles started slightly and opened his eyes.

"Ay, 'tis a bright light cummin'," whispered a feeble voice beside him.

"Do you need some water?" Charles asked, sitting up and turning toward the bed.

Bobby appeared not to hear him. Charles rose and immediately went for Maggie.

Maggie knew from the look on Charles' face that the moment had come. Her hand went to the trembling lip of her mouth as she rushed to Bobby's side.

"Catharine," said Jocelyn, "go for George. Tell him to ride for the doctor, then both of you hurry back here."

Already Catharine was out the door.

Charles put his arm around Jocelyn and they waited a few moments, then slowly followed Maggie into the bedroom. She was leaning toward the bed with her face close to Bobby's. They heard faint words coming from the bed, though there was no other sign of life.

" . . . don't ye fret fer me, Maggie me doo. I'm ay a happy man, an' I've had a happy life shared with ye. Ye're all a man could hope fer."

The voice was barely audible, what remained of the strength of its owner nearly spent with the simple expression of love. Maggie wept freely.

"Bobby . . . Bobby, you can't leave me yet. You will—"

"Lass, 'tis time the Master is wantin' me," whispered Bobby. "He's calling me t' *his* home now. Ye mustn't be anxious. 'Tis time I was leavin' yers, an' becummin' one o' the blossoms in *his* garden."

He closed his eyes and appeared to sleep for a while.

Catharine returned in twenty-five minutes. George arrived in forty. Jocelyn dozed in a chair in the sitting room. Charles read his Bible.

Presently Maggie entered. Her face was pale.

"Master Charles," she said. "Bobby wants you . . . he wants you all."

Instantly the four Rutherfords were on their feet and followed her.

As they walked in, Bobby's eyes were open, bright, and alive. He appeared more full of life than he had for months, as he truly was, for Life was rapidly approaching.

"Master Charles," he said as he saw Charles, stretching out a thin hand. Charles took it. "He wants me t' tell ye that ye're well on yer way t' the sonship of yer callin'. Ye faced the deepest agony a man can face— the rejection of his love by one of his own. But ye must ne'er forget why he gives some t' walk that painful road—'tis so ye can know his own father's heart a wee deeper than most. 'Cause havena we all done the same t' his own Father's love? So take comfort that ye have a deeper share in the divine grief o' creation. Don't lose heart, Master Charles . . . ye're his man, an' ye must be strong an' o' good courage, 'cause he'll overcome the world in the end."

Charles nodded and squeezed the white palm gently. He could not speak, however, for the fullness of his heart. Tears streamed down his face.

"Lady Jocelyn," whispered Bobby, now taking her hand as he had Charles', "ye mustn't give up hope fer yer wayward lass. She's his as much now as the day she was born an' ye held her wee form in yer arms. He knows yer pain. He's kept every one o' yer mother's tears in his heart. An' with them he's waterin' the seed in Amanda's own soul, so that one day 'twill bear the good fruit that the ill one tries to make ye give up on. So keep prayin', Lady Jocelyn, an' keep weepin' when ye need to, 'cause none of it's wasted. But weep with thanksgiving, fer yer prayers are the sun, an' yer tears are the rain, an' the Master won't forget a single one o' them. He'll cause them t' do their work on that wee seed that ye an' Master Charles planted long ago an' is still growin' in the lass's heart."

Jocelyn wept freely as he spoke.

"Ye don't know where she is," Bobby added. "But he knows, an' he's aye keepin' watch so that when the time comes, an' she's ready, he'll lead her back t' ye."

"Thank you ... thank you, Bobby," wept Jocelyn. "I will treasure every word you have said."

"Miss Catharine," continued Bobby, "ye're a joy t' the Master's heart fer ye have a pure an' trustin' spirit. But ye're young, lass. Winds an' storms'll aye cum t' shake an' test that purity an' that trust, as they do t' all. Be strong when they do, lass. Don't listen t' the lies o' the ill one. The pure always have their reward, though the world'll tell them they're fools. Their reward is t' see God—there can be no greater thing than that. So be strong, lass, as ye grow. Be God's daughter all yer days, just like me own Maggie."

He released Catharine's hand. With it she wiped both eyes several times as she stepped back from the bed.

"Master George," now said Bobby, reaching for George's hand in its turn, "ye're a fine young man t' do yer parents an' yer God proud. But like I said t' the lass, temptations are sure t' visit ye, fer they visit us all as we grow. Don't satisfy yerself, Master George, with a middlin' kind o' belief, but stand tall with a man's faith. An' when the temptations cum, send them back where they cum from, an' say, 'I'm God's man, an' I'll listen t' none o' yer lies!' Be strong o' faith, Master George, an' o' stout heart like yer father."

George stepped back.

Bobby's face had grown pale. The exertions of the four speeches had clearly taxed him. He laid his head back down on the pillow and closed his eyes, breathing slowly in and out. All five watched silently . . . and waited.

At length Bobby's eyes again opened a crack. Though his head could scarcely move, he appeared to glance about. When his eyes located Maggie, a thin smile came to his lips.

"Maggie, me doo . . ." he began. His voice was noticeably weaker than before.

Charles nodded to the others. They quietly left the room.

Five minutes later they heard a burst of sobs. Charles and Jocelyn sprang from their chairs and together reentered the bedroom. Maggie knelt beside the bed. Bobby's eyes were closed, but his mouth yet remained open a crack in the midst of whatever word had been on his tongue. Lingering traces of a final smile remained on his lips, nor had the glow yet altogether faded from his face.

They knew he was gone.

They waited another moment or two, then approached, took Maggie's two hands in theirs, and gently lifted her to her feet.

Each of the three then said a final good-bye to the man they loved with a kiss on the warm face, Jocelyn on the top of Bobby's bare shiny head, Charles on his wasted, whiskered cheek, and Maggie on the half-parted but now unresponsive lips.

Two minutes later the doctor arrived. It was another calling than his, however, that was needed now.

Maggie spent the next three nights at the Hall.

Timothy Diggorsfeld was sent for that same day to perform the farewell celebration.

For three days all Milverscombe mourned.

On the fourth day arrived occasion to rejoice—not in death, but for *life*.

By the appearance of the funeral, a stranger to the region would have concluded that nothing less than a duke had passed on. Never even had a full royal funeral been filled with such an outpouring of feeling for a man. It is not many communities who honor the simplest and best of their folk in such a manner, but this one did. The loss of the humble man of the cottage was felt by every man, woman, and child of the region, and those who had been there long enough to remember the rumors which had circulated about him years before could no more even remember the slightest cause for them.

Chiefly they gathered, not to grieve, but to celebrate the new life to which Bobby McFee had always looked forward and had now gone. Tears were of course shed in plenty, for sorely would they miss him, but the tears were accompanied with many smiles and much laughter.

With a man of faith like Timothy Diggorsfeld officiating, with a wife like Margaret McFee left behind, and with friends like Charles and Jocelyn Rutherford to give testimony of Bobby's impact into the lives of the generations that followed him, how could it be other than an occasion of praise and rejoicing? One after another spoke of now this, now that, in which Bobby's practical faith had touched them.

From the church to the graveside, the community then retired to the Hall, where the stories continued all afternoon and into the evening. By the time she lay down again in her own bed in the cottage that night, Maggie could feel her Bobby was with her still.

The loneliness in her heart thus made room for a new kind of happiness, for she saw how blessed she was to have been allowed to share her life with him.

PART VII

———— ✦✦✦ ————

Behind the Lines
1914

105
A Man's Decision

*T*he lone figure of a man strode slowly yet purposefully across a wide meadow which bordered a gentle hillside sloping up toward a region of woods. It was midafternoon. In his hand he held the envelope which had arrived from London about thirty minutes earlier.

Charles Rutherford knew the decision he made would affect his entire family, perhaps even the whole community. He was now fifty-five years old. His age alone would preclude his being expected to resume his commission in the Royal Navy unless the southern shores of Kent and East Sussex were actually invaded. No one had breached the Channel in 850 years. Napoleon had been unable to conquer Romney Marsh north of Dungeness, and the Germans were unlikely to make such an attempt now.

But Charles was a patriot, however unambitious as a politician. The military had always interested him more than politics. And the fact that his twenty-four-year-old son George was almost certain to serve had turned the elder Rutherford's thoughts in recent days more and more toward Winston Churchill's request. He loved his son with all his heart and was not ready to part with him just yet.

Perhaps a way might be arranged whereby they could serve together, he in the advisory capacity which his age and experience would make necessary, and George in more active duty on the same ship. If the navy wanted him, perhaps under such circumstances he might agree.

He had mentioned the possibility to Churchill. Now the first lord of the admiralty had replied.

His request had been approved.

A final decision must be made within the week, at which time George, with him or without him, would begin training with the British fleet.

Charles entered his prayer wood as he had so many times in the past. He paused and glanced pensively around him, knowing this might well be his last visit to this most beloved corner of the Heathersleigh estate for some time.

It was not a large meadow, hardly more than fifty feet by twenty-five or thirty. Its seclusion made it special, surrounded on all sides by thick pines and birches. The babbling little stream which came through added to the enchantment of the place.

He well remembered the day as a boy of seven when he had discovered it, thinking it the most delightful fairy-tale place imaginable. Throughout the remainder of his boyhood he had convinced himself that no one but he knew of it, though now he chuckled at the naïve notion. He had been a thoughtful and introspective boy, and this had been his childhood haunt, his retreat, his private grounds of play, his haven for solitude.

Here he had learned to dream. Here, after he was grown, he had discovered intimacy with God. Here he had learned to pray.

He had brought George here at fourteen. The boy understood the sanctity of the place and had come on his own many times since. He shared it with Catharine four summers ago, when he saw signs that her own spiritual self was quickening within her and coming awake. They had shared an afternoon that he would treasure as long as he lived.

He had always wanted to bring Amanda here too, to talk with her as only a father and daughter can, in hopes that perhaps the Lord might use the occasion to intrude into her life more deeply. Just being here had always made him somehow feel closer to God. That too was part of the mystery. He hoped it might have the same effect on her.

He had waited for a right moment which never quite seemed to arrive. The years had passed, Amanda had become silent and drifted away from them . . . and then suddenly she was gone. He never had come to the hidden meadow with her. It remained one of his deepest regrets.

He sat down on one of the three large boulders which appeared as though they had been tossed from the sky into the middle of the otherwise grassy spot, drew in a deep breath and slowly exhaled. He always felt more peaceful when he came here, though today matters of high import were on his mind. It was the ancient conflict between faith and defense of one's country, between the Master's words of love toward enemies and devotion to one's nation. Decisions had to be made, and he must know what his Father wanted him to do.

"Lord," he sighed, *"show me what you would have of me, what path you*

would have me walk in this hour of trial that has come to our land."

He paused and exhaled slowly again.

Today's prayers would not require many words. He could not have articulated his multitude of thoughts had he tried. The sigh came from a place in his heart too deep for words. But God's Spirit knew his inner groanings and would answer his deepest heart's desires by praying in his stead.

What lay before him was the agonizing choice between two of the four people he loved most dearly in all the world. Did he remain with his wife, or go with his son? It was a decision too grievous not to crush a tender and loving man such as Charles Rutherford. He would be unable to do either without a certainty that God was making the decision for him, and he obeying it.

Charles emerged from the wood an hour later and walked directly home. There were things to talk over and settle with Jocelyn and George. They would pray tonight as a family, along with Catharine. More than ever at this moment he regretted that their family was not whole.

He reached the little knoll just beyond the lawn which led the rest of the way to the house, then paused. Squinting his eye in the sun, unconsciously he sent his gaze along the drive leading toward the main road, as if the mere gesture of his look might cause his daughter to appear on the road on her way back toward them.

He was *always* looking for her, anticipating that moment when he might run to meet her and throw his fatherly arms around her and welcome her home. Past experience, however, did not rouse optimism in his heart. Nor was today different than hundreds of days before.

After a moment or two he pulled his gaze away from the road with a sigh, then continued on toward the Hall.

106
Welcome Face

•••

$\mathcal{F}$or several days Amanda was beside herself.

A change had come. The moment Mr. Barclay had spoken the words "I am afraid that will be impossible," all at once he seemed frightening and sinister. When she looked into his eyes now she saw the glint of submerged threat rather than warmth. Mrs. Halifax seemed distant and aloof. Suddenly everything had changed. She had become a stranger among strangers.

What was she going to do? *Was* this her new home now, as Mrs. Halifax had said? Was her past indeed behind her? But ... surely she couldn't stay here *forever*.

One warm tedious afternoon she lay down on her bed and fell into a lazy sleep. Her mind was so dulled by Mr. Barclay's influences that it was not even capable of dreaming. She didn't *want* to dream ... didn't want to think.

When she awoke the sun still shone into her room. No time seemed to have passed.

A voice intruded into her consciousness from somewhere in the house, soft at first as she came gradually awake, then more pronounced ... a strange yet familiar voice. As wakefulness increased, its sound spoke of sudden new deliverance in the midst of this dreary hopelessness.

It was a voice of help and comfort.

Suddenly she recognized it—*he* would know what to do!

She leapt off the bed, flew out of her room and along the corridor to the stairs, then recklessly down them to the entryway. There stood the new arrival greeting his mother and one or two others.

"Ramsay!" Amanda cried. A few tears of relief and joy attempted to escape eyes too long dry.

She ran into his arms, which opened to receive her. Suddenly she was safe again.

"When did you arrive!" she exclaimed.

"Only a moment or two ago," laughed Ramsay. "As you can see I have not even left the entry."

"Why didn't you let me know you were coming!"

"The war threw everything into a tizzy. It was all very hastily arranged."

"You can't imagine how glad I am to see you!"

"Come, everyone," said Mrs. Halifax, "we shall all have tea together. Amanda and I want to hear how you have been, Ramsay dear."

Feeling more secure than in a long while, Amanda kept close to Ramsay's side. He stretched his arm around her shoulder, gave her another reassuring squeeze as if to say all her worries were over now that he was here, and they followed Mrs. Halifax toward the kitchen.

107

Surprise Proposal

It was two days after Ramsay's arrival. He and Amanda walked slowly through one of Vienna's parks not far from the house. Amanda had been pouring out her fears and uncertainties upon Ramsay's sympathetic and understanding ears. She had no inkling that she had been the subject of a conversation between Ramsay, his mother, and Hartwell Barclay the day before, a discussion which was destined to change her life forever.

"I didn't know what would become of me," she said, "especially with all of Europe at war."

"You don't need to worry about a thing now," Ramsay replied. "I'll take care of you and make sure nothing happens to you."

"I've been so afraid, Ramsay."

"Afraid of what?"

"I don't know, everything's . . . so strange here."

"You've been safe with my mum. Vienna is not about to be overrun by the Russians anytime soon. You're safer here than you would be anywhere on the Continent."

"That's just it, I don't know if I *want* to be on the Continent."

"Where else would you want to be?"

"I want to go home, Ramsay."

"Home," he repeated. "But your home is with my mother and me now. *This* is your home. You have nothing to go back to."

The words plunged like a cold knife of harsh reality into Amanda's heart. Ramsay was right. It was just as his mother had said earlier. Where would she possibly go?

"But why can't we both go, Ramsay? Why can't *you* take me back? We belong in England together. You're as much English as I am. We could be happy there together, away from all this."

For a moment Ramsay seemed to flinch.

"Why can't we just go back to England?" repeated Amanda.

"Because the whole Continent is at war," he replied after a brief pause. "We would never make it. Don't you see—you're in danger, Amanda. You're English and the daughter of an important man. Now you're behind enemy lines. You *have* to stay here, out of sight."

"But what about you—you're English."

"I have dual citizenship."

Amanda turned toward Ramsay with confused expression.

"What do you. . . ? I don't know what you mean."

"I have both British and Austrian passports. I thought you knew. I can travel about freely anywhere I want."

The revelation silenced Amanda briefly. The question did not exactly raise itself to the level of her conscious mind: What *else* about this man don't I know? Nevertheless his words brought with them a sudden chill of discomfort.

They walked on.

"Are you part of all this, Ramsay?" Amanda asked at length.

She hadn't intended so blunt a question. She hadn't even consciously framed the idea to herself that something more than met the eye was going on here. But suddenly out had come the words. They hung momentarily in the air between them.

"Part of what?" he said.

"Of what's involved at the house, the secretive comings and goings, the peculiar people—did you know that the assassin Princip was there? He tried to kidnap me and take me to Sarajevo with him!"

"No, of course not," he replied, laughing off the suggestion.

"What is it all about, Ramsay? I've got to know if you're part of it."

"You know me better than that. I would never be involved with assassins."

"What about your mother?"

"Certainly not—what kind of a question is that? Heavens, Amanda, what do you think we are, revolutionaries and terrorists?"

"She said it was her house."

"What—no, you must have misunderstood her. Mum just knows people here—she's of Hungarian descent, you know. This is where we always stay when we come to Vienna."

Amanda nodded, wanting desperately to believe so simple an explanation could dismiss her misgivings.

"And in this part of the world," Ramsay went on, "well—there *are* more radicals and strange customers than one meets in England. You can't help running into them almost everywhere. No one here knew what Princip was up to."

Again they walked on in silence. Relieved somewhat by Ramsay's account, however, Amanda yet remained confused and on edge. Ramsay was the next to speak.

"There *is* a solution to all the troubles and uncertainty," he said.

Amanda glanced over at him. A flicker of renewed hope stirred within her.

"We could get married," he went on, then stopped and turned to face her.

Had she heard him right!

"As my wife you would be safe," Ramsay went on. "You too could apply for dual citizenship. Who knows, after we're married, perhaps then there might be a way for us to return to England."

"Ramsay, do you ... do you actually mean it? Do you really want to marry me?"

"Yes, of course," he replied with a light laugh. "I assumed you knew that long ago. I've merely been waiting for the right time. That moment has now come."

He took her in his arms, kissed her, then held her close.

"Marry me, Amanda Rutherford," he said, "and you never have to be afraid or without a home again."

So many thoughts floated back and forth in Amanda's brain in the few seconds following Ramsay's unexpected proposal. Somehow she did not feel as she had always expected to feel at such a moment.

"What about your mother?" she said drowsily. "Will she approve?"

"Of course. She is the one who suggested it. She said we ought not delay a moment more than is necessary."

Ramsay was probably right, thought Amanda. It was her only way out of this predicament. A war was on. What else could she do? She had dreamed of what it would be like to be married to Ramsay Halifax. After the ball in Cambridge, she had thought of it even more. She almost had expected him to propose that night. It was just that she hadn't heard from him in so long, she had begun to forget.

No doubt it was for the best. She probably loved him.

Maybe she had loved him from the very beginning without realizing it.

108
A Recollection

*M*aggie McFee sat slowly rocking back and forth in her favorite chair in the sitting room of the cottage. Her Bobby had now been gone two weeks.

She was slowly growing accustomed to the silence. But would she ever accustom herself to the isolation?

She knew this season of a woman's aloneness to be in the usual order of things. It was a time, as in youth, to kindle afresh one's vows to the Bridegroom of all believers.

She missed Bobby. Yet her thoughts of him were so pleasant—always with his smiling face and cheery disposition—how could she think of him and be sad?

As she glanced about, Maggie's eyes came to rest on a piece of unfinished tatting she had been working on the last time Catharine was here. And with Catharine in her mind, Amanda soon followed.

More and more these days she found herself reflecting anew on the daughter of Master Charles and Lady Jocelyn. Amanda's brief visit to them the previous March had been fortunate. Otherwise she would never have seen Grandpa Bobby again.

Had Bobby possessed some premonition of what was coming? He

had spoken to her almost with similar benediction as he had uttered on his deathbed to the others of her family. Maggie had only heard a portion of his words, for as she came upon Bobby and Amanda outside the barn, they had already been talking for several minutes. But the words remained with her, as if they contained more significance than he intended, or even knew.

"... recall when ye was here as a lass," Maggie had heard him from a distance as she slowly approached. "We spoke t' ye then about yer father an' the heritage that is yers on account o' his faith. 'Tis time ye woke up, lass ... woke up t' discover that heritage. Ye're wastin' the best years o' yer young life, lass, with this foolish rebellion o' yer heart toward the two best friends ye'll ever have in this life...."

Why Amanda had stood listening was a wonder. Even as a young-ster she had not put up with their sermonizing with such tolerance.

"... afore it's too late," Maggie recalled Bobby's voice. "Ye can't go back an' get the years ye waste, lass. Someday the pain an' regret'll come upon ye, and then ye'll shed bitter tears o' remorse. An' ye'll say, 'How could I have been so blind!' Open yer eyes now, lass. Don't wait too long. Ye got t' discover yer heritage. 'Tis different than folks think, dif-ferent than ye imagine. 'Tis a legacy ye're given t' discover, though it be hidden from yer eyes at present. A *hidden* legacy, lass, do ye hear me? Find it. Ye *must* find it!"

Now on this day, Bobby's words rang over and over in Maggie's brain.

A hidden legacy ... different than folks think ... ye must find it.

What could the words mean? Did they mean more than even Bobby intended?

109

Heartbreaking News

◆◆◆

𝒯he letter which arrived at Heathersleigh Hall fortuitously came when Charles was home after his initial training exercises at the naval facility at Portsmouth. He had not yet been assigned a ship, and would be home for an undetermined period of time. George was presently training in the Orkneys.

Jocelyn saw the familiar handwriting and tore open the envelope, hardly noting the Austrian stamp.

Moments later her face went ashen. She collapsed rather than sank into a chair. The letter fell to the floor. Charles stooped to retrieve it and read,

> *Mr. and Mrs. Rutherford,*
>
> *My husband Ramsay felt it proper that I inform you that he and I were married three days ago in a private civil ceremony in Vienna, where I have been living the last few months with Ramsay's mother, Lady Hildegard Halifax. You may be worried about me because of the war, but I assure you that I am safe. However, you will probably not be hearing from me again.*
>
> *Yours sincerely,*
Amanda Halifax

Charles exhaled a deep sigh of heartache, for he had come to recognize all the more clearly the character of those individuals with whom Amanda had become involved. After her brief return home in March, they had been hopeful that a change of her heart was at hand. This was indeed a severe and crushing blow.

He reached down and took Jocelyn's hand, pulled her to her feet, and slowly led her outside. It was time to seek the heather garden.

Jocelyn was already weeping as they slowly walked across the grass east of the Hall.

"Oh, Charles," she said, "I don't know if I can bear any more heartache. It seems everything we worked for and hoped for as parents was for naught."

What could he say? Never had he felt so low as a father, as a man, as a Christian. What had his faith accomplished if he could not even pass it along to his own children? What did it mean? What manner of man could be so despised by his own flesh and blood? Perhaps Amanda was right. Perhaps he *was* a hypocrite, an empty shell of a man spouting meaningless spiritual words of pretended faith that had no substance.

What comfort could he offer his wife? What did he have to give anyone!

They sat on the familiar bench. Both knew they should pray. But how could prayers rise out of such despondency and emptiness? For ten minutes husband and wife sat silent ... staring blankly ahead, stunned by the deepening shock of this devastating turn, so brusquely and unexpectedly delivered.

Everything had suddenly changed. Amanda was married. And they had not been part of it.

"*Oh, Lord,*" cried Jocelyn at length, "*how much more must we endure?*"

She paused briefly, then cried out in anguish, "*God, I want my daughter!*"

Jocelyn broke down in convulsive sobs the moment the words were out of her mouth.

Charles rose and walked a few paces away, tears streaming down his face, his heart in an agony of sorrow. He had no words with which to comfort his wife, for he had no words with which to comfort himself. Never had he been acquainted with such despair.

The cry of her frustration and grief briefly stilled the tumult of Jocelyn's heart. Presently she rose and followed her husband, slipping her hand into his. Slowly they made their way along the curving familiar trails of the heather garden.

"I know we ought to consider Catharine and George," Charles sighed at length, "and tell ourselves it *hasn't* all been for nothing. Yet I can't make that help ease the suffering I feel for Amanda. I feel like such a failure as a father, and as a spiritual example."

"I know," said Jocelyn. "Yet poor Amanda is going to suffer in the end most of all. As much as I hurt, I feel awful for her. She is the one who has jeopardized her future. When she wakes up and realizes what she has done, not only to us, but to herself, how she has thrown away her purity for a man who may not genuinely love her ... it will be a burden she will have to carry for the rest of her life."

"The poor girl ... the poor confused girl," said Charles. "Why ... why did she do such a thing!"

"Don't you think she was manipulated into it?"

"No doubt. But that doesn't change the fact that she is now married. I know everything Timothy told us about praying for her, and that God himself would continue to woo her, but it is so hard to hold on to belief after so long, seeing no results. And now this. I wish there were something we could do."

"What else can we do but keep praying for moments of clarity, and that her eyes would eventually come open?"

"It is so hard to pray with any kind of faith at all. We have been praying so long and hard. Why would God allow it, in the midst of so much prayer for Amanda? I don't understand. We prayed for protection ... and now this."

Charles sighed and shook his head.

"I have to tell you, Jocie," he went on, "I am very confused. This situation with Amanda is testing my faith to the depths. Not my belief itself, but my faith. I know God is good. If I didn't have that fact to hang on to, I sometimes think the despair would overcome me entirely. But if he is good ... then why are our prayers seemingly unheeded?"

"Perhaps because they are only *seemingly* unheeded," suggested Jocelyn.

Charles pondered his wife's words.

"I have heard you yourself talk many times," she went on, "about his larger purposes that we cannot see. Perhaps now we must begin to pray for Amanda's future, for how God might be able to use her—even use this present season of her life—to help other families and other young women *not* to experience such breaking and heartache."

"I'm certain you are right," sighed Charles. "But it seems that every time I pray for Amanda I must add the words, 'Lord, help my unbelief.'"

"I know, Charles. Yet we must continue to pray. 'Help my unbelief' is a legitimate prayer. It was after the man uttered those words that Jesus healed his son. Perhaps out of your own honest admission of weakness before God, he will work a miracle in Amanda's life. Even if our own hope is gone, we *must* continue to pray. Jesus told his disciples to pray and faint not."

In one accord, husband and wife stopped and, hand in hand, sank to their knees.

Their emotional entreaties on this day were silent. No audible expressions were capable of giving vent to the outpourings flowing through their hearts on behalf of their daughter.

110

Kaffe Kellar Again

*T*hough the British fleet commanded the seas, initial losses were heavier than anticipated. Off the coast of India, on September 10, six British steamers were captured by the German cruiser *Emden*. Two weeks later a German U-boat sank three British cruisers, the *Aboukir, Cressy*, and *Hogue*. On October 15, the British cruiser *Hawke* was sunk by another German submarine.

Meanwhile in Vienna, the blue haze of the Kaffe Kellar hung thinly suspended over the heads of its patrons as the cloud of war now hung over the map of Europe. Its clientele had shrunk and changed. Uniformed soldiers now made up many of its declining number.

The low voices at its now half-vacant tables were no longer discussing potential communist revolt but rather the very present war against England, France, and Russia.

Two months of fighting had resulted in nothing decisive. In the west, the German advance into France, in a wide sweeping von Schlieffen arc through Belgium had been halted at the Seine, the Marne, and the Meuse. Already the Germans had begun a slow retreat. A long, protracted struggle seemed in store. Their own Austrian army had just been badly defeated by the Russians at Lemberg in fierce week-long fighting.

A young man in his late twenties sat with two older individuals— a woman of Hungarian blood and an Englishman with pure white hair. The youth had been here many times throughout the years. But what he now heard exceeded all previous and naïve notions of socialist ideals. No more would he be a mere spectator and minor player in the coming of the new order. That had all changed the day after his arrival.

The ruling duo had been expanded to a leadership triumvirate of power.

He had been given a test and had passed it.

His own moment of destiny had come, and he had shown himself ready to step into it.

111
Arrows of Clarity
✦✦✦

*J*ocelyn awoke suddenly in the middle of the night. All about her was black and still. Not even a moon lit the sky outside. Charles slept soundly beside her.

Something had prompted her to wake.

Immediately her thoughts gathered themselves about Amanda. She knew she had been roused to pray.

"Lord, send a piercing arrow of light into Amanda's heart," she whispered before she had a chance even to think what to pray.

An urgency lay upon the mother's heart. Amanda was in need of light and truth at this moment. Jocelyn sensed it more than ever before.

"Oh, God," she prayed, *"bring dear Amanda awake. Open her heart. Send a moment of shining clarity into her consciousness. Make that moment of enlightenment explode and awaken decision, Lord. I have been praying for moments of clarity all along . . . now, Lord, illuminate something deep within her. Wake her will, Lord . . . wake her will!"*

112

Terrifying Discovery

*A*manda's eyes shot open.

The house on Ebendorfer Strasse was silent. What could possibly have awakened her?

Some sharp, stinging light had penetrated her brain from unknown regions beyond consciousness. For a few brief moments the mental stupor vanished. She was thinking more clearly than she had in years.

Ramsay was not in bed beside her. An inner compulsion told her to get out of bed.

She shook her head as if trying to clear her brain. Why did she suddenly feel so clear of thought?

Her mother's face came to her—smiling but urgent, as if trying to speak. Then in her mind's eye rose the face of her father.

No anger accompanied the vision. For the first time in recollection, with the reminder of his face came the fond memory that she had once loved him . . . loved him with all the affection of a daughter's heart.

How could she have forgotten? For an instant she was a little girl again, and he was her father.

Father. The word brought with it feelings of warmth and contentment, security and safety . . . and love.

All these thoughts and emotions passed through Amanda's brain in less than ten seconds. Then just as suddenly as they had intruded from some unknown place as she lay awake came the reminder of her present situation.

Now she remembered. Ramsay wasn't home when she went to bed.

Amanda shivered. The night was warm, but she felt suddenly very cold and strange.

What time could it be?

She rose for a glass of water. As she approached her sideboard, through the crack of her bedroom door, faint voices filtered into her hearing.

An impulse told her to listen.

Carefully she opened the door a crack. The voices came from the sitting room below. Its door must be open. She could just barely make out the words.

She crept along the carpeted floor, making not a sound, careful not to betray herself. Gradually the voices grew louder.

It was Ramsay and his mother. They were talking with Hartwell Barclay and, from what she could make out, another man whose voice she did not recognize.

Amanda strained to listen. Did she hear her name? Were they talking about her!

Now she heard the name of Princip's friend.

" . . . Mehmedbasic said he knew about the lighthouse operation," Barclay was saying.

"Impossible," replied Mrs. Halifax, ". . . no way to know."

" . . . might also know about the signals . . . have to change the code."

" . . . use only Morse," said the third man. ". . . U-boats have nothing sophisticated . . ."

"Don't worry, Generaloberst von Bülow," rejoined Barclay. "If we must, our people will find him . . . kill him before he can pass the information off . . . time the assassin got a dose of his own medicine."

Kill him! thought Amanda. Who were they talking about . . . Mehmedbasic?

" . . . if we decide to land an invasion . . . lighthouse . . . cannot be compromised . . ."

Amanda heard a door open below. Then footsteps. Another voice. It was Gertrut Oswald, the lady who always sat at the side door at night. She spoke at the entry to the sitting room. Amanda could hear her every word clearly.

"Mr. Halifax," she said, "there is a young lady at the door. She said you are expecting her—a Miss Grünsfeld."

"By all means, Gertrut, show her in!" said Ramsay, with obvious emotion, now hurrying out of the room. The new arrival, however, had not waited, but had followed Oswald. The two met in the corridor just below where Amanda stood.

"Ramsay!" said a female voice.

"Adriane darling!" said Ramsay.

In the brief silence which followed, in horror Amanda realized the two were in each other's arms!

"You made it without incident?" said Ramsay, leading the newcomer into the sitting room where the others waited. Oswald returned to her post at the side entrance.

"Yes, of course—hello, Mrs. Halifax," replied the young woman in a voice oddly familiar. "It is wonderful to see you again."

"And you, my dear," replied Mrs. Halifax. "We are glad to have you safe and sound at last."

In stunned shock and repugnance, Amanda could not believe her ears. She and Ramsay had been married less than two weeks!

They had . . . and now . . .

This must be a dream! A horrible nightmare . . . he would not . . . how could he do such a thing to her!

But they were talking again. In nauseating torment Amanda knew she must listen.

" . . . sorry, darling," Ramsay was saying, "but you will have to sleep alone—for a while, that is."

"A problem you have not told me about, Ramsay?" said the young lady.

"Only a minor one. But it will be taken care of before long."

Hot tears of shame, defilement, and mortification rose in Amanda's eyes. She had been duped . . . she had married a—

She didn't even know what to call him!

Suddenly she realized she knew the voice of the new woman!

Annie McPool deserves better than the likes of them! rang the words in Amanda's ears. *I was born for the opera.*

It was the actress Sadie Greenfield she and Ramsay had seen at the theater! But her real name was Adriane Grünsfeld—the name from the article!

The charges in the newspaper were true all along!

Ramsay had lied. He *did* have a German mistress in Morocco!

It was all too horrible! How could she have gotten mixed up in something so sordid and awful? And been convinced to write that horrible pamphlet.

She was going to be sick. She felt unclean, filthy, as if she had been defiled. Her own husband, the man she thought loved her, kissing another woman and calling her *darling*!

Words from her father's letter came back to her.

. . . listen to my cautions . . . dangers involved . . . these people are not what they seem.

Why hadn't she listened!

Tears burned her eyes, but not so bitterly as the disgrace and humiliation that burned deep in her heart.

Suddenly her thoughts were interrupted.

She heard her own name again!

" . . . use her for barter . . . now that she is securely ours . . ." It was Ramsay's mother speaking—her own mother-in-law!

" . . . English will pay handsomely for the return of Sir Charles Rutherford's daughter."

" . . . knows too much . . ." said Ramsay.

"She knows nothing," rejoined his mother.

She couldn't listen to any more! Involuntarily Amanda clasped her hands to her ears, but not before Barclay's reply reached her.

" . . . don't think I would actually turn her over . . . once they pay . . . find some means to eliminate her."

Barclay stopped abruptly.

"What was that?" he said. "I think I heard a sound."

Amanda heard his footsteps approach the door, then walk out into the corridor.

Terrified, she shrank back into the shadows. She could feel his presence below her looking up the stairway onto the landing above, probing the dark corners of the house.

He took one or two steps up the stairs, paused again listening, then seemed to think better of it, and returned to the others in the sitting room. This time he closed the door behind him.

Amanda now crept noiselessly back to her bedroom.

She climbed into bed. Sleep was impossible. She could do nothing but lie in trembling disbelief.

About an hour later the door opened. Ramsay entered, undressed, and climbed into bed beside her.

His body pressed close to hers. Heart pounding in terror, Amanda pretended to be asleep. She shuddered at his touch, fearing every moment that he would speak. He *must* know she was lying awake beside him!

Slowly the seconds passed, then a minute, then three. Gradually Ramsay began to breathe deeply. She felt his muscles relax. At last she knew he was asleep.

113

Ancient Mystery

It was the same night. Wakefulness had visited a third house. Arrows of sudden clarity were being launched earthward in many directions. Years of prayer at length were culminating in the release of heaven's answering rains.

In Heathersleigh Cottage, all at once Maggie McFee started out of a deep slumber. She had no idea that as she lay alert and questioning of the Lord, both Jocelyn and Amanda were likewise awake at the same hour.

Bobby's words filled Maggie's brain.

A hidden legacy . . . different than folks think . . . ye must find it.

With new revelation suddenly she knew what they must mean.

Maggie rose, turned on the light that Master Charles had installed in the cottage, and sought her great-grandmother's Bible.

Twenty minutes later she still sat, smiling to herself.

It had been here all along—all these years!

No one had ever realized what the simple message pointed to. How wonderful of the Lord to make use of her own husband's words to reveal the truth!

Again, as she had so many times before, Maggie prayed for Amanda. Indeed, on this night of Amanda's great need, she was bathed in the loving prayers of the two women who loved her more than any other in the whole world.

This will certainly change her history, thought Maggie to herself. *The day will surely arrive when the legacy will come to light, and when the Lord will make this revelation known. But what to do about it must be the Lord's to decide. I must do what he shows me to do, but I mustn't interfere with the Lord's plan for anyone else. That will be up to him . . . and to them.*

114

Into Vienna

*A*manda lay awake the rest of the night with only one thought in mind—she had to get out of here!

If she could just reach France. There she might wire her parents or Cousin Martha—anybody!—for money. But how to get across Austria-Hungary and Germany!

She lay the rest of the night as one paralyzed, knowing that next to her slept one she could no longer trust, whose mistress was somewhere under this same roof waiting for him until she herself was out of the way!

It was all she could do not to scream out in outrage and shame. Yet she had to lie motionless as each slow, lonely minute passed.

She must *not* wake him! One look, one word . . . and he would know that she knew.

Gradually a madcap plan came into her brain.

When morning arrived, still pretending to be asleep when he woke, she waited until Ramsay was gone. Then slowly she too rose and dressed.

There was already one actress in the house. Now there would have to be *two*. If she wanted to get away, she would have to give the most convincing performance of her life!

Summoning what little courage she possessed, she put on as normal a face as she could muster and went downstairs to breakfast. Ramsay sat with his mother at the table. At least Mr. Barclay was nowhere to be seen, nor the sensuous Sadie Greenfield. Amanda didn't think she could cope with the eyes of the one and the pretense of the other just now.

Ramsay and Mrs. Halifax greeted her as she entered. How could they not see the fear and deceit in her eyes! She sat down to her tea and did her best to throw a few occasional crumbs into the fragmentary morning conversation.

Fearing Ramsay would be suspicious of her every word, midway through as much breakfast as her knotted stomach could tolerate, and after he had divulged that he would be in and out most of the afternoon, trying to sound casual, Amanda spoke.

"Ramsay, could I . . . uh, have a little money?" she said. "I would like to go into town today."

"Of course, my dear," he replied. "What for?"

"I . . . uh, want to buy a new dress."

He glanced up from his newspaper.

"I need a dirndl," Amanda went on cheerily. "If I'm going to be Austrian, I ought to look the part, don't you think?"

Ramsay and his mother glanced at one another, then nodded their approval of the suggestion, delighted that Amanda seemed to be adapting so well to her new life.

"All right," said Ramsay, "A new dress sounds like a great idea."

"I will go with you, dear," said Mrs. Halifax.

"That is very kind of you," replied Amanda. Her heart was pounding. If only her quivering voice didn't betray her! "But I really like to be alone when I shop," she added. "Buying clothes . . . is so personal. Otherwise I get embarrassed and always come away with nothing."

The hint of a frown creased Mrs. Halifax's forehead. But it seemed a reasonable explanation. Reluctantly she consented.

Throughout the morning Amanda did her best to carry out her normal routine. Keeping to herself, she watched and listened. Ramsay gave her two hundred Austrian schillings. She still had ten pounds of her own she had secretly kept back when Ramsay asked for the rest of her money after their wedding. That still wouldn't get her across Europe. She must get her hands on more.

She saw no sign of the Greenfield woman, or whatever her name was, although she came upon a few whispered conversations. She only saw Mr. Barclay once. He was occupied most of the morning in meetings upstairs. Several uniformed men came and went throughout the day, but no one paid attention to her. About ten-thirty she dozed off in one of the downstairs sitting rooms.

Amanda awoke groggily. Gradually the nightmare of the previous night returned to her mind, and with it her plan. She rose from the chair and listened. Ramsay appeared already to have gone. His mother was talking with one of the servants, saying she would be leaving for about an hour as well.

This was her chance!

The conversation came to an end. Quickly Amanda sat down again and leaned her head back and closed her eyes. A moment later she heard a slight noise of the door swinging open. She felt Mrs. Halifax's gaze upon her. With great mental effort she breathed deeply in and out pretending to be asleep.

Several long seconds passed. Then the footsteps retreated.

Amanda opened one eye a slit. She was alone.

Mrs. Halifax ascended the stairs to her small apartment, then returned a few minutes later to the ground floor. Two minutes later the front door opened, then closed.

Amanda sprang from the chair and flew to the window. She peeked out a crack between the curtains. Mrs. Halifax hailed a taxi on the street.

Calmly, though with heart racing, Amanda left the sitting room and walked upstairs to her room, pulled out the smaller of her two bags from the closet, then frantically threw what she could carry into it. The day was warm, but she would have to take her heavy coat, for autumn was in the air. And her best walking shoes. As for the rest of the possessions she had brought on the cruise . . . she would have to leave them behind.

And money . . . she had to get more money.

She went to Ramsay's bureau and tore hurriedly through the drawers. Nothing.

Where did he keep money? There was no time to search further.

She crept into the corridor. Gertrut Oswald's room was just down the hall. She had heard her in the kitchen with Mrs. Halifax.

Amanda tiptoed toward her room. As lightly as she could, she knocked faintly. No answer. She tried the latch . . . the door swung in . . . there was no sign of Gertrut.

Amanda entered, glanced about, then rapidly began searching drawers and cabinets. Three minutes later she was on her way back to her own room.

She changed her shoes, put on her coat, took one last hurried glance about the room—which had briefly represented her future but would now forever remind her of a brief, bitter moment in the past—then picked up her bag, drew in a sigh of final determination, and walked into the hall and toward the stairs.

She reached the landing and started slowly down the stairs. She heard a few voices at the other end of the house and a floor above her, but still saw no one. For another few moments her luck continued.

One floor above suddenly a door opened. She heard Mr. Barclay's voice in conversation with two or three other men. They were walking toward the stairs!

As hurriedly as she dared, Amanda ran down the rest of the way to the ground floor and continued, half running, across the entry. She hurried toward the door. The voices above were almost in view.

She put her hand to the latch. What if Mrs. Halifax was just returning! She opened the door. No voice from Mr. Barclay came from behind her. No presence stared back from in front of her!

Quickly she stepped out, then carefully closed the door behind her.

She was walking down the steps now. She reached the sidewalk, turned left so as to avoid being seen from the side entrance, then hurried along.

Quickly she turned at the first side street, walking more rapidly now, changing directions randomly at every block.

Several cabs were parked ahead on the street. The first appeared empty and available.

Amanda ran toward it.

115

Maggie Prays

———— ◆◆◆ ————

*M*aggie's brain was alive with questions and thoughts, prayers and possibilities.

Like Amanda, who filled her thoughts, she had hardly slept a wink the rest of the night.

She had to write it all down, that much Maggie knew, for there was no telling when or how she would see Amanda again. Steadily the conviction had grown upon her that what she had been given this night was a revelation for the three young people of Heathersleigh. She did not know why. She must leave a new clue, just as the one she had discovered had been left for her.

Why so much time had elapsed . . . Maggie could not explain, other than by recalling that the Lord had his own timetables for the carrying out of his purposes.

"*Lord, I've been lax in my praying for them all,*" she began. "*Just because I've lost my Bobby doesn't mean I can lose sight of your business. There's still work to be done . . . your work. Amanda and Catharine and George are part of it, and so am I. Forgive me for not holding up my end these last days.*"

She rocked awhile longer, reflecting on many things.

"*And I haven't lost my Bobby anyway,*" she said after a few minutes, both to herself and to the Lord. "*He's only gone to be with you. So there's no better way for me to be with him than praying, for that keeps us both connected with you.*"

She closed her eyes and sat silent for many long minutes. When at length she began praying again, even her voice took on the sound of the ages. Little did she know how much her prayer resembled that prayed by her great-grandmother so many years earlier toward the same end. God's ways often require generations for their fulfillment. And this petition, prayed by many saints in many ways for many of his wayward ones, was at last approaching its appointed time.

"*Lord God,*" Maggie prayed, "*again I ask that you would draw the girl Amanda to yourself. Bring to a close this season of her prodigal sojourn in the far land spoken of by the Master. It is time, Lord. It is time for her to rise up and remember from whence she came. Bring all the mysteries connected with the Hall and the cottage to light, and in the end may good come of all that was done before. Prepare the lass Amanda even now for her part in it. Show her in your way and in your time what you want her to do. Bring her home, Lord . . . bring her home.*"

116

Suspicious Eyes

───── ♦ ♦ ♦ ─────

*W*hen Mrs. Halifax returned to Ebendorfer Strasse after about an hour, she felt immediately that something was wrong.

The look on Gertrut Oswald's face confirmed her suspicions.

"What is it, Gertrut?" she asked.

"The girl ... she left," replied the keeper of the door.

"Which girl?"

"The English girl ... Amanda."

"Yes—she planned to go shopping," replied Mrs. Halifax. "I was aware of it. How long ago was that?"

"About forty minutes. I heard the front door close," Oswald went on. "I went to look. Out the front window, I saw her just as she walked out of sight—"

Mrs. Halifax waited, not sure what was Gertrut's point.

"—she carried a bag."

"A handbag?"

"A carpetbag ... a traveling bag—"

Mrs. Halifax's brow clouded.

"—and she wore a heavy coat, a winter coat," added Gertrut.

Only a moment more did Mrs. Halifax delay.

"If you see Mr. Barclay, or if my son returns, tell them to wait for me," she said in a voice of command. Immediately she turned and again left the house.

She knew exactly which shops Amanda would be likely to find the kind of dirndl she said she wanted. She would go to each ... and quickly.

Whatever might be going on, she would not let Amanda out of the sight of one of them again until she had satisfied herself that the girl's loyalties were not wavering. But first she had to find her!

In less than two minutes Amanda's mother-in-law was seated in a cab speeding toward the city.

117

Chase

$\mathscr{A}$manda was running ... running ...

She had no idea where she even was. None of the streets looked familiar.

After a taxi ride of five minutes away from Ebendorfer Strasse, she told the driver to stop. She needed to save every penny for the train.

She got out. As soon as the cab disappeared she began walking in the general direction she thought might take her toward the station. Soon she was running, taking as many small streets as possible, hoping she wouldn't by remote chance encounter someone who recognized her.

Though she was well away from the house, she was terrified. Every face seemed watching her! Soldiers walked about everywhere.

In her confused state, it did not take many minutes before her sense of direction was completely turned around. But she had to keep going. She must get to the station. She broke into a run again, more befuddled than ever about where she was.

* * *

Mrs. Halifax returned to the house. None of the shops had seen Amanda.

Barclay and Ramsay awaited her.

"Amanda's gone," she said. "She never went to the city."

She explained what Gertrut had seen.

"The carpetbag and winter coat can only mean one thing," said Barclay. "Go after her, Ramsay—see if you can pick up her trail."

Already Ramsay was on his way toward the door.

"I'll check with the cabs along the street," he said. "You and some of the others spread out for a block or two around the house. Ask if anyone's seen her."

Ramsay ran quickly south on Ebendorfer Strasse, then left on Felder Strasse. He was certain such would have been Amanda's direction. A block farther, near the Rathaus, sat a row of taxis. He ran toward them and began questioning each of the drivers.

Had any picked up a young woman near here in the last hour? He gave a description of Amanda.

118

Too Close

♦ ♦ ♦

*E*xhausted, at length Amanda sat down on a stone embankment along the walkway where she found herself. The sleepless night was catching up with her. Her legs and head ached. With sinking heart she had the feeling she had seen this same street already today.

How could she possibly get to the station without taking another cab?

She rested four or five minutes.

Down the street a taxi approached. She rose on weary feet to hail it.

Wait! Why did it seem familiar? It looked like—

It was the very cab she had ridden earlier. Now she remembered . . . and this was the same street they had been speeding along when she had told the driver to stop!

She had done nothing but run around in circles!

Now the cab pulled over again . . . at the same spot.

She stood watching. The door opened. A man got out and paid the driver.

Ramsay!

Amanda turned and sprinted along the sidewalk. Ahead, the brick wall of a corner building would offer protection. She hurried around it, then stopped and leaned for a moment against the surface to catch her breath.

How could he possibly have known where to find her!

Carefully she poked her head out around the edge of the wall.

Ramsay had not seen her. He glanced in every direction as he walked. He was coming this way!

Amanda pulled her head back out of sight and tore off down the street in the opposite direction, the carpetbag swinging about like lead in her hand. She turned into the first alley she found.

Her step slowed. For a brief moment the opposite thought struck her. Maybe Ramsay had followed to *help*. Perhaps he was concerned. Briefly the haze of confusion returned. She should just go back to meet him. He would tell her what to do.

She turned and began walking back toward the corner. An immediate sense of relief filled her at giving up the fight. Ramsay would—

Stop—what was she thinking!

Of one thing there could be no doubt. Whatever was going on, he was in on it—why else would he follow her?

Toward the end of the alley Amanda now ran, turned again, then along the next street, left at the intersection—

A horn blared. She nearly stumbled in the middle of the street.

—right into a narrow alley.

She was exhausted. It was a struggle to force her legs to keep moving.

At the end of the alley she turned for a quick glance back.

No sign of Ramsay. All she could do now was keep going as she was, which was *away* from where she had last seen him.

After another ten minutes, with many turns through alleyways and streets but moving mostly in the same general direction, at last again Amanda sought a taxi.

An empty car approached and stopped. At least it was not the same one from before. She stepped inside and sat down.

"Südbahnhof," she said as the cab sped off.

119

Search

♦ ♦ ♦

*A*fter an hour Ramsay returned to Ebendorfer Strasse.

"I lost her," he said, explaining briefly his search. "After she left the cab, I spoke with one man who thought he had seen her. After that, not a trace."

"You looked everywhere?"

"I couldn't wander the streets forever. She could be anywhere."

"Where did the cab take her?" asked his mother.

"Nowhere. She drove for a while, then told the driver to stop."

His mother and Barclay shook their heads. Neither had they had success. Hartwell Barclay did not like surprises like this, nor loose uncertainties.

"Search the house," he said. "Tell everyone. Ramsay, go over your rooms with a fine-tooth comb. I want to know anything that is missing. Hildegard, talk to Gertrut and the other women."

They all dispersed. Ramsay went to his apartment. A minute or two later, he heard Gertrut walking past outside toward her room.

Five minutes later a shout was heard in Gertrut's usually taciturn voice.

"My money is gone!" she cried, running into the hall. "Three hundred schillings!"

"What about your room, Ramsay?" Mrs. Halifax asked him. "What did she take?"

"As far as I can tell, a coat, two changes of clothes . . . a few personal items."

"Too much to be accounted for by a shopping trip into the city. What about money?"

"Only what you saw me give her this morning. She had no more that I know of."

"Identification?" asked Barclay.

Ramsay nodded. "Yes, her passport is also gone."

"Wait," said Gertrut, standing in the corridor listening. "I just realized . . . I keep my passport in the same drawer with my money."

She ran back, then emerged thirty seconds later into the corridor.

"My passport is gone!" Gertrut announced.

"She is trying to leave the country!" exploded Barclay. "You fool!" he said to Ramsay, "how could you let her slip out from under your nose?"

"I was gone," he shot back. "*You* were the only one in the house when she made her getaway!"

In white fury, Barclay did not reply.

"How far would five hundred schillings get her?" said Ramsay's mother. This was a time for practicalities, not an argument.

"Easily into Switzerland or Italy . . . if not all the way to England."

"We've got to stop her!" seethed Barclay.

"The station," cried Mrs. Halifax, "—we'll try the station!"

120

Station

♦♦♦

*A*manda walked into Vienna's southern train station, wishing she hadn't already spent so much.

At least she was here now.

But where to go? She couldn't buy a ticket for Paris—Austria was at *war* with France! That border would surely be closed.

Maybe Italy. If she could get safely across the border, perhaps from there she could get to France, although she spoke less Italian than her smattering of German! As far as she knew, Italy was still neutral even though technically Austria's ally.

She looked about for the board where the train times were posted. *Any* route out of Vienna would do!

She found the schedule board and glanced up and down it.

Berlin . . . no.

Nuremberg . . . no.

Munich . . . no.

Was *every* train westbound for Germany!

Innsbruck, Salzburg . . . they were both still in Austria.

South—*Trieste* and *Venice* . . . that was her best chance to get out of Austria!

She turned and hurried to the ticket window.

"Fahrkarte, bitte . . . Trieste," she said nervously.

"Hin und Zurick?" asked the agent.

"Nein," she replied shaking her head.

"Fünf-und-achtzig schilling."

Amanda shoved one of the two hundred schilling notes Ramsay had given her through the window.

Eyeing her a moment, the man handed her back the ticket and two coins of change. *"Bahnsteige neun, vier uhr zwanzig,"* he said.

Amanda took the ticket and coins and turned away. Scanning the floor to get her bearings, she now walked through the station toward the tunnel leading to platform nine where the agent had told her the train would be. A few minutes later she arrived, then sat down to wait.

Four-twenty.

She glanced up at the clock. It was now ten till three.

In ninety minutes she would be safe.

121

Secret Business

◆◆◆

*T*here was one more item of business Maggie McFee knew she must attend to as well, just in case the Lord chose to take her to follow Bobby sooner rather than later.

The next day, therefore, to the amazement of all in the village who chanced to observe her at the Milverscombe station, wearing the finest dress she owned, Maggie boarded a train for Exeter.

No amount of expostulation, however, either that day or in the weeks to come, was sufficient to persuade Maggie McFee to divulge the nature of her business.

Somehow it was later discovered that the errand which had taken her to the city had to do with a certain solicitor's firm.

More than that was never known, Maggie's business in fact concerned two documents which thereafter lay in the solicitor's files for safekeeping. One was a letter she had written, which would not be opened until those eyes to whom it was addressed, and who also was the chief subject of the second document, were ready to know the truths which it revealed.

The general conclusion of the matter in Milverscombe was that Maggie's appointment must have had something to do with her husband's passing. That no one ever learned what might be the nature of that business only deepened the mystery surrounding the unknown antecedents of the old couple of Heathersleigh Cottage.

All the way from Exeter back to Milverscombe on the train, Maggie's heart was full of Amanda.

"We've got to pray," she said to herself. "We've got to pray like never before. Master Charles, her dear mother, myself, Catharine, George, all who know her . . . we've all got to pray. I feel that Amanda's in danger. But I know she's coming home. She might even be on her way right now.—O Lord," she said, breaking into whispered petition even as she sat gazing out the windows at the passing countryside, *"protect her and guide her footsteps. Keep evil people who would try to harm her away from her, Lord. Wrap your arms around her. Encompass her about with a hedge of thorns against the enemy. Send her to people, and send people to her—your people, godly men and women, to help her, point her toward truth, and bring her home."*

122

Waiting

❖❖❖

*I*n Vienna's Südbahnhof the time dragged slowly by.

Amanda felt her head drooping.

No! She couldn't doze off! She might miss the train. She must remain alert.

She shook herself and glanced about.

Why did it seem everyone was looking at her with suspicious glances? Suddenly she felt very, very *English*. Everyone must know the fact . . . and hate her for it. If only she had a dirndl now!

What would happen when she boarded the train, or tried to cross the border?

The passport of Gertrut Oswald listed her nationality as Austrian. Whatever broken German she could manage would give away in an instant that the passport wasn't her own.

She would have to keep her mouth shut and hope no one asked too many questions.

She was *so* tired. But she had to keep watch along the station corridors and the tunnel entries.

She looked up at the clock. Its two hands pointed to the four and the eight. She tried to make the face of the clock register in her weary brain. The four and the eight . . . twenty after eight.

No! It can't be! she thought to herself, jumping to her feet. She had fallen asleep! She had missed her train!

Quickly she glanced around in panic, then back at the clock.

Stop . . . what was she thinking? Her brain was playing tricks—the *little* hand was between the three and four. It was only three-forty! Was she going crazy in the midst of her exhaustion?

She sat back down with a sigh. Forty more minutes. The train should pull in anytime. Then she could board, find a seat . . . and wait.

Amanda sat for another ten or fifteen minutes, glancing along the track for any sign of her train's arrival. At length she rose again. She would go to the washroom one last time. A splash of cold water on her face might wake her up.

123
Final Encounter

$\mathcal{R}$amsay ran into the station glancing to his right and left. A minute later his mother and Hartwell Barclay followed him inside.

"I don't see her," said Ramsay. "We'll have to split up and check the three platforms. Mum, you take one through three—that tunnel's closest. I'll check four through six. The Paris line—no, that border would be closed. But Innsbruck leaves from five—she's probably making for Innsbruck! That's as far west as she could get directly from here. But, Barclay, just to be safe, you check seven through nine."

Immediately they hurried off in the direction of the three tunnels to the trio of platforms.

Feeling temporarily better from the cold water on her face, Amanda gave the attendant a few *groschen* coins, for which she was thanked by a scowl and grunt, then opened the door to return to the station.

She gasped in terror. She would know that white head of hair anywhere!

Hartwell Barclay stood with his back to her, less than twenty feet away! He was looking about the platform area!

Amanda shrunk back inside the small room. Another lady bumped and crowded past her with a rude remark Amanda couldn't understand. As the door opened and closed, she saw an engine followed by eight or ten coach cars slowing on the track facing platform nine where she had been waiting.

It was her train!

With a final screech the locomotive and cars came to rest. The doors opened and the departing passengers poured out.

And there stood Barclay between her and her way of escape.

What time was it—4:09 . . .

She pushed the door open a crack and peeped out. Barclay had wandered off along the platform, but not nearly far enough that she could yet risk leaving the bathroom.

Behind her, the voice of the irritable attendant shouted a flurry of foul words in her direction. She pretended not to hear, but knew well enough that she was being ordered off the premises now that her business was done.

She snuck another peek.

Again the door shot open. Another lady entered. A volley of angry shouts erupted behind her.

She might be safe now. She saw Barclay heading toward the tunnel back to the main part of the station. She crept out.

Suddenly he paused, then turned around for one last scan through the sea of faces. The gaze of his evil eyes probed straight in Amanda's direction. Yet something prevented recognition. Amanda spun about and tried to disappear in a crowd of passengers making their way across the floor. A second or two later she dared a partial turn of her head.

Barclay was still looking about. He seemed to know she was near. From this distance she could feel his frustration. His eyes glowed with black fire.

Then, just as quickly as he had paused a minute earlier, he spun about and disappeared into the tunnel.

Amanda darted for the train.

124

Toward Home

◆ ◆ ◆

The report of all three of Amanda's pursuers was the same. No one had seen her.

Ramsay thought a moment, then ran for the ticket window. He would interrogate the agent.

Two ladies stood in line before him. He pushed past and shouted his question to the man behind the pane of glass.

But they would have none of it. A rude torrent of rebukes flew at him. He could not afford a scene—he might never get the information.

Reluctantly he walked behind the women and stood waiting.

Frantically Amanda stood waiting as the conductor examined the tickets of those ahead of her. She glanced behind every few seconds.

At last she was next in line. . . . now she stepped forward and handed the man her ticket.

He glanced at her with an unfriendly expression.

"Trieste?" he said.

Amanda nodded.

"Identification."

She handed him Gertrut Oswald's passport.

He looked at the picture, a little more carefully than Amanda liked, then closed it and handed it back to her.

Quickly Amanda stepped up and onto the train, then hurried inside the coach to find a seat.

At last she sat down, closed her eyes briefly, and breathed deeply with exhausted relief.

Ramsay glanced up at the clock. Four-thirteen.

The second lady's transaction was interminably slow.

At last he reached the window.

It was four-seventeen.

"What trains have left the station in the last hour?" he shouted. Whatever reservoir of patience he possessed had been used up waiting for the two women, and he had none left to spare.

"Let's see," replied the man, glancing through the glass to the schedule board posted on the wall of the station and squinting slightly, "there was the Moscow—"

"Going west!"

"Berlin—"

"No, you fool, she would never go to Berlin."

"The southbound is scheduled at four-twenty, sir."

"That's got to be it."

"I am afraid you will not make it now."

"*I'm* not going anywhere, you idiot! Did you sell a ticket to a young lady?"

Briefly he described Amanda.

The agent nodded.

"What was her destination?"

"Trieste."

"*Trieste!*" repeated Ramsay. "What in the—"

He paused a moment.

"That's it—of course! The little vixen is smarter than I thought. She's making for Italy!"

In her seat, with great relief Amanda finally felt movement beneath her. A whistle sounded. The southbound Vienna-Trieste line began to jerk and creak into motion.

She leaned her head back and glanced out the window absently at the platform lined with men and women waving to those inside the train as it gradually picked up speed.

From behind them a figure she recognized now came sprinting out of the tunnel and onto the platform.

It was Ramsay!

She pulled away from the glass. But it was too late. Somehow he spotted her instantly among all the windows with faces pressed against them.

He raced shouting toward the train. But the engine was increasing in speed. Above the metallic clacking on the tracks she could faintly make out the word she saw on his lips.

"A - m - a - n - d - a ! !" came a great cry.

Behind him now labored two others out of the tunnel.

He pointed straight at her. The eyes of Mrs. Halifax and Hartwell Barclay followed his hand. For the briefest moment the flash of hatred from them met her answering gaze.

Then they were gone, disappeared behind the outside station wall. Suddenly the buildings of the city of Vienna rose in the distance.

The rhythmic clacking beneath her became instantly soothing and melodic.

Amanda sat back in her seat breathing deeply. At length her relief was complete. Could she dare believe that this horrible episode in her life was finally over?

Quickly the train picked up speed. Within five minutes they passed into the open Austrian countryside.

"I'm going home," said Amanda to herself. "At last I'm going home."

She paused briefly, then closed her eyes. This time, however, the reason was not for weariness, but to address one to whom she had not consciously spoken in years.

"God," said Amanda, *"help me get safely back to England."*

As she sped southward out of Vienna she had thus begun that most important journey of the heart, whose first steps begin with the recognition, however faint, that all is not as it could be, or should be, and that there is only one place to make it right.

Though around her the world was at war, and though she was alone in the middle of a foreign land, Amanda Rutherford was indeed already more than halfway home.

Notes and Acknowledgments

$\diamond\diamond\diamond$

The years leading up to the First World War were characterized by an extremely complex political landscape, with alliances constantly shifting and loyalties not nearly so fixed as the polarization which developed later in the twentieth century during the Cold War. This fact, along with the many additional societal forces explored in *Wayward Winds*—the rise of socialism and communism, nationalism, the increasing power of the working and middle classes, etc.—all combined to create a climate in which many fringe organizations, networks, and revolutionary societies flourished. The problem of "moles" and "sleepers" and spies loyal to Britain's enemies was very serious in the years before the war. The Serbian terrorist organization known as "The Black Hand" is factual. They trained the seven conspirators—including Gavrilo Princip and Muhamed Mehmedbasic—who plotted the assassination of the Archduke Franz Ferdinand and his wife Sophie. The Fountain of Light, however, and all the characters involved in it, is entirely fictional.

All the incidents attributed to the suffragettes are factual, including the account of Emily Davison's death at the 1913 Derby. A number of these incidents are described in more detail in *The Strange Death of Liberal England* by George Dangerfield. It might be of interest for the reader to know that later in her life Christabel Pankhurst became an outspoken Christian author and evangelist. The account of the assassination of Archduke Franz Ferdinand was fictionalized from the information provided in *Sarajevo* by Joachim Remak.

Some of the statements, as noted in the text with asterisks, attributed in conversation with Charles to Winston Churchill, and attributed to Churchill's thoughts, are loosely quoted from Churchill's actual words according to his detailed written account of the period, taken from *The World Crisis, Volume One*.

The following sources were very helpful in research for *Wayward Winds:*

Barraclough, Geoffrey, ed. *The Times Atlas of World History.* London: Hammond/Times Books, 1978.

Chambers, Frank. *This Age of Conflict.* New York: Harcourt, Brace, World, 1943.

Churchill, Winston S. *The World Crisis, Volume One.* New York: Charles Scribner's Sons, 1923.

Dangerfield, George. *The Strange Death of Liberal England.* New York: Putnam & Sons, 1935.

Remak, Joachim. *Sarajevo.* New York: Criterion Books, 1959.

Smith, Goldwin. *A History of England.* New York: Charles Scribner's & Sons, 1949.

Tillinghast, William. *Ploetz' Epitome of History.* New York: Blue Ribbon Books, 1883.

Tuchman, Barbara. *The Guns of August.* New York: Dell Publishing Co., 1962.

Vienna, A Knopf Guide. New York: Alfred A. Knopf, 1994.

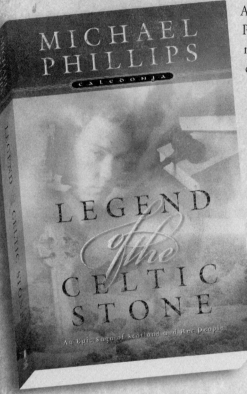